ONLY A KISS

There was a stillness about him; his features had hardened, his eyes had darkened. The strong pulse at his throat started an answering beat in her own body.

She had to say something, anything to break the charged atmosphere between them. "Your ideas about marriage are far different from mine."

The belt of her wrapper had come undone and she tied it snugly. But his eyes flared, and she recognized that the action had somehow challenged him.

"Very nunlike," he said, "but I am not an untried youth, Jess. There's no need to cover yourself as though a glimpse of your naked flesh will unleash the savage in me. I'm quite civilized, I promise you."

She backed up a step, not because he'd moved, but because she felt overwhelmed by him. He said he was civilized but that wasn't how he appeared to her in that moment. She was acutely aware of the strength and maleness of him. He wanted her to be aware. She could see it in his eyes.

She had to put a stop to this. "What is it you want, Lucas?"

He lowered his head to hers. "Just a good-night kiss, Jess," he said, his voice husky. "Is that too much for a man to ask his wife on their wedding night?"

The light from the candle cast an intimate glow. But it was his eyes that held her, eyes as dark as midnight, and just as dangerous. When his head dipped again, she moaned.

His firm, sensual lips curved in a faint smile. "It's only a kiss, Jess," he whispered.

Only a kiss. The memory of their last kiss set her blood on fire.

His mouth touched hers. Her stomach tightened and her knees went weak. And then he took the kiss deeper, opening her mouth to his intimate possession. . . .

YOU ONLY LOVE TWICE

ALSO BY ELIZABETH THORNTON

The Bride's Bodyguard
Dangerous to Hold
Dangerous to Kiss
Dangerous to Love

YOU ONLY LOVE TWICE

Elizabeth Thornton

BANTAM BOOKS

New York   Toronto   London   Sydney   Auckland

YOU ONLY LOVE TWICE

A Bantam Book / February 1998

ISBN 0-553-57426-4

Published simultaneously in the United States and Canada

Bantam Books are published by Bantam Books, a division of Bantam
Doubleday Dell Publishing Group, Inc. Its trademark, consisting of the
words "Bantam Books" and the portrayal of a rooster, is Registered in U.S.
Patent and Trademark Office and in other countries. Marca Registrada.
Bantam Books, 1540 Broadway, New York, New York 10036.

PRINTED IN THE UNITED STATES OF AMERICA

OPM   10 9 8 7 6 5 4 3 2 1

YOU
ONLY
LOVE
TWICE

PROLOGUE

HE WAS A MURDERER. HE FELT NO REMORSE, NO shame for what he'd done. Some things were worth killing for. If he had to, he would do it again.

Sister Martha was on her knees in the chapel during vespers when the voice came to her. At first, she hardly knew what was happening. She'd had almost a year of uninterrupted tranquillity and had come to believe that she had finally exorcised her curse. Now, as the haze in her mind gradually took the shape of words, she realized how premature her hopes had been.

Her fingers tightened around her rosary and her heart began to pound. Had she not been so weary from tending the sick in the infirmary, she would have known at once what was happening, and could have slammed the door on this intrusion. Now, he had entered her mind and the door was wedged open.

She must concentrate on her prayers. Her lips began to move. "Hail Mary, full of grace. Blessed be . . . blessed be . . ." She groped for the words and could not find them.

People were such fools. They looked at him and saw exactly what he wanted them to see. No one had ever suspected him of murder. He was too clever for them.

With every ounce of will she could summon, she tried to suppress the voice. But it wasn't a voice, not really. It was more like a presence, an uninvited presence that distilled its own thoughts inside her mind. She called it a voice for want of a better word. "Hail Mary . . . Hail Mary . . . Please, oh please . . ."

It was no use. He was taking her with him, traveling over old ground, returning to the scene of the crime. She knew what was coming. He'd taken her here before.

Darkness was all around them and a light rain was falling. There was nothing to see, but a wave of impressions flooded her senses. They were in a densely wooded area, and close by was a stream. She could hear the rain on the water, could smell the faint scent of wet vegetation and flowers. There was a house on a hill, a rich man's house, and behind them was another house.

She didn't want to go on with this, but she didn't know how to stop it. In desperation, she started on another prayer. "Our Father which art in heaven, hallowed be . . . hallowed be . . ."

He'd concealed himself behind a tree. He'd been running so hard, he was out of breath. His heart was thundering, but the hand that held the pistol was quite steady. Rage. Hatred. And a steely determination. She could feel his emotions as if they were her own. A shadow moved by him, and she braced herself for the report of the pistol shot, but she still jerked when it came.

When it was over, she let out a long shaken breath. She was trembling, and tears were streaming down her face. She told herself that it did no good to agonize over a murder that had taken place years ago. She didn't know who the principals were, didn't know if they were real or a figment of her imagination.

If they were not real, she was mad.

Her body was beginning to relax in blessed relief when the next impression came, electrifying her.

He wasn't a murderer by nature, but having murdered once he could do it again. In fact, he would do it again. His mind was made up.

Her mouth went tinder dry and a frisson of panic leapt along her spine. This was something new, something she had never imagined. And she was helpless to prevent it. She didn't know who he was, where he was. Dear God, this must not be allowed to happen.

It would take careful planning. This time, nothing must go wrong. He would make it look like an accident. Two murders in one small community might stir up a hornets' nest and that would never do.

She was not aware that she had risen to her feet, or that the other nuns had turned to stare at her.

"Don't do this!" her mind screamed. "For God's sake, don't do this!"

She sensed his shock of awareness, felt his mind blink as an eye blinks rapidly when surprised by the unexpected. Then a shutter came down and she was left with her own thoughts.

They were not comforting. She had just revealed to a murderer that she had a window into his soul.

C H A P T E R

1

SISTER MARTHA WAS IN THE GARDEN ON HER KNEES picking daffodils when Sister Brigid found her. Martha wasn't aware that she was being watched, and had stopped to turn her face up to catch the rays of the sun as they filtered through the budding branches of a sycamore. A moment later, she buried her nose in the bunch of daffodils she held in the crook of one arm. There was no doubt in Sister Brigid's mind what happened next. Martha's shoulders began to heave and she let out a choked sob. Sister Martha, the apple of the Reverend Mother's eye, was weeping her heart out.

The young novice hesitated to intrude on such a private moment. She was, moreover, shocked to see Sister Martha like this, and wondered if it had something to do with vespers last evening. Everybody, at least all the novices, were talking about how Martha had rushed out of the chapel as though she'd seen a ghost. And now this.

These displays of emotion were not like Martha. She wasn't like the other novices. For one thing, she was older, perhaps twenty-two or twenty-three, a good six years older than Sister Brigid. And for another, Martha seemed to live on a higher level. She was usually so serene. There was a good reason for this, as old Sister Dolores had let slip when she'd rebuked one of the novices for referring to Martha as "Sister Perfect." Sister Martha, she'd scolded, rounding on the culprit, carried a great sadness inside her. She couldn't talk about her childhood, or her family, or what had led her to choose the religious life as the other novices did. Her memory went back no further than three years, when she'd been brought to the infirmary after a terrible accident and had awakened not knowing who she was or where she'd come from. Even the name Martha wasn't her own name but had been given to her by the Reverend Mother because, like the Martha in the Bible, she was such a hard worker. The other novices would do well to take Martha as their example.

After that, Sister Brigid had begun to watch the older novice, and the more she saw, the more she'd come to admire her. Sister Martha might not mix with the other nuns, but actions spoke louder than words. No job was too menial or too dirty for Martha to take on. In fact, the other novices took advantage of her and could be counted on to disappear into cracks in the old convent's walls whenever the slop pails had to be emptied or soiled bedclothes had to be stripped and carried to the laundry. But not Martha. In Sister Brigid's eyes, Sister Martha was the Virgin Mary and the mother superior in one. She went in awe of her, but she also idolized her and had become her most devoted champion.

When it was obvious that the bout of weeping had come to an end, Sister Brigid kicked a pebble with the toe of her boot, sending it rattling along the flagstone path, in an awkward attempt to warn Martha that she was not alone. Martha, she knew, would not wish to be seen like this.

"Martha," she called softly, then a moment later, "Oh, there you are," and she slowly made her way toward the kneeling girl.

There were no tears in evidence when Martha rose and turned to face Sister Brigid. Her smile was untroubled. Her eyes were clear.

Sister Brigid said, "The Reverend Mother sent me to fetch you. Father Howie is with her."

"Oh," said Martha. "In that case, would you mind taking over? Sister Dolores asked me to gather daffodils to brighten the infirmary." She passed the flowers to Sister Brigid and turned to go.

"Martha." Sister Brigid swiftly touched Martha's hand. "Yes?"

Martha's expression did not invite sympathy, and Sister Brigid faltered. "Nothing. That is, will I see you later in the infirmary?"

"Of course."

Martha read the curiosity in the younger girl's eyes, but she made no attempt to satisfy it. She supposed that all the nuns would be avidly discussing her behavior at vespers last night. Sister Martha, the novice who never put a foot wrong, had fled from the chapel as though the hounds of hell were in pursuit.

She didn't want to lie, but she couldn't bring herself to tell anyone her closely guarded secret. Should she be so foolish, she had no doubt that the sympathy on Sister Brigid's face would turn to horror.

Witch. Freak. Lunatic. That's what everyone would think of her if they ever got to know of her Voice. Even now, they looked upon her as an oddity. Sometimes, she questioned her own sanity. But she knew her Voice was real. She knew. She also knew that after last night, she could not go on living this lie.

Her dream of taking her vows and becoming a member in full standing of the Sisters of Charity was now in ruins. That's why she had given in to tears. She knew what she had to do. She had to find a way to return to her former life and stop this nightmare from happening. It was the right thing to do. But part of her was a coward. The convent was all she knew. She felt safe here. In time, the other nuns would come to accept her.

It was too late to think about that now. She'd made her decision and she must stick to it.

When she entered the convent, she paused for a moment to absorb the familiar sounds and smells. Everything on this side of the building was muted. On the other side, through the great oak door, was the orphanage. Just thinking about the children made her feel better. She didn't have to earn their acceptance. They took her on trust.

Tears welled in her throat again and she swallowed hard to keep them at bay. Her mind must be calm and clear for the interview with the mother superior and Father Howie. She did not think they would turn from her in disgust if they knew about her Voice, but she was sure that they would not approve of the course she had decided to follow. They were the nearest thing to parents she knew, the good Father and the Reverend Mother, and had been since she'd awakened in the infirmary to see their kind, compassionate faces hovering over her. They would want what was best for her, would want to cure her of her curse, exorcise her Voice so that she would never be troubled by it again.

It was what she wanted, too. And it was what she feared more than anything.

She made straight for her own little room, with its whitewashed walls and bare wooden floor. The furnishings were sparse, a table and chair, a bed and a commode. The only splash of color came from the patchwork quilt she'd made with her own hands.

She had no possessions from her former life, nothing that might give her a clue to her identity. She hadn't been carrying a bag or a purse, nothing to identify her, when she'd been knocked down by a carriage right in front of the convent doors. The patchwork quilt was the only thing that was truly hers.

After removing the voluminous apron she'd worn to protect her habit, she wet a cloth from a pitcher of cold water, dabbed at her face and hands, then went to the small scrap of mirror on the wall to survey her handiwork. As she adjusted her wimple, her fingers gradually stilled and she became absorbed in her own reflection.

She was just an ordinary-looking young woman. There was nothing to distinguish her from the other novices. They all wore black habits and the white novice's wimple. Then why had the Voice come to her?

They had to be connected. She'd gone over it in her mind endlessly, and it was the only answer that made sense. They must have known each other in the past.

In the beginning, she'd thought her memory was coming back. Her Voice wasn't a Voice then. She saw pictures, vague images that meant nothing to her. She couldn't remember when the pictures and impressions had begun to form themselves into words, or when her Voice had become embittered. She'd tried to suppress it, but she couldn't always remember to be on her guard. Last night was the first time she'd tried to connect with it, and she never wanted to do it again. It was too dangerous.

It was all too bizarre to believe!

Maybe it was a figment of her imagination. Maybe her brain was more damaged than she knew. Maybe her mind was unhinged and she was slowly going mad. Maybe she should be locked up in an insane asylum for her own good.

He wasn't a murderer by nature, but having murdered once, he could do it again. In fact, he would do it again. His mind was made up.

A shudder ran over her, then another. Not even her imagination was that inventive. On that thought, she hurried from the room.

•   •   •

The mother superior broke off her conversation with Father Howie and smiled encouragingly as Sister Martha entered her office. The girl was young, but her composed manner gave the impression of someone older than her years.

"Martha." The Reverend Mother gestured with her hand and Martha crossed to the chair her superior had indicated.

She sat quietly, her hands clasped loosely in her lap, her calm gray-eyed gaze resting on Father Howie's face.

He was a little man with a long, thin face and, beneath black, bushy eyebrows, alert blue eyes with a decided twinkle in them. Father Howie had been a physician long before he'd become a priest, and had kept a watchful eye on Martha ever since she'd been admitted to the infirmary. The Reverend Mother was a feminine version of the little priest, though a few years younger, and anyone seeing them together knew at once that they must be related. Martha knew they were brother and sister.

He greeted Martha warmly. Her greeting was more subdued, but her lips were curved in a genuine smile. Father Howie took that smile as a great compliment. Martha rarely smiled.

As the Reverend Mother busied herself pouring out tea, the priest embarked on a flow of small talk to put Martha at her ease, but on another level of his mind, he was studying her intently.

Anyone looking at her would take her for the picture of the perfect nun. Not a hair was out of place. In fact, not a hair was showing from beneath the close-fitting novice's coif. Her black habit might be threadbare, but there wasn't a spot or wrinkle on it. Calm. Serene. Collected. That was the impression Martha gave, but it was a false impression. No one who had been through what this young woman had been through could be so untouched. He'd seen her when she was panic-stricken, when she'd awakened in the infirmary not knowing who she was. He'd been a frequent visitor to the convent then, and had been amazed at how well she had adjusted, amazed and skeptical. It had not taken him long to deduce that Martha's adjustment to convent life was based on fear of the outside world. He and the Reverend Mother had managed to calm her fears by assuring her that she could remain at the convent as long as she wished. The Sisters of Charity was not primarily a contemplative order but one of service to the poor, and there were always more jobs to do than hands to do them.

And here she had remained ever since, first as a lay sister and now as a postulant. Her dearest wish, as he'd understood, was to take her vows. But that was before last night.

The priest lowered his head and gave careful attention to stirring his tea. When he looked up, he said, "The Reverend Mother tells me that your memory is beginning to come back to you, Martha."

In her heart, Martha uttered a prayer of contrition for all the half-truths she was about to tell. "It seems that way, Father. But I wouldn't go as far as to say that my memory is returning. It's more like pictures and impressions that come to me, some vividly and others vaguely."

The Reverend Mother said, "Tell Father Howie what you told me after vespers, Martha."

Martha nodded. "I've seen some of these pictures before, but I didn't know what to make of them. Last night at vespers, I knew I was connected to them. They felt familiar to me." She was thinking of her Voice.

"Go on," said the priest quietly.

She breathed deeply and went back to the very beginning, before her Voice had begun to frighten her. There was a village, she told them, and beyond it a great castle. Between the village and the castle there was a house, a manor, and above the manor a hawk soared in flight.

There were orchards and a stream and softly rolling hills where sheep grazed.

There was more, much more—impressions she'd buried deep inside her and had forced to come to the surface in the long hours of sleeplessness the night before. She wasn't aware that as she spoke her face had become animated or that her voice had taken on an edge of desperation. She spoke for a long time, rarely pausing, giving them the carefully expurgated account she'd rehearsed in her mind. When she was finished, she sat back in her chair and looked anxiously at Father Howie.

"I wouldn't let it worry you," he said. "These memories, if they are memories, may mean something or they may mean nothing at all. Only time will tell."

The Reverend Mother smiled. "There's no need to be afraid, child. Whatever happens, no one can force you to leave here if you don't want to. I wouldn't allow it."

The Reverend Mother and Father Howie had misunderstood. Martha searched for the words that would convince them of her urgency without betraying too much. "You don't understand. I must find out who I am. I'm needed. Someone is calling to me. It's a matter of life and death." She touched a hand to her heart. "I sense it here. I must find out who I am and return to the life I once had."

When Father Howie and the Reverend Mother were alone, he rose, walked to a cabinet under the window and removed a glass and a half-empty bottle of brandy. After pouring himself a small measure, he took his chair again.

"I don't know why I indulge you," said the Reverend Mother.

The priest grinned. "Because I'm the elder. It's a habit you've got into, Lizzie." And he laughed at his own pun.

The Reverend Mother refilled her teacup. "What chance is there, John, of finding out who Martha is?"

"Short of Divine intervention, none, I should think. When she first came here, we made an exhaustive search to trace Martha's people, didn't we, and came up with nothing. She hasn't told us anything new that is really useful."

The Reverend Mother knotted her straight black brows. "I don't like the sound of it. 'Someone is calling me. It's a matter of life and death.' Quite frankly, it sounds as though she were . . . well . . . hallucinating."

"It's possible. It's not uncommon for eager young nuns to fall into trances. In fact, it happens all the time."

"Yes, but their visions are usually about the Virgin Mary or one of the holy saints. This is different. This doesn't sound like Martha. She's usually so levelheaded."

"You have a high opinion of that young woman, don't you, Lizzie?"

"I do, and I don't mind admitting it. You didn't see her when she was first brought to the infirmary. She'd been run down by a carriage, almost outside our door. Her arm and two of her ribs were broken. You wouldn't have recognized her face. Yet, she was very brave. We hardly heard a whimper out of her."

"An ideal patient, in fact," he murmured.

She shot him a sharp look. "There's a lot more to it than that. She was panic-stricken when she came to herself and realized she couldn't remember things."

"Yes, I was there."

"And her progress since then has been truly remarkable."

"You've certainly done wonders with the girl."

"I can't take the credit. Martha did it by herself. Most young women in her position would have been reduced to a quivering jelly. She has reserves of strength that few possess. I know she seems cold and reserved—"

"Lizzie, I'm not finding fault with your little chick, far from it."

"—but if you could see her with the children in the orphanage, you would know that there's more to Martha than shows on the surface. The children adore her. And she's indispensable to Sister Dolores in the infirmary."

"Yet, you discouraged her from taking her vows. Why, Lizzie?"

His comment brought the Reverend Mother up short. After a moment's reflection, she let out a sigh. "I was not sure of her vocation, and I saw no harm in delaying. She had lost her memory. If it had come back to her, she might regret the decision she'd made. The convent is all she knows. It's only natural that she would be afraid of the outside world. Here, there is peace and harmony, and useful work to do. It suited Martha. But that is not a vocation."

Father Howie's head was cocked to one side. "Did I ever mention," he said quizzically, "that you are very wise?"

The Reverend Mother smiled. "I don't feel wise, John. In fact, I feel . . . I don't know . . . puzzled, uneasy. For three years, Martha has been happy here. Now, suddenly, she is desperate to return to her former life." The Reverend Mother shook her head. "It would be different if she had regained her memory. Then she would know who her friends were. I don't want her to leave here as things stand."

"I don't think there's much fear of that happening. As I said, she hasn't given us nearly enough to go on. However, there's no use fretting about it. If the good Lord wants Martha to return to her old life, He will clear a path for her."

"And I," she said, giving him a level look, "shall pray that the good Lord will deal gently with her."

She was reaching for the teapot when they heard a cry from the corridor, then the sound of running footsteps. There was a pounding on the door, and at the Reverend Mother's command, a nun entered.

Sister Brigid's face was flushed with excitement. She was breathing hard and could hardly say her words fast enough. "Reverend Mother, it's a miracle! You remember the woman who was brought to the infirmary yesterday? She's come round, and—oh, you'll never guess what's happened!"

Both the Reverend Mother and the little priest had risen to their feet. They exchanged a quick look.

"It's about Sister Martha, isn't it?" said the Reverend Mother.

Sister Brigid did not hear the note of fatalism in the mother superior's voice, but Father Howie did, and he grinned ruefully. "I think," he said, "your prayers are about to be answered, Lizzie, though not, perhaps, in the way you anticipated."

Sister Brigid gave them a radiant smile. "Yes, it's about Sister Martha. The woman recognized her! Only, she's not Martha. Her name is Jessica Hayward, and she is mistress of Hawkshill Manor, near Chalford on the river Thames."

C H A P T E R

2

LUCAS BROUGHT HIS HANDS UP TO COVER HIS EARS AND flipped to his side. There was no relief. The sound of drums grew louder and louder till he thought his head would split. Someone called his name. Groaning, he forced his eyes to open the merest slit. The light was so blinding, it took him a moment or two to take stock of his surroundings. The first thing he recognized was the chamber pot that sat on the table beside the bed. The soldiers lined up on the mantelpiece turned out to be empty brandy bottles. Dirty dishes were stacked high on a chair. The stench of stale sweat and cheap perfume made his stomach heave.

As memory began to return, he let his eyelids droop. He was in the Black Swan. Three, maybe four days and nights drowning his sorrows. And, if he was not mistaken—he groaned again when he felt the soft, womanly contours wriggle against his back—a little bit of an orgy thrown in for good measure. That part, he couldn't remember. He'd wanted oblivion and oblivion was what he'd found.

The drums resolved themselves into a pounding on the door.

"Lucas! Open the door!" His cousin Adrian's voice.

"We know you're in there!" And his younger cousin, Perry.

Lucas shut his eyes tight. If he didn't answer, maybe they would go away.

"Bloody hell!" This came from the soft, womanly contours as she hauled herself up. "Will ye stop yer bawlin'! Yer friend is dead t'the world."

"Open the door at once!" Adrian's voice.

"All right! All right! Hold yer horses."

Lucas heard Millie? Lily? muttering under her breath. "Rich, they calls 'im! Rich, my arse! I's yet to see any coin." She grabbed Lucas's shoulder and shook him hard. "I wants m'money. T'weren't my fault ye were so sotted wi' drink ye couldna rise t'the occasion." There was a thoughtful pause. "And who is Jess?"

That did it. With a roar of rage, Lucas shot out of bed. His anger dimmed a little when he saw the fear in the woman's eyes, and it dimmed even more when it registered that she had the face and form of a blue-eyed Venus. If he couldn't rise to the occasion with Millie? Lily? there was no hope for him.

Christ, when had he got to be so maudlin?

Jess! That one word revived his anger. Teeth gritted he looked around for his clothes and discovered he was still wearing them, except for his coat and boots. His coat was on the floor as was the woman's garments. He reached for his coat, found his purse, extracted a sovereign and tossed it to the girl. He wasn't surprised when she gasped with delight. A crown was the usual rate of exchange for the favors of the Black Swan's barmaids, as he should know.

"Lucas, open the door!"

Lucas bit out something crude and pithy and the door

handle stopped rattling. He picked up the clothes on the floor and threw them at the blue-eyed Venus. "Dress yourself," he said tersely, then he went to the window, opened it wide and breathed deeply. It didn't help. He still felt like a used mop. One step—there wasn't room to swing a cat in this box that passed for a bedchamber—took him to the washstand. He poured the jug of cold water into the tin basin and, cupping his hands, filled his mouth with water, drank greedily, then doused his face and head.

Millie kept one eye on him as she dressed. Lucas Wilde was a regular customer at the Black Swan, but he rarely came upstairs with any of the barmaids, more's the pity. He was tall, muscular, and with darkly handsome looks that made a girl's heart beat just a little faster. Poor sod. She'd heard that he'd never been the same since he'd lost the girl he wanted to wed, which puzzled her, because that girl's name was Bella, not Jess. She couldn't imagine any woman in her right mind choosing another man over him, yet, that's what had happened. But that was before he'd unexpectedly come into a title. He was Lord Dundas now, a belted earl, whatever that meant. Even in his cups, he was a real gent, and generous to a fault. She looked at the gleaming sovereign in her hand and made up her mind that next time she would make it up to him.

"Ready?" Lucas managed to arrange his face in a smile.

Millie nodded, scrambled from the bed and allowed him to lead her to the door.

When the door opened, Perry charged into the room, then came to a sudden halt. In looks, he took after Lucas rather than his brother, Adrian. At twenty-three, he was eight years younger than Lucas, but just as tall. He had the same thick, wavy hair and brown eyes, but Perry's hair was fair while Lucas's was dark.

There was, however, one major difference between them. No shadows from the past touched Perry's young life, and it showed in his ready smile and clear, untroubled eyes. Life was meant to be enjoyed. The only wrinkle that sometimes bothered Perry was that Lucas and Adrian were his joint trustees—and a bit too tight with the purse strings to suit him.

"Whoa," he said, and blocked Millie's exit. He cupped her face with one hand and smiled into her eyes. "Now here's a pretty filly," he said. "Tell me, sweeting, did my cousin—"

The sentence was never completed. Lucas shot out a long arm and grabbed Perry by the collar. "Perry," he drawled, "mind your manners in the presence of ladies."

Perry shrugged free of Lucas's grasp and sketched the barmaid an elegant bow. "Perry Wilde, at your service," he said, and winked broadly.

"Millie Jenkins," she replied, batting her eyelashes, "and likewise, I'm sure."

"Now that's what I like to hear," beamed Perry.

Millie went off in a gale of giggles. Adrian shut the door, and Lucas's eyes shifted to him. In spite of being cousins, the only physical resemblance they shared was their dark coloring. Adrian had the face of a poet and the lean, supple body of an acrobat. He had the annoying habit of always managing to look as though he'd just dressed up for a night on the town. He was born fastidious, thought Lucas dourly. Even as a boy, Adrian had never forgotten to wash behind his ears.

Their interests were as different as their looks. Adrian was happiest in the city where he could pursue his various hobbies—the theatre, the opera, his gentlemen's clubs and, above all, women. He, Lucas, had sworn off women entirely.

So what was he doing here?

Adrian said to Lucas, gesturing to Perry, "My strategy for civilizing this barbarian isn't working. He's had three Seasons in London and the only town bronze he's picked up still smells of manure."

Perry laughed. "I hate London and town manners. I'm a country boy like Lucas. What's wrong with that?"

"Lucas never forgets that he's a gentleman."

"If," said Perry, "this is one of your lectures on good breeding, Adrian, you can stow it. You're forgetting that I know all about you and Lucas and the scrapes you got into when you were my age. I've a long way to go before I catch up to you."

Perry had been wandering around, and had come to a halt by the table with the chamber pot on it. His nose wrinkled, then he looked up and started to laugh. "Good God, Adrian! Is this the mark of a gentleman? This piss pot is brimming."

Lucas did not join in the laughter as he normally would have. His eyes were hot. His head was throbbing. And he did not care to be discovered during one of his bouts of debauchery, especially not by Adrian. Even now, he could feel Adrian's eyes on him, assessing, weighing, seeing more than he wanted him to see. Perry was different. He didn't know him as well as Adrian knew him, and simply took everything at face value.

Every muscle ached as he took the two steps to the washstand. "As you can see," he said, "I'm fine. I don't know what you hoped to accomplish by barging in here." There was a sliver of soap on the stand. He ignored the filthy rag that lay beside it and used his hands to work up a lather to soap his face.

Adrian said quietly, "It's about Jessica Hayward."

Lucas went as rigid as a board. Breathing became difficult. His shoulders sagged. Without being aware of what he was doing, he dried his face and hands with the filthy rag. When he could find his voice, it was no more than a hoarse whisper. "She's dead. Is that what you're trying to tell me?"

Perry opened his mouth to answer but a look from his brother silenced him. "Jess is not dead," said Adrian. "In fact, she's very much alive."

The soapsuds must have got into his eyes. Lucas blinked rapidly to dispel the sting. "She's alive," he repeated. "How do you know?"

"Perry found out. I'll let him tell you the story."

Perry glanced uncertainly at Adrian, then spoke to Lucas's back. "Jessica Hayward rode into Chalford yesterday morning, in a horse-drawn wagon, accompanied by two nuns, if you can believe it. She went straight to your attorney's office in Sheep Street and picked up the keys to Hawkshill Manor. As far as I know, she's there now."

"At Hawkshill?"

"So it would seem."

There was a moment of complete and utter silence, then Lucas pivoted to face his companions. "Who told you this?"

Perry was mystified by the harsh tension in his cousin's face, and he stammered a little before answering. "I saw her with my own eyes. At first, I didn't recognize her. Her garments were . . . well . . . plain, serviceable, you know what I mean. I would have taken her for a serving maid, except that she has the air of a great lady." He chuckled. "Yes, Jessica Hayward a lady! But that was before I recognized her."

"You spoke to her?" asked Lucas sharply.

"Well, of course I spoke to her. I'm not a country oaf, whatever you and Adrian may think. And the scandal had nothing to do with me. I wasn't even here when it happened. If you remember, I was away at Oxford. It was during term."

"Perry," said Adrian, "just get on with it."

"What? Oh, well, as I was saying, I spoke to her. I can't remember exactly what I said . . . just the usual pleasantries—that I wouldn't have known her, and was she staying long, that sort of thing. That's when she told me she was taking up residence at Hawkshill."

While Perry had been speaking, Lucas had been utterly still. Now, he exploded into motion. Despite the con-

fines of the room, he began to pace. "All this time . . .
wondering . . . then, just like that"——he snapped his
fingers——"she rides into town and takes up residence in
Hawkshill." Suddenly halting, he turned to look at
Adrian. "How is this possible? Hawkshill belongs to me
now. Shouldn't I have been consulted?"

Adrian shrugged. "Your attorney asked me to pass
along the message that he'd found tenants for Hawkshill,
but no one knew where you were, not even your mother.
So Perry and I came down here to take care of things."

Lucas said incredulously, "By advising my attorney to
rent a property of mine to Jessica Hayward?"

"Ah, no. It's rented to the Sisters of Charity. They're
an order of nuns that do good works. They are going to
set up an orphanage in Hawkshill——you know, for home-
less children. Since the house was deteriorating from neglect, your attorney jumped at the chance of letting it. All
that remains is for you to sign the papers. As for Jessica,
no one was more surprised than I when Perry told me it
was she who had collected the keys."

"Nuns!" snarled Lucas. "What has Jessica Hayward to
do with nuns?"

Perry said, "I can answer that. She's been living with
them for the last three years, in their convent in London.
Leastways that's what she told me."

No one moved. No one said anything. The only thing
that ruffled the silence was the sound of Lucas's breathing. Finally, he said, "Are you saying Jess is a nun?"

Perry shook his head. "No, I'm not saying that. But
she's helping them set up the orphanage, or something.
We only spoke for a few moments."

Lucas breathed deeply. "Well, she can't stay at Hawkshill."

Perry snickered then stopped abruptly when two pairs
of hostile eyes fastened on him. "No, indeed," he stammered. "That would only start people talking."

Adrian walked to the door and held it open. "Perry, I

think coffee is in order. Why don't you go down to the taproom and reserve a table for us? Lucas and I will be down in a few minutes."

"But the taproom will be empty at this time of day. There's no need to reserve a table."

"Perry."

"Oh, all right then. I can see when I'm not wanted."

There was no real resentment in Perry's voice. He enjoyed a certain closeness with Lucas and Adrian, but only up to a point. Before he was out the door, his expression had brightened. He was thinking of Millie Jenkins and wondering if he would find her in the taproom.

Lucas sat on the edge of the bed and began to haul on his boots. When the silence lengthened, he glanced up at Adrian. He spoke harshly. "Say what you have to say and get it over with."

Adrian paused for a moment to take snuff, looked deprecatingly around the room and, since the only chair was cluttered with dirty dishes, propped one shoulder against the closed door.

"I thought you were over these black spells?" When Lucas did not reply, he went on. "One minute you were the life and soul of Lady Melrose's party and the next you had disappeared off the face of the earth."

"I left you a note."

"Ah yes, a note that told me nothing, not even where I could find you if something came up."

"I'll do better the next time." Lucas rose and reached for his coat.

Adrian sighed. "I was hoping there wouldn't be a next time. You know what everyone thinks, don't you? They think you're still not over Bella."

"That's ridiculous."

"Is it?"

"You know it is! You're as thankful as I am that she chose Rupert over us."

Adrian gave a genuine smile. "That's an odd thing to say when Rupert is one of our closest friends."

"You know what I mean," said Lucas irritably, wondering what the hell he really meant.

"Yes," replied Adrian. "At heart, we're romantics, while Rupert is ruled by his head."

"Now you're talking in riddles," snapped Lucas.

"Am I?"

Lucas gave his cousin a level look. "My black spells, as you call them, have nothing to do with Bella."

"As I am well aware. Lucas, when are you going to stop blaming yourself for what happened?"

"I don't want to talk about it, all right? How do I look?"

Adrian stared at his friend gravely, then shook his head. "There's no reasoning with you when you're in this mood."

Just as grave, Lucas replied, "Not when you talk nonsense, and not when I feel as though I'd just been kicked in the head by a horse. You did mention coffee?"

It took a long time before Adrian's lips curled in a reluctant smile. "You look like hell," he said. "What did you expect after wallowing in this dung hill for the best part of a week?"

"A week?" Lucas's brows rose. "That long?"

"You don't remember?"

"Vaguely. How did you know I was here?"

"Your steward saw your horse in the Black Swan's stable and was good enough to tell me. He knew we were all worried about you."

Lucas's eyes narrowed beneath the black slash of brows. "If I had wanted you to know where to find me, I would have told you."

As soon as the words were out, he regretted them. Adrian was far more to him than a cousin. They'd been friends since they were infants. As boys, they'd done everything together, gone to the same schools, followed the family tradition of attending Oxford University. They'd served in the same regiment, fought in the Spanish Campaign and had both sold out after Waterloo. They'd loved and lost the same girl, Bella. Now that they were older, they were not so close, but they were still good friends. Adrian deserved better of him.

Trying to make amends, he said flippantly, "If I promise to be a good boy and stay out of mischief, will that satisfy you?"

Adrian let out a bellow of laughter, making Lucas wince. "That's more than I would dare ask," said Adrian. "You might demand the same of me."

"At least we understand each other. Shall we go?"

Adrian straightened, but he did not move away from the door. "One final word of advice?"

That was the trouble with making amends. People always took advantage. As stoically as he could manage, Lucas said, "What now?"

"Stay away from Jessica Hayward. Remember what happened the last time you tangled with her. She's—"

Lucas's voice slashed across Adrian's words. "Jessica Hayward has a lot to answer for. I'm not looking for trouble, but if she crosses swords with me, she'll regret it."

Adrian stepped to the side and allowed Lucas to open the door. "As stubborn as a jackass," he muttered. "Haven't I always said so?"

In the taproom, the coffee was already waiting for them, as well as hot, buttered rolls that were straight from the oven. Perry did most of the talking. Adrian watched Lucas and was not surprised when after only a few sips from his cup, he pushed back his chair and rose.

"I'll see you back at the house," he said.

Adrian reached for a buttered roll and said casually, "You're making a mistake."

"That's a matter of opinion."

Perry said, "But where are you going?"

"To take care of some unfinished business," said Lucas.

CHAPTER
3

JESSICA HAYWARD. SHE PAUSED TO SAVOR THE SOUND OF her name, then went back to kneading the dough for the day's bread. She still found it hard to believe. She didn't feel like a stray anymore. She was a real person, Jessica Hayward, and she'd come home.

Not that Hawkshill Manor belonged to her. It had been sold to Lord Dundas to pay off her father's debts. That was one thing that had come as a great disappointment to her. She had no living relatives. She still didn't know what had taken her to London.

The sudden sting of tears took her by surprise. It was stupid, of course, but she'd hoped . . . She blinked them away. So she was an orphan, just like their boys. It couldn't possibly matter to her, because she couldn't remember her parents. But it did matter. Before Mrs. Marshal, the woman at the infirmary who had recognized her, had filled in the blanks, she'd begun to weave fantasies about her family. She'd imagined her homecoming. She would be like the prodigal son returning from a far country and her parents would throw a party in her honor. She would be surrounded by her brothers and sisters and cousins and uncles and aunts, and there would be great rejoicing throughout the land. Then she'd learned that she had no living relatives. Her mother had died when she, Jessica, was an infant and her father not long before she'd turned up at the convent.

So much for her fantasies.

She shook her head. She should be grateful just to be here. And now that she was home, she would meet people who had known her from before. Then she would have the answers to all the questions that teemed inside her head. And now that she was in familiar surroundings, maybe her memory would start to come back to her.

She stopped kneading, and glanced around the kitchen. If only she could remember . . . Impatient with herself, she went back to kneading her dough. The important thing now was the work she and the sisters had to do, and Hawkshill Manor was ideal for their purposes.

Manor was too grand a word for this dilapidated red-brick building. One could tell that Hawkshill had once been a working farm, but that was before it had fallen into decay. And a working farm it would become again if the Sisters of Charity had anything to do with it. It was a dream the mother superior had long cherished—to train the older boys in the orphanage for a trade, and everything had fallen out, so she'd said, as though it had been ordained.

Ordained. Jessica couldn't help smiling. All that meant was that when Father Howie had made inquiries on her behalf, he'd discovered that Hawkshill had lain empty for three years and could be rented for a song. So not only could Jessica return to her home with the sisters to keep an eye on her, but the mother superior's dream could be realized as well.

The landlord obviously had no interest in the place. His house was only a mile along the road and could be seen from their attic windows but, according to the attorney, Lord Dundas had no use for Hawkshill's buildings and had bought the property because its acreage adjoined his own estate. This being the case, there was a good chance his lordship could be persuaded to waive the rent if he thought it was in a good cause. Lord Dundas was known to be a very generous man.

And so here they were, the advance party, she and Sisters Dolores and Elvira, along with old Joseph, the burly former pugilist turned convent doorman who was now their watchdog. It was their job to get Hawkshill ready before their boys arrived. She wondered how the boys would react when they saw her as she was now. She was no longer Sister Martha, no longer in the garb of a novice. Deep down, she'd always suspected she had no calling as a nun, and now she knew it. She was plain Miss Jessica Hayward, and dressed to suit her new station in life.

Her new station in life. She absently dipped one hand into the crock of flour by her elbow, rubbed her hands together and began to divide the dough into three equal parts. She would not have been human if she hadn't been avidly curious to know about her friends. She'd met one already, Mr. Perry Wilde. Yesterday, he'd stopped her in Sheep Street and had seemed really pleased to see her. It had been an awkward moment for her. She didn't want anyone to know she'd lost her memory. As irrational as it was, she was ashamed, fearful. She didn't want fingers pointing at her or people whispering behind her back, saying that she was odd. What she wanted more than anything was to be treated as an ordinary girl.

Oh yes, just an ordinary girl! If they ever got to know of her Voice, they would do to her what they'd done to Joan of Arc.

Time and enough to think of that later. For the present, it was her job to bake the bread. And when she'd finished with that, there were strawberry tarts to make. In fact, there was no end of work to keep her busy. The house looked well enough from the outside, but inside it was a shambles. The day before, after they arrived, they'd done no more than clean out the kitchen and one of the bedrooms. When Sisters Dolores and Elvira returned from Chalford, where they'd gone to fetch supplies, they were going to tackle the rest of the house, with Joseph doing most of the heavy work. Meanwhile, he was out searching for firewood and she had bread, scones and pies to make.

She worked quickly now, patting the dough into three loaves and covering them with a damp cloth before setting them aside. There were no eggs to be had, so she used milk to brush the surface of the scones she'd just made, and grasping the long wooden paddle at the side of the fireplace, she eased them into the brick oven. The heat from the fire was scorching hot, and when the scones were in place, she shut the door with a snap and swiftly stepped back. It took only a few moments to set out the ingredients for her strawberry tarts.

She straightened and stretched her spine. The table was too low for comfort, and if she was going to do most of the cooking, which seemed likely, one of the first things they would have to do was replace it or she would end up with a permanent backache. To ease her aching muscles, she took a few paces around the kitchen, then wandered into the breakfast room and into the front hall.

There was a long, cracked pier glass between two doors, and though she always avoided looking at herself when the sisters were there, she had to admit that nothing in the house fascinated her half as much as that looking glass. There were no mirrors in the convent that were bigger than a thumbnail. Until now, she'd never seen a full-length reflection of herself.

The girl in the looking glass stared solemnly back at her. Jessica moved closer and traced the reflection of her eyes, her brows, her nose, her chin. She smiled, she frowned, she turned this way and that to get a better look at herself. Though she was by no means sure, she thought her best feature might be her hair. It was the color of honey and the curl could only be tamed when she did it in a long plait, as now. Her figure—she removed her apron and set it on a bench—she thought was too thin. The high-waisted spotted muslin hung on her loosely. She pinched it between her fingers to get a smoother fit. That was better. She wondered if that nice young man she'd met on Sheep Street thought she was pretty.

This was vanity. She shouldn't be thinking these thoughts. The mother superior was right. Idleness was an invention of the devil. She should get back to work.

She was reaching for her apron when she heard the clatter of a horse's hooves on the approach to the house. Her heart gave a leap. It might be that nice Mr. Wilde, coming to call, or a friend who had heard from him that she was back in Hawkshill. Nerves fluttered in the pit of her stomach. Breathing deeply, she opened the door and stepped onto the porch.

When she saw the horse and rider, she felt a shiver of alarm. The man on the horse looked as though he might have stolen it. The horse was a magnificent beast—black glossy coat, streaming mane, muscles that moved and rippled as it climbed the slope. Its rider was the opposite. He slouched in the saddle. His clothes were disheveled; his hair uncombed; his face unshaven. But it was his expression that alarmed her more than anything. His brows were down and his jaw was tensed. This was definitely not a friendly visit.

Her mind made a lightning connection. He must be one of those Gypsies or tinkers—"those thieving rogues" as Sister Dolores called them—who had encamped in Hawkshill while it had lain empty. It was their mess she and the sisters were now forced to clean up. Joseph had warned her they might return and had advised her on how to handle it. This called for a show of strength.

Swinging around, she darted into the hall and snatched up the old blunderbuss that lay, primed and ready, behind the door. Then she walked out of the house to face the intruder. A show of strength, that's all the blunderbuss was. She wasn't supposed to aim it at anyone. If worse came to worst, she was to fire it into the air and that would bring Joseph to her.

The stranger reined in a few yards away. He didn't dismount, but sat at his ease, eyes narrowed on her speculatively, as a panther might eye a rabbit that had suddenly strayed into its path.

He spoke first. "I swore I wouldn't come here. Curiosity got the better of me, that and an irresistible urge to welcome my new tenants."

His meaning hardly registered. She was puzzling over the sneer behind the words and the insolent twist to his mouth. He was angry about something, and she couldn't think what. She hadn't done anything. He was the one who was trespassing.

He leaned forward in the saddle and gave her the same insolent smile. "Didn't my attorney tell you? I own Hawkshill now."

"*You* own Hawkshill?" She could hardly credit it. This was their landlord, this unkempt, disreputable-looking wild man? She shook her head.

"Oh, it's perfectly true. Ask my attorney if you don't believe me. I, Lucas Wilde, am the owner of Hawkshill."

Wilde? That was the name of the young man she'd met in Sheep Street. They must be related. "You are Lord Dundas?" she asked incredulously.

"Aye, a lord now, Miss Hayward, and rich enough to buy and sell my neighbors ten times over." He edged his horse forward. "But life is full of these little ironies, don't you think?"

He might look like a Gypsy but he spoke like a gentleman. Lord Dundas. It must be true. Now she understood the condition of the house. It was just like its owner.

The conviction that he was telling the truth hardly reassured her. From the look of him, she would have said that he'd been drinking.

She'd dealt with drunkards before, when she and the sisters had combed the stews of London for abandoned children. But on those occasions, she'd been dressed in her nun's habit. Even the most ramshackle dock worker showed respect for the Sisters of Charity. She wasn't wearing her habit now.

She eyed him warily. He was their landlord and she didn't want to get his back up. At the same time, she knew that drink made a man unpredictable. As a subtle reminder that she wasn't as defenseless as he might think, she inched the gun into the crook of one arm.

His response was a low rumble of laughter. "Careful," he said, "you might hurt someone with that thing," and without taking his eyes off her, he slowly dismounted and tethered his horse to the hitching post.

She backed up a step, giving herself room to maneuver in case she had to get off a shot to summon Joseph. "The sisters aren't here," she said, "only our man, Joseph." The reference to Joseph was another subtle reminder that she wasn't as defenseless as he might think. "And I have no authority to act for the sisters."

He arched one brow. "Yes, I heard about the nuns, but I can hardly believe the story I was told. Why don't you explain it to me in your own words?"

"There's not much to tell. We're going to bring some of our boys from the orphanage here, to teach them how to run a farm or apprentice them to local tradesmen, you know, so that they will have a chance of improving their lot when they leave here."

"Just you and the nuns?"

"Oh no. We'll hire people to help us."

He laughed harshly. "And you expect me to believe that?"

When he took another step toward her, it flashed

through her mind that he was far more dangerous than she'd realized. Now that he was only a pace away, she saw things she hadn't noticed before. He was in the grip of some powerful emotion he could hardly control. He stood there, staring at her, jaw clenched, hands fisting and un-fisting at his sides.

She heard the catch in her throat and was aware that her pulse had leapt. If he wanted to, he could really hurt her. But she had the gun.

His voice was husky. "Why? Why did you come back?"

"I told you. For the children. We're going to teach them to be farmers, or help them learn a trade."

"Was it for the title? The money? Did you think the past wouldn't make a difference? Answer me, Jess."

Whatever he knew of Jessica Hayward obviously wasn't to her credit. She didn't have time to think about that now. He was closing the gap between them, forcing her to retreat. Her next step took her into the hall.

She moistened her lips. "Lord Dundas—"

He acted as though she'd struck him. "Christ, if you call me that again—"

He was reaching for her, and she jerked up the gun, pointing it straight at his chest. He stopped dead in his tracks. "I know how to use this," she said, trying to control the wobble in her voice. "I'm warning you, don't come any closer."

The hard planes of his face gradually softened and he laughed low in his throat. "Now this is more like the Jess I know." He spread his arms wide and took another step toward her. "Go on, then. Pull the trigger. You can't miss me from that distance. Aim for here." He touched his heart. "What's the matter, Jess? Have you lost your nerve?"

She aimed for the floor, shut her eyes and squeezed the trigger. Nothing happened. It was a mistake that cost her dearly as she knew the moment she opened her eyes. His face was livid with color and his lips were pulled back, baring his teeth.

"Christ! You vicious little bitch! If you had remembered to cock that firing piece, you would have emasculated me."

Though she quailed before the thirteen stone of quivering masculine outrage that loomed over her, there was just enough of Sister Martha in her to be outraged as well. "Blasphemy," she coldly informed him, "is not tolerated in this house."

"The hell it isn't!"

With a suddenness that caught her off guard, he grabbed for the gun and with one yank wrested it from her hands. She had the presence of mind to give him a hard shove, then she took off. She heard another violent oath, then the thud of his boots as he came after her. Panting as though her lungs would burst, she flung into the kitchen and made straight for the paddle beside the brick oven. Without waiting to take aim, she swung it in an arc and caught him a glancing blow on the shoulder. He staggered and cursed, but still came on. There was no stopping this man! She swung the paddle again, missed, and sent the crock of flour she'd set out on the table tumbling to the floor. A fine brown powder floated up.

He gave one of his infuriating low laughs and lunged for her. She swung at him again. This time her paddle collided with the pan of strawberry jam and sent it spinning. It hit the mantel with a resounding thud and exploded in a shower of gooey crimson rain. It rained on the ceiling, it rained on the floor. It rained on him, it rained on her.

Hands on hips, he threw back his head and hooted with laughter. "If you could only see yourself!"

She didn't care what she looked like, not when she was facing a madman. Her eyes were trained on him, watching his every move. Her hands were clenched around the paddle, holding it like a lance. When he came at her, she went for him, but he neatly sidestepped her. As she charged by, he grabbed her from behind, pinioning her arms to her sides, and he lifted her effortlessly off her feet. She bucked, she kicked, she twisted, she squirmed. She could not budge him. He was squeezing her so hard she thought she would suffocate. In a blind panic, she dropped the paddle. Almost at once, the pressure of his arms eased.

When her feet touched the floor, he slowly turned her to face him. "What in hell's name did you think I was going to do to you?" he demanded, giving her a rough shake.

She didn't have the breath to answer him. She was using the dregs of her strength to strain as far back as his hands would allow.

"Dammit, will you stop squirming?"

She stopped squirming.

His brows were a dark slash. His eyes moved slowly over her face. "You're frightened of me," he said, "really frightened."

She wheezed out, "You attacked me."

He gave a crooked half smile. "Jess, you were the one with the gun. You provoked me. You know you did."

He was using the tone of voice she, herself, sometimes used with the children in the orphanage, when she wanted to soothe their fears. He didn't seem like a dangerous lunatic now. In fact, that crooked half smile made him look almost harmless. With that thought, some of the tension drained out of her. She shrugged helplessly. "I thought you were mad."

"And I thought you were . . . sweet."

When he reached out with his hand, she jerked back. "Don't!"

His hand dropped away. Something came and went in his eyes, pain, regret—whatever it was, it made her feel less threatened.

"It's only a blob of jam," he said.

She brushed her face with her hand. "Jam?"

"Allow me." Again, his hand reached for her, but this time she didn't flinch away. With the pad of his thumb, he removed the sticky substance from her chin. "Jam," he said, showing it to her. Then, with eyes holding hers, he spread the jam on his tongue and swallowed.

The muscles in her throat contracted involuntarily. She felt the swift rise and fall of her breasts. A strange expectancy gripped her. As his eyes continued to hold hers, her heart began to pound.

He let his breath out slowly. "It's still there, isn't it, Jess? You feel it, too. Is this why you came back? Is it, Jess? *Is it?* No, don't push me away. I won't hurt you. I just want to hold you."

She didn't resist when he drew her into the circle of his arms. Something stirred in her, something that went beyond memory. Her brow wrinkled as she searched his face. Here was someone who could tell her all she wanted to know about Jessica Hayward. Then his dark head descended and she froze as his mouth touched hers.

Before she could draw a breath to protest, every fiber of her being was electrified. The terror she had experienced only moments before at the hands of this man was forgotten, as were the rules she was sworn to uphold as a nun. Sister Martha might never have existed for all the impression she made on Jessica. The kitchen of Hawkshill Manor slipped quietly into oblivion. The only reality she was sure of was the rightness of being in his arms. Her mind might not recognize this man, but there was something in the deepest reaches of her psyche that was profoundly affected. In that moment, she could have sworn he was as familiar to her as the beat of her own heart.

She was captivated by the gentleness of the powerful arms that held her; she was enthralled by the reverence of his lips as they moved on hers. He kissed her again and again, each kiss sweeter than the last. Her lips softened beneath the pressure of his, and her hands moved of their own volition to slide over his shoulders and into his hair.

That small act of surrender changed everything. He tore his mouth from hers and covered her face with hard, random kisses, her throat, her breasts. His chest rose and fell rapidly. Air rushed in and out of his lungs.

"Jess," he whispered hoarsely, "Jess."

She cried out when he lowered her to the table, then she relaxed as he came down beside her. She wasn't afraid. Memories that were born and bred into every cell and sinew of her body had taken over.

He was staring down at her through the veil of his thick dark lashes.

"I trust you," she whispered, and the truth of it awed her.

He went perfectly still. "You trust me?"

She nodded.

With a savage oath, he pulled to his feet. A muscle clenched in his jaw and the violence was back in his eyes.

Shocked, she rose to her elbows. "What did I say?" she cried out.

He lowered his head till his face was within an inch of hers. "You have a poor memory," he said, snarling the words. "That's exactly what you said the last time. I lost Bella because of you, and for what? A toss in the hay that didn't amount to much."

His sneer became more pronounced when he straightened and began to adjust his clothing. "For God's sake, tidy yourself. And get off that table before someone walks in here. Or is that what your scheming little mind is hoping will happen? If you think I can be browbeaten into marrying you, you can think again."

Jessica's scattered thoughts were beginning to come together, and the more they came together, the more appalled she was. She was the lunatic, not he! With a gasping cry, she scrambled off the table and stared at it in horror, wondering what on earth could have possessed her to go so far. Burning with shame, she turned to face him.

The contempt in his eyes goaded a temper that she had not known was there. "I didn't invite you here," she said. "You invited yourself. And as for browbeating you into marriage, I'd sooner take my vows."

His mouth curved in an unpleasant smile, then he turned on his heel and strode for the door. At the threshold, he turned back. "You still haven't answered my question. Why did you come back? And don't give me that faradiddle about the boys from the orphanage. That may do for the nuns, but it won't do for me."

She lifted her chin a notch and looked him squarely in the eyes. She wanted to shake him as much as he had shaken her. "I came back to find a murderer," she said.

All the color washed out of his face and his eyes flared. In a low, driven tone, he said, "I want you out of here. Oh, the nuns can stay, but you go. Get back to your nunnery, Jess. There's no place for you here. If you won't go willingly, I'll make you go. Do I make myself clear?"

He didn't wait for her answer, but slammed the door as he left.

CHAPTER
4

THE ATTORNEY PASSED THE DOCUMENTS TO JESSICA, sat back in his chair and gave her a moment to absorb what she was reading.

Finally raising her eyes, she said, "Two thousand pounds?" It seemed like a fortune. This was the residue of her father's estate after taxes and various obligations had been discharged.

"Naturally, it's invested," said Mr. Rempel. "You'll have a small income, and if you're careful and leave the capital intact, it should be enough for your needs." He shook his head. "There should have been more, much more, but your father was not exactly a provident man."

Jessica felt as though a weight had been lifted from her shoulders. When she'd come into town in answer to Mr. Rempel's brief note, she'd feared he would hand her an eviction notice signed by Lord Dundas. Three days had passed since he'd threatened to drive her out of Hawkshill, but so far he'd taken no action against her. Now, he could do what he liked and it wouldn't matter. She could move out of Hawkshill and take lodgings in town. Modest lodgings, but she was used to that.

She hadn't been prepared to like Mr. Rempel when she'd entered his office. A great deal had changed in five minutes and she looked at him with different eyes. He was small and rotund, the picture of a congenial country gentleman who spent more time out of doors than he did at his desk.

"I didn't expect anything like this," she said, handing him back the documents.

He misunderstood. "No. As I said, your father wasn't a provident man. If it had not been for Lucas there would have been even less of an estate to pass on."

Her shoulders involuntarily stiffened. "What does Lord Dundas have to do with my father's estate?"

"When Hawkshill went up for sale, Lucas bought it for far more than it was worth."

"Why would he do such a thing?"

"Why?" The attorney picked up a pen and studied it carefully. "You'll have to ask Lucas that question." He looked up and shrugged. "I've known Lucas since he was a boy. He has always been openhanded, even when he was poor and living off the charity of his relations. He felt responsible, I suppose, perhaps even guilty, though no one blamed him for what happened to your father that night."

"What happened to my father?"

He looked at her in surprise. "You don't know?"

She shook her head.

"It was in all the papers, oh, not just the local papers, but in the London *Gazette* as well."

"I didn't see them." When he hesitated, she went on. "Please, don't spare my feelings. I have to know."

He looked down at his hands. "He was shot to death by some assailant as he made his way home from a local tavern. Shot in the back, to be precise."

She felt as though the ground beneath her feet had

suddenly shifted and she was tottering on the edge of a black hole. She had never imagined anything like this.

All she'd known was what the woman in the infirmary had told her, that her parents were dead. Mrs. Marshal had said nothing of murder. Perhaps she hadn't known. Or perhaps she had known but hadn't wanted to upset one of the nuns who was nursing her.

The solicitor was watching her, waiting for her to react to the news he'd just broken. A normal girl would have feelings; a normal girl would break down in tears, or rant and rage about this horrible thing that had happened to her father. But she wasn't normal. She had no memory of her father. Then why did she feel so shattered?

"Miss Hayward, are you all right? Can I get you a glass of water? Brandy?"

The attorney had half risen from his chair and she made an effort to collect herself. "No. Thank you." She managed a smile. "I'm fine."

He sank back in his chair.

She swallowed hard. "Who did it?"

"No one was ever apprehended."

"When did it happen?"

"In the late summer of 1815."

"What date?"

"August sixteenth. I remember the date because it was my wife's birthday."

And on the eighteenth, two days later, she had been knocked down by a carriage in front of the convent. She sat there staring mutely up at him as the thought sank into her mind. "And where was I?"

"Where were you? Don't you know?"

He was looking at her curiously, almost suspiciously. There was no way out of it. She had to tell him the truth.

"I don't know because I've lost my memory as the result of an accident. I remember nothing before I awakened in the convent of the Sisters of Charity. And that was three years ago."

"You've lost your memory?"

"I didn't even know my own name until a few weeks ago. A patient in the infirmary recognized me. Until then, I was Sister Martha. Now I'm Jessica Hayward, but I know nothing about my life before I was a nun. I don't even know what I was doing in London, or how long I'd been there before the accident."

His mouth was agape and he was staring at her as though she'd sprouted another head. It was exactly the reaction she had feared, and it made her squirm.

He closed his mouth. "By damn!" he said. "I think you're telling the truth! No wonder no one could find you. Who would have believed that Jessica Hayward would have ended up in a nunnery?"

She didn't allow herself to become diverted. "Mr. Rempel, when exactly did I leave Chalford?"

He hesitated then said, "My memory is uncertain about the exact sequence of events. Constable Clay is the person you should ask."

"But surely you can tell me whether it was before or after my father's death?"

"You disappeared the same night your father died," he said. "Your bed had not been slept in. That's all anyone knows."

She stared at him blindly as a confusion of thoughts raced through her brain. "The same night," she said faintly.

He leaned forward, clasping his plump hands on the flat of his desk. "Listen to me, Miss Hayward. Start afresh somewhere else. You have the funds to do it, oh not on a grand scale, but modestly if you're careful."

"Why should I do that?"

He shrugged. "People gossip, you know how it is. You've been away for three years. There's been a great deal of speculation about you."

She waited expectantly, and when he remained silent, she said, "You must see how it is with me. Without my memory, I feel lost. Anything you can tell me can only help me to get my bearings."

"I know very little," he said, "and most of what I know is based on hearsay. No, Miss Hayward, I'm not the person to ask."

She was sure he could tell her plenty if he had a mind to. Ignoring that for the moment, she said, "But you do know about my father's death. How did it happen?"

"He'd been drinking at the Black Swan. He was on his way home when he was set upon and was shot to death."

"Why should Lucas Wilde feel guilty—that is what you said, isn't it?"

"Lucas has no need to feel guilty. Anyone could have killed your father. It might have been poachers or footpads."

"Then what did you mean when you said that Lucas blamed himself for what happened to my father that night?"

"They quarreled, just before the tragedy happened. Your father wasn't armed when he left the Black Swan, so he wasn't in a position to defend himself. Lucas had taken his pistol away from him. You need not look like that. Lucas was completely exonerated at the inquest."

Her breath came quick and fast. "Oh, I don't doubt it. The noble Earl of Dundas would have many friends in high places."

He spoke abruptly. "He wasn't an earl then. He was plain Mr. Wilde. Miss Hayward, let me give you a word of advice. Don't go around casting aspersions on Lucas's character. He's well liked in and around Chalford, and you'll only make enemies for yourself."

She bit back an angry retort. The attorney was right. She had to tread carefully here.

"I'm sorry," she said. "I don't know what to think, but I shouldn't have jumped to conclusions. Tell me about my father. Where did the attack take place?"

He sighed and shook his head, obviously impatient

with her persistence. "He took a short way home, by the bridle path that goes through Hawkshill's woods. If you want to know more, I suggest you ask at the tollbooth. Constable Clay was on duty that night."

"And what did Lucas and my father quarrel about?"

He stood up, abruptly bringing their interview to an end. "Constable Clay will be able to tell you more about that, too, but if I were you, I'd talk to Lucas first."

She could see from his expression that he would not answer any more questions. Smiling to mask her frustration, she allowed him to usher her to the door. She held out her hand. "Thank you for taking care of my affairs, Mr. Rempel."

He clasped her hand and held on to it, preventing her from leaving. "There's a lot you don't know, Miss Hayward, and it's not my place to tell you. The more I think of it, the more convinced I am that you should talk to Lucas before you come to any decision about your future."

When she stepped onto the pavement, she began to tremble. Everything was coming together. It was her father's murder she had seen over and over again. That explained her connection to her Voice. Her father's murder, not some stranger's. And two days afterward she was run down by a carriage in London.

Nothing would convince her that these events were unrelated. She didn't believe in coincidence, not on this scale. Then what had happened? Where was she when her father was murdered and how had she got to London?

Her next thought had her reaching for the door lintel to steady herself. Perhaps everyone in Chalford believed that *she* had murdered her father and had run away to escape the consequences. And what could she say in her own defense? That her *Voice* was responsible? What *Voice*? Where was he? *Who* was he?

Many minutes passed as she groped in her mind for something, some memory to guide her. There was nothing. All she had to go on were cold facts. And the most significant thing she had learned so far was that Lucas Wilde had quarreled with her father just before the murder. And she could not forget Lucas's expression when she'd told him she'd come back to find a murderer. He had something to hide, that's why he had warned her away.

He wasn't the only one who had warned her away. The attorney had advised her to start afresh somewhere else. It seemed that neither she nor her father had had many friends among the good people of Chalford. In the last three days, no one had come to call. No former friends had descended on Hawkshill to welcome her home. This wasn't how she'd imagined it would be. Maybe she hadn't fitted in here any more than she'd fitted in at the convent.

When she realized where her thoughts were leading, she straightened her shoulders and lifted her chin. She didn't have the time or energy to waste on useless self-pity. She'd returned to Chalford with a purpose and she would do well to remember it.

She had taken only a few steps away from the solicitor's door when a horse and rider turned the corner of Waterside Street into Sheep Street. It was Lucas. He had yet to see her, and she quickly stepped into the doorway of a draper's shop where she could watch him unobserved.

On this occasion, he was equal to his horse, more than equal. His loose-limbed grace was pleasing to the eye. In fact, everything about him was pleasing to the eye. He was immaculately turned out in a dark gray coat and doeskin breeches. The powerful muscles in his legs and thighs rippled as he directed his horse. Today, he was wearing a hat, and beneath its broad brim his clean-shaven, handsome face was wreathed in smiles.

The smiles were for various townspeople who had business in Sheep Street. There were many who called out a greeting to him as he walked his horse up the hill. There was no question in her mind that Lucas Wilde fitted in. He was the last person anyone would suspect of murder. But that's exactly what her Voice had told her during vespers.

People were such fools. They looked at him and saw exactly what he wanted them to see. No one had ever suspected him of murder. He was too clever for them.

A fierce determination suddenly seized her. She would unmask him. As God was her witness, she would unmask her Voice! He had shot her father in the back, as if he were vermin. No one deserved to die like that. Her Voice was a monster.

For just a moment, she felt such a pang of grief that she wanted to cry. She'd never given much thought to the victim in the vision her Voice had passed on to her. All she'd felt was the natural regret and horror she would feel for anyone who'd met a violent end. But now she wondered what was going through her father's mind at the moment of death. Was he afraid? Had he suffered? Were his last thoughts of her?

Blinking rapidly, she turned on her heel and struck out toward Chapel Street. It wasn't the way she wanted to go, but she had no wish to come face-to-face with her landlord. A short detour would take her to the Black Swan. She'd passed it on the way to the attorney's office when she'd stopped to watch the Morris dancers on the banks of the river Thames. The Black Swan was the tavern Mr. Rempel had mentioned, where Lucas and her father had quarreled.

It was market day, and in the Black Swan's inner courtyard, what seemed like a regiment of horses were tethered to hitching posts. Jessica passed the entrance to the courtyard and boldly entered the inn by the front door. Finding no one at the desk in the hall, she followed the sound of voices to a glass door on her left. She took one step into the room and abruptly halted. Though the place was crowded, there wasn't a lady in sight except for the young women who were waiting on table.

Someone at her back exclaimed her name and a sea of faces turned to stare at her. Jessica did not hear. She was intent on visualizing the quarrel that had taken place between Lucas Wilde and her father all those years ago.

The room couldn't have been well lit. This was a Tudor building with small windowpanes and dark crossbeams supporting the low ceilings. The bar was at one end with tankards of ale set out for the barmaids to serve. Some gentlemen were drinking at the counter.

She had the scene well impressed on her mind, but something intruded, something that startled her. She was here, too, not as she was, but as she'd been as a very young girl. She was desperately unhappy about something. Lucas left his friends and came toward her.

"You shouldn't be here, Jess."

She didn't know if it was a memory or simply her imagination.

"You shouldn't be here, Jess."

A hand on her arm turned her around. Lucas Wilde was glowering down at her, not the Lucas of her reverie, but someone infinitely more menacing. It took her a moment to come to herself, to distinguish reality from fantasy. Then she was puzzled. She had left him on Sheep Street. How had he got here?

"You followed me!" she said furiously.

He ignored her outburst. "In the name of God, Jess! What the devil do you think you're doing here?"

"I have business here," she said sharply.

"Believe me the kind of business you'll find here won't be to your taste."

A movement on the stairs caught his eye and he stepped in front of her, blocking her vision. She circumvented his maneuver by standing on tiptoe to peek over his shoulder. A couple were descending the stairs. The girl was adjusting the drawstrings on her bodice. The man's arm was draped around her shoulders, and he was nuzzling her ear. When they passed into the taproom, Lucas turned on her.

"See what I mean?"

Jessica did, and her face was red, but she held her ground. "I've been in worse places than this when I was a nun, looking for parents who had abandoned their children."

"I don't care what you did as a nun. You're not a nun now, and this is Chalford. Let's go."

She stuck out her chin. "I'm not leaving here till I talk to the landlord."

Whatever Lucas was about to say was forestalled when one of the barmaids caught sight of him and hailed him by name. "It's me," she said, smiling broadly as she set down the brandy cask she'd obviously just brought up from the cellar. "Millie Jenkins. 'Ave ye time for a quick one, luv? This one's on me. I owes you, and Millie Jenkins always pays 'er debts." Her eyes flickered to Jessica. "You must be the new girl. Come to take Flora's place, 'ave ye?"

Jessica didn't know whose face was redder, hers or Lucas's. He stood stock-still for a moment, darted her an uneasy glance, then bared his teeth in a pathetically false smile. "Some other time, Millie," he said. "My friend and I were just leaving."

He grabbed Jessica's arm and propelled her to the rear of the building. "We'll go out the back way," he said curtly. "Perry has his curricle waiting."

Jessica was sorely tempted to put up a struggle, but her memory of the last time she had struggled with this man was still too vivid for comfort. Humiliated beyond words, she allowed him to have his way.

CHAPTER
5

PERRY HAD POSITIONED THE CURRICLE CLOSE TO THE back door and was standing by the horses, holding them steady. Lucas didn't give her time to climb into the curricle, but swept her up in his arms, tossed her in and sprang up beside her. When he had the reins in his hands he said, "Perry, mount up."

Fuming, Jessica watched as the nice young man who had greeted her effusively on her first day in Chalford quickly mounted Lucas's great black stallion. Perry Wilde obviously found the situation humorous. His eyes were twinkling and he was grinning even more broadly than the barmaid in the taproom. Millie Jenkins, she thought, and sniffed.

"This should give us a semblance of respectability," said Lucas, and ignoring Perry's disbelieving laugh, he flicked the reins and urged the matched chestnuts through the arch that gave onto Waterside Street.

There were no houses on the other side of the street to block Jessica's view of the river Thames, and she had a glimpse of punts and barges bobbing on the water, and on the near bank, children feeding the swans. Then her view was obscured as Perry nudged his horse into position, close to her side of the curricle. She had time to give him one long, aggrieved look then she clutched for the side of the curricle when Lucas suddenly sent his team flying toward the Oxford road. Their pace was so furious that everything flew by in a confusion of hedgerows, cottages and the occasional vehicle and rider. Nor did Lucas slow his pace until they had turned off the main thoroughfare and into the approach to Hawkshill. Here he drew rein.

"My thanks for the loan of your curricle, Perry," he said. "Why don't you go on and I'll meet you back at the house?"

"What?"

"I'll meet you back at the house," said Lucas pointedly. "I'll return your curricle to you then."

"But I want to talk to Jess."

"You can talk to her later, after I've had my say."

"But—"

Lucas snapped, "What I have to say is for Jess's ears only. Now, go away."

Perry's face flushed to the roots of his blond hair, making him look very young, and Jessica felt a wave of indignation on his behalf. She'd learned a great deal about Lucas and his family in the last three days, courtesy of old Joseph who had struck up an acquaintance with some of Lucas's tenants, and she thought that it was a pity his tenants could not see their master now. Just why Lucas Wilde was so well liked was a mystery to her.

Lucas gave a crooked half smile. "Perry, I have an apology to make to Jessica, and it's going to be difficult enough without you listening in."

It was an olive branch of sorts, and Jessica did her part to help Perry save face. "And I," she said tartly, "have a few choice words I wish to say to Lucas."

Perry grinned. "All right, all right," he said. "You've

convinced me. I'd only be in the way." With a cheery wave, he wheeled his mount and trotted off.

As soon as Perry was out of sight, Lucas turned on her. It was the moment she had been waiting for, too. Eyes snapping, she cried, "You have no right to treat me like this. This is an abduction, that's what it is."

"I didn't hear you screaming for help when I smuggled you out of the Swan. You should never have gone there."

"How was I to know it wasn't what it seemed?"

"You must have seen there were no females there when you entered the taproom."

"There were women there. They were waiting on tables."

He snorted. "Aye, women, and that's putting it politely."

She breathed slowly, seething. "You would know more about that than I."

Her angry words were met by silence. Lucas was staring at her oddly. Finally, he looked away and said, "About Millie Jenkins . . ."

"What about her?"

He cleared his throat. "It's not what you think, that is, I know the girl by sight, I mean, I've met her . . ." His brows came down. "Hell and damnation, Jess, I know what you're thinking, and you've got it all wrong. At any rate, I'm sorry she accosted you like that, sorry for what she said to you, and that's the only apology you're going to get from me."

It was her turn to stare. Why he thought he owed her an explanation for Millie Jenkins was beyond her comprehension. Did he think that just because she had allowed him to kiss her she would care? She wasn't so naive.

"There's no need to apologize," she said. "I've had worse things said to me in the taverns of London. Nuns are not so sheltered as you seem to think. As for your relationship with Miss Jenkins, that means nothing to me."

He grinned wickedly. "Are you sure about that, Jess?"

"Perfectly." Her tone was frigid.

"You're not still in love with me?"

Jessica was speechless. When she could find her voice, she said hoarsely, "When was I ever in love with you?"

His eyes narrowed on her face. "If you're trying to convince me that you've lost your memory, you'll have to do better than that."

It took her a moment to think this through and when she did, she saw red. "You've been to see the attorney," she said. "He told you that I'd lost my memory." She breathed deeply. "I find that appalling. It's highly unethical for an attorney to gossip about one client to another, and if it isn't, it ought to be."

In contrast to her impassioned tone, he spoke slowly and reasonably. "Rempel does not gossip about one client to another, so don't get your bowels in an uproar over nothing. It was the sisters who told me that you'd lost your memory. All Rempel did was warn me that your next stop was likely to be the Swan."

She bristled with hostility. "You were at Hawkshill?"

"Just after you left."

"You have no business spying on me!"

She glanced at his face, then glanced away. He wasn't looking at her as though she'd sprouted another head, and she couldn't detect pity in his expression, either. She didn't know why his opinion of her mattered so much, but it did.

In a more moderate tone, she went on. "If you wanted to know anything, you should have come to me."

"I'm here now, and I'm asking you outright—is it true what I've been told? Have you lost your memory, Jess?"

She asked incredulously, "Do you really think I could fool the nuns for three years?"

He shrugged. "I'm not saying you weren't injured in the accident, but when you came to yourself, it's possible you decided that a life of contemplation with the nuns was much easier than the life you had here."

He obviously knew nothing of her particular order of nuns or what was involved in looking after children. Did he think they had an army of servants to do all the work? And what did he know of a life of contemplation, especially for someone in her situation? A blank mind, a blank past, a blank name. Her throat closed as she remembered her first few months in the convent, when she'd lived in hope that someone would claim her—a father, a mother, a brother, a sister. Someone. Hopes and dreams, that's what had kept her going, and when hope faded, the awful despair.

Things were different now. She was a real person, with a real name. She had a history. Maybe her memory would never come back to her, but she could at least try to fill in the blanks. And in three days, she'd come a long way.

Her eyes flicked to Lucas. She would be much further ahead if Lucas Wilde would only consent to answer a few questions. "Lucas," she said, trying for a conciliatory tone, "what do I have to do to convince you I'm telling the truth?"

"You can begin by telling me when, exactly, you found out that your father had been murdered."

It was on the tip of her tongue to tell him that she'd found out, not half an hour ago, from the attorney. Then she saw his trap. She'd recklessly told him that first day back that she'd returned to Hawkshill to find a murderer. If he'd visited Hawkshill and questioned the nuns, he would see that there was a discrepancy in her story.

"I was told in the convent," she said, and made herself remember to breathe.

"By the woman who recognized you?"

She saw where he was leading and tried to circumvent him by going on the attack. "You did go to Hawkshill to spy on me! Well, you won't get any answers from the sisters, because they don't know anything. I . . . I didn't tell them about my father. I . . . I just couldn't."

After studying her expression for a moment, he said, "That's not all. Explain if you will what happened between us three days ago. If you'd lost your memory, I would be a stranger to you. So how do you explain that you came damn near to allowing me to take you on the kitchen table? Does that sound as though you'd lost your memory?"

She was appalled. "Are you saying we were lovers?"

His eyes moved slowly over her face. After a moment, he let out a breath. "No, we weren't lovers. But I would like to know what's going on. If you didn't know who I was, why did you fall into my arms when I came out to Hawkshill?"

Relief shivered through her. She sniffed and offered an explanation she thought he might accept. It was as close to the truth as she was willing to go. "You attacked me. I was frightened and confused. Then you took me in your arms. I didn't know what I was doing, where it was leading." She looked directly into his eyes. "I know nothing of men. If I was ever in love with you, I have no memory of it."

"Is the past gone forever, Jess, or will your memory come back?"

She was silent for a moment, but deciding it was a serious question, she answered him seriously. "They told me that my memory would probably come back in a few days, but that was three years ago. Then they said it might come back to me suddenly, in one fell swoop. Or it might never come back."

He stared at her then said softly, "I'm still not sure that I believe you, Jess."

"Why would I lie about a thing like that?"

"A convent would be a good place to hide, would it not?"

"Hide?" She sat up straighter. "From what?"

"From me."

She jerked at his words, knocking his elbow, and the horses reared up.

"Now look what you've done," he roared, holding his team steady.

She was breathing hard. There was something there, a memory, just out of reach. "You quarreled with my father the night he was murdered. Don't deny it. The attorney told me."

"Why should I deny it? It all came out at the inquest. And there was a full house that night. About twenty people witnessed the fight."

"You took his pistol away from him so that he could not defend himself."

The words jerked out of his mouth. "I took his pistol away from him so that he would not kill me."

"What did you quarrel about?"

"You, of course. You told him that we were lovers in a deliberate attempt to trap me into marriage."

She gasped. "I told him? I can't believe I would do such a thing unless . . ." Her face blanched, and she stammered, "unless it was true."

His face darkened. "What kind of man do you think I am? Of course it wasn't true! I was going to marry Bella. Then your father came barging into the Black Swan and that was that."

"I'm sure I had no part in it. I'm not that sort of girl."

"How do you know if you've lost your memory?"

She looked up at him with a stricken expression. "Lucas," she breathed out, "are you saying that I was a . . . a scarlet woman?"

There was a heartbeat of silence before he answered. "No, Jess. All I'm saying is that you were sweet on me."

The breath she'd been holding rushed out of her lungs as relief swamped her, then she sucked it in again when she saw the humor in his eyes. "Just tell me what happened that night," she snapped, then, remembering that she'd decided to be conciliatory, "Tell me. Please. I have to know."

He hesitated then said, "I was not long back from the war and was drinking with friends in the Black Swan's taproom, celebrating my engagement to Bella Clifford. Soon after my friends left, your father entered. He'd been drinking and was in a towering temper. You'd told him, so he said, that we were lovers. He accused me of ruining you for other men. There was a fight. When he pulled his pistol on me, I took it away from him. He left. Shortly after, I left, too."

She was shaking inside. "Why would I tell him we were lovers if it wasn't true?"

He studied her face for a moment, then exhaled an exasperated breath. "Because, from the time you were a girl in pinafores, you'd set your heart on me. Everyone knew it. In fact, it was a great joke in Chalford. I tolerated your attentions because, well, I didn't want to hurt your feelings. You were only a young girl, and I was flattered, I suppose, that you hero-worshiped me. But that night, you went too far."

This unflattering picture of herself made her writhe, but she couldn't deny it. She was remembering how she'd felt when Lucas had kissed her and she'd practically allowed him to take her on the kitchen table.

She lifted her chin. "It wasn't all one-sided," she said.

"No," he said simply. "It was easy to ignore you when you were a child, but . . ."

"But what?"

He turned his head to look at her. "But when I came home from the war, you were all grown-up."

His eyes were locked on hers, and she felt it again, the irresistible tug on her senses. He felt it, too. She heard the catch in his breath, saw the way his lids grew heavy. Not again. Dear Lord, not again.

"Jess," he whispered.

She caught his wrist, preventing him from touching her. "Why did you buy Hawkshill, Lucas?"

"What?"

"You heard me."

His lips thinned. "Why does anyone buy a property that adjoins his estate? I wanted your acreage."

"The attorney says you paid more than Hawkshill was worth. Was it blood money?"

He swore. "Blood money for what?"

"Murdering my father."

"One more crack like that and I'll put you over my knee and paddle your backside."

"That's no answer. The attorney said you felt guilty because you'd disarmed my father and he couldn't defend himself. Is that true?"

He nodded. "That's about it."

His answer was a tad too pat for her liking. "There must be more to it than that."

He looked as though he were ready to explode. "Look, I wanted your acreage and I paid a fair price for it. That's all there was to it."

"Where did you get the money? The attorney told me you were living off the charity of relatives then. So where did the money come from?"

"Rempel doesn't know when to keep his mouth shut. I borrowed it from friends."

"Oh, don't worry! I had to pry everything out of the attorney. He wouldn't answer my questions. That's why I'm asking you. What friends?"

"Rupert Haig for one. My cousin Adrian for another. They'll tell you."

"Do you know what I think, Lucas? I think you're lying."

He spoke through clenched teeth. "There's a lot you don't know, Jess, or you wouldn't speak to me like that."

"Then tell me!"

"I wanted to provide for you in case anything happened to me. Yes, I felt guilty about your father because I'd taken his pistol away from him. What's wrong with that? And you have to understand how it was with us. My God, I'd been looking after you since you were a scrawny brat. You looked up to me. I felt responsible for you. Somebody had to. Your father was a wastrel. He never gave a thought to your welfare."

Her breath was coming thick and fast. "Don't you dare speak ill of my father! What would you know about him? You were a soldier! You were away at war."

"And you've lost your memory. He was a gambler, Jess. He drank too much."

Tears were shimmering in her eyes. "So he wasn't a saint. But he kept me with him. He didn't abandon me to some distant relative who would have used me as a drudge. I could have earned my own living, as a governess or . . . or a lady's companion. He must have wanted me with him."

Something flickered briefly in the depths of his eyes before his expression became veiled. "So that's the way of it," he said.

"What does that mean?"

"Your father . . ."

"What?"

He shook his head. "Maybe you're right, but that's not how it seemed to me at the time."

His placating words came too late to stem the tide of emotions. "My father was brutally murdered," she cried, "and I'm not going to let this rest till I find out who was responsible."

Several moments elapsed before he said anything. "Do you really think I'm capable of murder, Jess?"

It didn't matter what she thought. She was playing against long odds, and she had to take chances. "You had motive and opportunity."

"What motive?"

"You were in love with this girl, Bella. I think my

father threatened to tell her about me. You didn't want to lose her. That's why you killed him."

"Tell her?" He laughed harshly. "It was too late to keep anything from her after that brawl. Everybody there knew, or thought they knew, that we were lovers. And it was a damn lie! You wanted to ruin things for Bella and me. And you succeeded. Soon after you left Hawkshill, Bella married my best friend, Rupert Haig. That's what your lies did, Jess."

"If it wasn't true, why would I tell my father?"

"Why?" He leaned closer so that they were glaring eye to eye. "Because you were infatuated with me. You thought I'd be forced to marry you. You wouldn't be the first female to try and compromise me."

Oh, she could well believe it, and for some odd reason the thought inflamed her. "If you didn't do it, I think you know who did. Who are you trying to protect, Lucas?"

He rubbed his eyes tiredly. "Who the hell do you think I'm trying to protect? You, of course. Don't you understand anything? The murderer was never caught. If you stir things up, he may decide to do away with you, too. And there's something else you're not taking into your calculations. You disappeared the same night your father was murdered. No one knew where you were. For all anyone knows, you could have murdered him."

He dropped her at the front door of the house. She was in too much of a daze to respond coherently to his parting words. Her brain felt as though an electric current had passed through it. Thoughts chased each other in a frenetic jig. She didn't know what to hold on to or what to let go.

This wasn't the time to think about things. She heard voices coming from the breakfast room, which was now also their communal office. After removing her bonnet, she forced her lips into a serene smile and went in.

The nuns were sitting at the table, making entries in

one of the ledgers. Sister Dolores, close to sixty, was tall and thin with a sallow complexion and the most eloquent dark, bushy eyebrows that Jessica had ever beheld. Her stately manner and air of authority had earned her the nickname Sister Duchess. When she told a patient he was going to get well, so the novices joked among themselves, he hastened to obey her or he died in the attempt. Sister Elvira was about ten years younger and was small and chubby. Her domain was the orphanage, and though she never gave up on a child, no matter how hardened, she was no one's dupe, either. She was an odd mixture of saintliness and worldliness and the novices had dubbed her Sister Solomon. It was Sister Elvira who was in charge of Hawkshill.

When Jessica entered, the nuns broke off their conversation. In the last few days, ever since the jam incident, there had been many such aborted conversations between Sisters Dolores and Elvira. They were curious, and when Jessica remembered the state of the kitchen when they'd walked in, while she was scraping jam from the ceiling, she wasn't surprised. She hadn't told a lie. She'd said she'd inadvertently hit the bowls on the table with the bread paddle and they had let it go at that. But it wasn't in Sister Martha's character to be careless, and she'd been aware ever since of the nuns covertly watching her. It wasn't done in an unkindly way. The Reverend Mother had appointed them to be her guardians, and guard her they would, come what may.

"How did things go with the attorney?" asked Sister Dolores.

"Very well. My father left me some money. I'm not an heiress, but I'm not destitute, either. Sister Elvira, you seem very pleased with yourself."

Sister Elvira beamed at Jessica. "That's because our landlord was here earlier this morning. He's promised to have our lease all properly signed and notarized by the end of the week. Not only that, but—oh, I swear the man is an angel—he also offered to take six of our boys under his wing and apprentice them to his own people. The blacksmith, the farrier, the gamekeeper . . . I forget who all."

"Lord Dundas promised to sign the lease?" asked Jessica incredulously.

"He did," replied Sister Dolores, "and we are to have Hawkshill for a nominal sum." She patted the empty chair beside her and, when Jessica was seated, went on. "He said that he had business in town with his attorney and that if he saw you he would drive you home."

"Well, he did," said Jessica crossly. "I . . . I suppose he asked a lot of questions when he was here?"

The nuns exchanged a quick glance. "He was curious about us, about our order and our boys," replied Sister Dolores.

He was curious about *her,* thought Jessica sourly. "And you told him I'd lost my memory?"

"It came up in the conversation."

Sister Elvira said, "There's nothing to be ashamed of, Jessica. And Lord Dundas was very sympathetic to your plight."

Sympathetic! He had all but called her a liar. Her brows pulled to a frown. "I'd be careful about taking anything he says too seriously." When the nuns stared at her in surprise, her cheeks went pink. "I mean, when he speaks to his estate manager, perhaps he'll change his mind about placing our boys."

They were like two alert sparrows watching a worm. Jessica squirmed uncomfortably. There was no getting around it. She had to tell them what she'd learned in town before they heard it from another source.

But there was something she had to clear up first. Breathing deeply, she said, "I didn't tell you that my father was murdered."

"We understand, Jessica," said Sister Dolores. "It must have been a great shock to you. We told Lord Dundas that you'd probably heard it from Mrs. Marshal."

"Well, it was a shock," said Jessica, and marveled at her facility with evasions and half-truths, "but there were more shocks waiting for me this morning when I visited the attorney." And without giving them time to consider or ask her to elaborate, she plunged in.

"The thing is," she said, "I've learned that Lucas, that is, Lord Dundas and I were not the best of friends when I left here. And it's no exaggeration to say that he doesn't want me here now." She told them about Lucas's quarrel with her father and how he blamed her for trying to trap him into marriage. She told them about her father's murder and how she had disappeared the same night. The sisters were so sympathetic and so accepting that everything poured out of her as if of its own accord.

When she had finished speaking, Sister Dolores studied her thoughtfully. She wasn't a woman to speak without thinking. At length, she nodded, as though satisfied with what she'd heard. "That's more or less what Lord Dundas told us."

Jessica's head came up. "He *told* you?"

Sister Elvira said, "He thinks you should leave this place, Jessica, and start afresh somewhere else."

"Oh, he does, does he?" Jessica knew her tone was hostile and she made a conscious effort to soften it. She wasn't angry at the sisters but at Lucas Wilde for deliberately trying to get them on his side. The offer to place their boys was probably a bribe to persuade the sisters to get rid of her. "And why should I leave this place?"

"To avoid any unpleasantness. People are bound to gossip. Those were Lord Dundas's words."

"How very kind of him to think of me," replied Jessica sweetly. "However, I came to Hawkshill to find out . . ."

"To find out?" prompted Sister Elvira.

"To find out about myself," Jessica went on seamlessly, "and until I do, I'm not going anywhere."

She expected an argument and got none. In fact, the sisters approved. It was their conviction that the whole enterprise had been inspired by God, and it was their duty to follow where He led.

Somewhat chastened by the sisters' blind faith, Jessica left them to begin preparing the evening meal. She didn't feel put upon by having to do most of the cooking herself. They had agreed on the division of labor from the beginning. The kitchen was her domain. The sisters did most of the washing and cleaning and were out a good part of the day, knocking on doors to beg or buy whatever was needed to set up for the boys' arrival. They didn't have the money to purchase all they wanted, but that didn't dampen their spirits. They expected the good Lord to provide and, to their way of thinking, He did. They'd already acquired some odds and ends of furniture, one milch cow and her calf and a handful of brood hens.

It was Joseph's job to take care of the stock and generally keep the place in good repair. Before he'd become a professional fighter, he'd been a farm laborer. He didn't say much, but Jessica could tell it suited him very well to be back on the land.

She donned her apron and stood for a moment or two in the middle of the kitchen floor in silent contemplation. There was so much to think about, so much to worry about. Of all the shocks she'd had today, the one that weighed most heavily on her heart was the brutal murder of her father. "Papa," she whispered into the silence, trying to think herself into the part of a loving daughter. There was no answering chord in her memory.

She stayed there for a long while, staring into space, then frowned as she remembered that moment in the

Black Swan when she'd had an impression of herself as a young girl. What had she been feeling? She'd been panicked until Lucas had left his friends and come toward her.

Was it a memory? What did it mean? And why would she remember Lucas but not her father?

Scarlet woman. No. It couldn't be true. Even without her memory, she knew she wasn't that sort of girl. Then what sort of girl was she?

Her eye fell on the kitchen table. Gritting her teeth, she picked up her skillet and slammed it down.

In the breakfast room, the black-robed nuns listened to the rattle of pots and pans that emanated from the kitchen. Sister Dolores's eloquent eyebrows rose a notch at every clatter; Sister Elvira's lips were turned up in a complacent smile.

"She's not the same girl she was three days ago," said Sister Dolores.

"No," agreed Sister Elvira. "I think we'll be seeing less and less of Sister Martha as time goes on."

Sister Dolores rested her chin on the back of her hand and gazed into space. "What did you think of Lord Dundas?"

"I liked him. He seemed genuinely interested in our work."

"Strange that he should offer to sign our lease. I had the distinct impression, when he first arrived, that he'd come to evict us."

Sister Elvira's bright eyes gleamed shrewdly. "Oh, I don't think there's any doubt of that."

Sister Dolores slowly turned her head and her dark brows knitted in a perplexed frown. "Then what made him change his mind?"

"The good Lord, of course, and . . ."

"And?"

"Well, we did play upon the poor man's conscience. It's

a powerful combination, the good Lord and a good conscience, as we should know."

"Mmm. You don't think Jessica had something to do with it?"

"Of course Jessica had something to do with it, but I doubt that Lord Dundas is aware of it." Sister Elvira chuckled. "With Jessica not remembering anything, he'll have to court her all over again."

Sister Dolores's jaw went slack. "Your imagination is running away with you, Sister Elvira."

"Would you like to bet on it?"

"You heard Jessica. Her father tried to force Lord Dundas to marry her and he refused."

"I heard her," agreed Sister Elvira, "but I know what my eyes tell me."

Nonplussed, Sister Dolores simply stared.

Sister Elvira, who had more experience of the world and its wicked ways than Sister Dolores, knew when she was on to a good thing. "Three to one says it will be a summer wedding."

Sister Dolores gasped. "I think you've taken leave of your senses!"

"For mercy's sake, it's only toffees we're betting. And it wouldn't be the first time. Besides, the mother superior will never get to hear of it. Who would tell her?"

"That's not what I meant. Jessica doesn't even like Lord Dundas. That was patently obvious."

There was the sound of breaking glass in the kitchen. Sister Elvira leaned toward the other nun, till they were practically nose to nose. "Four to one," she whispered.

"You're a bad influence!"

"Treacle toffees," Sister Elvira threw in, shamelessly exploiting one of Sister Dolores's few weaknesses.

"The kind your nephew supplies you with?"

"The same."

"And what's my stake?"

"Those sugar plums your niece sends you on your birthday."

Sister Dolores smiled a slow, calculating smile. "You're on," she said.

CHAPTER
6

AFTER LUCAS HAD SEEN JESSICA ENTER THE HOUSE, HE turned the curricle around and made for home. He paid little heed to his surroundings. His mind was engrossed with thoughts of Jessica.

She'd lost her memory. When the nuns had told him, he hadn't believed it; he hadn't wanted to believe it. In fact, he'd been downright suspicious and had questioned them at length. They thought nothing of the inconsistency he'd found in Jess's story, and he couldn't tell them about how Jess had melted in his arms, as if she'd left him only yesterday. But as soon as he'd left Hawkshill, he'd rushed to Chalford to confront Jess in person. Then he'd found her in the Black Swan and they'd got off on the wrong foot.

She'd lost her memory. That's not how it had seemed to him three days ago when he'd practically taken her on her kitchen table. And for three days, he'd stewed about things. When she'd gone missing all those years ago, he'd combed the county for her, he'd combed London, but he'd never thought to look for her in a convent. And all this time, he'd lived in dread that the constable or one of his friends would knock on his door and tell him that her body or her bones had been found. That's why he'd been enraged when she'd turned up three years later, safe and sound, with nary a word to him in all that time.

But if she'd lost her memory, that would explain everything.

He had to accept it. For one thing, nuns didn't tell lies. And for another, Jess was different. In fact, he hardly recognized the Jess he knew in this Tartar of a woman. The Jess he knew had hero-worshiped him. She'd looked up to him from that day, on the church steps, when some upstart girls had taunted her with not knowing how to read and he had sent them scurrying to the sides of their mamas with a look.

He'd never really paid much attention to Jessica until then. She was simply a neighbor's child who was allowed to wander the countryside at will. While other girls of twelve were learning their alphabets, sewing their samplers and generally learning how to conduct themselves as young ladies, Jess was left to her own devices. William Hayward was notorious throughout the neighborhood even then. He was an inveterate gambler, and an irascible, unpleasant sort of man who had managed to alienate all his neighbors. As a father, he was worse than useless, but no one could ever tell Jess that. For some reason that he could never fathom, Jess had idolized her father.

Something else he could never fathom—why he had decided to take a hand in things. He was a young man of twenty. He had other fish to fry. But there was something about the misty-eyed waif even then that had aroused his protective instincts. Or it might have been the result of his upbringing. Though there was never any money to spare, his father could always be counted on to give a helping hand to anyone in trouble.

For whatever reason, he'd jumped in with both feet.

First, he'd had a word with his mother, and when his mother could not persuade Hayward to take Jessica in hand, he'd enlisted the constable's aid. And the constable had made life so difficult for Hayward that he'd been glad to send Jess to the Dame's school in town.

It was only natural that after that he would take an interest in her progress, only natural that she would be flattered and look up to him as her champion. By and large, he'd regarded her devotion with a kind of amused tolerance, even when it sometimes proved annoying. But all that changed not long before he went off to war, when Jess cornered him in his stables.

And he was never to regard Jessica Hayward with amused tolerance again.

He'd tried to let her down gently—hadn't he always?—but Jess being Jess, naturally she'd taken advantage. He remembered he was telling her that one day she would fall in love with someone who was right for her, someone nearer her own age, when she'd thrown her arms around his neck and kissed him.

He was smiling when her lips touched his. This was Jess's first kiss, he remembered thinking, and he didn't want to spoil it for her. And it seemed right, somehow, that he should be the man to give it to her. His next thought had shocked him. What he really wanted was to be her first lover.

He was so stunned by this appalling revelation that it had taken him a moment or two before he could think clearly. Then he grasped her shoulders to push her away, but it was too late. He didn't know how she managed it, but she toppled him on the hay and rolled with him. He would have laughed had he not heard Adrian and Bella calling him by name. To say that he was guilt stricken didn't do justice to how he'd felt.

He and Jess were in his stable, in broad daylight, on the floor of an empty stall. She was on her back with her skirts hiked to her thighs, and he was planted solidly between them. It was a miracle that the closure on his trousers was still buttoned.

When the stable door creaked open, Jess opened her mouth, and he knew exactly what was going through her mind. The little vixen had set a trap for him. She was going to call out so that Bella would find them in *flagrante delicto,* more or less. And that would have put paid to his chances with Bella.

He'd had the presence of mind to cup her mouth with his hand to silence her. And moments later, when he heard Bella and Adrian walking toward the house, he'd given Jess a shaking she would not soon forget. Then, he'd sanctimoniously lectured her on the perils of arousing a man's passions. And when she'd still protested that Bella didn't really love him, that she was all wrong for him, that she could never make him happy, he'd deliberately and cruelly told Jess that it was too late. He was deep in love with Bella and always would be.

He'd thought he was speaking the truth, but in hindsight, he could acknowledge that Jess had been far wiser than he. A good part of Bella's attraction was that she'd been the most sought-after girl in the county, and for some inexplicable reason she'd favored him over her other suitors. Such was the vanity of youth. If her father had been as easily won over, he and Bella would have been married at once. But Sir Henry had put his foot down. He'd wanted something better for his darling daughter than an adventurer who lived from hand to mouth. So he, Lucas, had gone off to war to make his fortune; Bella had vowed to remain constant, and there was no turning back.

But it hadn't been Bella's image that had haunted him as he'd chased the French out of Spain. It was the image of the misty-eyed waif who'd sworn her undying love for him. He became obsessed with her, but it wasn't an obsession he was willing to tolerate. This was Jessica Hayward! She was little more than a child! He should be shot for having these carnal thoughts! Then there was Bella. He'd asked her to marry him. They weren't formally betrothed, but they had an understanding. A man of honor did not go back on his word. Though he might live to regret it to his dying day, he had to marry Bella.

When he came home in the summer of '15, after Waterloo, he was firmly resolved to do the right thing. By this time, Bella's father had softened, and he was ready to give his blessing to their marriage.

Fate, however, had other plans. Adrian and Rupert had arrived home weeks before he did, and what they told him made him furious. Jess was practically a recluse. She had no friends. He went to Hawkshill looking for William Hayward, but it was Jess he found. And later, that same night, Jess told her father a pack of lies, and Hayward cornered him in the Black Swan.

He'd been so angry he'd wanted to throttle Jess. But that was before he knew that her father had been murdered and that she had disappeared. And for three years, he'd gone through hell, wondering what had become of her.

Now he knew, but he didn't know what he was going to do about her. It was still there, this strange magnetism that had always drawn them together. And Jess was no longer a child. And Bella was no longer between them. Jess might not know it, but they were standing on the edge of a precipice. The thought made him grin.

He was still thinking about Jessica when he arrived home. Perry was waiting for him in the stable yard.

"You've got company," said Perry, nodding to the vehicle and its team of horses that sheltered under a stand of oaks. "Bella and Rupert," he added gratuitously, as though Lucas would not recognize the distinctive blue and gray livery of Rupert's coachmen. "They arrived in Chalford this morning, heard the news about Jess and dropped everything to rush over here to . . . now what was it Bella said? . . . oh yes, to lend their support." He grinned. "What humbug! She's foaming at the mouth. Just thought I'd warn you."

When Lucas alighted from the curricle, Perry jumped into it and took up the reins. Lucas said, "You're not coming in with me?"

"Hell, no! That is, thank you, no. I've already made my apologies. Anyway, Adrian's there to play host until you show up." And with one of his insufferably cheery grins, Perry cracked the whip and the curricle took off in a cloud of dust.

Lucas wasn't surprised. Perry was always complaining that he, Adrian and Rupert were a bunch of old fogies. When they got together, all they ever talked about was the war or the good old days.

Old fogies, Lucas thought with a chuckle. Perry had never seen them in battle, when they'd been fearless warriors. But now look at them. Adrian was a pleasure seeker; Rupert was a country gentleman devoted to growing his prize roses; and he . . . he supposed he was drifting.

When he entered the drawing room, he paused just inside the door, undetected, listening to the conversation. The subject was Jessica, and Bella was doing most of the talking.

A truly beautiful woman, thought Lucas. Her brilliant blue eyes were enhanced by the blue of her gown; dark ringlets framed a flawless face. But her beauty no longer affected him. He had learned over time that behind that lovely façade was a vain, small-minded woman, but since she was Rupert's wife he put up with her.

Adrian caught sight of him first. "I was just telling Rupert and Bella," he said, "that you'd gone down to Hawkshill to give the nuns notice to quit. What kept you?" He looked more closely at Lucas's face then sighed. "So you didn't give the nuns notice to quit. Now why am I not surprised?"

Lucas sliced his cousin a silencing look and ignored the taunt.

"Lucas!" exclaimed Bella. She had risen from her chair and was holding out her hand. "We just heard the news and came right over. Adrian says it's true, that Jessica Hayward really is a nun."

He dutifully took her hand and pressed a kiss to it. Though she looked serene, he could feel the tension in her rigid fingers. "Bella," he said, "as lovely as ever, I see. And no, Jess isn't a nun." He repeated what the sisters had told him. "She never took her vows. She's good with children and is helping the sisters until the orphanage is established."

He turned to greet Rupert, and this time there was genuine warmth in his smile. Rupert was as fair as his wife was dark. He was tall and slender with a slight stoop to his shoulders. In dress regimentals, there was no finer-looking soldier. Dressed as he was now in the casual clothes of a country gentleman, he looked like a prosperous farmer. The look was deceiving. Rupert had been born to wealth and privilege.

Rupert said, "All is well with you, I trust?"

"Why shouldn't it be?"

Rupert searched Lucas's face. "You left town so suddenly, without a word to anyone."

"Some unexpected business came up," replied Lucas curtly. When Rupert's brows rose, he said in a humorous tone, "Ask me that question when there are no ladies present and I'll give you a different answer."

"Ah," said Rupert and a knowing glint lit up his eyes. "It's time you settled down with one woman, Lucas!"

Adrian cut in rudely. "I'll thank you, Rupert, not to meddle. Don't put ideas in his head."

"You don't want him to marry?"

"As his friend, yes. But as his heir, no."

As soon as the laughter died away and Lucas sat down, Bella said impatiently: "We were all shocked to hear that

Jessica Hayward had come back. What's her game, Lucas? What is she up to?"

Rupert said, "Give the man time to catch his breath, Bella." He smiled into her eyes. "We're all anxious to hear about Jessica. Now sit down and let Lucas gather his thoughts."

After a few sips of brandy, Lucas told his friends as much as he knew about Jessica's time with the nuns, ending with what he'd learned that morning about the carriage accident and her subsequent loss of memory.

When he finished speaking, Bella demanded incredulously, "And you believe her?"

Lucas didn't know why the question irritated him since he'd initially had his doubts as well. He said carefully, "The nuns confirm Jess's story. And it makes sense. Why else would she stay away for three years?"

"Why?" Bella's laugh was brittle. "Because of the lies she told. Because she was afraid to face the consequences of those lies. Because she knows if she shows her face here, she'll be shunned." Bella breathed deeply. "I could go on and on."

"Then why has she come back now?"

Her voice rose a notch, as did her volume. "Jessica Hayward always had plenty of nerve. She's setting her cap for you, Lucas, now that she knows you have come into a title and a fortune. She's a devious little witch, and if you don't watch your step, she may succeed this time where she failed before."

Adrian chuckled and Bella rounded on him. "What?" she demanded.

"Jessica Hayward," he said, "is not the girl we all knew. She is no longer infatuated with Sir Galahad here." He jerked his head to indicate Lucas. "In point of fact, she took an instant dislike to him, so much so that on their first encounter at Hawkshill, she pointed a loaded gun at him and pulled the trigger. Luckily, the gun did not go off."

Bella gasped. Rupert chuckled.

"It's worse than that," said Lucas gloomily. "Not half an hour ago, she practically accused me of murdering her father."

There was a long silence, then Rupert began to laugh. He stopped when he caught Lucas's eye. "Sorry, my friend," he said. There wasn't a shade of apology in his voice. "But isn't this what you always wanted, to cure her of her infatuation? It seems you've succeeded. I don't know why you're looking so glum. No one would ever suspect you of murder, whatever the girl says."

Lucas looked first at Adrian, then at Rupert. "If I had shot William Hayward, it would not have been in the back. That was a cowardly act."

There was another long silence, then Rupert said in his easy way, "Yes, I've thought about that. Whoever murdered William Hayward in that reprehensible way is scum, and deserves nothing but our contempt."

Bella said impatiently, "Whoever murdered William Hayward did the world a good turn, and you're all hypocrites if you say otherwise." Having disposed of William Hayward's murder in these few terse words, she returned to the topic on her mind. "So, Jessica Hayward is staying at Hawkshill? Is that what it comes down to, Lucas?"

He said quietly, "I can't turn the nuns out. They're hardworking, self-sacrificing ladies who will be an asset to our community." He shrugged helplessly as he groped for words. "Besides, if I turn them out, they'll simply find another house in the area, so they might as well remain at Hawkshill. It's lying empty and I have no use for it."

Bella rose and began to pull on her gloves. "There's going to be gossip and it won't be pleasant." She gave him an acid smile. "The nuns may be an asset to our little community, but they don't move in our circles. And neither will Jessica Hayward. She never did, and after the scandal she created, no respectable lady would dare open her doors to her. Poor girl, I can almost feel sorry for her."

The gentlemen had all risen politely to their feet. Lucas brushed a speck of lint from his sleeve. "The doors of this house will always be open to Jessica," he said mildly. He looked at Bella with eyes that were wide and clear. "For one thing, my mother was always fond of Jess, and when she comes down from London, I know she'll wish to see her again. And for another thing, I don't believe Jess told her father those lies. I think William Hayward concocted that story by himself to get money out of me."

Bella said stiffly, "This is the first time you've mentioned that theory, Lucas."

"Is it? Let's just say, now that I've had time to think about it, that theory sounds good to me."

Rupert was frowning down at a loose button on his coat. "I've always liked Jessica," he said, "yes and felt sorry for her too. She didn't have much of a life with that father of hers." He looked up and smiled at Bella. "I know when you've had time to think about it, dear, you'll see that Lucas's way is best." He turned to Lucas. "Our doors will be open to Jessica as well."

Lucas's eyes flicked to Bella. Her smile didn't give much away, but he sensed her inner struggle as she fought to master her fury. Finally, she said, "If Jessica has changed her ways, then of course, I'll do my part to help her become accepted." Then abruptly to Rupert, "Come along, dear. I promised Cook I'd go over menus with her this afternoon, and you know how the silly woman can't do anything without direction."

Lucas and Adrian stood on the drive watching Rupert's carriage disappear from view.

Adrian said thoughtfully, "So you're convinced Jessica has lost her memory?"

"I'm convinced," replied Lucas.

When he did not elaborate, Adrian went on, "If you're

looking to re-establish Jessica's reputation, you'll need the help of a suitable female."

"Who, for instance?"

"What about the vicar's wife? She's a good sort."

"I'll bear that in mind. Why do you look so serious?"

"I'm thinking of Bella. She'll make mincemeat of your Jess."

"*My* Jess?" said Lucas darkly.

Adrian let out a hoot of laughter and clapped Lucas on the shoulder. "Lucas, a blind man could read you, and I am not blind. A word of advice?"

"Stow it, Adrian."

Another hoot of laughter. "Just make sure that history doesn't repeat itself."

On the drive home in the carriage, Bella kept up a flow of small talk, never once mentioning what was really on her mind. But that was only for the benefit of the coachmen, in case they should overhear and carry tales out of school. No one was going to say that Bella Haig's nose was out of joint because Jessica Hayward had returned to the area. She'd been made a laughingstock once before. It wasn't going to happen again.

As soon as they alighted from the carriage and the coachmen drove off to the stable block, she said, "I don't know why we must spend every summer in this backwater when we could be in Brighton with the Prince Regent. He asked me particularly if we would be going there this year."

Rupert's voice was mild. "I'm as sorry as you, m'dear, but we really can't disappoint our people. They expect us to be present at their Tenants' Ball."

"Why can't they hold it in August?"

"They'll be too busy with the harvest. Besides, it's a tradition that's been in my family for generations."

Bella's lips thinned. For the most part, Rupert was an indulgent husband, but on one thing he always stood firm.

When they came into Berkshire, they must reside in the house that had been in his family for over two centuries, the house where his grandfather had raised him. Tradition was something her husband prized.

It was nonsense, of course. Her late father's house, which was far superior to this pile of moldering bricks, had been sold off. And now, for more than half the year, she was forced to endure rooms the size of closets, smoky chimneys, and plaster that fell from the ceilings in chunks whenever someone slammed a door.

They had the money to rebuild the place from cellars to rafters, but Rupert wouldn't hear of it. The house in London, he always reminded her, was hers to do with as she wished. She couldn't fault him there. No expense had been spared to turn the house in Grosvenor Square into her own private palace. And it wasn't her money that had gone into it, either. Nothing had surprised her more, after her marriage, than to discover just how wealthy Rupert was. It was known, of course, that the Haigs had money, but the Spartan life he had shared with his grandfather in this dreary house had given no hint of how much. She didn't know why people would choose to live like this when they could do whatever they wanted.

When they entered the Great Hall, her lips tightened even more. She hated the dingy place with its dark paneling and small windows. Other people lived in airy Palladian mansions that boasted Greek columns and white marble. There was no point in mentioning it to Rupert. He would only reply that this was a Tudor manor, that it was a house with character and that marble and Greek columns were highly overrated. What did he know about it? If they were good enough for the Prince Regent, they were good enough for her.

When Rupert mentioned that he was going to the conservatory to tend his roses, she asked him sweetly if he would mind coming to her parlor so that she could speak to him in private. She waited till he had closed the door.

"I could hardly believe my ears," she cried, "when you said that our doors would be open to Jessica Hayward, and after all that she did to me!"

Rupert sat on the arm of a chair. "I was thinking of you," he said. "How would it look if you cut the girl? People would say that you were still in love with Lucas or that you were jealous of Jessica."

"I don't care what people say," she cried out.

"You don't mean that. You care a great deal about what people think of you, and so do I."

His calm tone inflamed her. "You are wrong! I don't care!"

"Don't you?" There was no smile now, no gentle manner. His features had set like granite. "Well, I do. I mean what I say, Bella. I won't have our name dragged through the mud. I won't have my wife act in a vulgar manner. I'm not asking you to make the girl your special friend, but you will act in a way that does credit to this family."

She was more shaken than she cared to admit. He rarely used this tone of voice with her, and when he did, it reminded her of her father. Pushing the memory away, she lifted her chin. No one could speak to her like this. "Jessica Hayward did me a great wrong," she said, "and I shall never forgive her for it."

He got to his feet. "I'm not asking you to forgive her. But you will be civil to her. That's all I ask." At the door, he turned back and gave her one of his sweet smiles. "Did I tell you that I've developed a new strain of rose? I'm naming it 'Arabella' in your honor. It's a true, vivid crimson and has as perfect a bloom as I've ever seen. Hardy, too. In fact, it reminds me of you."

Anger shimmered through her. Did he think he could bribe her by naming a rose after her?

When she was alone, she sat down on a sofa and folded her hands. The white on her knuckles stood out starkly. A few hours ago she'd been in London; she was happy. Now look at her! She was as tense as a coiled spring.

Chalford always did that to her. In London, she was a different person, but here she sensed all the subtle signs that convinced her she could never be one of "them." Her father had warned her that quality was what counted in this provincial society, and rank and beauty could take her only so far. Well, if she wasn't a lady of quality, she didn't know who was. She was a woman who took care of herself. She was always dressed in the height of fashion; she knew all the best people; her parties were the talk of the town. Yet in Lucas's drawing room, she'd been made to feel that Jessica Hayward, a girl who should have forfeited everybody's good opinion by her lurid past, was more highly thought of than she.

Even her own husband had betrayed her.

Just thinking about it made her boil. She was the one who had been wronged. Then why did no one stand up for her? She'd waited for Lucas for four years. She'd never expected it to be that long before he came home from the war. Four years during which time all her friends were marrying one by one. People were beginning to think of her as a spinster. But she'd loved Lucas. And as time wore on, it became more and more difficult to change her course. People would have said that she'd wasted the best years of her life waiting for him. They would have laughed at her. So, she persevered.

Then the scandal had blown up in her face. She'd been made to look ridiculous and that was something she never forgave.

Her father had been even more livid than she. He'd never wanted her to marry Lucas. Rupert had always been his first choice. Though Rupert would never inherit a title, his pedigree was impeccable. He had money. He was a war hero. So she, a woman who could have any man she wanted, had accepted his proposal.

And this was her reward?

She took several long breaths and forced herself to relax. She'd spoken in the heat of the moment when she'd told Rupert she didn't care what people said about her. She did care. She cared passionately. But she also cared passionately about punishing anyone who had slighted her. Lucas had paid his debt when he'd lost her to Rupert. But Jessica Hayward . . .

Jessica Hayward had always been a thorn in her side. She'd been a strange child; a little busybody if the truth were known. But she couldn't tell anyone the truth because it showed her in a bad light. It was because of Jessica Hayward that her own father, Sir Henry, had given her, Bella Clifford, the most sought after girl in the county, the thrashing of her life.

He'd discovered that someone in the house had been stealing porcelain objects and silver trinkets, and he'd blamed one of the footmen when, in fact, she was the culprit. She'd been too terrified to say anything, and so the footman had been duly charged, convicted and transported to the colonies for the crime. Somehow Jessica Hayward had stumbled on the truth. She'd tattled to Sir Henry and the result was he'd thrashed his only daughter and had bankrupted the little jeweler in Chalford who had bought all the trinkets from her. And, to keep Jessica Hayward's mouth shut, he'd paid off her father—with money that Hayward had immediately drunk and gambled away.

If Sir Henry had given his daughter a reasonable allowance in the first place, she wouldn't have been forced to take things. It wasn't as if she were stealing. After all, she'd inherit these things eventually. It was all a great to-do about nothing.

After that, she'd been very careful to stay away from Jessica Hayward. But she'd spread stories about the girl and had turned people against her. With Lucas away at the war, it was easy to do. There was no one there to protect her.

Then Lucas had come home . . . and Jessica Hayward had turned the tables on her. No one did that to her and got away with it.

Calmer now, she leaned back in her chair and closed her eyes. Many minutes passed before the pout on her lips curled into a smile. She opened her eyes. She would do as her husband asked. She would open the doors of Haig House to Jessica Hayward, but she would do it with a vengeance.

C H A P T E R
7

AFTER DINNER, JOSEPH WENT OFF TO HIS WORKSHOP IN the barn while Jessica and the sisters cleared up the kitchen. When the dishes were dried and put away, the sisters sat at the table and spread out a rug they were in the process of making from long strips of old clothes. The nuns did most of the talking, and Jessica listened with half an ear as they reeled off the names of some of their neighbors who had offered to come out to Hawkshill and help repair the place.

But Jessica had other things on her mind, and after donning her shawl, she unobtrusively slipped outside. In the cobblestone yard, she paused for a moment, deliberately opening her senses to everything around her. The tang of mint and lemon came to her from the overgrown herb garden. When she turned her head, she caught the not-unpleasant scent of farm animals and newly mown grass. In the soft glow of twilight, the outbuildings didn't look so rundown.

She slowly traversed the length of the yard to the barn,

desperately searching for something she could recognize. There was nothing. Everything about Hawkshill was as unfamiliar to her as it was to Joseph and the sisters. What was worse was that she had no recollection of her father, either, and if Lucas was to be believed, she was better off not knowing.

Impatient with the sudden sting in her eyes, she opened the barn door and went in. Joseph was at his bench, examining one of the wheels from the wagon. He looked up at her entrance and gave her a toothless grin. He'd been expecting her, and so had the mare. Tulip whinnied to attract Jessica's attention.

"She wants her sugar," said Joseph.

He was a big man, with muscular arms and shoulders and thick-knuckled hands. Jessica could easily discern the fighter he must have been in his prime. He never spoke of that life, but she'd heard that he'd given it up when he'd accidentally killed an opponent.

He set the wheel down. "Heard about your pa and it's sorry I am, right sorry."

It shouldn't matter, Jessica told herself. It was foolish to grieve for a father she couldn't remember. "That's all right, Joseph," she said. "It happened three years ago, and I don't remember him."

He wiped an arm over his brow. "I can't remember my pa, either, and from what I knows, it's a blessing. Light's not so good. Better stop now."

This was typically Joseph, thought Jessica. He said what he had to say and not one word more. He didn't go in for displays of emotion or hand out advice. This was as close as he would come to doing either.

As he tidied away his tools, she looked around the barn. It was spotlessly clean. The cow and her calf were huddled together in one pen, and in another, Tulip was standing by the bars, eyes soulfully trained on Jessica. Laughing, Jessica approached, felt in her pocket and produced a small lump of sugar. Tulip puckered her lips and swiftly gobbled it. Jessica laid her cheek against the mare's neck and inhaled. She loved the smell of horses.

"You's country bred." When she looked up, Joseph went on, "You's no fear of animals. Now the sisters"—he flashed another toothless grin—"they's afeared to go into the henhouse."

Jessica laughed. It was perfectly true. The sisters would rather muck out the barn than face an angry hen who didn't want to give up her eggs. But if she was country bred, she had no memory of it.

Leaving Joseph to tidy away and lock up, she wandered outside. This was the moment she'd been waiting for, when her chores were done and she had time to explore.

She walked beyond the outbuildings, downhill, toward a forest of trees that seemed faintly menacing in the fading light. When she came to the bridle path, she halted. The way down was soon lost to view in the dense underbrush and stands of trees. She was sure that somewhere down that path, her Voice had lain in wait for her father as he'd made his way home from the Black Swan.

Her heart picked up speed and her breathing became quick and shallow. She gave one last look behind her, to the cluster of buildings that made up Hawkshill. It all looked so safe and solid. The fading rays of the sun were caught in the manor's many small-paned windows and winked back at her. Below her, everything was in shadow; everything was silent. With a long, trembling breath, she picked up her skirts and started down the incline.

For the first little while, the shadows blurred and flickered, but as her eyes became accustomed to the gloom, she could see her way quite clearly. The path was wide and smooth and was obviously still in use. At one point, it branched off to the right. Here she stopped, not because she was uncertain of the way, but because she knew that if she followed the fork, it would take her to Lucas's house.

Walton Lodge. She said the name softly, hoping to evoke a memory of the place, but all that came to her was what the sisters had told her over dinner. The Lodge, Lucas had told them, had been his principal residence until he'd come into his uncle's title and fortune. Now he owned a house in London and an estate in Hampshire, but Walton Lodge would always be his home, and it had given him a great deal of pleasure to fix it up, when he'd had the money to do it.

There was a mother and a young ward, the sisters had told her, but they lived in London. It was a comforting thought. She did not think Lucas's mother would welcome her back with open arms, not after what she'd done to her son.

She swallowed a soft sound of distress. What kind of girl would do such a thing? Not the kind of girl she wanted to be. When she'd returned to Hawkshill, she hadn't expected to be the most popular girl in town, but she hadn't expected this, either. If she could travel back in time, she would give that girl a good shake.

Or had Lucas exaggerated? She hoped he had exaggerated. She *prayed* he'd exaggerated. That was the trouble with losing your memory. Anyone could tell you anything and you wouldn't know what to believe.

Then why had she no friends? Was it just because it was early days yet, as the nuns said? One friend would be enough to satisfy her, a girl her own age, someone who would be glad to know she had returned.

You disappeared the same night your father was murdered. No one knew where you were. For all anyone knows you could have murdered him.

Lucas's parting shot drummed inside her head. Did people really suspect that she had murdered her father? Is that why no one had come out to Hawkshill to welcome her back? Well, she knew she hadn't murdered her father, but how could she explain about her Voice? She couldn't, of course.

With a shudder of apprehension, she turned her back on the Lodge and looked down along the bridle path. Hawkshill might not be familiar to her, but this shortcut into town was. She'd been here many times with her Voice. In fact, her Voice had given her a map to follow. She closed her eyes, trying to get her bearings.

Behind her was a manor with a hawk soaring over it— that had to be Hawkshill. There was a rich man's house on a hill. Lucas's house? She didn't think so. When her father was murdered Lucas wasn't a rich man, and the Lodge was not grand enough for the impression she had been given. There was a castle off in the distance, Windsor Castle, of course. It was the most prominent landmark in the area.

She opened her eyes and breathed deeply. She took one step, and another, then her pace quickened and she went forward as if propelled by an invisible force. She was vividly aware that each step took her closer to her destination, but she wasn't afraid. Her mind and senses were finely honed, poised for the moment of recognition.

The shadows were deepening as the sun slipped below the horizon. A branch whipped at her face, but she pushed it away and ran on. She could hear the stream now, rippling over rocks, just as she'd heard it from her Voice. Her heart was thundering. She was out of breath. This was exactly how her Voice had felt the night he'd lain in wait for her father. She was close, so very close . . .

The muffled report of the pistol shot stopped her in her tracks. It took her a moment to realize that the sound came from inside her head. Blinking rapidly, one hand pressed to her heart, she looked around her. At this point, the trees were thinning, and the path leveled out. About twenty yards ahead, the vista opened up, and the clouds on the horizon, dappled with the purple haze from the setting sun, gave the impression of a range of mountains off in the distance.

She turned to look back the way she had come. If Lucas was her Voice, he must have taken a different route to get here ahead of her father. Then he'd hidden behind a tree in this very spot, and when her father passed him, Lucas had shot him in the back.

It was logical, but it was all wrong. It was all wrong because she didn't want to believe it. She didn't want Lucas Wilde to be the murderer.

She was still staring along the bridle path, trying to remember every detail of the attack as her Voice had told it to her, when she became aware that she had unwittingly opened herself to him. He was there, at the very gates of her mind, thinking the same thoughts as she. Her body went as rigid as a length of iron. She stopped breathing. Every ounce of willpower went into erasing her own thoughts so that he wouldn't detect her presence.

He was puzzled. One of the images she had passed on to him was unfamiliar, and he had paused to think about it. She sensed his confusion, his growing uncertainty, and finally his suspicion. After what seemed like an eternity, she felt him blink mentally, as though someone had recalled him to another conversation. He lingered one moment longer, then he was gone.

She stayed as she was, unmoving, terrified to draw a breath. When she was quite sure that she was alone with her thoughts, she began to shake.

Hardly aware of what she was doing, she left the path and sought the protection of the trees. Supporting herself against the trunk of an oak, she drew air greedily into her lungs. When her fear had ebbed a little, she sank down on her knees and tried to put her thoughts in order.

This wasn't the first time she had given herself away. At vespers, when her mind had screamed at him not to murder again, he'd sensed her presence. One intrusion into his mind he might put down to mere imagination, but not two. She would have to be more vigilant in future. There must be no unwary moments, no more openings for her Voice to enter her mind. If his suspicion became a conviction and he got to know of her existence, he might deal with her as he'd dealt with her father.

She'd learned something from this encounter. She was on the right track. This was the murder her Voice had relived countless times in his mind. If she could only discover who her Voice was, she would know who had murdered her father.

She let out a long sigh and rose to her feet. She didn't know how to go about proving who had murdered her father. If the constable hadn't solved the crime, how could she possibly hope to do it? Maybe the constable could point her in the right direction, though. That's what she would do. As soon as she could be spared from Hawkshill, she would go into town and question the constable.

On that note of resolve, she drew her shawl more snugly around her and made for home.

Later that night, as she lay tossing in her narrow bed, she felt the presence of her Voice, as soft as a whisper. But she had taken care to shutter her mind and there was no way in.

C H A P T E R
8

IN THE FOLLOWING DAYS, JESSICA WAS KEPT SO BUSY that all thoughts of the constable were crowded out of her mind. The first batch of boys was due to arrive by the beginning of June, and there were more jobs to do than she, Joseph and the nuns could manage. She was tired but she was also keyed up. Soon, their boys would be here. She was good with children. She was needed. Her work at Hawkshill was important and left little time to think about herself.

Lucas was a regular visitor, but he came in the role of their landlord, and though he spoke to her in passing, he did not seek her out. He had brought thatchers and slaters with him to fix the various roofs, and carpenters to build new privies and mend broken sills and doors. A time or two, when they were shorthanded, he removed his coat, rolled up his shirtsleeves, and set to work with the men. She could hear them from her kitchen window as she prepared the noon meal. There was good-natured masculine banter at his lordship's expense, and she could feel her own lips turn up when Lucas replied in kind. As was to be expected, his credit with the sisters couldn't get any higher. It was "Lord Dundas this" and "Lord Dundas that," and they'd taken to thanking the good Lord at evening prayers for sending such a generous benefactor.

They'd also taken to watching Jessica and Lucas whenever their paths crossed, and more often than not, this was when the workers and Lucas trooped into her kitchen to eat the meal she had prepared. The banter, then, became subdued, and she was aware of the veiled looks and speculative glances directed at both herself and Lucas, not only from the nuns, but from the workmen as well. She didn't know whether they expected her to pounce on Lucas and kiss him or box his ears. It made her all hot and bothered, as though she weren't hot enough with the heat of her labors, making the mountain of pies, potatoes, stews and puddings these men devoured.

Lucas took it all in his stride. As she and the nuns hovered around the table, setting down the big platters of food and generally fetching and carrying for the ravenous men, he would occasionally catch her eye and wink. It was very hard to keep a straight face, but all she had to do was remind herself that these men thought she had once tried to compromise Lucas and that brought her down to earth.

Neighbors began to call. The first to arrive were the vicar and his wife, John and Anne Rankin. They appeared at their door with boxes of clothes and bed linens that their congregation had collected in anticipation of the boys' arrival. Others soon followed their lead, among them the apothecary, Wilson, and his wife, and surprisingly, the attorney, Rempel, and Mrs. Rempel. The general goodwill and generosity of their neighbors went a long way to quelling any fears the nuns may have harbored about their reception in the area. In fact, though they had always gone about their work cheerfully and without complaint, now the sisters' spirits seemed to soar.

There was nothing they could not do, would not tackle, and it afforded Jessica and old Joseph no end of amusement to see Sisters Elvira and Dolores march with raised brooms into the henhouse to do battle with the startled hens for their precious eggs.

Though Jessica was as happy as she could remember, it was inevitable that she would suffer a few pangs when visitors greeted her by name and she did not recognize them. She felt awkward and shy when they had to introduce themselves, all the more so because she felt she had this horrible reputation to live down. But there was more to her discomfort than that. She wondered how she would feel when she finally came face-to-face with her Voice. Would there be a moment of truth? An instant of heart-stopping recognition? Would they know each other? And she would search each new face with a shiver of apprehension.

But no such moment occurred. Everyone was very nice, very ordinary. The only time she'd experienced that moment of recognition was with Lucas, and everything within her rebelled at the thought that he might be her Voice. She couldn't explain why she felt this way. She hardly knew him. But logic could not control what she felt deep inside.

Sometimes, she would stop what she was doing and look around Hawkshill, her gaze moving from one friendly face to another, and it would seem inconceivable that a murder had taken place only half a mile down the bridle path. No one spoke of it; no one referred to her part in her father's quarrel with Lucas or to her subsequent disappearance. She'd been missing for two nights before she'd turned up at the convent. Where had she been? What had made her go to London? She could not begin to guess what had driven her to such lengths. And no one would answer any of the oh-so-tactful questions she put to them. They were either being evasive or they did not know.

She mentioned her frustration to Perry, Lucas's young cousin. There was no one from her former life she felt half as comfortable with. They were the same age, he was open and friendly, and along with Lucas, he was their most regular visitor.

"People are just being considerate," he said. He looked at her keenly. "Have you been going around asking questions, Jess?"

"I've tried. Oh, don't worry, I'm very diplomatic. But no one will tell me anything."

"Lucas doesn't want you asking a lot of questions," he said.

She bristled at this. "Why doesn't he want me asking questions? Does he have something to hide?"

"Don't be daft! He's thinking of you. He doesn't want anyone to upset you."

"Well, I am upset! No one will talk to me, not even you."

This startled a laugh out of him. "Have it your own way. What is it you wish to know?"

What she learned from Perry only confirmed what Lucas had told her. As a young girl, she'd been infatuated with Lucas and had relentlessly pursued him. As for the night her father died, Perry could not help her there. He'd been away at university at the time and what he knew he'd been told by others. He told her something else. Bella, he said, was Chalford's leading light. They were bound to meet sooner or later.

This morsel of information filled Jessica with anxiety. No one had mentioned that Bella lived in Chalford. She'd assumed, hoped, that after her marriage, she'd moved away.

She thought of the girl she'd once been, infatuated with a man promised to another, a vixen who would heedlessly lie to get her own way, and she cringed. She couldn't recognize that girl as herself and didn't know what she could say to Lucas's Bella to atone for what she'd done.

The next time she saw Lucas, he was standing in the shade of one of Hawkshill's tall oaks, watching footmen unload a wagon of supplies that two gentlemen had just delivered. She was dispensing fresh lemonade to the thirsty helpers, and eventually made her way over to him. Deciding that diplomacy would not work on Lucas, she asked him point-blank if what Perry had told her was true.

"Yes, Bella is here in Chalford," he said. He accepted the glass of lemonade she held out and took a long swallow. "This is her home. Where else would she be?"

"I gathered . . . I understood . . . I thought she lived in London."

"Only for part of the year. When the Season is over, she and Rupert always return to Chalford."

"I see," she said.

He turned slightly and gave her a slow, searching appraisal. "What is it, Jess?" he asked softly. "Didn't you realize you'd have to face Bella sooner or later? And not only Bella. My mother will be here in a day or two and—"

"Your mother!"

"Didn't you know I had a mother? I thought Perry would have told you."

"The sisters told me, but they said she lived in London with . . . with a young relative."

"Ellie is my ward. My mother and Ellie usually spend the summer here with me. Don't look so stricken. As far as I know, my mother has no quarrel with you. But Bella—ah well, that's a different story. I wouldn't like to be in your shoes when she catches up to you."

This was said with so much relish that she was taken aback. In the last little while it had seemed to her that he had softened toward her, had even come to like her. Now she saw that she had assumed too much.

Lucas moved and she tensed. "Don't look so scared," he said in a different voice. "No one is going to hurt you. Not unless they want to make an enemy of me."

"Fine words!" she flared, the hurt strangely turning to anger. "Don't pretend you care! I'm not forgetting that you said you would drive me out of Hawkshill. You made all kinds of threats if I did not leave. You implied . . . oh . . . all sort of things," she ended lamely. She felt perilously close to tears, and would have bolted for the house if he had not blocked her path.

"Does this seem like driving you away?" he said, gesturing to encompass Hawkshill and the transformation that was taking place, thanks to him.

"I'm only repeating what you said."

"That was a long time ago, Jess. At least three weeks." He rubbed his neck. "A lot can happen in three weeks. Maybe I've changed my mind."

"Why, Lucas? Why would you change your mind? What are you really up to? Why are you nice to me one moment and nasty the next?"

He had a stupid grin on his face, but he was looking beyond her. "Ah," he said, "here are two gentlemen who are eager to see you. Jessica, you won't remember Rupert Haig, but I'm sure he remembers you."

She spun around and saw the two gentlemen who had been overseeing the unloading of the wagon. The one with fair hair was bowing, and she curtsied awkwardly. She had an impression of intelligent gray eyes and a warm smile, then Lucas's words registered and she hurriedly looked away. This was Rupert Haig, *the* Rupert Haig whom Bella had married? Through the confusion of her own thoughts she heard his pleasant voice saying that his wife would be calling on her when things were more settled at Hawkshill. Meantime, Bella was donating an assortment of supplies—oatmeal, potatoes, sugar, candles, he didn't know what all—which he hoped would come in useful.

Bella Haig's generosity brought guilty color rushing to her cheeks, and she stammered out her thanks.

"And this," said Lucas, "is my cousin Adrian Wilde. You already know his brother, Perry."

He was the most handsome man she had ever seen. A lock of dark hair fell across his brow and his brown eyes were assessing her in a thoroughly masculine fashion. "So this is Perry's Jessica," he said. "Miss Hayward, I hardly recognize you." He laughed. "Now I begin to understand. Perry did not exaggerate."

"Perry," she said, "has been a good friend to me."

When she looked at Lucas, she could see that the provoking man had turned nasty again, for some inexplicable reason. The good sisters appeared then and invited everyone into the house to take refreshments. For the next thirty minutes, Jessica took part in a conversation of which she could not later recall a single word.

The boys arrived on one of the warmest days they'd enjoyed so far that summer. The countryside seemed to put on its best show to welcome them. Clover and buttercups bobbed their heads in the pasture that was due to be scythed. Honeysuckle trailed over low stone walls and exhaled its sweetness in a husky bouquet. The swallows had returned and they wheeled and dived overhead. The ever-present robins and sparrows had teamed up to form a choir in the topmost branches of nearby oaks. Even their pony entered the spirit of the thing. Tulip pricked her ears, crossed the pasture at a slow trot and neighed a welcome as she reached the fence post.

Everyone was milling around the yard talking and laughing at once as the boys, with their scrubbed faces and in their Sunday best, spilled out of the two hired carriages that had just arrived from London. Sister Brigid was one of the first to alight. There were also two young priests who would be moving on once the boys were delivered.

The boys had almost immediately let fly with a barrage of questions.

"Sister Martha, why aren't you wearing your robe?"

"Joseph, is it true you're going to teach us 'ow to be farmers?"

"Sister Elvira, where's the privy? I's got to use the privy."

"I'm starved. Where's the grub?"

"I wants to ride the 'orse. Sister Dolores, can I ride the 'orse?"

They did not stop talking as they trooped into the house. The ride from London had been a grand adventure. Such luxury! Such comfort! Such convenience! With a chamber pot under the seat! This last had obviously been the greatest marvel they'd ever encountered as Sister Brigid confirmed with a roll of her eyes. Jessica laughed. She felt as excited as the boys, and she was glad that the young nun was to be part of their little community. Jessica genuinely liked this young novice. She'd never heard Sister Brigid complain, never heard her gossip about another nun. She was by nature shy, but she also knew when to stand her ground.

It was an hour before they could all catch their breaths, an hour of arguing over who should sleep where, of stowing belongings and washing the grime of the journey from little hands and faces. And when they finally took their places at the trestle tables that had been pushed together to make one long table in Hawkshill's main parlor, a lump formed in Jessica's throat. Her eyes traveled over the little faces that glowed with anticipation and she would not have recognized them as belonging to the same boys who had been brought to the convent so short a time ago.

The boys were between seven and ten years old but they looked younger. They were small for their age, and their thin, undersized bodies had been in great demand by masters who had used them as chimney sweeps or sewer boys. Until they'd been rescued by the nuns, these children had rarely seen the light of day. They'd been abused or abandoned by their parents, easy prey for unscrupulous men.

But they were in safe hands now. She shifted her gaze to take in the sisters and Joseph and her heart swelled with gratitude. They looked rather comical, Joseph with his toothless grin and the sisters like crows in their black robes, but their looks were deceiving. They were saints and they were warriors rolled into one. She'd found a safe harbor with them, and so would these boys.

That thought stayed with her through the hubbub of dinner and the quiet time of vespers. Later, when the children were sleeping, she donned her shawl and slipped away to be with Joseph, as she'd got into the habit of doing since their first night at Hawkshill. He didn't say much, but what he did say always struck a chord within her.

Tulip was in her stall and whinnied to Jessica for her lump of sugar. Joseph was planing a piece of wood at his workbench. It was here, Jessica thought, that she felt a sense of the familiar—Tulip nuzzling her fingers; the smell of farm animals and hay; someone at a bench hammering or sawing, just like Joseph. Her father, maybe. Maybe this is why she liked this quiet time of the evening. Maybe this is where she and her father had done all their talking.

"Boys all settled?" asked Joseph, abruptly bringing her thoughts round.

She nodded and approached the bench. "They're worn out with excitement. They've only just arrived and already they're eager to be out in the world, you know, as apprentices learning a trade, as stable boys or in service, and the sisters agree with them."

"And you don't?"

She let out a sigh. "I don't know. I suppose the sisters know best. But I can't help thinking of what our boys have been through. They've found a safe harbor with us. I'd like them to stay here as long as possible. They have plenty of time to learn a trade."

Joseph picked up the board he'd been planing, held it at arm's length and examined it from all angles. "Harbors are good," he said.

"My thought exactly."

"But ships weren't built for harbors." He put down the plank, looked at Jessica and gave her a toothless grin. "Ships be meant to sail the ocean, whatever the dangers. Our boys knows this."

She could almost hear the chord strike within her.

CHAPTER
9

HER PARENTS' GRAVE WAS IN SAINT LUKE'S CHURCH-yard on the outskirts of town. The headstone was a small square of granite, with nothing inscribed on it but names and dates. The plot was well kept, but there were no flowers or plants adorning it. It didn't look neglected, but it didn't have the little touches that the other graves had—a stone vase, an urn, an ornament—to make it look loved. It brought a lump to her throat.

Jessica had brought flowers with her, white daisies that grew in profusion around the foundations of Hawkshill. Kneeling down, she set them in front of the headstone. Mary Hayward, her mother, had died at the age of twenty-six, when she was only three. Her father had been close to fifty when he'd died. She knew very little about their life together, but she knew more now than she'd known a few days ago. Sister Brigid had discovered an old box in the attic, and the box contained her father's effects.

There was nothing of value in the box, but Jessica

would not have parted with its contents for a king's ransom. There were books and papers and other odds and ends that were of little interest except that they'd once belonged to her father. What she treasured most were her father's watch with his initials inscribed on the back, his gold ring, and two letters he'd written to her mother, both from London, but two years apart. For the most part, they dealt with the buying and selling of horses. Though she was disappointed with their impersonal tone, Sister Elvira declared that there was nothing unusual about that. Men were shy of expressing their feelings on paper. The important thing was, he'd mentioned his daughter by name. "Tell baby Jess that Papa will be home soon," he'd written.

Those few words had acted on her like a flood after a long drought. Something deep inside her had bloomed. And, of course, she'd turned into a watering pot. But nothing escaped the sharp eyes of small boys, and she'd been forced to tell a white lie. She had a trifling cold, she'd said as she blew her nose for the tenth time in as many minutes.

Tell baby Jess that Papa will be home soon. She let the words turn in her mind, hoping to unlock her memories. One memory would do. But try as she might, she could not find the key to that locked door.

She trailed her fingers across the headstone. Perhaps there was no sense of recognition, but there was an affinity, she told herself fiercely. Her father must have loved her or why had he kept her with him? He could have farmed her out to some family who would have been glad to board her for a small fee. William Hayward must have wanted her with him. And on the last night of his life, it had been his daughter he'd been thinking of. He'd only done what any responsible father would do to right a wrong against his child.

She stood and stared down at the gravestone for a long time, then finally turned away to retrace her steps. Only then did she become aware that she was not alone. A young girl was kneeling at a gravestone close to the stone gates. Her hands were clasped in prayer, and she was as oblivious of Jessica as Jessica had been of her. Suddenly she turned and looked up.

Jessica gave an apologetic half smile. The girl's eyes were blank, then they suddenly blazed with hostility. In the next instant, she jumped up and hurried away.

Taken aback by that look of open dislike, Jessica could only stand and stare. Finally coming to herself, she looked at the gravestone the girl had been kneeling beside— *Bragge,* she read, two generations of Bragges were buried here, but, of course, the names meant nothing to her.

She was still standing on the path when another figure entered by the stone gates, but this lady had a warm smile on her face. "Jessica?" she said. "Jessica Hayward? Ellie said that you were here. Oh, forgive me, my dear. I'm Rosemary Wilde, Lucas's mother."

Jessica's heartbeat picked up speed. This beautiful lady was Lucas's mother? It didn't seem possible. She was too young. There wasn't a thread of silver in the glossy brown hair that peeped from her bonnet. Her figure was as lithe as a girl's. The lines on her face were laugh lines and added expression to a lovely complexion.

"Lucas's mother," repeated the beautiful lady, but slowly this time.

Jessica willed herself to say something, but all she could manage was a breathless, "Oh!"

"You must forgive Ellie," said Lucas's mother, ignoring Jessica's frozen state. "She should have brought you to me, but I suppose she was overcome with grief." She gestured to the gravestone they were standing beside. "Ellie's whole family is buried here, except for her brother, Philip. You remember . . ." She shook her head. "What am I saying! Of course you don't remember the Bragges. They had a house on Waterside Street. Poor Philip died at Waterloo. He and Lucas were very close. The first thing Ellie does, whenever we return to Chalford, is to come here and pay her respects."

Jessica's brain was beginning to thaw. "How sad," she said, and looked down at the white roses that had been arranged in a stone vase.

Mrs. Wilde looked past Jessica, to her parents' grave. "I knew you, of all people, would understand." She smiled at Jessica. "But this isn't the place to have a conversation." She slipped her arm through Jessica's and began to lead her through the gates. "We arrived yesterday evening and Lucas has told us so much about the good work you and the nuns are doing. You must tell me when is the best time to call, or better yet, you must come up to the Lodge."

She went on in this vein as they came out onto the road, and Jessica realized gratefully that Lucas's mother was trying to smooth over the awkwardness of their first meeting.

Ellie was sitting in an open carriage. Her eyes were no longer hostile, but they weren't friendly, either.

"May we drive you home, Jessica?" asked Mrs. Wilde.

Jessica pointed to the wagon with Joseph sitting up front holding the reins. "We still have some errands to run," she said. She didn't add that she was on her way to call on the constable to probe for clues to her father's murder.

Rosemary Wilde waited until the carriage had turned onto the main thoroughfare before she spoke to Ellie. "What did you say to Jessica, Ellie?"

"I didn't say anything, Aunt Rosemary."

Rosemary smiled. "What? No word of greeting when you came face-to-face in the churchyard?"

"No. I . . . I was close to tears and didn't want to speak to . . . to anyone. Why do you ask?"

She wasn't quite sure that she believed Ellie. For one thing, she looked guilty, and for another, Ellie was jealous. She was at a difficult age, having just turned sixteen, and couldn't make up her mind whether she was a child or a woman.

It was Lucas who, in all ignorance, had set Ellie off.

Last night over dinner, he'd talked a great deal about Jessica and Hawkshill and the fine work the nuns had started there. This had put poor Ellie's nose out of joint. Ellie was in the throes of first love, and Lucas was the man she was smitten with.

Ellie wasn't the only one suspicious of Lucas's interest in Jessica Hayward. So was his mother. Rosemary thought back to when Jessica was a girl. Lucas had paid attention to Jessica, but it hadn't been a lover's attention. He'd been more like an older brother. She herself had always been fond of Jessica. The girl had a way with her. She was tenderhearted. And when she gave her loyalty, she never faltered. Though Lucas wouldn't agree with her, she'd found Jessica's devotion to her father quite touching. And her devotion to Lucas had been understandable. He must have seemed like a knight in shining armor to a girl who was used to fending for herself.

Then Bella Clifford had moved into the area, and Lucas had fallen for her. Jessica had not liked Bella, and neither had she—Bella was completely self-centered; no one's feelings mattered but her own; her servants were afraid of her. But no one could tell Lucas any of this, least of all his mother. But she'd known it was only a matter of time before Lucas saw through Bella's lovely façade. If he hadn't gone off to war—things might have turned out very differently.

"Aunt Rosemary?"

"Yes, Ellie?"

"Don't you think that Hayward woman should know she's not wanted here and leave? After all the harm she's done?"

"What harm did she do?"

Ellie said indignantly, "She told lies about Lucas! He lost Bella, and he'd loved her for years."

"Did he? I'm not sure now that he did love Bella."

Ellie was shocked. "Then why did he get engaged to her when he came home from the war?"

She'd said too much. Ellie was too young to understand that love was rarely the driving force in a man's life. With some men, it was money. With others, it was prestige. With Lucas, it was honor. Bella had waited for him for four years. He would never go back on his word. In fact, his most scathing contempt was reserved for anyone who broke a promise or a vow.

She felt as though someone had just walked over her grave, and she shivered.

"Aunt Rosemary, what's wrong?"

She cleared her expression. "Nothing, dear. I was just thinking of what Lucas told us: we're to put the past behind us and accept Jessica as we find her. So be careful of what you say to her."

"Whatever Lucas says, I can never forget the past!"

Mrs. Wilde did not reply to this passionate outburst. The carriage had come to a stop outside the circulating library on Waterside Street. She glanced out the window, then her gaze became riveted. A distinguished-looking gentleman in his late forties had just exited with a book in his hand. He didn't look up or notice her carriage, but turned on his heel and struck out along Waterside Street.

Her heart turned over. He shouldn't be here. She would never have come down to Chalford if she'd known that he was here. They had an understanding. Chalford was hers for the summer months. He came down for the hunting season. Then what was he doing here?

Ellie said, "Who is that gentleman, Aunt Rosemary?"

"Sir Matthew Paige," she murmured, and just saying the name out loud brought her to her senses. "I haven't seen him in years." She went on brightly. "Now let's see if we can find Mr. Scott's latest novel."

• • •

Jessica was in a towering temper when she left the constable's office, not so much by what she'd learned but because the constable wouldn't take her seriously.

As soon as she was seated in the wagon, she turned to Joseph and said scathingly, "I'm rapidly coming to the conclusion that my father must have shot himself. According to Constable Clay, there is no one in Chalford who would stoop to such a cowardly act. The people here are all saints. Oh no, the malefactor must have come from a neighboring town, or even London, you know, one of my father's gambling cronies. It wouldn't surprise me if the murderer turned out to be the man in the moon."

Joseph looked sympathetic and flicked the reins. Tulip started forward.

Many minutes later, she said, "Lucas found my father's body. Can you believe that? Lucas found the body, and he said nothing to me."

"Stands to reason he would have found it."

Jessica looked at him sharply. "What do you mean?"

"The bridle path. How else would his lordship get home?"

This deflated her anger somewhat. "All the same," she said, "there's something here that's not right. No one has anything to hide or so Constable Clay would have me believe, but in the next breath, he tells me not to stir things up. There's something he's keeping from me, yes, both he and Lucas, and I haven't a clue what it is."

"Mayhap it has nowt to do with you or your father."

She gave him an "et tu Brute" look and pressed her lips together. Her pique did not last long. Joseph had a way of putting things into perspective. She was getting worked up about nothing. And the information she had managed to pry out of the constable wasn't all bad.

"No one seriously suspected me of murdering my father," she said at length. "In fact, they feared something had happened to me, too. The whole town turned out to search for me." She looked down at her hands. "I hadn't realized . . . that is . . . people can be so kind."

"Even his lordship?" asked Joseph with a sly smile.

Her brows flew together. "It was his lordship," she said tartly, "who gave me the impression that I was suspected of murdering my father."

"But you knew you were innocent."

"Well, of course I did. I knew all along it was—"

"What?"

She'd known it was her Voice. "Impossible," she said.

When they turned into the drive to Hawkshill, her eye was caught by some movement high up on the ridge that ran along Lucas's property. Two riders had emerged from the trees, a man and a woman. She recognized Lucas at once but not his companion. They drew rein and Lucas dismounted. When he went to help the lady, she slid from the saddle and seemed to stumble. Lucas's arms went around her.

Then they kissed. Full on the lips.

Jessica dragged her eyes away and glanced at Joseph. He had seen it, too. She wasn't going to say anything. She was determined not to say anything, but the words came out of her mouth anyway.

"Who is she, Joseph? Do you know?"

But Joseph either did not know or he wasn't telling.

It was the smell of smoke that awakened her. She sat up, momentarily dazed, then she jumped out of bed. Down below in the farmyard, their wagon was blazing like a pitch torch. Calling for Joseph and the sisters, she covered herself with a shawl and went tearing down the stairs.

Joseph was already there. He grabbed for her as she raced to the wagon. "There's nowt to be done, lass. It's beyond saving."

"How did it happen?" she cried out.

"Someone did it on purpose."

"Someone did it on purpose?" she said faintly. "How can you be sure?"

He went down on his haunches and pointed. "They set the fire under the wagon, see? And I can smell the pitch." He straightened and wiped the sweat from his brow. "I should have locked the wagon away, but I never reckoned on anything like this."

Her eyes darted around the farmyard. The chickens were squawking; the mare was whinnying and the cows lowing. "Tulip," she cried, and took a step toward the barn but Joseph held her back.

"Barn's as tight as a tollbooth," he said. "They couldn't do no harm there."

The sisters joined them moments later, but when they heard the boys calling out from upstairs, Sister Brigid was sent back to calm them.

"It could be worse," said Sister Dolores. "It could have been the barn or even the house."

Still, the thought that someone wanted to hurt them was appalling.

As the nuns conversed in hushed tones, Joseph went off to patrol the area. Jessica was hugging herself, numb in spite of the scorching heat from the wagon. This was meant for her, not for the nuns, not for the orphanage boys, but for her, Jessica Hayward. She could sense it in every pore in her body.

When Joseph came back, his expression was somber. "They've wrung a chicken's neck," he said, "and hung it over the front door. Damn ruffians, if you'll pardon the expression, Sisters. Boys from the village, I'd say. If I catches up to 'em, I'll wring *their* necks."

"Lord Dundas will have to be told," said Sister Elvira. "He'll know what to do."

"Shouldn't we send for the constable?" asked Jessica quickly. Maybe *now* he would take her seriously.

Sister Elvira turned to Joseph. "What do you think, Joseph?"

After a moment's hesitation, he nodded. "Why not? A night or two in the tollbooth is just what them rascals deserves."

They stood around the yard until the wagon was reduced to a smoldering, blackened skeleton. Joseph wouldn't go back to his bed, but set up a pallet in the barn with his blunderbuss for company. If the ruffians came back, he would be ready for them.

The moment Jessica was back in her own room, she threw herself on the bed and stared at the ceiling. She was remembering the constable's warning not to stir things up. It was the same warning Lucas had given her.

CHAPTER
10

SHE HAD A MUTINY ON HER HANDS, AND THE LITTLE monsters had chosen the wrong moment to get her back up. She had a headache. It had been a terrible day. She'd had words with the constable again when he'd arrived this morning to investigate the burning of their wagon. She was running late. She was at the end of her tether. And the boys were taking advantage.

"You will eat the food I have prepared for you," she declared, "or you will sit at that table till doomsday."

Knowing that she had just made a blunder did nothing to improve her headache. "Never make empty threats," was one of the cardinal rules Sister Elvira had laid down.

The boys glared at the food on their plates. The ringleader, Pip, a scrawny little brat of eight, folded his arms across his chest. It was the signal for the others to follow suit, and now six horrid little wretches sat around her kitchen table with folded arms and mutinous expressions darkening their small faces.

Jessica changed tactics. "Now come along, boys," she

said coaxingly, "eat your dinner. It will make you strong like . . . like Joseph."

"I ain't eating no toads," said Pip. "They're slimy."

Jessica was ready to tear out her hair. "They are not toads! How many times do I have to tell you. They're sausages. You like sausages, don't you? That's all they are. Sausages cooked in a pudding."

"Then why d'you say, 'toad in the 'ole'?" This was Martin, Pip's younger brother.

"Because 'toad in the hole' is the name of the dish." And she wished she'd never mentioned it.

"Well, they don't looks like sausages to me!" piped up another voice.

"That's because I cut them into slices." When there was no response, Jessica retreated a little. "All right," she said brightly, "let's forget about the toad . . . the sausages in batter. Drink your milk and eat plenty of bread and butter, then you can go and join your friends."

"I don't likes the milk. It tastes funny."

"It's farm milk," she protested. "It's fresh and creamy, that's all."

"Well, I don't likes it!"

"And," another voice piped up, "the butter tastes funny as well."

Arms akimbo, Jessica surveyed her charges with patent dislike. They'd lived in hovels. They'd been abused, starved and beaten. And they had the gall to find fault with the wholesome, nourishing food she had taken the trouble to cook for them? Ungrateful wretches! No wonder their parents had abandoned them.

It was a wicked thought, but knowing that it was wicked didn't make her feel any better. "Fine," she said, "then you'll sit there till . . . till I say you can leave." Then, as an afterthought, "Wouldn't you like to be with the other boys? Wouldn't you like to help Joseph build a new wagon? Or you could help the sisters weed the vegetable plot."

"Not if we 'as to eat this slop."

Pip, again, the ringleader. And to think that these boys had all been specially chosen to come to Hawkshill because the mother superior thought they were the most promising! If she had her way, she would send them back on the next stage.

Well, they wouldn't wear her down. And just to show them she meant business, she stomped to the great granite sink, rolled up her sleeves and began to wash the dirty pots. They could sit there forever for all she cared. She knew one thing: if she backed down now they would take advantage of her forevermore.

Zzzz.

Jessica jerked, and water from the pot spilled down the front of her apron. She put the pot down and slowly turned. "Who made that sound?" she asked in a dangerously soft voice. The little monsters knew that she was terrified of bees and wasps.

Six innocent faces stared back at her.

When no one answered, she turned back to the sink and started over. They weren't going to get a rise out of her.

Zzzz.

Her lips turned up. They really were little monsters, but maybe she deserved it. She'd been like a bear with a sore tooth ever since she'd seen Lucas . . . no . . . that kiss had nothing to do with it . . . ever since she'd had a set-to with the constable yesterday. And the visit he had paid them today had only aggravated her temper. Joseph had left a message for him and when he got it, the constable had ridden hell-for-leather to Hawkshill.

She was surprised that his horse could hold him. Constable Clay was built like an ox. He was old, older than Sister Dolores, but what really annoyed her was that he didn't seem interested in solving her father's murder, any more than he was interested in their burned-out wagon.

And he had a temper.

"I expected to find you all murdered in your beds," he'd roared. "You called me out for a burned-out wagon? This is child's play! A mischievous prank! I have more important things to see to than this."

The sisters and Joseph had been chastened, but not she. And when she'd found herself alone with the constable, she'd told him exactly what she thought of him—and a few other things she shouldn't have said.

Zzzz.

Those boys were incorrigible! No. They were only mischievous, and after all they'd been through in their short lives, it was a good sign.

"Sister Martha," said Martin, "there really is a wasp in your kitchen."

She turned. "Really?" she said brightly, as though wasps meant nothing to her. "Where?" There was no wasp. She shook her head. "I can take a joke, but you really mustn't tell lies."

"But Sister Martha—" said Pip, just as the door was flung back on its hinges, making them all jump.

Lucas entered, scowling. "I just came from Chalford," he said, "where I happened to bump into Constable Clay." His voice rose to a roar. "You damn well accused me of—"

"Lord Dundas!"

Her sharp reproof cut him off short. He looked at the boys. "Out!" he said and held the door for them.

The gleeful boys began to rise from their places. "Sit down!" said Jessica in her most imperious manner. When the boys slowly sank back, she looked at Lucas. "They are not going anywhere," she said, "not until they eat what's in front of them. If you wish to speak to me, you may wait in the little parlor. It's behind the dining room."

"I'll wait here," he replied in a voice that brooked no argument.

No one moved. No one said anything. Six glum boys

stared at their plates. Jessica went back to washing her pots.

"So what's wrong with your dinner?" asked Lucas, enlightenment finally dawning.

Pip answered him. "We're not eating no toads," he said.

"Sausages!" shrilled Jessica. "They're sausages. How many times do I have to tell you? 'Toad in the hole' is only a name. It doesn't mean . . . oh, eat your dinner and let's have no more of this nonsense."

Again, no one moved. After a long interval of silence, Lucas's lips quirked. Finally, he said, looking at Pip, "Give me your plate."

Pip handed over his plate and Lucas shoveled a huge forkful of sausage into his mouth. After a moment, he said, with his mouth still full, "Who said these were sausages?"

"Sister Martha," chorused the boys.

"Sister Martha?" His brows rose, and he looked at Jessica. "Well, Sister Martha is mistaken. These are toads, all right."

Jessica glared at him. Now they would never eat their dinner.

"I know," said Lucas, "because I eat toads all the time."

The boys gasped.

He swallowed the mouthful of sausage and started on another. "Well, all soldiers do. And prizefighters, like Joseph. That's how we get to be soldiers and fighters. But sniveling little weaklings of boys never do. And when they grow up, they become sniveling little weaklings of men. And do you know what? Joseph and I make short work of them. Now, eat your dinner."

The boys reluctantly picked up their forks and began to jab at the sausages in the pudding, but they did not eat. Jessica flashed Lucas a superior smile. He grinned back at her.

"And," said Lucas, "the first boy to finish can have a ride on my stallion. That is, when I finish my conversation with Miss . . . er . . . Sister Martha."

"A ride on a stallion!" Pip drove his fork into the pudding, came up with a sausage and gingerly tasted it. "It ain't 'alf bad," he said, and drove his fork in again. The other boys needed no further encouragement. In a matter of minutes, they had cleaned their plates and would have charged out the door had Jessica not reminded them of their chores. In double-quick time, they cleared the table, stacked the dishes, then whooped out of the kitchen like an Indian war party from one of the stories she'd read to them at bedtime.

Jessica glanced longingly at the open door. It belatedly occurred to her that she and Lucas were alone in the house. If she'd been thinking straight, she would have left with the boys. Her gaze quickly returned to Lucas when he took a step toward her. "That was bribery," she said. "We don't use those tactics here."

"What does it matter? I helped you save face. You should be thanking me."

And she would have, if she weren't angry with him. He was stalking her, and that made her nervous. As he advanced, she retreated, carefully keeping the table between them. "They'll be expecting a reward the next time—"

"Stop prevaricating," he suddenly yelled. "You know why I'm here."

"If it's about Constable Clay—"

"You know damn well it's about Constable Clay. You accused me of murdering your father. Don't try to deny it. Clay told me himself."

Had she gone that far? She'd said a lot of things to the constable in the heat of the moment. "He must have misunderstood. All I said was that he should keep an open mind. He's known you and your friends forever. He's prejudiced in your favor. Look how he came running to you today."

He put his hands on the flat of the table and leaned toward her. "You also accused me of setting fire to your rickety old wagon and wringing the neck of your scrawny chicken."

Her hand fluttered to her throat. "I was making a point," she cried out. "I was trying to get him to think like an officer of the law. He should be suspicious of everyone and everything, and not take what his friends tell him at face value."

His eyes narrowed on her face. "What's made you change your mind about me, Jess?" A light came on in his eyes. "I saw your wagon, yesterday, from the ridge. That's it, isn't it? You saw me on the ridge."

"Listen!" she hissed.

He straightened. "What is it?"

Zzzz.

"A wasp!" she shrieked. "There it is! Lucas, help me!"

She batted her hands in front of her face, then came charging round the table, straight into Lucas's arms. Her momentum carried him backward and they both went tumbling to the floor.

The wasp buzzed over their heads and out the door that slowly swung inward.

"Hello? Hello? Is anyone at home?" The voice was cultured and belonged to the woman who had kissed Lucas when they were riding on the ridge.

Lucas hauled Jessica to her feet. "Bella!" he exclaimed. "What the devil are you doing here?"

Jessica had expected to be embarrassed when she finally met up with Bella again. After all, she felt horribly guilty for what she'd done. And to have been discovered rolling on the floor, entwined in Lucas's arms, exceeded her worst nightmares. But the kind of shame she experienced now was new to her, and she was ashamed of being ashamed.

She was sitting in a straight-backed chair opposite Bella in the small parlor. Lucas was on her right and Sisters Elvira and Dolores were to the left of her. As the conversation went on around her, she watched Bella's keen eyes search out every blot and blemish, and as she mentally pounced on them, Jessica winced. She was seeing things through Bella's eyes and she was ashamed, ashamed of herself and her work-worn hands and service-able garments, ashamed of the parlor with its threadbare carpet and oddments of cast-off furniture that their neigh-bors had passed on to them, ashamed of the chipped cups and saucers and the misshapen biscuits the boys had helped her bake. Everything was shabby and run-down, and either she had never noticed it, or it had never mat-tered to her until now.

She looked at Bella and saw perfection. There wasn't a hair out of place; her skin was flawless; her white muslin gown with its short blue Spencer jacket looked fashion-able and expensive. Bella even smelled expensive. Jessica was well aware that the loveliness did not penetrate below the surface. Since they'd entered the parlor, Bella had dominated the conversation. She'd asked a few perfunc-tory questions about Hawkshill, then she'd turned the conversation on herself. She dropped the names of famous personages the way their boys dropped their aitches. Bella wanted to impress them. Jessica knew all this and it didn't seem to matter. In Bella's presence, she felt diminished.

She couldn't help looking at Lucas to see what effect Bella had on him. He was watching Bella intently and Jessica wondered if he was still in love with her. A splin-ter seemed to pierce her heart, and when Lucas turned his head to look at her, she quickly averted her gaze.

Bella had now returned to the topic of Hawkshill, but her eyes were as busy as ever, and this time they had come to rest on Sister Elvira. In one long, comprehensive stare, she absorbed everything about the little nun, her plump face with its sparse eyelashes, her rotund figure in its grubby habit, and she dismissed her with a flick of her lashes. Jessica thought of the tireless hours the sisters worked, their self-sacrifice, their pleasure in simple things, their unshakable faith, and a spark of resentment ignited inside her. Bella had wanted to make her feel small and she'd succeeded. Maybe she deserved to feel small for what she'd done. But she would tolerate no insult to the nuns.

Bella's eyes suddenly narrowed on her, and Jessica's spine stiffened. "As I said," said Bella in her beautifully modulated voice, "we are all eager to do our part to make a success of Hawkshill." She paused dramatically. "And I have come up with the idea of a subscription ball."

"A subscription ball," said Sister Elvira carefully.

"Oh, it won't cost you a penny," said Bella. "I've talked it over with my husband and he thinks it's a wonderful idea. We'll host it, of course, and have invitations printed." She laughed. "We wouldn't want just anyone attending, now would we? But at the door, when guests present their cards, they'll have to fork out the price of admission. And after the ball, we'll turn over the money we've made to Hawkshill."

Sister Dolores said, "We're always short of money. I think that's a splendid idea. How kind of you to think of it."

Sister Elvira slipped her hands inside the sleeves of her habit and maintained a thoughtful silence.

Lucas leaned forward, arms on his knees, hands clasped together. "And when are you thinking of holding this ball?"

"As soon as it can be arranged," said Bella. "In fact, the sooner the better. Rupert *will* have his Tenants' Ball, you know, so it must be before that."

"Why not after?" said Lucas.

"Why should we wait?" countered Bella.

Lucas glanced at Jessica, then turned back to Bella. "I'm not sure that Jessica is up to such a grand event."

"My dear Lucas, I shall be there to help her." She smiled at Jessica. "And this is an ideal way to reintroduce her to Chalford society."

Jessica had been following the conversation carefully. She'd known something was coming, but not this. Her initial surprise at Bella's generous offer was quickly swallowed up in shock. They were expecting *her* to attend? She couldn't do it, not without the sisters, and she knew perfectly well that they would not go. She wouldn't enjoy it. In fact, it would be purgatory. If she ever knew how to dance, she had forgotten it. She didn't know how to go on in society, how to make small talk, how to . . . She didn't know what was expected of her, and it terrified her. And she had nothing to wear.

Bella knew all this, and she had offered to help her.

Aye, and pigs could fly.

Lucas spoke to Sister Elvira. "I must advise against it."

"But why?" asked Bella with a light laugh.

"For the reason I've already given. Jessica isn't ready for such a grand affair. She's been a nun for three years. She doesn't know how our world works. A ball for Jessica would be like a debut, a coming-out. Afterward, she would be expected to take her place in society." He chanced a quick look at Jessica and said abruptly, "She's not ready for it, that's all."

The shame that Bella had heaped upon her by mentally pouncing on every blot and blemish in sight was nothing to the chagrin Jessica experienced now. It seemed that nothing escaped Lucas's sharp eyes, either. She had a vision of herself driving around Chalford in her shabby clothes in Joseph's shabby wagon paying calls on elegant ladies, and afterward, receiving them in Hawkshill's shabby parlor, and she knew that Lucas spoke the truth. Moreover, he had done no more than say exactly what she had been thinking. But now she began to realize how

Lucas must see her and she was torn between a desire to run from the room and a strong urge to hit him.

Bella's eyes were wide and innocent. "But Lucas," she protested, "I only want what's best for Jessica. And this will give everyone a chance to see that all is forgiven and forgotten between us, as well as raise money for Hawkshill."

He said evenly, "I don't dispute that. But I want what's best for Jessica, too. And I say no."

Temper glinted in Bella's eyes. "In that case the ball will go forward without Jessica. But mark my words, people will talk."

That did it! Not only were they talking about her as though she were invisible, but no one thought to consult her wishes on the matter. She had no more desire to go to Bella's grand ball than fly to the moon.

The words of refusal trembled on her lips, but she could not say them. The thought that both Bella and Lucas expected her to make a fool of herself got her dander up. She might not have learned the social graces in the Convent of the Sisters of Charity, but she wasn't ignorant of the rules governing good manners. Convent life was far more disciplined in that respect than Lucas seemed to realize.

There was something else at work in her. She was no longer Sister Martha. She was Jessica Hayward of Hawkshill Manor. She was William Hayward's daughter. It was time she acted like it.

"Of course I'm going," she said. "It's not as though the ball is in my honor. No one will expect me to dance every dance or be the life and soul of the party. Besides"—she was remembering what Joseph had said to her about ships and a safe harbor—"I can't hide away here in Hawkshill forever."

Sister Elvira finally broke her silence. "Mrs. Haig is right," she said. "People will talk if Jessica does not attend the ball, particularly since its purpose is to raise money for our work." She gave Jessica a smile that made up for much of the hurt she'd experienced in the last little while. "And Jessica is right as well. It's time, Jessica. How wise of you to know it before I did."

"So that's settled, then," said Bella sweetly, and her eyes flashed with the thrill of triumph.

Shortly after, she left in a rustle of skirts and a cloud of perfume. Lucas went with her, but he returned within minutes. He wished to speak with the sisters in private, he said, giving Jessica a very straight look. She kept her back ramrod straight as she left the room.

Jessica slopped the mop in a bucket of water, squeezed it out, and carefully angling the long wooden handle, swabbed the last patch of her kitchen floor. Upstairs, pandemonium reigned. It was long past the children's bedtime, but they refused to go to sleep. They hated Hawkshill, hated the country. Everything was different. The milk was too creamy, the butter was too rich. They loved the farm animals, but not the chores that went with them. They were homesick for the sights and sounds of the only home they knew. London.

She couldn't think why she'd expected it to be different. It was exactly the same when they'd removed the children from hovels that weren't fit for pigs. It was familiar, and they were terrified to embark on something new.

The children and she had a lot in common. No woman should be terrified to go to a ball. And terrified or not, she couldn't back out of it now. She had too much pride. Oh, if only she'd kept her mouth shut!

Now, things were going to change. Lucas had seen to that in his private tête-à-tête with the sisters. They were sending to the mother superior for more nuns to help relieve Jessica of some of her duties, and her protests were completely ignored. There was more, much more. Her small income was to be spent on new gowns. From now

on, when she went into town, she would use the buggy
that his lordship had very kindly offered for the nuns' use.
They were to enlist the aid of Anne Rankin, the vicar's
wife, to teach Jessica the steps of the dances and generally
tutor her in what passed for good manners in Chalford's
society. The list went on and on.

So now she knew that she hadn't been mistaken. Lucas
saw her as an object of pity and ridicule. Much she cared!

A burst of laughter from the room upstairs brought
her head up. In another week or so, the children would
forget about London. Not everything was unfamiliar to
them. They knew the nuns, and that counted for something. And Sister Brigid was a great favorite. Very soon,
they would be calling Hawkshill home.

But where was home for Jessica Hayward? That was
the question.

She straightened her mop and stood it on the end of its
long handle. After curtsying to it, she counted out the
measure, one two three, one two three, and began to
waltz around the room. She dipped, she circled, she fluttered her eyelashes and laughed up at her handsome partner when he paid her a compliment. She felt light-headed.
She was having a wonderful time.

Her fantasy was shattered by a slow hand-clap. Horrified, she froze, then spun to face the intruder. It was
Lucas, as she'd known it would be.

"What do you want?" she asked rudely. To cover her
embarrassment, she turned her back on him and moved
her bucket and mop to the side of the kitchen.

He was watching her closely. "Didn't Sister Elvira tell
you? I'm to be your tutor, you know, teach you the steps
of the waltz for Bella's ball."

She scowled at him. "Sister Elvira said nothing to me."

"She must have forgotten."

She was excruciatingly aware of his immaculate appearance and her own filthy apron. Quickly removing it,
she hung it on the back of the kitchen door. "Anne

Rankin has agreed to teach me the steps," she said. Her back was still to him. "So you needn't trouble yourself."

When she turned around, he was only inches away from her. The man could move with the speed and silence of a panther. Her back was to the door and she couldn't get past him without touching him.

"It's no trouble," he said. "You're good with a mop. Let's see how good you are with a real man."

His cocky grin and the tone of his remarks incensed her. "Let me pass, Lucas."

The smile left his eyes and he stepped aside. She moved to the sideboard and began to put away dishes. Lucas let out a long sigh.

"You saw Bella and me up on the ridge. That's it, isn't it?"

She gave him one look, then went back to her chore.

He went on. "She must have known you were watching us. That's why she kissed me. There's no need to be jealous. It was only a peck, for heaven's sake."

And it incensed her more that he could read her so well. She thrust out her chin. "You don't have to explain yourself to me."

"Good, because that's the only explanation you're going to get."

He waited, and when she made no reply, he went on. "You're peeved because I said you weren't ready yet to go to Bella's ball. I was thinking of you and only you."

"I appreciate the thought," she said sweetly.

When he took a step toward her, she quickly retreated. He frowned and put his hands on his hips. "Now, what's got into you?"

"You didn't come here to teach me to waltz. Sister Elvira didn't forget to tell me you were coming. So why are you here?"

He smiled sheepishly and shrugged. "Not to have my wicked way with you as you seem to think, Jess." When she didn't smile, he said, "We never did finish that conversation we were having when Bella so rudely interrupted us. The constable told me you were asking a lot of questions."

She kept her back straight and her eyes trained on his. "Someone murdered my father. How can I find out who did it if I don't ask questions?"

"You told Constable Clay I was still your prime suspect."

"I suspect everyone."

His eyes narrowed to slits. His tone was lethal. "I did not kill your father."

"Perhaps not, but I think you know who did." The words surprised her as much as they seemed to disturb him. She hadn't realized that that was what she was thinking until she'd opened her mouth. It wasn't the first time these thoughts had occurred to her, but somehow they'd slipped to the back of her mind.

His eyes glittered and he spoke harshly. "We've been through this before. You don't know anything, Jess."

The words came easily now that she'd begun to put her thoughts in order. "There's some kind of conspiracy going on. No one wants me asking questions about my father's death, not the constable, not the attorney, or you or your friends. Only Perry gives me a straight answer, and that's because he's not involved. He wasn't here at the time."

"So you're still at it," he ground out, "still stirring up trouble by asking your incessant questions."

"Wouldn't you ask questions if your father had been murdered?" she cried out.

"Maybe your father deserved to die."

Something twisted in her breast, and quick tears flooded her eyes.

He cursed softly. "Look, I'm sorry. I shouldn't have said that."

"My father was not as black as you make him out to

be," she cried. "Maybe he wasn't the best of men, but I thought the world of him."

"How can you know if you've lost your memory?"

"The constable told me."

His face was gripped by a curious tension. Suddenly turning, he made for the back door. She went after him.

"Who murdered my father, Lucas? Who?"

"Christ, do you never give up?" He grasped her by the shoulders. One shake from those powerful hands sent the pins in her hair spilling to the floor. "Leave the past alone, Jess. Too many good people can be hurt by it."

She stared into his face. "Who are you protecting, Lucas?" she whispered.

His eyes were almost black. "What if I said I did it, Jess? Would you hand me over to the constable to be hanged? That's what they do with murderers, isn't it?"

Her throat felt as though she'd swallowed a bale of cotton. She'd never thought it through that far. She shook her head. She could never do that to him.

"And if I *am* the murderer, aren't you afraid of what I may do to you? Look at these hands, Jess. See how powerful they are? They could snuff out your life very easily. You should run from me while you still have the chance."

His voice was low and intense, mesmerizing her. She looked at his hands, at the thick, blunt fingers, then looked into his eyes. When his hands wrapped around her throat, she shuddered.

"You can't call out now, can you, Jess? It's too late. Just a little pressure on your throat and it will be all over for you."

His thumbs caressed her throat and tilted her chin up. He lowered his head till his face was only inches from hers. Tears welled in her eyes as she looked up at him.

"Jess," he whispered, "Jess." Then he covered her lips with his.

She was seduced by his gentleness, overwhelmed by the soft pressure of his mouth. She didn't want to fight him;

she wanted to console him. She didn't think he was a murderer. She'd wanted to hurt him and she'd succeeded. But she didn't mean it, she didn't mean it. She'd never felt safer in her life. With a little cry of surrender, she wrapped her arms around his neck and kissed him back.

He angled her against the door and rubbed his body suggestively against hers. She arched into him, inviting more. He gave her what she wanted. His hands caressed her breasts, rubbing them softly, creating a hunger in her to equal his own. His tongue began thrusting into her mouth to match the rhythm of his body, and where he led, she followed.

Suddenly, he released her and took a step back. He smiled crookedly. "Now that's the kind of kiss that means something to a man," he said. "What you saw with Bella was hardly worth so much jealousy, now was it, Jess?"

He lifted her away from the door as though she were a sack of feathers. "Oh, and no need to thank me for the lesson in masculine anatomy. Consider it my pleasure," and grinning, he left the room.

She stewed for a full minute after he'd gone. Suddenly turning, with a flick of her wrist she whacked the mop and sent it spinning. Then she marched out of the kitchen, up the stairs, into her bedroom, and she shut the door with a bang.

CHAPTER
11

ON THE NIGHT OF THE SUBSCRIPTION BALL, WHEN Jessica heard Lucas's carriage pull up outside Hawkshill's front door, she was seized by a full-blown panic. What a fool she'd been to think she could pull this off! It was her vanity that had led her into this quagmire. She'd wanted to show Bella and Lucas that she was equal to anything. And it wasn't true. Her head was buzzing with a confusion of unrelated facts. During the last two weeks, Lucas's mother and the vicar's wife had taken it upon themselves to teach her everything she needed to know to mix in Chalford's polite society, and now everything she'd learned had turned into a jumble. She couldn't remember a thing. She would disgrace herself and they would all see her for what she was—a fraud. Then how would she face her kind patronesses? And the reverend sisters? And Joseph? And the boys? And the mother superior? And—

"That should do it," said Sister Brigid, pushing the last

pin into Jessica's upswept curls. She stood back to admire her handiwork. "Now, turn around."

Jessica turned from her reflection in the brand-new looking glass, the only looking glass in Hawkshill, to face the nuns. When no one said anything, she anxiously searched each face.

Sister Dolores's mouth was a round O. She stole a look at Sister Elvira, and her brows wiggled. "You don't think . . . ?" She patted her flat chest.

"Certainly not!" said Sister Elvira tartly. "Would you have our Jessica stand out like a sore thumb? As the apostle Paul said, " 'When in Rome, do as the Romans do.' "

"I didn't know Saint Paul said that," said Sister Dolores.

Sister Elvira chuckled. "Well, perhaps he didn't, but he certainly used words very like them. Now stop fingering your gown, Jessica."

Jessica stopped trying to hoist up the edge of her bodice to cover what seemed to her an indecent expanse of bare flesh. "Listen!" she said.

They listened.

"I don't hear anything," said Sister Dolores.

"That's just it," said Jessica. "Where are the boys? What are they up to? That's what I'd like to know."

"It's long past their bedtime," said Sister Elvira soothingly. "They're not up to anything. They're sleeping like little angels, that's all." She looked a question at Sister Brigid.

The novice nodded. "They were sound asleep last time I looked in on them."

Jessica was not convinced. The horrid little monsters had lost no opportunity these last two weeks to mock her at every turn. They were up to something; she just knew it.

The sound of the door knocker sent her thoughts scattering and she sucked in a breath.

Sister Dolores smiled complacently. "That will be Lord

Dundas," she said. "How very kind he is to offer to take our Jessica to the ball in his own carriage."

They heard the sound of Joseph's footsteps crossing the hall and a moment later the low murmur of masculine voices.

Jessica jumped when Sister Elvira put her hands on her shoulders. The little nun looked deep into her eyes. "Jessica," she said, "I want you to forget all the rules you've learned in the last little while. Don't give them another thought, and I mean that sincerely. Just be yourself. Do you understand?"

She didn't, but she nodded anyway.

"But," quipped Sister Dolores, "don't forget the most important rule."

"To raise money for Hawkshill," said Jessica.

There was a moment of complete silence, then the room erupted in a gale of feminine laughter.

"To enjoy yourself!" declared Sister Dolores. "This is a ball, for heaven's sake. Don't forget to enjoy yourself."

Jessica was swept out of the room on another gale of laughter, but as she began to descend the stairs, her laughter died away. Lucas was waiting for her at the foot of the stairs, looking as handsome as she had ever seen him. His magnificently tailored dark blue jacket hugged his broad shoulders. His pale blue waistcoat, heavily embroidered with white fleurs-de-lis was, to her, the height of sophistication. He looked lean and fit.

He was in conversation with Joseph and had yet to notice her. Joseph saw her first, and his jaw dropped. Lucas turned to see what Joseph was staring at and his words trailed into silence.

His gaze roamed over every curve and contour on her body and lingered on the hollow between her breasts. Then his eyes jerked up to meet hers. It took a moment before Jessica realized that the gleam in his eyes was one of profound masculine appreciation. She let out a soft sigh. Everything was going to be all right.

She curtsied; he bowed; and as the nuns began to speak, she slipped by him to allow Joseph to drape her dark satin cloak around her shoulders.

"Well, Joseph," she said softly, "have you no words of wisdom to impart before I leave for the ball?"

"Aye," he said thoughtfully.

"What are they?"

He showed her his fist. "Just remember to keep your guard up."

He gave her one of his toothless grins and she turned away with a smile. Then they were outside, with Lucas leading the way to his carriage and the nuns following in their wake. It was twilight, and Jessica was sure she heard a nightingale singing high overhead in one of the mature oaks. Her panic had subsided. Her spirits were soaring. It was a night made for—

Then she heard it. The creak of one of the upstairs sash windows as someone opened it. She'd just known she wouldn't get away without one of those little monsters trying to take her down a peg or two. And in front of Lucas, too! And his mother and ward in the carriage, listening to every word! How could they do this to her?

"Sister Martha? Sister Martha?" Pip's voice.

With a tooth-grinding smile, Jessica turned to look up at Pip's dormitory and was taken aback to see boys at every window, grinning down at her.

"Three cheers for Sister Martha," yelled Pip at the top of his lungs, and all the boys chanted, "Huzzah! Huzzah! Huzzah!"

"I agree," murmured Lucas in her ear.

"Angels," she said, "they're absolute angels," and blushing profusely, she entered the carriage.

On the drive to Haig House, her nerves gradually settled. There was so much to see and as Lucas pointed out places of interest, she forgot about herself. There was a small awkwardness with Ellie, who was pouting because this was her first ball and she wasn't allowed to dance at it, but other than that the time passed pleasantly.

When they crossed the river onto the old Priory Road, they fell into line in a procession of carriages that were all bound for the ball.

"There's Haig House," said Lucas at one point and Jessica craned her neck to get a view of it from the carriage window.

It was set on top of a bluff overlooking the river, and its lights blazed like a beacon in a sea of twilight.

Jessica's misgivings rushed back and she swallowed nervously. Lucas leaned over and covered her hand. "I predict," he said, "that you'll be the belle of the ball."

She might not be the belle of the ball, but by the time the first interval rolled round, Jessica was feeling quite giddy with her success. She wasn't exactly besieged with partners, but there were more than enough to go around, and she was content to sit this one out, a rather boisterous country dance.

Seated on one side of her was Lucas's mother, and on the other side was Anne Rankin. These were her mentors and constant companions in the last two weeks. Tonight, they were her chaperones. They were kind, and generous, and Jessica liked them tremendously, but they could also be tyrants—especially Anne. It was thanks to Anne's bullying that she knew how to dance tonight at Bella's ball.

Anne leaned toward her. She was a sandy-haired, freckle-faced lady, around the age of Lucas's mother. "Did you know, Jessica, that the roses are named for Bella?"

Jessica looked around the Great Hall. White satin panels were draped from ceiling to floor, and the banks of crimson roses made a dramatic contrast. The footmen were in livery to match—white powdered wigs, crimson coats and white satin breeches.

Anne went on. "They are a new strain that Rupert developed himself."

Jessica knew that Anne was putting her through her paces, testing her facility in small talk. "What a lovely gesture," Jessica said. There was a silence. Obviously something more was required of her. Anything she had to say about Bella would only shock her two patronesses. That left Rupert. "But," she went on, searching for inspiration, "I'm not surprised. Bella is very fortunate to have such a devoted husband."

Both her companions beamed at her, then returned to what they really wanted to talk about, which was the pregnancy of Anne's elder daughter. So much for small talk. But Jessica didn't mind. Small talk was reserved for acquaintances and strangers. Friends gossiped or could ignore each other and nobody cared.

This last thought sent her glance to the gallery where Lucas had spent much of his time this evening. He wasn't there. If he was on the dance floor, she would eat Bella's cloyingly sweet-smelling roses. He'd danced only one dance tonight, the opening waltz, and that was with Bella.

Not that she expected him to fawn over her. Lucas's mother had told her that a gentleman did not dance with the same lady more than twice in one evening. Surely, he would want to dance at least once with her? Perhaps he hadn't noticed that the gown she was wearing was no hand-me-down but the creation of a London modiste and subsequently embroidered by the nuns in tiny white vines along the hem?

The sisters had been in such a twitter as they'd dressed her for the ball. She knew they would be waiting up for her when she got home, wanting to know what his lordship had said to her, word for word. They were such romantics, Sisters Elvira and Dolores. They were confusing Lucas with Prince Charming. Hah! If they ever discovered that he'd kissed Bella, they would be aghast. Just as surely as they would be ecstatic if they ever discovered that Lucas had kissed *her*.

"Do your lips always move when you're lost in thought?"

At the sound of Lucas's faintly mocking taunt, her head jerked up. She hadn't heard or seen his approach. She'd been remembering how he had kissed her. Even now, her heart was still thundering and her throat was dry. She knew she was blushing.

Lucas's brows climbed. "Perhaps you were praying," he said, and his eyes glinted wickedly. "Then pray no more, fair lady." He made an elegant bow. "Here I am, Lucas Wilde, at your service."

She suddenly realized that he was flirting with her, and that she was expected to flirt back.

Anne Rankin coughed; Lucas's mother surreptitiously poked her in the ribs. She had to say something. She rose and made a curtsy that King George could not have faulted and she said the first thing that came into her head. "They say that God answers prayer in mysterious ways. And now I believe it."

There was a moment of complete silence, then Lucas threw back his head and laughed. Anne Rankin tittered. Mrs. Wilde smiled.

"Well done, Jessica," said Mrs. Wilde. "You've learned your lessons well."

Lucas spoke to his mother. "With your permission, ma'am, I thought I'd take Jessica out on the terrace for a breath of fresh air."

"Jessica?" asked Mrs. Wilde.

"Thank you, my lord," said Jessica, still glowing from the knowledge that she'd said something witty. "There is nothing I would enjoy more."

As Lucas led Jessica away, Anne sat down in Jessica's chair. "Now tell me again there's not a romance brewing," she said mischievously.

Rosemary was watching the couple's progress through the crowd. "I don't know, Anne, I really don't know."

"You don't know!" exclaimed Anne in some astonishment. "What have you and I been doing these last two weeks, and the sisters too, if it's not to prepare Jessica to take her place as Lucas's wife?"

Rosemary turned to Anne with a smile. "I'm not saying that Lucas's affections are not engaged. It's Jessica I worry about. I'm not sure that she loves my son. She's very reserved about showing her feelings."

"Well, of course, she is! A girl in her position! She likes him, that's obvious. And love can come after marriage, as you and I both know."

"True," said Rosemary, but this was one topic she was not willing to pursue. Her eye alighted on Ellie, and she went on, "If you are right, Ellie is going to be even more difficult than she's been these last weeks. She's been impossibly rude to Jessica."

Anne looked at Lucas's ward and sighed. She was in a group of young people, but her eyes were trained on Lucas and Jessica. She was a pretty girl but the expression on her face was not pleasant. Anne said, "She's infatuated with him, I suppose?"

"I didn't realize how severely until Lucas began to take an interest in Jessica. Now Ellie's sunny disposition has flown out the window. She's turned into a sullen, moody girl, and I don't know how to manage her."

Anne patted her friend's arm. "She's very young, Rosie. She'll get over him."

"The sooner the better, as far as I'm concerned."

Out on the terrace, Lucas was propped against the stone balustrade, enjoying the sight of Jessica. She looked ethereal in her floating gauzes with her hair piled in tiny curls on the crown of her head. He itched to remove the pins in her hair and run his fingers through those golden tresses. He wanted to do a lot more than that.

She was looking at the marquee that had been set up on the lawns where they would soon sit down to supper, then she turned her head and studied the many illuminated paths that led through the shrubbery, and the couples who, like themselves, had come out for a breath of fresh air.

"What is it, Jess?" he asked softly. "Why do you look like that?"

"How do I look?" she asked lightly.

"I don't know exactly how to describe it, but I've seen that look on your face many times. It's wistful and searching. Sometimes, it's quite desperate."

She tried to laugh, but the sound that came out of her mouth was mirthless. "I'm curious about Haig House. I'm curious about everything, and everyone. Isn't that natural for a girl who has lost her memory?"

"You're looking for something familiar, is that it, Jess? Something you recognize? Something to shake your memories loose? A familiar face, perhaps? Or a place? Or an experience of déjà vu?"

His perceptiveness startled her. That was exactly what she'd been looking for. It was always the same when she met new people, entered a new house, or saw new vistas. She was desperate to find the thread that would lead her out of this terrible labyrinth of unknowing. But that was only part of it. She was searching for the face that belonged to her Voice.

Her next thought jarred. If anyone but Lucas had said those words, her suspicions would have been instantly aroused. It seemed as though he could read her mind.

She gave herself a mental shake. Her Voice would not give himself away so blatantly. He would take care to say nothing that aroused her suspicions. Unless he was testing her. But he wasn't Lucas. She refused to believe he was Lucas.

"What have I said, Jess?"

She put a brake on her thoughts and smiled. "This is a

ball," she said playfully. "And I refuse to think serious thoughts at a ball."

He had never seen her look so fragile. The wide gray eyes that were fixed on his were far more eloquent than she knew. The messages he read there made him want to scoop her up in his arms and carry her to a safe place where nothing and no one could ever hurt her again. He wanted to tell her that there would be other memories, happy memories, if she would only let go and let him take care of her.

"You're right," he said. "This isn't a night for serious discussions, not when I am looking at the loveliest lady at the ball."

Something, his words, the way he was looking at her, made her troubles lose their grip, and she felt suddenly dizzy with happiness.

"I wish the sisters and our boys could be here too," she said.

"Oh? Why?"

She gave him one of her rare, shy smiles and he could feel the power of it all the way to his loins.

"Because," she said, "they despaired of me ever mastering the steps of the dances. It wasn't easy, you know, with only nuns and small boys as partners."

"How did you ever persuade the boys?"

"Bribery," she said. "A penny a dance. I owe them a shilling apiece. We ran into some trouble learning the waltz, though. The nuns were afraid it might be improper. In the end, Joseph won them over."

"Joseph?" he said carefully. "How did he do that?"

"He danced the waltz with Sister Elvira. They were so comical, we couldn't stop laughing. Our boys, of course, made fun of the whole thing. After that, no one could think of the waltz as anything but a huge joke."

Lucas's shoulders began to heave and he shook his head. "Sometimes I wonder whether Hawkshill is run by nuns or by inmates of an insane asylum."

"That's what we wonder, too. The nuns, I mean."

When his smile faded, so did hers. He came away from the balustrade and held out his arms. "Let's find out about the waltz, Jess. Let's see if it's a joke."

When she'd refused to dance with him in her kitchen, she'd been embarrassed because he'd caught her at the worst possible moment. Tonight was different. She wasn't wearing a filthy apron, and he hadn't found her waltzing with a mop. The gown she was wearing was as lovely as any she'd seen tonight, except for Bella's perhaps, and the partners she'd danced with were all eligible young gentlemen.

She stepped into his arms with a dazzling smile, confident that she wouldn't disgrace herself. She'd practiced all the dances until she was step-perfect.

Her smile faded a little as his arm encircled her waist. He'd removed his gloves, and as his hand settled against the small of her back, she could feel his heat pass from his body into her own.

"Put your left hand on my shoulder," he said softly and Jessica obeyed. "Now put your right hand in mine."

She was wearing long white gloves, but they didn't seem to offer any protection. His hand was charged with a special kind of energy. And the sight of that powerful masculine hand cradling her own fragile fingers did something peculiar to her insides.

"Now look at me, Jess," he murmured.

She heard the huskiness in his voice, and her own throat tightened. She looked up at him. His eyes were heavy-lidded, sleepy, mesmerizing, and her own eyes began to close.

"Don't forget to breathe," he said, and chuckling, he swung her into the waltz.

There was no music, but she didn't need music. She moved instinctively. It seemed the most natural thing in the world to be closely held in Lucas's embrace, her body swaying intimately against his. She could feel the hard muscles of his shoulders beneath her fingers, and his powerful legs brushing against her skirts as they moved to a beat only they could hear. Even their hearts seemed to beat as one. In the distance, someone laughed, but she cared nothing for that.

His lips brushed her ear. "That will do for now," he said, and his arms slowly dropped away.

She opened her eyes and blinked up at his smiling face.

"Don't look so crestfallen, Jess," he said. "There will be another waltz after supper, and I'm claiming that waltz for myself."

It took a moment before his words cleared the mist in her brain. "But Lucas," she said, "I've promised that waltz to someone else."

"You did *what*?" His brows were a black slash. "Then you'll have to unpromise it."

"I can't do that. A promise is a promise."

"Who is it? Perry, I suppose. He's done this as a joke because I warned him off, I warned them all off. The first waltz I was obliged to give to our hostess. But the second waltz belongs to me."

"Well," she snapped, "it's a pity you didn't warn *me*. And it's not Perry."

"Then who the devil is it?"

"He's one of Bella's London friends."

His name was Rodney Stone, and he'd been her first partner that evening. He was very elegant, far more elegant than Perry or any of the Chalford crowd, and she'd been flattered when he'd asked her to keep the second waltz for him.

"His name?" demanded Lucas

She looked at him suspiciously. "Why do you want to know?"

"Why do you think? So that I can tell him that you gave away my waltz by mistake."

She gasped. "You can't do that!"

"Just watch me!"

"It's against the rules."

"Whose rules?"

"The rules your mother and Anne Rankin have drummed into my head this last week."

"I make up my own rules."

"Lucas," she said, trying to soften him with a smile, "I can't break a promise, but—"

"For heaven's sake, Jess, I'm not asking you to break a betrothal or a marriage vow. It's only a waltz."

"There are other dances I'd be more than happy to dance with you."

"I don't do country dances."

"You don't . . . but why ever not?"

"I've never bothered to learn the steps."

"Then why didn't you ask me to save you the waltz?"

"Because, you little shrew, I didn't expect you to—"

He fell silent.

"You thought I'd be a wallflower," she said tonelessly.

"I didn't expect you to be so much in demand. That's all I meant."

She looked back toward the glass doors that gave onto the ballroom, and thoughts chased each other through her head. Aside from Mr. Stone, the only partners she'd had all evening were either Lucas's friends or Perry's. Now she could see that it was all Lucas's doing. He was a good man, a kind man. He'd done it for her sake. But she would rather be ignored than pitied.

"Jess," he said, and reached for her. "Don't—"

Whatever Lucas was about to say was lost when someone called his name from the glass doors. It was Ellie. His hand dropped away and he smiled at his ward. "What is it, Ellie?"

As Ellie came up to them, Jessica blinked away the betraying moisture in her eyes. The girl's smile was warm, but it was meant only for Lucas. Ellie never wasted her smiles and conversation on her. The thought that at least she knew where she stood with this curiously hostile girl was comforting in an odd sort of way.

"It's time to go in for supper," said Ellie. She tossed her dark ringlets and darted Jessica a deeply suspicious look before turning back to Lucas with a brilliant smile. "You promised to take me in to supper."

"And so I shall," he said easily. "And Miss Hayward also." Then more formally, "That is, if you are free to join us, Miss Hayward?"

He was doing it again, making sure she wasn't a wall-flower. She should be grateful, but all she felt was this hole where her heart should be.

"Jessica?"

She accepted by inclining her head. Ellie had already burst into speech in an attempt to draw Lucas's attention to herself.

"We'll talk later," Lucas said in a soft aside, but this time she did not nod her head.

The ball was almost over when Lucas was joined by Bella on the gallery. "I thought I saw Adrian and Rupert with you," she said.

"You did," he replied without taking his eyes off the dance floor. He had a clear view of Jessica and the young man who had stolen his waltz. They were taking their places on the floor.

"Then where are they now?" asked Bella, temper blinking briefly in her eyes. She wasn't used to being ignored.

"Mmm? Oh, they went to the billiard room, I believe."

His eyes narrowed unpleasantly on the young man who was partnering Jessica. He was a fop! A beardless, baby-faced fop!

Between sips of champagne from the long-stemmed glass in her hand, Bella said, "Jessica has turned out to be . . . quite a pretty girl, don't you think?"

His eyes moved to Jessica. "*Pretty* isn't the word I would use," he said.

Bella moved behind him and took up a position on the other side of the rail. It was, thought Lucas, a deliberate attempt to move his attention from Jessica to herself. He didn't mind indulging her. For one thing, his eyes had been straying too frequently to Jessica all evening, and for another, he supposed he was being insufferably rude in ignoring Bella.

He gave her his full attention. Her dark hair was swept off her face and pinned back by a garland of tiny white rosebuds; the gown she was wearing might have been made of spun gold. He would have appreciated her beauty more if he didn't know her so well.

Bella cocked her head to one side and looked up at him through the sweep of her lashes. "How would you describe her?" she asked archly.

He looked over the rail again. The orchestra had given the opening chord, and as the fop bowed, Jessica curtsied. It was a formal curtsy, far more formal than they were used to in Chalford. She might have been one of the queen's ladies-in-waiting. The thought made him smile.

"There is no one," he said, "that I admire more."

He wasn't exaggerating, and this wasn't something new, either. Even when she was a young girl, he'd admired Jess's pluck. If she made up her mind to do something, she would do it. She'd made up her mind to attend Bella's ball, and here she was.

There was another reason he admired her. She'd stuck to her guns. "A promise is a promise," she'd said, and she'd meant it.

"I think that between us," said Bella musingly, "we have managed to restore Jessica's reputation. Of course, she still lacks some of the social graces, but that will come in time."

He did not respond, because what he wanted to say could not be said to a friend's wife. Bella was livid because she'd hoped Jess would make a fool of herself. She hadn't taken Sister Elvira into account. She hadn't realized how wise Sister Elvira was, and that she would not dream of allowing her little chick to enter the world without being properly equipped.

If only Sister Elvira were four stones lighter and thirty years younger, he could easily fall in love with her.

"Why are you smiling?"

He erased the foolish grin. "I was thinking of Jess," he said. And just to add salt to the wound, he added, "Tonight is quite a triumph for her."

"A triumph? Really?" She laughed lightly. "Who are her friends? Who are her dancing partners? I'll tell you who. They're *your* friends, Lucas. If not for you, Jessica Hayward would be completely passed over tonight. I don't think much has changed in the last three years. She's still an awkward girl."

"The trouble with you, Bella," he said pleasantly, "is that you don't recognize quality when you see it. The social graces can be learned. What Jess has cannot be learned. It cannot be bought or sold. It doesn't matter whether she's dressed to the nines or in sackcloth and ashes. She's quality and that's what people respond to."

Her fingers tightened around the stem of her glass, but she had the sense to keep her mouth shut. She couldn't afford to make an enemy of Lucas. He had too much influence in Chalford, too much influence with her husband.

Her eyes reproached him. "Naturally," she said, "I will do everything I can to help Jessica. That's all I meant, Lucas."

He plucked an invisible speck of lint from his sleeve. "Naturally, Bella. Now if you'll excuse me, I have an important appointment in the billiard room."

She stayed at the rail, sipping her wine through clenched teeth, trying to look unaffected in case anyone was watching.

CHAPTER
12

DANCES, THOUGHT ROSEMARY WILDE, SHOULD BE EX-clusively for young people, and only young people. For people of her age, there were too many memories, there was too much nostalgia, too great an awareness of the passage of time. It seemed like only yesterday that she would have been dancing the night away, crestfallen if she missed a single dance. And now look at her! She was reduced to the role of a chaperon. Where had time gone?

She wasn't unhappy, and she certainly wasn't bitter. She was in a reflective mood, she decided. She'd spent the whole evening thinking about other people—Lucas, Jessica, Ellie—and just for these few minutes it felt good to concentrate on herself. If she didn't, no one else would. She'd been deserted. Lucas, she knew, hated dancing and would be with his friends in the billiard room now that he'd done his duty; Ellie had gone off with a crowd of her friends to look at the roses in the conservatory, and Jessica was on the dance floor, waltzing with some young man. Even Anne had deserted her. She was with her husband.

They were a couple. And though they were kindness it-self, and always tried to include her in whatever they were doing, she didn't want to be tagging along all the time like a piece of extra baggage.

Her eye was caught by her reflection in one of the long pier glasses between two windows. No one was watching her so she sauntered over and took a good look at herself. If she didn't, no one else would. Once a woman had passed the full bloom of youth, no one spared her a second glance.

A stray thought entered her head before she could sup-press it. She wondered what Matt would think of her if he could see her now. Fifteen years was a long time. She shook her head and sighed. Matt was the real reason for all this introspection. Anne, without knowing what she was doing, had been keeping her informed. She'd casually mentioned to Anne that she'd caught sight of Sir Matthew leaving the circulating library on Waterside Street and Anne's reply had stunned her.

"Oh, now that his year of mourning is over, I think we'll be seeing a lot more of him," said Anne. "Well, we all know that Olivia, poor thing, preferred London, but with her gone, there's nothing to stop him from making Matchings his principal residence. After all, it is the most magnificent house in the county. I always thought it was a great shame that it was left empty for half the year."

She'd also learned that Sir Matthew had gone to Lon-don on a business matter, but if he could make it back in time for Bella's ball he would be here.

Silly old woman! she silently chided her reflection in the mirror. *So much trouble with your appearance tonight, and for what? Matt isn't here, and even if he were, you would be the last woman his eye would be drawn to. His mistress is half your age. You're old, Rosemary Wilde. Better get used to the idea.*

Another reflection joined hers in the mirror and her heart stopped beating. Matt! He was no more than ten feet away from her. And he had seen her. In fact, he was closing the distance between them.

"Rosemary?"

When she was sure she had command of her breathing, she turned slowly to face him.

"Rosemary," he said. "I thought it was you." Then, "Rodie," as though savoring the pet name only he had ever called her. "Fifteen years is a long time, yet it seems like only yesterday."

She answered him with composure, but her heart was beating painfully. She felt as tongue-tied as a young girl with her first beau. And that was stupid. She wasn't a young girl, and she wondered if he was shocked by what the years had done to her.

The years had been kind to him. There were lines in his face, and his dark hair was threaded with silver, but oddly enough, this only made him seem more manly. He'd always been too handsome, and now that flaw had been corrected. He was taller than she remembered, but his eyes were the same, a brilliant blue and fringed with long, dark lashes.

"Walk with me?" he said.

She put her fingers on the back of the arm he offered and allowed him to lead her outside. He made a remark about the extensive work Rupert had done to the grounds and she answered him vaguely. But her thoughts had taken a different turn. She was remembering the first time they'd met, when they were both out riding. He was a new neighbor and she'd taken an instant liking to him. Their friendship had become more meaningful when they'd discovered they both had invalid spouses. Her husband had had a stroke. His wife had broken her spine in a riding accident. No one else understood their loneliness and frustrations, and since they couldn't talk to their partners about them, they'd confided in each other. She hadn't understood what was happening when their eyes would meet and hold in a roomful of people, or when her spirits would lift just because he had walked into a room. They'd fallen in love long before they were aware of it.

They were silent as they descended the steps leading onto the lawns. It was dark now, but the gardens were well lit, and by tacit consent they chose one of the flagstone paths that wound along the bluff. Small talk didn't seem appropriate, and there was no way she could voice what was really on her mind.

"I'm going to change all the rules between us, Rodie," he said, "and I thought I should warn you first."

The seriousness of his tone alarmed her. "What rules, Matt?"

He took a moment before replying. "Now that my period of mourning is over, I intend to become a more sociable animal, take in parties, balls, that sort of thing. So you can expect to see a lot more of me. And when we meet, I hope we can put the past behind us and be natural with each other."

She swallowed hard. She thought she understood. He had no children. He would want to marry again, choose a woman who was young enough to bear him sons. That's why he would begin to attend social functions—to find a suitable bride. He was telling her as a courtesy, and it really wasn't necessary. They meant nothing to each other now.

"I understand," she said.

"What do you understand?"

"A man in your position will want to marry and have heirs."

He said quietly, "I have heirs, Rodie. A brother, Nephews. I wanted children once, but not now. I want to do other things with my life." He stopped speaking suddenly and turned to face her. "Do you still hate me, Rodie?"

"Matt, I never hated you."

"Did you not?"

"No. It was simply that we could no longer be friends."

"Can we be friends now?"

"What would be the point?"

"It would be more pleasant for both of us when we meet at gatherings like this, as we probably shall."

The prospect of other evenings like this one when she would have to pretend to be indifferent to him chilled her to the marrow. "Friends?" she said. "That would be impossible, Matt, but at least we can be friendly."

"Why can't we be friends? Because your son still hates me?"

"We never talk about you," she said quickly.

"Are you never lonely, Rodie?"

His abruptness as well as the question itself took her aback, and she faltered before answering. "Of course I'm never lonely. Life has been good to me. I have my family and friends."

A long pause ensued, then, "Aren't you going to ask me if I'm ever lonely?"

There was no need to ask. She already knew the answer. He'd remained with his wife, but he hadn't been faithful to her. He'd always kept a mistress. But in this last year after his wife's death, he'd embarked on a frenetic round of pleasure.

She spoke lightly because it was too awkward and painful to reveal what she really thought. "Matt, I know you're not lonely. People talk, and I have ears. You never lack for female companionship. And your latest mistress—" She stopped abruptly.

He gave her a searching look. "You know about Madaleina?"

Madaleina Cartier was an opera singer and the leading light of the King's Theatre, and she was no older than her own son. "Everybody knows about her, Matt. You're not exactly discreet about your *affaires*."

He smiled ruefully. "What reason do I have to be discreet? I have no wife, no children, no one who would be hurt by my indiscretions. In short, Rodie, nobody cares."

A lump formed in her throat and that appalled her.

Once they'd been lovers, but now this man was a stranger to her. She shouldn't be feeling like this.

She smiled serenely into his eyes. "Don't explain yourself, Matt. Not to me. There's no need. I should go back. My ward must be wondering where I am. No, don't come with me. I'd rather go alone. Please."

She didn't exactly run from him, but she did move swiftly. When she came to the terrace, she hesitated. Jessica was there with the young man she'd been dancing with earlier. The last thing they'd want was a chaperon hanging on their sleeves. There was the conservatory, but Ellie was there with her friends. Ellie wouldn't welcome a chaperon, either. Men had it so much easier. They could always retreat to the billiard room or the card room. She had nowhere to go where she could think her thoughts in private.

There was, of course, the ladies' cloak room.

With a breezy smile and a wave to Jessica, she crossed the terrace and entered the house.

Jessica's eyes were thoughtful as she watched Lucas's mother enter the house. Mrs. Wilde's smile was unnaturally bright. She seemed distracted. She was going against the stream, pushing past guests who were coming outside to take in the fireworks display that would begin shortly after the last dance. Jessica returned her gaze to the walk from which Mrs. Wilde had emerged, and she sensed something, but whatever she sensed stayed tantalizingly out of reach.

A warm breeze touched her skin and she raised her head, listening, watching, as if the breeze were trying to tell her something. There was nothing to tell. It was all very ordinary. Servants were going about their business, clearing up the debris of the sumptuous supper the guests had consumed. The walls of the marquee flapped in the breeze; lanterns were hung from the trees and winked like distant stars as they disappeared into the dense shrubbery; laughter floated over the lawns, and she could hear a horse whinnying from one of the many carriages that were stationed along the drive.

She looked at her escort and saw that his lips were moving. Mr. Stone was talking to her. She blinked and gradually came back to herself.

". . . a walk in the fresh air might do the trick," he said.

She was immediately contrite. She'd forgotten all about poor Mr. Stone. They'd been dancing the waltz when he'd suddenly stumbled and put a hand to his brow. The heat was too much for him, he'd said, and so they'd come out to the terrace for a breath of fresh air. And no sooner was she on the terrace than her mind had wandered to another partner and another waltz, and how very differently she had felt in *his* arms.

She should have been thinking of Mr. Stone. He really did look rather hot. His fairish red hair and the flush on his skin made him seem very young. But boyish or not, he was dressed in the height of fashion. His peacock blue coat was so snug that she didn't know how he'd managed to dance in it. Perhaps that was part of the trouble.

She heard the catch in his breath and she said anxiously, "Are you sure you wouldn't like to sit down, Mr. Stone? I could ask one of the footmen to fetch you a glass of water or a glass of wine."

"No, really, I'm feeling much better." He felt in his coat pocket, produced a handkerchief and began to mop his brow. "It was the heat. It's cooler out here. Shall we walk?"

He didn't offer his arm, but it was evident that he took it for granted that she would accompany him. And she had no objection. She'd learned from her mentors that in lieu of a dance, a gentleman might ask a lady to promenade around the ballroom, or go for a walk, or simply sit the dance out and talk. And anyway, she couldn't possibly leave Mr. Stone when he was unwell.

They left the terrace and strolled along the driveway where all the coaches were stationed. Mr. Stone did most of the talking. Jessica's eyes kept straying to the shrubbery. She felt something, sensed something, but again, whatever it was stayed out of reach.

At one point, she glanced over her shoulder. They'd turned the corner of the drive, and the house was no longer in view. Even the carriages had thinned out. Her steps slowed and finally halted. She hadn't realized they'd come so far.

"I think we should go back," she said.

She didn't hear his answer. A flare suddenly streaked across the night sky and exploded in a thousand little stars, illuminating the whole countryside.

"My carriage," said Mr. Stone. "Haven't you been listening to me, Miss Hayward? I'll drive you back to the house in my carriage. Then I think I must go home."

Jessica glanced at the carriage he indicated. It seemed isolated and— Without warning, a wave of something dark and malevolent slammed into her. There was a roaring in her ears and she felt as though she were suffocating. But everything in her mind was crystal clear. Nothing was as it appeared to be, not Mr. Stone and certainly not the unremarkable carriage.

He wanted her in the carriage. Not Mr. Stone. Her Voice. He wanted her in that carriage. Then he would deal with her later. Even now, he was on his way to her. He wasn't aware that he was betraying his thoughts. His emotions were too strong, too violent. One thought came to her loud and clear. He would do anything to be rid of her.

Mr. Stone had taken hold of her arm. "Don't turn missish on me now," he said. "I've been wanting to kiss you all evening."

It was an act, a pretext to allay her fears. He didn't want to kiss her. He wanted to get her into that carriage.

"Please, no," she said. "I must return to my friends.

They'll be wondering what's happened to me." She tried to free herself, but his grasp only tightened.

"You weren't worried about your friends a moment ago. A kiss. That's all I want. Come to the carriage with me and I'll drive you back to the house."

She fought back the panic and tried to think. She remembered Joseph's parting words to her. *Keep your guard up at all times.* It hadn't been a joke. Oh, why hadn't she paid more attention?

"I don't know what's come over me," she said. "I feel faint."

He relaxed his grip. "You'll feel better in a moment. Let me help you to the carriage."

Jessica seized her advantage. She sagged against him, then brought up her knee with all her might. He blocked her blow, but it landed on his thigh and one hard shove sent him sprawling on his back.

"Get her!" he shouted to his coachman.

Jessica acted instinctively. She took a flying leap into the shrubbery and landed on her hands and knees. Thorns like spikes tore at her face and became embedded in her filmy gown. She didn't wait to recover from the shock of her fall. She heard two sets of footsteps converging on her, and throwing off her shoes, she took off like a hare.

Her first thought was to find a place to hide, but as another flare exploded, turning night into day, she put every ounce of will and strength into outrunning her pursuers. She knew they were gaining on her, but she didn't dare look back. She was making for the house. It wasn't far now. Please God, it wasn't far now.

Shadows of trees blurred and wavered. She saw a light and sobbed with relief. Suddenly, the ground gave way beneath her and she went tumbling into space. She put out her hands to save herself, but when she hit the ground, her momentum carried her along. One hand buckled under her, and she came down heavily on her side. She would have screamed at any other time, but terror gave her an ironclad will and the scream died in her throat. If she gave herself away, they would find her, and that determined malevolence would be unleashed against her. The very air she breathed was thick with his presence. That's what she had sensed all evening.

She lay there for a long time unable to move for the pain that stabbed at her side. Her wrist ached and she feared she might have cracked a rib. But it was terror that brought tears to her eyes, not pain. At any moment, she expected rough hands to be laid on her and haul her to her feet. It was no use. She couldn't go on. Then she heard Stone's voice, a sinister whisper, wafting to her out of the darkness, calling her by name, and she forced herself to concentrate.

There was no light from fireworks to guide her now, only the pale glow of the moon. The light that she'd tried to reach winked tantalizingly a little way to her right. It might as well have been a sun in some distant galaxy.

Close by a twig snapped, then another. Her eyes frantically searched the gloom. A boulder or a bush, she could not tell which, lay just ahead. Biting down on her lip to stifle a moan, she slowly hauled herself to her knees and began to crawl. Inside her head she was praying.

Lucas, she thought. *Oh, Lucas.*

C H A P T E R
13

I N THE BILLIARD ROOM, THE GENTLEMEN WERE FILING
out one by one. Lucas was putting the cues away when
Adrian entered.

Adrian shook his head. "I like a game of billiards as
well as anyone, but this is going too far. Lucas, you've
been holed up in this room for hours on end."

Lucas's reply was drowned out by the sound of an
exploding firework. When there was silence, he grinned
and said, "Time always passes quickly when one is enjoying oneself. But you're wrong about the time, Adrian.
I've been here for half an hour and not a minute longer."

"Whatever. At least your friends always know where
to find you at a ball." He looked at his watch. "Any
moment now, Rupert will come through that door." He
took a long swallow of the champagne in his glass, then
smiled slowly. "I sense woman trouble, and I commiser-
ate, I really do. On the other hand, I'm delighted to ob-
serve that at long last a woman has the power to shake
you out of your complacency."

Lucas grunted. "I do not have woman trouble," he said. "Jessica has got the wrong idea about something, that's all. And when she's in a more reasonable frame of mind and I explain things to her, she'll come round."

Adrian's eyes danced. "How little you know women!"

"Well, we can't all have your vast experience," replied Lucas dryly.

"Oh, I've sworn off women. I've decided they're more trouble than they're worth."

"Now what has brought this on?"

Adrian took another swallow of champagne then held his glass up to the light and studied it carefully. "She's married, Lucas, and she loves honor more than she loves me. Need I say more?" He glanced at Lucas. "Now why are you frowning? Is it because I've lost my heart? No? Then it's because she's a married woman." He shrugged helplessly. "It's not so unusual, surely? I believe it happens in the best of families."

The lighthearted banter was at odds with the serious look in Adrian's eyes, and Lucas was at a loss for words. Adrian's affairs were legion. He was the greatest flirt on God's earth. No woman held his interest for long. And he had always given married women a wide berth.

He looked at his cousin now and realized how much he had taken for granted. Adrian was never serious. Life was all a game to him. When had he last looked deeper than Adrian's ready smiles and sardonic wit?

Adrian sighed. "It's not the end of the world, you know. Hearts don't break. But at least I know now that I do have a heart." His smile flashed as the door opened and Rupert entered. "As I was saying," he went on, "here comes Rupert right on cue, if you'll excuse the pun."

Rupert laughed. "I knew I'd find you two in here," he said.

"See what I mean?" said Adrian, and the laughter was back in his eyes. "We're old fogies, as Perry keeps telling me, and too predictable for words."

Lucas was watching Rupert. "What is it? What's wrong?"

"Nothing too alarming. Your mother is outside. She wishes to speak with you, that's all."

Lucas did not wait to hear more.

In the corridor, his mother came to meet him. "It's Jessica," she said. "I can't find her in this crowd."

"Perhaps she's watching the fireworks display."

Rosemary shook her head. "No. I've just come from there. Bella said she saw her with some young man, but she doesn't know who he is."

"Not know who he is? Surely she knows whom she invited to her own party?"

"Apparently not. I'm sure there's nothing to worry about. Perhaps they took a turn in the grounds. The paths are well lit and there are plenty of people strolling about." The anxious look in her eyes belied the calm in her voice.

Adrian and Rupert came out of the billiard room in time to see Lucas and his mother moving quickly along the corridor.

"What's that all about, d'you suppose?" asked Rupert.

"Jessica Hayward. What else would set Lucas off like a rocket?"

Rupert said, "I always wondered about his interest in that girl. D'you think . . . ?" He let the unasked question hang between them.

"What I think," said Adrian, "is that I don't know what to think anymore. Come on, we'd better see what he's up to."

They met Perry on their way out. He was with a party of friends coming from the card room and looking pleased with himself. "What is it?" he asked, seeing the expression on his brother's face.

"Nothing," replied Adrian, and brushed by him.

Perry watched them leave. "He always says that to me," he muttered to no one in particular, then, after a moment's indecision, he went after them.

• • •

Lucas was on the path that led to the little pavilion. There were several illuminated walks in the grounds, and he'd set his friends to comb every one of them. This one was the longest, and he'd chosen it precisely because it ended at the pavilion. He reasoned that if a man wanted to take liberties with a woman, it was the perfect setting. Rupert had built it on the best vantage point to view the hills and valley, right on the edge of the bluff. Even at night, the view was picturesque, for the lights of Chalford could be seen below, off in the distance.

He didn't know why he was so panicked. Whoever had gone off with Jess would be out of his mind if he did more than try to steal a kiss. On the other hand, he might have heard some of the rumors about Jess and decided she was fair game. If that was the case, he would personally break every bone in the bastard's body.

"Jess!" he shouted. "Jess!"

Silence.

Logic told him that Jess was all right, but he could do nothing about the visceral fear that chilled him. Images tried to intrude and he quickly suppressed them. But he began to run.

He was sprinting like an athlete when he rounded the last bend in the path. Ahead of him was the pavilion. It was open on all sides and the lantern should have been lit. He pulled up short just outside. There was no lantern. No one was there. And just a few yards farther on was the rail at the edge of the bluff.

He walked to the rail and looked down. There was nothing to be seen, nothing to hear. And he knew full well that Jess could not have gone over, not unless she'd done it deliberately. She would have had to climb over the rail first. But the rail did not extend all the way round the bluff.

Desperate now, he strove to silence his harsh breathing.

Every sense was heightened for a sound or cry from Jess. Then he heard it, the faint whimper of someone in pain.

"Jess!" he yelled and raced from the path into the undergrowth.

The sight that met his eyes had him snarling. Sir Matthew Paige was bending over Jess. He had a lantern in his hand, and Jess was on the ground, her back against a granite boulder, cowering away from him.

"What the hell do you think you're doing? Get away from her!"

Sir Matthew straightened. Lucas jumped into the small depression that Jess had fallen into and sank to his knees beside her. She looked up at him with eyes dulled with pain and shock. Blood was trickling from one corner of her mouth; her face was lacerated with deep scratches; the gown he had so much admired was filthy and in tatters. She had no shoes.

Sir Matthew said, "I was in the pavilion when I heard what I thought was an animal in pain. So I took the lantern and came to see what it was. You arrived almost as soon as I came upon her."

Lucas didn't answer him. "It's all right, Jess," he said. "I'm here now. You're safe."

He acted without conscious thought and began to test for broken bones. She moaned when he touched her left wrist, and cried out when he gently pressed his hands against her ribs. When he was satisfied that he had discovered all her injuries, he looked up at the older man.

"Leave the lantern and go back to the house. Find Dr. Vale and bring him here. Last time I saw him, he was in the card room. She may have broken her wrist and a rib. Tell the physician I said so. He'll know what to do."

Sir Matthew opened his mouth as if to say something, but Lucas cut him off. "We can talk later. Go, man, and hurry."

He turned back to Jessica, and after removing his coat, he eased it around her shoulders. She moaned. "I know, I know, it hurts," he said, "but I don't want you catching a chill. Jess, I must ask you: Did he rape you?"

She shook her head.

Lucas had been almost sure of her answer. Her gown was ripped but her underclothes were intact. It might not be the gentlemanly thing to do, but he'd checked when he was feeling for broken bones.

"Who was he, Jess? Give me his name."

She wasn't sure if she answered him. Now that she was safe, she wanted to slip into that blessed oblivion where there would be no more pain or fear. But she dared not give in to oblivion. It wasn't over yet. She could still feel his presence.

"Rodney Stone," said Lucas, repeating what she'd said to him. "What did he do, Jess? Tell me what happened."

"He tried to lure me to his carriage, but I fought him off. He came after me." Sobs choked her voice. "If you had not found me, he would have abducted me."

"It's all right, Jess. You've nothing to fear. He's long gone by now. In the morning, I'll find him and . . ."

Lucas's soothing words washed over her. It wasn't Rodney Stone she was thinking of, but her Voice. His anger was abating, and his thoughts were becoming more difficult to read.

Then her Voice went out like a light, and there were other voices to distract her, many voices, and Lucas's bellowing above the rest.

"For God's sake, man, did you have to bring the cavalry?" He scowled as a crowd of curious spectators followed Sir Matthew and Dr. Vale into the light. "Stand back! Stand back, I say, and let the doctor do his work."

Adrian and Rupert detached themselves from the press of people. Perry was right behind them. They spoke in undertones among themselves.

Jessica looked up at the sea of wavering faces, then moaned when someone lifted her and eased her down on her back.

A sharp rebuke burst from Lucas. "Watch what you're doing, for God's sake!"

Dr. Vale paid no attention, but continued to examine his patient. At each cry and whimper, Lucas flinched. The crowd grew silent.

Finally, the doctor said, "She has fainted, Lucas, and it's for the best. Let's get her back to the house as quickly as possible. I shall examine her more thoroughly there. No, don't carry her. It's best if she lies prone."

They used Lucas's coat as a makeshift stretcher. Lucas took one sleeve and Adrian the other. Rupert and Perry grabbed the coattails. Sir Matthew went ahead to clear the way as more and more guests came to investigate the strange report that was spreading like wildfire.

Lucas's face was set and grim on that long, careful walk to the house. Inside, he was trembling. It had occurred to him that if she had not fallen into that depression, she might have gone over the edge of the cliff.

The ball was over, but no one was in a hurry to leave. Guests crowded into the Great Hall as if it were a theater and they the audience. When some tried to follow them up the stairs, Rupert barked out an order. Footmen jumped and quickly ran to do their master's bidding, herding the guests well back.

Bella met them at the top of the stairs. She was with Lucas's mother and Ellie. When she saw Jessica, she put a hand to her throat. "Good God! I only just heard. What happened to the girl?"

Rupert answered something vague and soothing.

Bella's eyes snapped. "Only a fool would go off with a man she did not know. What did she expect?"

Rupert jumped in before Lucas could annihilate her, and his words lashed out, taking everyone by surprise. "If you have nothing useful to say, madam wife, I suggest you keep your mouth shut."

Lucas was aware of his mother's searching look flicking between Jessica and himself.

"In here," she said, leading the way to a door that stood open. "Mrs. Rankin is helping the maids set things up."

Anne Rankin's face blanched when she saw Jessica.

"She fainted," said Lucas.

Anne moved quickly to the bed and pulled back the covers.

When they had placed Jessica on the bed, Lucas stood there, looking down at her, his hands clenching and unclenching at his sides. Her face was paper white, making the deep scratches and abrasions stand out more vividly. She looked so defenseless, with her tousled hair tumbling around her shoulders.

Dr. Vale was ushering everyone out. Only Anne Rankin was allowed to stay. "Lucas?" he said crisply, and held out his coat to him. When he saw how reluctant Lucas was to leave, he softened his tone. "It's not as bad as it looks. At the most, a cracked rib and a broken wrist. She'll be up and walking before you know it. No, really, Lucas, there's nothing to worry about."

Dr. Vale was referring to Jessica's physical condition. But there was more to consider. He knew what people would be thinking and saying about Jess's latest escapade. They wouldn't blame the man for what had happened. Like Bella, they'd blame Jess for bringing it on herself.

"Lucas, I must attend to my patient."

Lucas tore his eyes from Jessica. "What?"

"I must take care of Miss Hayward."

"Aye, someone must!" he said savagely, and left the room.

VOICES INTRUDED ON HER CONSCIOUSNESS, FLOATING around her in hushed tones, soothing voices that stilled the initial leap of alarm as she slowly came to herself. There was nothing to fear here. She knew these voices, knew the gentle touch of the hands that tended her. They belonged to the nuns of the Sisters of Charity. As her fears faded, she drifted into sleep.

She moaned when a sharp pain suddenly stabbed her side. Someone had raised her head from the pillow and was holding a cup to her lips. She obediently took a sip, then another.

"It looks as though you've sprained your wrist and bruised your ribs." Sister Elvira's voice, matter-of-fact, cheerful, instilling confidence. "You had a nasty fall and you'll feel the effects for a day or two. Nothing serious, nothing to worry about. You'll be up and about before you know it, and Sister Dolores left a bottle of her famous elixir to dull the pain. I have to go back to Hawkshill, but if you need anything, Sister Brigid will be right here beside you. That's right, drink it down and off to sleep with you."

Soothing sounds—the rustle of a habit; the clink of a cup on a saucer; a clock ticking; her own shallow breathing. She slept.

It was brighter now, and there were other voices in the room.

A young voice, petulant. "I don't see why Lucas is running around the countryside trying to find this Mr. Stone. What has Lucas to do with this woman? Why can't Adrian find him, or Perry?"

"Hush, Ellie. Not so loud. The little nun may come back at any moment." Bella's voice. "He feels responsible, I suppose."

"But why should he? She's not one of us, is she? I mean, I know she was a nun and all that, but that doesn't excuse what she did. Mariah Hicks told me that her mama has forbidden her to speak to Miss Hayward after this."

"I'm not surprised. People have long memories and Jessica Hayward wore out her welcome here a long time ago. But there's nothing wrong with her bloodlines, so I suppose she is one of us."

"What do you think that man did to her?"

Bella exhaled a short, sharp breath. "I have no idea, but I'm sure that whatever it was, she brought it on herself."

The door handle rattled and Jessica raised her lashes. Sister Brigid entered carrying a tray. Lucas's mother was with her, and she was holding towels and a jug of steaming water.

"I met Sister Brigid on the stairs," she said. "The poor girl's hands were full, so I relieved her of these." She set the towels and jug on the washstand. Jessica couldn't keep her eyes open and her lashes swept down. "You know, Bella, I think you should assign a maid to run and fetch for Sister Brigid. It would be too distressing for Jessica if she should awaken to find herself alone in unfamiliar sur-roundings."

"But I did assign a maid!" Bella made a small sound of exasperation. "The stupid girl was probably detained by one of my other guests and did not know how to get out of it. Well, it's not surprising. The house is like a hostelry this morning, with everyone breakfasting at different times before they set off for town. I really shouldn't be here. There are a score of things that require my atten-tion. I'll look in later once things have quieted down."

After Bella had left, Mrs. Wilde said, "How is Jessica this morning?"

Sister Brigid set her tray on the table beside the bed. "She had a restless night, but the doctor says that she's not seriously hurt. She should be on her feet in a day or two."

"Thank God for that! Come, Ellie, I'm sure we're only in the way here. Oh, Sister Brigid, please tell Jessica that I hope her recovery is swift. Poor child, she looks as though she has been at the wars."

The door closed. There was a moment of silence, then, "Assigned a maid, indeed! If she did, I never saw her! The sooner we're back at Hawkshill . . ." Sister Brigid stopped. "Oh, Sister Martha," she said. "You're awake."

Lucas did not come to see Jessica until late that afternoon. She was taking tea, sitting at her bedroom window in a borrowed dressing gown with her arm in a sling when he was shown in. She'd slept for most of the day, and though she was eager to see him and greeted him with a smile, her head still throbbed and her side jarred every time she tried to move. But it wasn't only the pain that made her stiff and slow. Her ribs were bound so tightly that she could hardly fill her lungs with air.

He spoke in pleasantries for a moment or two, then asked Sister Brigid if she would mind giving him a few minutes' private conversation with her patient. Jessica carefully set her cup on its saucer and nodded her assent.

She was as anxious to speak privately with Lucas as he was with her.

He was smiling when he pulled up a chair and sat facing her. "I understand from Dr. Vale," he said, "that your injuries amount to one sprained wrist, possibly some bruised ribs and several scrapes and cuts?"

"Never mind that now," she said. "Tell me about Mr. Stone. Did you find him?"

"Ah yes, Mr. Stone. The young man who tried to lure you to his carriage."

There was something about Lucas that puzzled Jessica. No spark of sympathy warmed his eyes. She said carefully, "He may not be using that name now."

"Why should he not? Has he done something wrong?"

His voice was laden with enough sarcasm to make her wary. She cleared her throat and said, "What happened, Lucas? What's wrong?"

"Nothing is wrong. In fact, everything is fine. I'm satisfied now that I know exactly what happened. Last night you were not coherent. Oh, I'm not saying you told any lies. Let's just say I misunderstood you, shall we, Jess?"

She started to say something and faltered. Though his words were cordial, his manner frightened her. "You found Mr. Stone and he denied everything. Is that it?"

"I found him all right, and in essentials your stories are the same."

"He confessed? What did he say?"

"You shall hear for yourself."

She frowned when he rose and went to the door, then she jerked in shock when she recognized the young man who entered at Lucas's bidding. Rodney Stone was the picture of a guilty schoolboy. His face was flushed; his shoulders were hunched; he could hardly look her in the eye.

"My dear Miss Hayward," he said, then stammered to a halt. "My dear Miss Hayward," he said, "I hardly know how to begin to apologize. All I can say in my own defense is that I mistook . . . that is . . . I should never have tried to kiss you."

Not for one moment did Jessica believe this contrite mask. She looked appealingly at Lucas and cried out, "He tried to drag me into his carriage!"

Mr. Stone said quickly, "You told me you were feeling faint. I didn't know what else to do."

Lucas said quietly, "Is that true, Jess?"

"Yes, but that was only a subterfuge to make him think I was helpless. I wanted to take him off guard." Her breasts rose and fell, and she used her good arm to support her ribs. "When I pushed him away—"

"*Pushed* him, Jess?" Lucas's expression was as hard as flint. "Didn't you, in fact, attack Mr. Stone?"

"Yes," she cried out, "because I knew he was up to no good. He came after me, Lucas. He and his coachman both."

"I talked to the coachman," said Lucas, "and he's above suspicion. He's worked at the local livery stable for more than a year. He didn't come after you, Jess. He didn't even see you."

Mr. Stone said, "I knew you had panicked, and I feared you would come to grief. I'm truly sorry that my actions, which were meant for the best, only added to your terror. I had no idea that you really thought I meant to harm you. To be perfectly frank, I thought the best thing I could do was leave. And that is what I did."

She looked directly at Rodney Stone. "If Sir Matthew and Lucas had not found me when they did, you would have abducted me in that carriage."

A look of horror crossed Mr. Stone's face. "Miss Hayward, you are mistaken." He looked at Lucas. "I made no attempt to abduct Miss Hayward. We went for a walk. That's all."

"You lured me! You told me that you were unwell."

"And so I was, but the walk in the fresh air cleared my head."

"He deliberately lured me to his carriage, Lucas."

Mr. Stone looked helplessly at Lucas. "I should never have tried to kiss her, sir." He squared his shoulders. "Naturally, I shall make whatever amends you see fit."

Jessica felt a knot of dread in the pit of her stomach when she saw the cold, set expression on Lucas's face. Then he turned to Mr. Stone and the hardness melted.

"This has all been a most unfortunate misunderstanding," he said. "Any normal girl would have known not to go so far from the house, but Miss Hayward has led a more sheltered existence than most. The less said about this business the better. I shall tell our friends that Miss Hayward went for a walk and lost her way. And that is no more, no less than the truth."

"You may count on my discretion, sir. Miss Hayward, my humble apologies. The error was all mine. I mean that most sincerely."

Lucas was staring at Jessica, daring her to contradict him. "We accept your apology. Good day to you, Mr. Stone."

Mr. Stone bowed. "Lord Dundas. Miss Hayward."

Before the door had closed, Jessica was trying to rise. She managed to get to her feet, but she had to brace herself against the table for support. "Lucas, you can't let him leave just like that."

"Give me one good reason to stop him."

"He's distorting the truth!"

"Is he lying?"

"Not in so many words. But I know what I know!"

"Did you or did you not go with him to his carriage?"

"You know I did, but I didn't realize we were making for his carriage."

"Did you tell him that you felt faint?"

"Yes, but that was to get away from him. I didn't trust him."

"Yet you trusted him enough to go with him to an

unlit part of the drive. What made you change your mind?"

She'd changed her mind because she'd had a sudden and overpowering sense of evil. She'd known that her Voice had set a trap for her. She'd felt his presence, his determination, and finally his anger.

None of this could be confided to anyone, least of all the man who was staring at her with such scorn. She collapsed into her chair and stifled a whimper as the dull pain in her side suddenly flared.

"He changed," she said weakly. "He wasn't as nice as he'd been before. A woman knows about such things. Call it instinct or intuition, but I knew he was up to no good."

"He tried to kiss you, and you panicked. Now that, I might be prepared to accept."

She said vehemently, "Would I have been so desperate to escape from him if that's all it was?"

He boxed her in by bracing one hand on each armrest. "Do you know what I think, Jessica, what I *really* think?"

She shook her head.

"I think you were so angry with me that you tried to pay me back by going off with Mr. Stone. I think you may have flirted with him and got more than you bargained for."

Her voice was no more than a shaken whisper. "I wasn't angry with you, Lucas. If I was angry with anyone, it was with myself. I'd hoped for too much. I wanted . . . well, it doesn't matter what I wanted. But I swear I wasn't angry with you."

He straightened and gazed down at her with a perplexed frown. "You weren't trying to make me jealous?"

"No, Lucas."

"Or pay me back?"

"No."

"You didn't flirt with him?"

"No! Is that why you're so angry with me?"

He let out a long sigh. "God, I don't know what I think anymore."

She watched him as he stood there, staring out the window, and she said softly, "Why do you believe him before you believe me?"

He turned back to her. "I don't, Jess. I think you are both telling the truth as you see it."

"He's lying, Lucas," she said simply.

"Jess . . ." He shook his head and let out another long sigh. "Listen to me. Would a man who had tried to abduct you hang around Chalford for your friends to apprehend him? Would he come here today and offer marriage to make amends? I, for one, cannot believe it."

Her eyes widened. "Offer marriage? He wouldn't go that far."

"But he did—didn't you hear him?—when he said he'd make amends in any way I saw fit?"

She hadn't understood the reference, but now that Lucas had pointed it out to her, she didn't know what to think.

She put her hand to her throbbing temples. "I thought . . ."

"What did you think?"

She tried to recall the exact sequence of events of last night. If she were detached, she would have to say that Mr. Stone hadn't forced her to go with him, or attacked her. He'd done no more than try to kiss her. In fact, she had attacked him. But she wasn't detached, and she knew what she knew.

Or did she?

She had been so sure of what her senses told her when she'd seen the carriage, but now Lucas was forcing her to see things in a different light. Was she mistaken about Mr. Stone? She might admit to that much, but she wasn't mistaken about her Voice. Last night she'd heard him loud and clear.

She jumped when Lucas suddenly sat down beside her

and took her good hand. "Jess," he said, and shook his head.

"What?" His smile looked unnatural, strained, and that alarmed her even more. "What is it, Lucas? Tell me!"

"You were making great strides until this unfortunate incident. The people of Chalford had come to accept you. They like you, Jess."

He seemed to have difficulty finding the words and she said nervously, "And I like them, too. Go on."

"There's bound to be talk after last night." He was frowning down at her hand. "Don't ask me why, but people always blame the woman in such cases."

"I thought you blamed me, too. You were so angry."

He smiled ruefully. "I was angry because I've been up all night, worrying about all the things that might have happened to you. If I blame anything, it's your inexperience. You're too trusting. But that's not the point I am trying to make."

"What is the point?"

"The point is, you can't remain at Hawkshill forever. You are not a nun, Jess, and you'll never be a nun. The sisters know this. You're not even baptized in the Catholic faith. You're Church of England, the same as I." He stopped abruptly and uttered an unintelligible sound, then said, "How the devil did I get onto that? I'm not explaining myself very well. What I wanted to say was, you must think about your future and what you will do, where you will go when you leave Hawkshill. Jess, I have a solution."

His nervousness alarmed her. Her head began to swim, and she put a hand to her brow to steady herself. "But Lucas, the convent is all I know."

"That's what I mean. It's not enough, Jess, and—My God, you're trembling."

He rose abruptly, poured a glass of water from the

carafe on the table and raised it to her lips. "Drink," he said.

She took a few sips, but her stomach began to heave and she pushed his hand away. "I think," she said, "you had better send Sister Brigid to me. I'm going to be sick."

When Lucas entered Bella's drawing room, the buzz of conversation immediately ceased. They were all taking tea—Rupert, Adrian, Perry, Bella and Ellie. When she saw him, Ellie jumped up and ran toward him. "I wanted to see you, but everyone said I should stay here until you had talked to that woman."

She looked pale and Lucas touched her frown with one careless finger. "That woman has a name, Miss Hayward, and to please me, you will use it, Ellie."

He took the chair between Adrian and Rupert. "Where is my mother?"

Rupert said, "Sir Matthew came by and drove her home."

Lucas turned to stare at Rupert. "Sir Matthew? And she went with him?"

"Why shouldn't she?"

Lucas was aware that everyone was staring and he shrugged negligently. "I thought she would wait for me."

He accepted a cup of tea from Bella, whose gloating silence spoke volumes, and that got his back up. Had she planned the whole thing herself, she couldn't have hoped for a more disastrous end to Jess's debut.

Well, this was a setback for Jess, but it wasn't the end of it, not nearly the end of it. In fact, it was only the beginning.

He would marry her, of course. That would simplify everything, and not just for himself, but for Jess as well. She would be under his protection. No one would dare point fingers at her or snigger about her behind her back. When she was his countess and living in the lap of luxury, she could pay off old scores if she wanted to, thumb her nose at people like Bella who'd always looked down on her.

Not that Jess would. That wasn't her way. If she were a different kind of woman, he could dangle his title and fortune in front of her to tempt her into marrying him. What he had to do now was come up with reasons that Jess would accept. He couldn't see himself telling a former nun that the real reason they should marry was because they couldn't keep their hands off each other.

He stifled a laugh and took a sip of tea. At length, he said, "I don't know why everyone is looking so glum. It's just as I told you. It was all a misunderstanding. Jessica did not do anything wrong. She went for a walk and fell into a hollow in the ground. I found her right afterward."

Bella was provoked into ungluing her lips. "Hah! No one is going to believe that story!"

"I believe it," said Rupert.

"It doesn't matter what anyone believes," said Lucas. "Jess will be treated with respect, or I'll want to know the reason why."

Ellie's face was whiter than before. "But everyone knows how you feel about her, Lucas."

He turned his head to look at her. "Who have you been listening to, Ellie?"

"No one in particular." Her eyes slid to Bella, then back to Lucas. "It's what everyone was saying last night."

Perry and Adrian had been conversing in an undertone. Perry rose. "Come along, Ellie," he said. "Let's take a walk in the rose garden. The grown-ups want to speak in private."

"I'm not a child!" she protested indignantly.

When no one responded to this, she stalked from the room. Perry went after her.

Adrian was the first to break the silence. "How did you find Mr. Stone?"

"It wasn't too difficult, after I came to the conclusion that he hadn't run off to London. I see by your smile,

Adrian, you've guessed just how far I'd traveled before I had the sense to turn back."

"How far did you get?" asked Rupert.

"To Henley, and each hostelry on the way told the same story. No carriage had pulled in to change or water the horses."

"Then what happened?" asked Adrian.

"Then," said Lucas, "I returned to Chalford, and made the rounds here." He yawned. "Do you realize I've had only two hours' sleep since last night? I found him in the Rose and Crown, just as he was dressing for breakfast."

"Was he surprised to see you?"

"Very."

Surprised wasn't the word for it. Young Stone had been shocked out of his wits. Lucas hadn't been in the mood to hear explanations when he'd burst into the room. He'd grabbed Stone by the throat and flung him against the wall. If Stone had fought back, he would have thrashed him, but he couldn't thrash a man who wouldn't defend himself. But it took some time before he'd calmed down enough to hear him out.

"Well," said Adrian, breaking into his train of thought, "don't keep us in suspense. Why is he still breathing?"

Lucas laughed. "Because," he said, "all he did was try to steal a kiss from Jess. She panicked and ran. Then she got hurt in the fall. Mr. Stone never laid a hand on her."

Everyone was silent. Lucas drank his tea. "There is something I have been meaning to ask you," he said, looking at Rupert. "Who exactly is Mr. Stone?"

Rupert shrugged. "I don't know him. It was Bella's ball. I did not add him to the invitation list. Bella?"

Bella shook her head. "I don't know him either, but I'm sure I've seen him around town. Perhaps Perry knows him."

Lucas straightened in his chair. "Are you saying that you did not invite him to your ball? Then how did he get in without an invitation card?"

"I always have extra cards to hand out to young, eligible gentlemen, to give to their friends. That's why my balls are such a success. There are always more gentlemen than ladies present. No girl is ever a wallflower at my parties."

"Unmarked cards?" asked Lucas. "So anyone could fill in his own name?"

"Why, yes."

"Who did you give these cards to?"

"Perry for one. My cousin Philip, for another. Young gentlemen of rank and breeding who can vouch for the friends they invite. Is it important?"

"No," said Lucas. And it wasn't. The matter was closed and the sooner it was forgotten, the better it would be for Jess.

"Just a moment," said Rupert, abruptly rising. "In all the confusion, I've forgotten to give you the good news. Our subscription ball has raised close to two thousand pounds. Just think of it—two thousand pounds! And it's all Bella's doing. This calls for more than tea. Let's break open the champagne."

No one really wanted champagne, but out of respect for Rupert, they filled their glasses and drank to Bella.

Rodney Stone looked down at his boots and cursed. One of the heels had broken off. He couldn't walk like this. Setting his grip on the grass at the edge of the path, he found a rock and smashed off his other heel, then tossed them both into the river. He cursed again, picked up his grip and walked on.

He understood the need for secrecy, but thought that this was a hell of a way to achieve it. He wasn't used to walking and it was a fair distance to the rendezvous. The tow path was muddy, and he could hardly see his way in the fading light. But his partner-in-crime wasn't taking any chances. They mustn't be seen together. And after his run-in with Lord Dundas, he could understand why.

He suppressed a shudder. God, when Dundas had walked in on him this morning, he'd had the shock of his life. It had never occurred to him that the girl would set anyone on him. Up till that point, he hadn't done anything wrong. She was the one who was at fault. He couldn't believe the way the earl had carried on, and all over nothing. If Dundas ever suspected the truth . . .

He couldn't wait to get out of Chalford. He didn't feel safe here. He wouldn't put it past Lord Dundas to come looking for him again and the prospect terrified him. Obviously, it alarmed his employer as well. A boy had hand-delivered a note this morning with explicit instructions. He was to pay his shot at the Rose and Crown and come to the rendezvous tonight where he would find a horse waiting to take him wherever he wanted to go. *After* they had settled matters.

The words *settled matters* worried him. He'd botched the job and now it seemed likely that he wouldn't be paid in full. He wasn't going to let that happen. It wasn't his fault that the stupid bitch had taken fright just before he'd got her into the carriage. He still didn't know what had put her wise to him. Everything had been going according to plan. She'd swallowed the bait like a fish with a worm. Once he had put her in the carriage, he would have taken her to the rendezvous, then rushed back to the ball. Then he was to make his way to his own carriage and leave, which was exactly what he'd done. God, if the earl ever learned that there were two carriages involved and not one, he would be a dead man.

He shook his head. The poor man actually believed the girl was a lady. To save his own skin, he'd played along with him, when what he'd really wanted to do was laugh in his face. Stupid bitch! Why had she suddenly gone off like one of the rockets at the bloody fireworks' display? This was going to cost him dearly.

He licked his lips, imagining what was in store for her.

He wouldn't mind being the one to tame her. One thing was sure. She would give her captor a rough ride.

If she'd been a decent girl, he might have had a few qualms. But she wasn't a decent girl. In spite of her airs and graces, she was a soiled dove. He knew the type. Once they got a taste for that life, they couldn't give it up. They were more depraved than the lowest men.

He came to a fork in the path and branched left, away from the river. He stopped suddenly as a thought struck him. Maybe it wouldn't cost him dearly, not if he played his cards right. That cow of a woman obviously had Lord Dundas wrapped around her little finger. A hint to his employer that he might be tempted to go to the earl with what he knew might loosen the purse strings. It was worth a try.

For the rest of the way, he imagined what it would be like to have a regular supply of money. He would go to the best tailors, the best brothels, and the best gaming houses. And he wouldn't be stingy with his friends. If there was one thing that could be said about Rodney Stone, it was that he was generous to a fault. That's why he had so many friends.

The building was a dark silhouette against the horizon. He left the path and climbed over a low wall. His accomplice was waiting for him.

"Did anyone see you?"

"No. I followed your instructions to the letter."

"Good. This way."

Stone passed under an arch and was overcome with a strange, uncanny dread. "I think someone just walked over my grave," he said.

The blow on his neck sent him to his knees. The next blow finished him off.

Jessica sat straight up in bed. Her heart was pounding, the fine hairs on her neck had risen, her pupils were dilating. "Voice?" she said.

Lucas blinked the drowsiness from his eyes, and rising from the chair, swiftly crossed to the bed.

"What is it?" he asked. "Are you in pain? Did you hear something?"

Jessica looked at him blindly. "Voice?" she repeated.

"It's just a dream," said Lucas soothingly. He reached for the carafe of water on the table beside the bed, poured out a glass, and brought it to Jessica's lips.

Jessica drank the water and sank back against the pillows. "Where am I?"

"Haig House. Did you forget? Shall I fetch Sister Brigid? Her room is right across the hall. It will only take me a moment."

He could see awareness slowly fill her eyes. Her lower lip quivered. "Lucas, hold me."

"Jess!" He sat on the edge of the bed and gathered her in his arms. "What is it, Jess?"

"I don't know! I don't know! Don't leave me! Lucas, promise you won't leave me."

"I promise," he said soothingly. "I promise." But she would not settle until he had stretched out beside her on the bed.

She nestled trustingly against him. "I'm frightened," she whispered.

"It was only a dream."

"A dream?"

"Just a dream."

Jessica gradually relaxed. Her eyes closed.

Lucas remained as he was for several minutes, then tried to slip from her grasp. Even in sleep, she wouldn't allow it. He couldn't help smiling. "Jess, what am I going to do with you?" he whispered. His eyelids grew heavy and he closed his eyes.

In the morning, when she awakened, she had no memory of her dream, but she had plenty of other things to worry about. The vicar and his wife were framed in the doorway looking a ghastly shade of green. Perry was right behind them, with his eyes huge in his head. And Lucas was stretched out on her bed, under the covers, snoring his head off.

"We only slept together," she said in her own defense. She dug Lucas in the ribs to waken him, then retreated behind a wall of silence.

CHAPTER
15

JESSICA SLEPT A GOOD DEAL OF THE TIME, AND WHEN she was awake, she felt so groggy she could barely lift her head from the pillow, and she wondered whether her grogginess was self-induced so that she wouldn't have to face the enormity of what she'd done. Her waking thoughts were more than she could bear, and she would turn her head into her pillow and moan in mortification.

The aftermath of that horrible morning when she'd awakened to find Lucas in her bed and the vicar and his wife framed like two stone pillars in her doorway was a blessed confusion of fragmented memories—Lucas rising from her bed and conversing with their visitors with all the assurance of someone who had just risen from the dinner table; Sister Elvira, sympathetic and inflexible at the same time, telling her everything would work out for the best, and later, Lucas, equally sympathetic and inflexible, asking her to marry him. Only, he hadn't asked; he'd told her that there was no getting out of it after they'd spent the night together in her bed.

And it was all her own fault.

She kept reassuring herself that no one could make her do what she didn't want to do, and she didn't want to marry a man who didn't love her. When she was feeling better, she would straighten everyone out, beginning with Lucas. But Lucas had gone off to London on some business or other, and the thing had taken on a life of its own. Visitors came and went in a stream, all of them wishing her happy or making some other reference to her approaching marriage, and her feeble protests might as well have been spoken to an empty room.

With Lucas gone, she felt isolated. She was by turns afraid of her Voice and afraid that she might be losing her mind. What if there was no Voice? What if there was? Thoughts came and went in a dizzying confusion.

She didn't like Haig House. She wanted to go home to Hawkshill. She missed the boys. She missed the nuns. But to all her entreaties, Sister Elvira had given her a gentle but emphatic no. She was Lord Dundas's affianced wife. She couldn't go back to her old life as though nothing had happened. When Lord Dundas returned, he would take charge of things and decide what was to be done. In the meantime, Sister Elvira said, she had written to the mother superior to inform her of Jessica's changed circumstances.

One visitor whom Jessica was always pleased to see was Perry. Only when he visited the sickroom did she feel that she was talking to a rational human being. He didn't see why she should have to marry Lucas, either. He wasn't tactful. In fact, sometimes he was frank to the point of rudeness. It made a welcome change from people who wished her happy but wouldn't look her in the eye.

In the second week of her convalescence, Perry arrived when the whole house was a hive of activity. This was the night of the annual Tenants' Ball, and though the only guests would be local people, it absorbed all of Bella's energies, as it had done for several days. As a result, she rarely came to visit Jessica.

"You shouldn't marry Lucas if you don't want to, Jess," said Perry.

They were sitting on either side of the table in front of the window, and Perry moved his chair to get a better look at her face. "One good thing has come out of it, though. The gossip has been scotched."

She said miserably, "Is it generally known, then, that Lucas was discovered . . . you know . . . in bed with me?"

"Good Lord, no! If it *had,* then of course you would have to marry him. What I meant was the gossip about you and Mr. Stone. Now that people know you and Lucas are engaged, they've forgotten about that other episode."

"What are they saying about Lucas and me?"

"They're saying that it's a love match."

A love match. She would have laughed had she not felt so miserable. Her memories were hazy, but one thing she *did* remember. When Lucas had proposed to her, the word *love* had never been mentioned. He had given her many good reasons why they should marry, but at the end of it, she was left with the distinct impression that he would be better off if he hired a governess to look after her, or a nurse, or maybe both.

"What I can't understand," said Perry, "is what Lucas was doing in your room so late at night."

"He only intended to stay for a few moments. But he was exhausted. He'd been up most of the previous night looking for Mr. Stone."

"But to fall asleep in the same bed! That is inexcusable."

She opened her mouth then thought better of what she was going to say. Lucas had told her not to offer explanations or make excuses. They had done nothing wrong.

Perry went on. "This is worse than the episode with Mr. Stone. And after what happened between you and

Lucas all those years ago, you'd think he'd take more care not to be caught in a compromising position with you. There's more to this than meets the eye."

For a moment, her interest was piqued, but she allowed it to die. It was one thing to believe in her Voice, and another to see sinister motives where none existed. Lucas was beyond suspicion. He'd been alone with her when Sir Matthew had gone off to fetch the doctor, and he'd done everything to make her comfortable. He was not her Voice. Everything in her nature recoiled from such a suspicion.

Rodney Stone was not her Voice, either. He couldn't be. He had no connection to Chalford or her father. He'd frightened her, but she had brought that on herself. It was her Voice she had sensed when she'd looked at the carriage. The only reasonable explanation for her distrust of Stone that came to her now was that she'd panicked when her Voice had slipped into her mind and she'd made connections that simply did not exist.

If there was a Voice. Now that she'd been proved wrong about Mr. Stone, she was beginning to mistrust her own judgment. Brain damage was always a possibility, she'd heard Father Howie tell the Reverend Mother in her first few weeks in the convent. If she was suffering from brain damage, then there was no Voice, she had no sixth sense, no intuition or ability to read people or situations. On the other hand, if her brain was not damaged . . . and so it went on.

Perry was waiting for her to say something. "You may be right," was all she said.

"And the thing about Lucas is, when he gets an idea in his head, he's unshakable."

"I know."

He patted her hand. "Don't look so miserable, Jess. If worse comes to worst, I'll offer for you myself."

She was startled into laughter, then stopped abruptly

when a spasm of pain gripped her side. Her bruised ribs were healing, but she wasn't better yet.

"I'm not joking, Jess."

"But . . . but why would you do such a thing?"

He colored up. "You won't remember this, but a long time ago we were friends. I mean, when we were children. There weren't any boys my own age to play with, and, well, you could climb trees and scrap with the best of them. We always got along together."

"I was a tomboy?" she asked, diverted by this picture of herself.

He grinned. "You used to box my ears when I called you that. You had quite a temper, Jess."

She looked at him curiously, this fair-haired young man who looked like a younger version of Lucas. There was something about him that was very appealing. It warmed her to think they had once been friends. "What happened to our friendship, Perry?"

He shrugged. "I went away to school. When I came back, you were smitten with Lucas. You weren't climbing trees anymore. We quarreled. It's the only time I remember boxing *your* ears."

She thought she was going to laugh, and braced her ribs, but tears welled up.

"Now what have I said?" Her hand was resting on the table, and he reached out and covered it with one of his own.

She managed a smile. "I wish I could remember those days, but I can't. But there's one thing I shall never forget, and that's your kindness to me when I really needed a friend." She impulsively raised his hand to her cheek. "I won't take you up on your rash offer, so you can stop shivering in your boots."

They both laughed, but in the next moment, Perry dropped her hand and pulled back with a start. Jessica turned to see what he was looking at, and she too pulled back with a start. Lucas and his mother and ward were standing just inside the door.

Lucas's gaze held hers as he closed the distance between them. His eyes, so like Perry's, had undergone a transformation. They were as black as thunderclouds, and when he bent his head to hers, she braced for the lash of his temper. What she got was an openmouthed kiss that shook her all the way to her toes—slow and proprietary.

When he straightened, she was breathing hard and her cheeks were as crimson as the velvet drapes around the bed. Lucas regarded her for a long moment and slowly smiled. Thoroughly flustered, she looked beyond him to his mother and ward. Mrs. Wilde was smiling also but Ellie wasn't. In fact, her look was savage.

"I'm glad to see you are recovering, Jessica," said Mrs. Wilde. She took the chair her nephew offered her. "Thank you, Perry. Ellie and I were wondering where you had got to."

"Um, I always look in on Jessica at this time of day."

"Yes. So Bella told us."

Lucas took a chair and moved it close to Jessica. Seating himself, he said, "I asked Perry to keep an eye on my betrothed in my absence, Mother. Where is Sister Brigid, by the way?"

It was lightly spoken, but Jessica felt the reproach. Once again, she'd been caught breaking one of society's cardinal rules. She was entertaining a gentleman caller—if one could call Perry that—with no one to chaperone them. And she, of all people, should know better. Would she never learn?

She forced a smile. "Mrs. Haig asked her to take care of one of the maids who has a bad toothache. I think it needs to be pulled. She'll be back soon."

Lucas reached for the hand that was bound at the wrist, her left hand. "I've brought you something from London," he said. "A betrothal ring."

Jessica looked down at the ring he had slipped on her

finger, a single sapphire set in a band of gold filigree. It fitted her perfectly. An image flashed into her mind, a fragment of a memory, or a dream. *Don't cry, Jess. I'll buy you a sapphire ring.* She searched for more, but the more she searched, the more the memory faded.

Lucas said, "If you don't like the ring, Jess, you have only to say so. I'll get you another."

"I do like the ring," she said. "In fact, it's quite lovely."

She looked at Lucas, then his mother. She couldn't accept the ring. She should say something before it was too late. But she couldn't bring herself to shame Lucas in front of his mother.

"It's lovely," she repeated lamely.

There was a commotion at the door, and Sister Brigid entered followed by Sister Elvira.

"We met on the stairs," said Sister Brigid, then, "Oh, what a beautiful ring!"

The sisters swooped down on Jessica and duly admired the ring. Jessica was hardly aware of how she responded. Her head was beginning to swim.

"I don't believe in long engagements," declared Sister Elvira, "and neither does the mother superior. A letter arrived from her this very morning. She says, well, she says a lot of things but . . ." She could hardly keep still for excitement, and rocked back and forth on her heels. "You can read for yourself. This letter is for you, Jessica."

Jessica broke the seal and slowly read the letter. She wouldn't have recognized the Reverend Mother in these few terse sentences. It was a command from a superior. The gist of it was, Jessica must marry Lucas Wilde for the good name of their order.

"What does it say?" asked Lucas.

She stared blindly at the letter, then looked up. "The Reverend Mother says we must marry at once."

Her eyes moved from one face to another. The sisters were smiling radiantly; Lucas was watching her as a cat watches a mouse; Ellie looked as though someone had just slapped her, and Perry's face looked like thunder. Only Lucas's mother showed a spark of sympathy. She patted Jessica on the shoulder, rose to her feet and began to adjust her shawl.

"Your Reverend Mother sounds like a very sensible woman to me," she said. "However, I won't have it said that Jessica and my son married under a cloud. There's been enough gossip already. Don't you agree, Lucas?"

He regarded his mother quizzically. "What are you suggesting, Mother?"

"This will be no hole-and-corner affair, as though you and Jessica have something to be ashamed of. This will be a wedding to remember."

"If I may make a small suggestion," interposed Sister Elvira diffidently.

Jessica knew that look, and she sat up straighter. *Watch her,* went through her mind. Though she loved Sister Elvira dearly, the little nun's looks could be deceiving. She wasn't always as soft and motherly as she appeared. She could be as hard as iron with a boy or a novice when she thought that boy or novice needed a push in the right direction.

When Lucas's mother nodded, Sister Elvira went on. "This will be a difficult transition for Jessica, and all the more so if she stays in Chalford. Here, she doesn't know whether she is Sister Martha or Jessica Hayward. I want her to have the best chance possible. You have a house in London, I believe. May I suggest that you take Jessica there?"

Jessica felt as though the ground had shifted beneath her. "But . . . but I can't leave Hawkshill," she protested. "I have work to do there. I can't leave our boys just like that."

Sister Elvira bent over her and, as she did when she wanted to make a point, looked deeply into Jessica's eyes. "I don't mean that you should live in London forever, Jessica. You will always be welcome at Hawkshill. But first, take some time to get accustomed to your new role. Don't be in a hurry. And there's no need to look so sad, my dear. When one door closes, another opens. Isn't that what we nuns always say? Your work won't be finished, Jessica. You'll simply be moving into another sphere."

Mrs. Wilde said, "Sister Elvira has a point. All things considered, a London wedding might be exactly what we need. We'll open up the state rooms in Dundas House. Jessica will need bridal clothes—we'll have to arrange that as soon as possible. And when she's ready to travel, she must come up to London and live with us."

"But Aunt Rosemary!" Ellie's voice intruded like the fractious cry of a child who has been forgotten.

"Yes, dear?"

"N . . . nothing." Ellie hung her head.

Jessica had eyes only for Lucas, and she put everything into that look. She appealed to him, she pleaded; her look spoke volumes and eddied with messages that only he could understand. And she said only one tremulous word. "Lucas?"

Lucas held her gaze for a long time then, releasing her, turned to the other occupants of the room. "I'd like to speak to Jessica in private," he said.

When they were alone, he took her hand in his and kissed the tips of her fingers. "Listen to me, Jess," he said. "It will be all right, you'll see. I'm not an animal. All right, so I got carried away when I saw you with Perry a moment ago, but that doesn't mean anything. When we are married, I will treat you with complete restraint and respect. You've been a nun for the last three years and of course I'll take that into consideration. Our marriage will be on your terms. I'll give you as much time as you need before I claim my conjugal rights, and it will be up to you to say when. Does that make you feel better?"

So much for looks that spoke volumes and eddied with messages that only he could understand! How could one man be so dense? That's not what she wanted to hear. She snatched her hand back.

"You don't want to marry me," she said crossly, "so why are you so determined to go through with this?"

"Not want to marry you?" He looked astonished. "Of course I want to marry you."

"Why?" she asked hopefully.

"Because," he said, "I have never wanted a woman as much as I want you."

Then he kissed her chastely on the lips and left her.

The Tenants' Ball was in full swing when Lucas made his way to the billiard room. He'd just looked in on Jessica and found her fast asleep. He'd wanted to stay, but had thought better of it. He wasn't exhausted tonight, and if she persuaded him to stretch out beside her, he couldn't vouch for the consequences.

He'd compromised her. In all innocence, he'd compromised her. Maybe he should feel guilty but he couldn't pretend to something he didn't feel. All things considered, their being discovered in bed together was just the push Jess needed to do what she really wanted to do anyway. He didn't know why women had to make everything so complicated. She'd been reluctant to marry him for all the wrong reasons. He could do so much better for himself; his friends would be aghast if he married her; she didn't know how to be a countess; she blamed herself for everything.

If she'd told him that she didn't want him, he might have accepted it. No he wouldn't, because he wouldn't have believed her.

His grin faded as that thought led to another. When he'd walked in on Jess today, he'd been shocked at the change in her. She seemed thinner, paler, and there were dark circles under her eyes. Her injuries had not been that serious, and two weeks had passed since the accident. She should have been blooming with health, not fading away, and he wondered whether Bella or someone else had said something to upset her.

The sooner they were married, the better it would be all round. Sister Elvira was right. What Jess needed was a complete break from her old life. She was going to have pretty things. She was going to learn to enjoy herself. She wasn't going to lift a hand to do anything if she didn't want to. It was her turn to be pampered and looked after, and whether she liked it or not, by God, he was going to see that she was.

He knew what had brought this on.

When he'd gone up to London to investigate Rodney Stone, he'd also decided to pay a long-overdue visit to the convent of the Sisters of Charity. At first, the mother superior was suspicious. She'd heard from Sister Elvira of how he'd compromised Jess and meant to marry her, and she was not impressed. If, she'd said, public opinion made it impossible for Jessica to continue with her work at Hawkshill, she could always return to the convent and take up her life there.

Perhaps he'd said too much. Hell, he knew he'd said too much. But the thought of Jess spending the rest of her life in a convent had provoked him into telling the little nun a few home truths about her pet. Jess, he'd told the Reverend Mother, didn't have the temperament to be a nun. She was a warm, vibrant woman who was made to have a husband and children. And if he didn't take her on, he didn't know who would, or who else could manage her. Then she'd be stuck in the convent for the rest of her life, and if that was what the mother superior wanted for Jess, then she didn't know Jess half as well as she thought she did.

He'd gone over that interview in his mind many times, and he still could not fix on exactly what he'd said to win the mother superior over. He'd expected to be shown the door. Instead, the Reverend Mother had given him a tour of the convent, and when they'd returned to her office, she'd offered him a glass of brandy. And for the next half hour, they'd talked about Jess.

The girl that she described was nothing like the Jess he knew. Sister Perfect? The nun who never put a foot wrong? He just couldn't see it. Nor could he imagine Jess in the convent's stark interior, following the disciplined life of a nun.

She hadn't had much of a life with that father of hers, but she'd been free to come and go as she pleased. And as for being afraid of life, Jess had reached for it greedily with both hands. And he had helped her as he'd watched her grow up, not because he'd felt sorry for her, but because he'd been captivated by that engaging child.

Nothing had changed and everything had changed. They no longer shared the same memories, and it was, in some respects, like starting over. As the mother superior had pointed out, he must put all thoughts of the girl he'd known from his mind and remember that all this new Jess remembered was her life as a nun.

He accepted the theory; it was putting it into practice that was difficult. *Our marriage will be on your terms.* Had he really said that? He hoped he could live up to his promise.

When he turned into the corridor leading to the billiard room, he had to dodge past a slightly tipsy and amorous maid. Rupert's Tenants' Ball wasn't exactly what he was used to. It was a rollicking affair where, for one night of the year, the tenants and their masters were supposed to be on an equal footing. It made the serving girls bold and their quarry, such as himself, head for cover.

When he opened the door to the billiard room, he saw that he wasn't the only gentleman who had taken cover. A cloud of tobacco smoke was trapped under the ceiling. The babble of voices dimmed at his entrance, then rose again when it became clear that he wasn't a footman with reinforcements for the empty glasses that many of the gentlemen clutched.

He bumped into someone and turned with a smile of apology. The smile slipped when he saw who it was. "Sir Matthew," he said. He'd thought Sir Matthew had gone home.

Sir Matthew nodded. "Dundas," he acknowledged, with all the warmth of an iceberg.

There was no getting out of it. They had to exchange a few words. "I thought," said Lucas, drawling the words, "that you were fixed in London till the hunting season."

"And I thought," said Sir Matthew, drawling the words, "that the last girl you would marry would be Jessica Hayward. But your mother tells me that it's a love match. Congratulations, Dundas."

Everyone in their vicinity laughed. Lucas laughed with them, but what he really wanted to do was smash his fist into that handsome face. He didn't care for the implication that this man and his mother were on friendly terms again. In fact, it downright infuriated him.

He couldn't quell the bitter memories that the sight of this man always revived. He was no longer that idealistic boy of sixteen, he reminded himself, no longer so easily shocked. But he couldn't help what he was feeling. Sir Matthew had been his father's friend, or so he'd pretended. He'd also been his mother's lover. The memory of their betrayal was as vivid now as though it had happened yesterday.

His father had taken a turn for the worse and his mother was out sketching somewhere. He'd scoured the countryside looking for her, and had ended up in Sir Matthew's palatial estate. He'd come to Sir Matthew for help, because he was a friend of the family, and he didn't know where else to turn. He found them in the summer house.

Even now, he could still feel the shock of discovery wash through him. He'd looked up to Sir Matthew, he'd thought the world of him. He was a constant visitor to the house, and had spent many hours with his invalid father.

But he should have known that what brought Sir Matthew to the Lodge was not someone who was twice his age. It was the young, pretty wife he had been after.

He hadn't waited for his mother. He'd told her about his father, then turned on his heel and let her find her own way home. He had never mentioned that episode in the summer house, but he'd made it clear that she could not have both her son and her lover. Afterward, he'd avoided Sir Matthew like the plague.

The men at the billiard table put down their cues.

"Care for a game?" Lucas asked the older man.

Sir Matthew looked at the billiard table, then back at Lucas. He smiled. "Why not?" he said pleasantly.

They chalked the tips of their cues like two duelists preparing their pistols for combat. It was a melodramatic thought, and had his opponent been anyone but Sir Matthew, Lucas would have laughed at himself. He was in deadly earnest, and try as he would, he could not summon his usual grace. It was only a game, and it was more than a game.

They tossed a coin to determine who would start. Sir Matthew won. He played with all the charm and carelessness that was the mark of a man of breeding. When one shot went wild, Lucas took over.

His eye and hand had never been steadier. His resolution was like iron. Shot by shot, he hammered the ball home. When he came to the shot that would decide the contest, he looked over at his opponent.

Sir Matthew was very much at his ease, one hip propped against a table, his cue held loosely in one hand. His eyes were quick with intelligence and there was irony in his smile.

"No quarter asked or given, I see," he said.

Lucas lined up the ball and drove it home.

He left the billiard room feeling like the loser. Not only had he to accept Sir Matthew's congratulations for a game well played, but he also had to shake the man's hand. Sir Matthew had known what he was doing. He'd stuck out his hand and Lucas had been forced to take it.

He passed the stairs and debated whether he should check on Jessica again. He was on his way up when his mother appeared on the landing above him and began to descend the stairs.

"I just looked in on Jessica," she said. "She's still sleeping."

Lucas tucked his mother's hand into the crook of his arm and descended the stairs with her. He was aware of her searching look and he smiled into her eyes. "I made up my mind to take the most beautiful woman in to supper," he said. "So here I am to escort you. Now, let's find Ellie."

They passed Sir Matthew in the hallway, but mother and son were so involved in their own conversation that they did not seem to notice him.

Her eyelids felt as if they were weighted with lead. She lay there, trying to force them open, when every cell in her body was demanding that she go back to sleep. Laudanum . . . The word floated through her mind. That's why she couldn't marshal her faculties; that's why she was lying here like a stone when something was far wrong.

She dredged up the remnants of her willpower and slowly opened her eyes. Though she was groggy and the room was in darkness, she knew where she was. This was her bedchamber in Haig House. There was some kind of dinner party going on. No. The Tenants' Ball. That was it. If she hadn't felt so unwell, she would have been downstairs as one of the guests.

The strains of a country jig drifted up to her. She could hear voices and laughter, but they were muted. But that's not what had awakened her. She could smell roses, not real roses, but something sickly and cloying.

Bella's perfume.

She jerked to an upright position, and the pain in her

side made her gasp. Her head was swimming. "Bella?" she whispered. "Bella?"

The silence was frightening.

And not only the silence. None of the candles was lit. The drapes had been drawn. Sister Brigid should have answered her, or one of the maids. They would never have left her alone in the dark. At the very least, they would have left a candle burning for her.

She eased over the edge of the bed and stumbled to her feet. She was doing it again, doing what she'd done with Rodney Stone. There was a logical explanation for everything, if she would only concentrate. And all she need do was pull the bell rope and a maid would come running. Then the candles would be lit.

She crossed the room in slow, uncertain steps. She was reaching for the bellpull when she heard a sound—something dropped with a soft thud on the carpeted floor. Before she could cry out, a blow sent her sprawling. She fought down nausea and a wave of pain as she twisted to avoid the next blow. There was no blow. The door opened and closed, and she heard footsteps receding along the corridor.

She was alone.

It was a long while before she moved. Rising first to her knees, then to her feet, she steadied herself with one hand on the wall and breathed deeply. Finally straightening, she yanked on the bellpull, then walked to the bed and sat on the edge of it.

Bella had been hiding behind the bed drapes. But why? Bella must have blown out the candles, then hidden behind the bed drapes.

It didn't make sense. This was Bella's house. She didn't have to steal into someone's room like a thief in the night. She could go anywhere she wanted.

The door opened and a maid with a candle entered. "Oh, miss," she exclaimed, "your candles have gone out."

Jessica watched as the maid lit the candles on the mantelpiece.

The maid turned to look at her. "Can I get you something, miss?"

Jessica couldn't smile though she tried. "Thank you, Eliza, but the candle is all I wanted. Oh, and I think something dropped on the floor."

The maid dutifully searched where Jessica pointed, and a moment later came up with a pair of shears. "How did the mistress's shears come to be here?" she asked ingenuously.

Long after the maid had gone, Jessica sat on the edge of the bed with a hand pressed to her aching temples. In that moment, she would have given anything to be Sister Martha again, and back in the serene surroundings of the convent of the Sisters of Charity.

CHAPTER
16

THREE WEEKS LATER, LUCAS AND JESSICA WERE MAR-
ried in the great reception room of Dundas House.
In deference to the bride's wishes, there would be another
service at the convent, to bless their union, when Father
Howie returned from his papal mission to Rome. But that
would be a private ceremony. On this occasion, the drawing room was filled with friends and guests.

As Lucas slipped his ring on Jessica's finger, he wondered why it had taken them so long to reach this point.
She was his wife, finally, and if he'd had any sense, she
would have been his wife seven years ago when she'd
cornered him in his stable and tried to compromise him
just as Bella and Adrian walked in. For years, he'd trivial-
ized what he felt for her. How could he have been so
blind? And now he had got what he deserved. He was the
one doing the chasing. The old Jess would have been
crowing in triumph. This Jess . . . this Jess . . .

She was one of the loveliest women he had ever
known. Her long-sleeved gown was of pearl gray silk.

The flowers on her short veil and in her bouquet were delicate white lilies, culled from his own hothouse. At her throat she wore his bridal gift, a simple gold cross studded with sapphires to match her betrothal ring. A shaft of sunlight was captured in her hair, and each strand shimmered like a golden thread. Given the occasion, he shouldn't be having the thoughts that were beginning to crowd into his mind.

She was looking up at him, repeating her vows, her huge gray eyes fearful and questioning at the same time. In all the years he'd known her, he'd never been able to resist that look. It stirred something in the profoundest reaches of his psyche. That's how it had all started. It would have been better for him, better for them both, if he *had* paid attention to that look and the effect it had on him.

Jessica noted his serious expression, and her heart sank. If he was having second thoughts about their marriage, he was a tad too late. And she wasn't to blame. She'd given him plenty of chances to back out of it, and he'd pushed on. Well, they just had to make the best of it now.

She was good at making the best of things, as the mother superior had reminded her only yesterday. She'd awakened in the infirmary, the Reverend Mother told her, not knowing who she was or how she had got there. But by degrees, she'd made a new life for herself. It was the same in marriage. Every bride faced the same fears that she faced now. Her task was to create a new role for herself as Lucas's wife.

She gave a start of surprise when Lucas dipped his head and kissed her on the mouth. "Don't look so frightened, Lady Dundas," he whispered. "This is supposed to be a joyous occasion. Smile."

Sister Martha, and now Lady Dundas. Would she ever know who she truly was?

She smiled as the cleric pronounced them man and wife, and turned them to face the assembled guests.

• • •

During the reception that followed, Jessica did not betray how uncertain she felt. She had a role to play, and she played it as well as she could. It wasn't too difficult. Lucas's mother had rehearsed her well. It was a matter of pride to get the protocol right among so many people of rank. Everyone was kind and friendly . . . with three exceptions: Ellie, Perry and Bella. Ellie was sulking, Perry was in a temper, and Bella had turned into a green-eyed monster.

From the corner of her eye, she saw Ellie flounce out of the room. With a face like thunder, Perry went after her. Jessica sighed. It was very wearing having two unruly young people constantly underfoot, young people who wore their hearts on their sleeves. She was beginning to see just how tedious she must have been as an adolescent.

Her gaze shifted and came to rest on Bella. She was the center of a group of people, holding forth on some topic that obviously enthralled her little audience, but her eyes were avidly searching the room, pouncing on all its treasures.

It was ironic. At Hawkshill, when Bella's eagle eye had pounced on every flaw, she, Jessica, had been ashamed of the shabbiness of the place. Now, Bella's eyes were popping out of her head at everything she encountered—the priceless Titians on the walls, the Sevres porcelain, the Aubusson carpets and, most of all, the stately Corinthian columns and peerless Adam interior. She should feel vindicated, if not triumphant. But all she felt was pity. Bella had something that could not be bought, and she wasn't even aware of it. A husband who loved her. Rupert was by her side, a sad little smile on his face, as though he knew he could never be dashing enough for Bella's taste.

She couldn't help remembering that night in Haig House when Bella had attacked her. The more she'd thought of it, the more certain she'd become that it *was* Bella. She was so unnerved that when Lucas arrived the next morning and told her they were leaving that day for London, she would have promised him anything if he would just get her out of there. And he'd made it easy for her to save face. Their marriage would be on her terms, he'd promised.

I've never wanted a woman as much as I want you, he'd told her.

Want, not love. It was only as she watched Rupert with Bella that she began to see the difference. Lucas did not dote on her.

Conversations went on around her. She talked, she smiled, but her thoughts frequently strayed to Hawkshill and the last time she'd been there. Maybe she shouldn't have gone back, but she hadn't wanted the boys to think that she was deserting them. It had been a great trial all round. Joseph said that if they didn't stop their weeping and wailing, he'd be forced to build an ark, just like Noah. When she'd leaned out of the carriage window to wave goodbye, Joseph had said, quite seriously, for her ears only, "Three cheers for Jessica Hayward."

"Not Sister Martha?" she'd quizzed.

He shook his head. "I's putting my money on Jessica Hayward."

His parting words made her feel warm all over.

Someone made a remark about the house and she dragged her thoughts back from the past. It was a lovely house, she agreed, and looked around her. Though the interior was too rich for her taste, she could still admire it. Inside it was all Sienna marble and gilt-edged columns. Outside, it was a handsome neoclassical mansion. The house was in the heart of Mayfair, but the west windows overlooked Green Park, giving the impression that they were in the country—even with Piccadilly, the busiest thoroughfare in London, only a short walk away.

"Why so pensive?"

She looked up to see Lucas watching her. "I was admiring your house," she said.

Lucas gave a cursory glance around the room and grinned down at her. "It's a far cry from Hawkshill and your convent, isn't it, Jess?"

"That doesn't make it better, Lucas, only different."

The smile left his eyes. "Why the sharp tone, Jess? I thought you liked it here. It's what you told my mother."

"I do like it," she said. "But I was also happy where I was."

Realizing that she'd sounded critical, she started to explain, but was interrupted by other guests.

At one point, finding herself alone, she wandered into the dining room where an array of delicacies was set out on long tables covered in white damask. Crystal and silver glittered brilliantly under the lights from the chandeliers. The footmen were in their dress livery—powdered wigs, white satin breeches and silver coats. The orchestra on the platform was playing something measured and stately. There was much laughter, and voices rose to be heard above the music. Jessica thought her face would crack from so much smiling. Her head began to ache. She passed through an arch into the Crimson Room, and the first person she saw was Ellie.

She was silhouetted against the Venetian window, wearing a gown that Jessica considered far too old for her. It was a low-cut embroidered blue silk that showed a great expanse of white bosom. Her hair was heavily crimped and threaded with pearls. She was a pretty young girl, but she was trying hard to look older.

Jessica's first impulse was to slip away unseen. Ellie was all sweetness and light when Lucas was present, but when he wasn't, she didn't hide her dislike.

Her glance shifted to Ellie's companion who was looking right at her. It was Perry. There was no getting out of it now. She had to join them.

Her smile slipped a little at Perry's first words. "I hope you can talk some sense into her," he said in a low, driven tone. "She's been moping in corners all evening. People are beginning to notice."

Ellie's anger was equal to his. "Oh, why don't you mind your own business!"

"I am minding my own business. Lucas told me to look after you."

"I have a headache. That's all it is."

So had Jessica, and it wasn't getting any better. "Perry," she said, cutting off his next retort, "would you mind bringing me something to eat? A sandwich would do. I haven't eaten all day, and I'm famished."

"What?"

"A sandwich," she repeated. "Ellie, would you like something?"

Ellie held out her glass of strawberry cordial. "Yes," she said. "You can exchange this for a glass of champagne."

Perry grinned. "I'd have to answer to Lucas if I did. Drink your tonic, Ellie. It's good for growing children."

"Why you . . ." He was gone before Ellie could complete her sentence, and she turned her flashing eyes on Jessica. "I suppose you've come to gloat?"

Jessica was aware of the stares of people close by, and she said quietly, "I'm not gloating, Ellie. In fact, I feel rather awkward among these grand people. This is not exactly what I'm used to."

"No, but you'd like to become used to it, wouldn't you, Jessica? Well, you'll never fit in. You don't belong here. But I suppose you don't care now that you're a countess."

Jessica had been searching the crush of people for Lucas, and she saw him talking to Rupert and Adrian on the other side of the room. She had begun to raise her hand to attract his attention, but at Ellie's words, she stiffened and turned to face the younger girl.

"I didn't marry Lucas for his title."

"No, you married him for his money."

"That's not true."

"Isn't it? You have a peculiar way of showing it. But Lucas is no fool. He's on to you, too."

Jessica stared at her blankly. "I don't know what you mean."

"The clothes you ordered from Mrs. Marsh? I've watched the boxes arriving at the house all week. Lucas says that at this rate, you'll make him a pauper."

The quick tears that flooded Ellie's eyes took the edge off Jessica's annoyance. When she was Ellie's age, she'd made a fool of herself over Lucas, too. She wished, now, that she'd had an older sister or some female relative to put her straight about a few things.

"Ellie," she said quietly, "Lucas and I are married now. We exchanged vows. You must learn to accept it."

"He'll never love you," Ellie cried passionately. "He's been in love with Bella for years. She's everything that you can never be."

Jessica's sympathy was rapidly evaporating. "I don't want to be like Bella and neither should you. You're a lovely young woman. I don't know why you would want to be like someone else."

Enlightenment suddenly struck her. Ellie was trying to make herself over into the kind of woman Lucas could love. Her clothes, her hair, her mannerisms were all modeled on Bella. "Oh Ellie," she said, "don't throw away your most precious possession. Just be yourself."

Ellie appeared not to hear her. "Ask Lucas about his black spells. Ask anyone. They'll tell you that he's still not over Bella, and that's why he suffers from fits of depression."

Torn between the desire to box Ellie's ears and the need to avoid a public scene, Jessica said tersely, "Ellie, you're not yourself. Can't we discuss this later?"

"But you got him, didn't you, Jessica? And you didn't care how you did it. I don't believe for a minute that Rodney Stone wanted to marry you. I think you planned it together, to trap Lucas."

At least Ellie didn't know that Lucas had been discovered in her bed. That was something, she supposed, or Ellie might have broadcast it to the world. Still, her cheeks were burning. Everyone was looking at them, and Ellie was making no attempt to keep her voice down. Since she was Ellie's target, she decided that the thing to do was remove herself from the battle zone.

"Excuse me, Ellie," she said, "I have guests to attend to."

As she moved past Ellie, the girl fell against her and tipped her glass of cordial down the front of her gown.

Jessica looked down at the spreading stain on her beautiful bridal gown and her temper ignited. She reached for Ellie and caught her by the wrist. "You spiteful child." Her voice was low, but quivered with emotion. "You did that on purpose."

Ellie wrenched out of her grasp. "It was an accident," she cried out. She looked around wildly and saw Lucas coming toward her. Her voice rose shrilly. "It was an accident, Lucas, but Jessica won't believe me."

When Lucas came up to them, Ellie flung herself at him, and sobbed uncontrollably into his shoulder. His arms came around her in a protective gesture.

"It's all right, Ellie," he said soothingly. "Jessica knows it was an accident. Now say you're sorry and let that be the end of it." Then to Jessica, "What in blazes is going on here?"

Jessica was as cold as ice. "It wasn't an accident," she said. "She did it deliberately."

Lucas's gaze flicked to the gawking spectators, then narrowed on Jessica. "For God's sake, unfreeze your face. She's only a child. Ellie, apologize to Jessica."

Ellie turned tear-bright eyes on Jessica. "I'm sorry, Jessica, truly sorry. Please say you forgive me."

Jessica's voice did not warm. "If you're sorry, Ellie, then of course I forgive you."

Perry arrived carrying two plates of delicacies. He took

one look at Jessica's white face and set them on the nearest table. "What's going on?" he demanded. "I could hear Ellie's voice from the next room."

Ellie began to weep in earnest.

"My God, this is beginning to turn into a circus." Lucas spoke to Perry. "Take Jessica to her room, and when she's changed, see that she comes back to her guests. I'll take Ellie to my mother. Come along, Ellie." The harsh tone had softened. "So you ruined Jessica's dress. It's not the end of the world. I'll buy her another."

"No." Ellie's head was tucked into the crook of Lucas's shoulder as they walked away. "I'll replace it, out of my pin money."

Lucas's laugh wafted back to Jessica.

She was trembling from head to toe. She looked at Perry. "She did it on purpose," she said.

"You don't have to tell me," he replied. "What Ellie needs is a good shaking. But try and tell Lucas that."

His words helped relax the tight knot in the pit of her stomach. She managed a smile. "I think Lucas just gave us an order."

Perry chuckled. "It's one of the things he does really well. But you and I were never much good at obeying him."

"Things are different now."

His smile faded. "Yes. Very different. Whose fault is that?"

Before he could say more in this vein, she cut him off. "Shall we go?"

They used the servants' staircase to avoid curious eyes. Perry waited outside in the corridor while Jessica entered her room. It was less elaborately decorated than the rooms on the ground floor, but she still found it intimidating. Her few possessions had been moved into it only that morning, but it didn't feel like her room. In fact, she felt like an impostor in this grand setting.

Moving quickly, she crossed to her dressing room.

There was a bellpull for summoning the maid, but being waited on hand and foot was something Jessica was not accustomed to, and she began to undress herself.

Her fingers stilled when she looked into a cheval mirror and saw her reflection. The red stain fanned out from the bodice all the way down to the hem. It would fade when it was cleaned, but it would never be the same again.

I'll buy her another dress.

She didn't want another dress. She wanted *this* dress. It was her wedding dress. She would have packed it away and taken it out occasionally, perhaps to wear to a grand affair or perhaps for her own daughter's wedding, if she should be so lucky as to have a daughter. A sensitive man would have understood, but not Lucas.

Impatient with the tears that were threatening, she quickly stripped off her gown and went to the wardrobe to choose another. There were plenty to choose from. Gowns for every occasion and in every fabric—muslins, silks, sarcenets, and twills. Ellie was right about all the boxes that had been delivered to the house in the last week. But that wasn't her doing. The dressmaker had come to the house to take her measurements. Then Mrs. Marsh had conferred with Lucas's mother and this was the result. Most of her own garments had been donated to the Parish, to be distributed among the poor. Even her underthings had been replaced.

She fingered her chemise. Silk. The pleasure she had taken in prettying herself up for her wedding was now shattered by Ellie's outburst.

She reached for a lavender muslin and quickly donned it. As she turned to leave, her eye was caught by a splash of color. Neatly folded on the back of a chair was the patchwork quilt she had made in the convent. She snatched it up, marched into her bedchamber and spread it over the foot of her bed. At the door, she turned back to survey her room and her eyes were instantly drawn to the splash of color on her bed.

That was better. Jessica Hayward refused to be intimidated. One way or another, she'd make her mark on this house.

And on Lucas Wilde.

"What were you and Ellie quarreling about?"

Perry's question brought her chin up. "That's between Ellie and me," she said.

He kept pace with her as she descended the stairs. "Ah, so it was Lucas. Be careful of her, Jess. She's a jealous little cat, and unlike me, she doesn't know when to give up."

These little hints that he was enamored of her were beginning to get on her nerves, and she said crisply, "I would hate to lose your friendship, Perry, but unless you can speak to me like a brother, our friendship ends here and now."

She halted her descent and turned to face him. "And I would hate that to happen, because I have so few friends."

His black look gradually softened. "I am content to be your friend," he said.

She smiled. "Thank you, Perry."

As they continued down the stairs, she said, "Perry, what can you tell me about Lucas's black spells?"

He said darkly, "I suppose Ellie told you."

"So it is true."

"That's all in the past. Now that he's married, he'll change his ways." To her questioning look, he replied jokingly, "Not many married men I know go off carousing for weeks at a time. Their wives won't let them."

She didn't tell him he was telling her more than she knew. "I'm told he's nursing a broken heart." They had come to the half landing, and Jessica halted. "Well? Is it true?"

He looked away. "Lucas doesn't confide in me, Jess, but Adrian doesn't think so."

She was desperate to know more and that made her speak plainly. "Explain to me, Perry, the difference between loving a woman and wanting her."

Perry's cheeks went red. "We shouldn't be talking like this."

"Perry," she said, appealing to him, "I know nothing of men. You're my best friend. If you don't tell me, how shall I ever find out?"

He shifted from one foot to the other, but he couldn't resist that appealing look. "A man loves only one woman," he said, "but he can want many. You're the kind of woman a man loves, Jessica. The other kind, well, they're just a convenience, a means of slaking his thirst."

A frown puckered her brow. "Why am I the kind of woman a man loves?"

"Well, because you're the kind of woman a man respects."

"And a man doesn't respect the women who slake his thirst?"

"Not generally speaking. As I said, they're just a convenience." He dislodged his neckcloth as though it were too tight. "Did Ellie bring this on? I could wring her neck! No more questions, Jess. I've said enough as it is."

She reluctantly let the subject drop. "I shouldn't be too angry with Ellie," she said. "From all I've heard, I was very like her when I was her age."

He was relieved to change the subject. "Oh, you were dead set on Lucas, if that's what you mean—but the similarity doesn't go any further. From the day she was born, Ellie was spoiled. Her parents were older, and they doted on her. And when they died and she went to live with her brother and his wife, she ruled the roost there, too."

"Philip Bragge and his wife, Jane? And they died, too."

Jessica had heard the tragic story from Lucas's mother.

First, Ellie's sister-in-law, Jane Bragge, had drowned in a boating accident on the river Thames, and a few months later, Jane's husband, Philip, had died at Waterloo. He'd been Lucas's comrade and close friend. That's why Lucas had been named as Ellie's guardian.

"Then Ellie was foisted on Lucas," said Perry, "and—"

"Foisted!" she exclaimed. "Perry, that is unkind."

"Well, unkind or not, it's the truth." He looked at Jessica, and shrugged helplessly. "Maybe it was unkind. What I should have said was that Ellie chose Lucas to be her guardian."

"She *chose* him?"

"It was either him, Adrian or Rupert, because of their pact, you see."

"What pact?"

"Didn't you know? Before the battle, at Waterloo, they swore an oath that whoever survived would take care of the other's dependents. It's quite common among soldiers before a battle. And these four were close friends. Poor Philip was the only one who died."

"Ellie must have been desolate when that happened."

"Well, yes. But my point is that Lucas was there, and his mother, and they carried on the tradition of spoiling her. I mean, everyone feels sorry for her, and she makes the most of it."

There was something in what he said, but she knew from her experience with the sisters that orphans were desperately unsure of themselves. Sometimes it made them clinging, and sometimes it made them test the patience of a saint.

And she was no saint.

"And what about me, Perry," she said. "Was I spoiled, too?"

"In a way. You had more freedom to come and go than Ellie, more freedom than most girls."

"I wish I could remember those days," she said. "I wish . . ."

"What?"

"I wish I could remember my father. What was he like, Perry?"

He thought for a moment then shrugged. "You thought the world of him. That much I do remember. But—"

"But what?"

"Jess, I really can't remember. Much of the time, I was away at school."

She said lightly, "Perry, you're not going to hurt my feelings by telling me the truth. I know my father was a gambler and he drank too much. I know he wasn't well liked in Chalford. But that doesn't tell me what he was like as a father."

"I remember," he said carefully, "that whenever he returned from London, he brought you presents."

Her eyes lit up. "What kind of presents?"

He laughed. "Geegaws, trinkets, that sort of thing. Girls' stuff. Jane Hicks practically fainted when you told her that your father had bought you silk underthings. Oh, and there was a sapphire ring that you wore on a chain around your neck because it was too big for you. All the girls were green with envy, as you meant them to be."

This picture of herself delighted her, and she hugged herself as laughter bubbled up. "Oh, I can well believe it!" she exclaimed. "From what I've heard, I'd say I was a little monster when I was a child. I think my father must have been too lenient with me."

"He was certainly that. Leastways, that was my mother's opinion."

She nodded. "I suppose it was hard for him, bringing up a child on his own."

She stopped speaking when she realized what she was doing. She was just like the children in the orphanage, building her father up to be something he was not. But *her* father hadn't abandoned her. He might not have been the best of fathers, as Lucas said, but he wasn't all bad, either. He couldn't have been.

She smiled up at him. "I was a tomboy, you said."

He nodded. "The Hawkshill Hoyden, I called you, and you practically bashed my brains in."

"And did that stop you calling me names?"

He grinned. "I've got more gumption than that. I also called you 'Witch,' but that was no fun. It only made you cry like a girl."

She frowned. "Why did you call me a witch?"

He shrugged. "You used to play tricks on me, pretend you had second sight, that sort of thing."

"What kind of tricks?"

"Well, once, when my dog was lost, you told me where to find him, yes, and charged me a penny for the information."

Her heart was beating rapidly and she put a hand on the rail to steady herself. "That doesn't sound like a nice thing to do."

"No, it wasn't. After all, we were friends, yet you charged me the same as everybody else."

This was lighthearted banter on his part. Jessica was deadly serious, though she tried not to show it. "I charged people? What people?"

"Some of the neighborhood brats. Judge Hicks's daughter for one. She was at school with you, and, oh, I forget who all."

"I charged them for finding things they had lost?"

"Sometimes, but you also told fortunes, and that was your undoing. You told Phoebe Fulham that her grandfather was going to die, and he did. Oh, don't look so stricken. Everybody knew he was going to die except us children. Lucas said you probably overheard some grownups talking and used the knowledge to enhance your budding career as a soothsayer."

"A soothsayer," she said faintly.

"That was Lucas's word. We children just called you 'Witch.' "

"I suppose," she said carefully, "Lucas put an end to my career?"

"Well, of course he did. He was angry, but not half as angry as I was when he pointed out that you'd probably stolen my dog and locked him up in the Hendersons' barn just to get money out of me. I was ready to bash *your* brains in."

She laughed with him. "Why didn't you?"

"Oh, Lucas said he would deal with you. I don't know what he said, but I do know you paid everyone back. And that was the end of your career as a witch."

"I see."

She was very quiet as they descended the rest of the stairs. When they came to the door to the ground floor, she detained Perry by placing her hand on his sleeve. "Perry," she said, "I've been thinking about Rodney Stone."

"Rodney Stone! Good grief, what has brought this on?"

She hovered on the brink of telling him everything. He was her friend; he was kind; he had her best interests at heart, and she was so tired of keeping everything to herself.

"What is it, Jess? Why do you look like that?"

She hesitated to say the words because she was afraid that he wouldn't believe her, then everything would change between them. Perry was so uncomplicated, so down-to-earth. She didn't want him to think she was unhinged.

"Ellie mentioned him," she said, "and I've been thinking about him ever since."

"Ellie would! You mustn't blame yourself for what happened, Jess."

"Oh, I don't." Her eyes were very wide, very clear. "The more I think about it, the more convinced I am that

Mr. Stone was up to no good. For my own peace of mind, I have to know the truth. Will you help me, Perry?"

He shook his head, but when he saw her imploring expression, he gave a resigned sigh and said, "What is it you want me to do?"

"Find out all you can about him, who his friends are, that sort of thing. I think someone may have put him up to it, just to discredit me." When he began to shake his head again, she said desperately, "Perry, I have to know. The uncertainty is driving me mad. If I could, I would make inquiries myself. But that's impossible."

"But Lucas investigated Stone and found nothing to discredit him. Didn't you believe him?"

"Of course I did. But Lucas's investigation was superficial. I think Mr. Stone is hiding something, and I want to know what it is."

There was an interval of silence, then Perry said, "Lucas won't like it."

She inhaled a deep breath and let it out slowly. "Lucas must never know," she said.

Adrian pocketed the envelope Lucas had just handed him. "There's no need for this, you know," he said.

They had wandered out to the gardens to enjoy a quiet smoke, as many gentlemen had. They were a little apart from the others, standing by the iron rail that marked the boundary of Green Park.

"Of course there is," said Lucas. "Jessica is now my wife. I'm the one who should provide for her. It's my decision to turn Hawkshill over to the convent, so it's only right that I should pay for it. That bank draft cancels my debt to you. That's all."

"But the money for Hawkshill was never a loan. It was part of our pact to provide for Jessica. It was a debt of honor."

Lucas inhaled and blew out a plume of smoke. "I don't remember any pact," he said, "and neither does Rupert."

Adrian murmured, "Point taken. But before we leave this subject, there's something I want to say to you. Jessica was asking me some questions in there"—he nodded in the direction of the house—"about Philip and Jane Bragge."

"What of it?"

Adrian shrugged. "If she's still digging into the past, that could be very unpleasant for all of us."

Lucas shook his head. "You're forgetting that I was her prime suspect. She would hardly want to see me hang now that she's my wife. It's Ellie she is curious about, which is only natural."

Adrian grinned. "You never did tell me how you convinced Jessica to accept your proposal. I thought her mind was made up to refuse you, in spite of your being discovered in *flagrante delicto*."

Lucas scowled. "Perry told you that, I suppose?"

"Now don't look like that. I am his brother and he was brokenhearted. Who else would he confide in? No one else knows. And it's only calf love. He'll get over it."

"He's making a bloody spectacle of himself!"

Adrian drew on his cheroot then flicked the stub into the shrubbery. "He's only following in our footsteps." He clapped Lucas on the shoulder. "Don't you remember the widow Watkins? We were going to fight a duel over her until we found out Squire What's-his-name was bedding her. And we were heartbroken—"

"Adrian, we were only fourteen."

"—until Sally Mathers came along. In case you've forgotten, she was the blacksmith's wife, and we were both madly in love with her. We fought that one out with our fists."

Lucas chuckled. "Then her husband thrashed the living daylights out of both of us, and we were friends again."

"And when Bella came along, we fought about her, too."

Lucas propped one shoulder against the trunk of a tree. "What in Hades has brought this on?"

"Weddings always make me nostalgic," said Adrian soulfully. "Especially this one. With you down, I feel my days are numbered. We always did everything together. I suppose it's only a matter of time before someone bags me, too."

Lucas looked at him steadily. "What about your latest love, the one who is married?"

Adrian gestured with one hand. "Oh, that," he said airily. "That's old history. Didn't I tell you? I'm in love with Lady Caroline Howard. Off with the old, on with the new. That's my motto. But we were speaking of Perry."

"What about Perry?"

"Well, if he has to fall in love, I'm glad it's with someone like Jessica who'll let him down gently. But you never did answer my question."

"What question?"

"The one about Jessica. What made her change her mind about you?" He peered into Lucas's face then hooted with laughter.

"What?" said Lucas stiffly.

"You persuaded her with logic. Am I right?"

"What's wrong with that?"

"Oh, nothing," said Adrian. "If you don't know, I can't explain it. But if I were you . . ."

"What?"

"Try kisses, you idiot," and with another laugh, Adrian turned away and strolled toward the house.

CHAPTER
17

SHE WAS AT HER DRESSING TABLE AND HAD JUST FIN-ished braiding her hair when Lucas passed her door. She recognized his voice and the lighter tones of his valet. When she heard a door closing farther along the hall, she let out the breath she hadn't known she was holding.

This wasn't an ordinary wedding night, she reminded herself, and she and Lucas had said their good-nights some time ago, when the last of their guests had finally departed. Lucas's mother was there, as was Ellie, so she and Lucas hadn't exchanged more than a few words before he'd gone to check that the house was locked up for the night. Which was just as well. She hadn't wanted to talk to him. If he had even looked at her the wrong way, she would have snapped at him. That's what came of bottling everything up inside her and putting a good face on things.

She had unstoppered a bottle of perfume when she heard sounds coming from the dressing room, and her hand jerked. Quickly restoppering the bottle, she set it down and listened. Doors opened and closed, there was the murmur of voices then there was silence.

I've never wanted a woman as much as I want you.

She gave a teary sniff, stomped to her bed and threw off her negligee. The sheets were cool and smelled faintly of lemon. Propped against the pillows, arms folded, she contemplated her new domain.

She might as well douse the candles. Lucas wouldn't be coming to her, not if he possessed a particle of intelligence. A man did not snub his wife on her wedding day, then expect her to fall into his arms at night. Besides, he'd promised that she would be the one to decide when their marriage would become a real one. He must have known from the look she'd given him when she'd said good night that she'd as soon see him roast in hell.

She would never have had such wicked thoughts when she was a nun.

Another sniff. She wasn't being unreasonable, she told herself. Ellie had deliberately poured the glass of cordial over her bridal gown and Lucas had rewarded the girl by letting her absorb his attention for most of the evening. He should have known better than to neglect his own wife.

Who was she trying to fool? Ellie was only a small part of it. She'd been brooding on Perry's words all night long. *A man loves only one woman but he can want many.*

Well, now she knew exactly where she stood. She was a convenience, that's what she was.

That thought was revolving in her mind when the door to the dressing room opened and Lucas entered. He was wearing a dark maroon robe, belted at the waist, but what caught Jessica's eye was the bottle of wine in one hand and the two glasses in the other. The second thing she noticed was the big smile on his face.

The smile was definitely a mistake. It made her feel like a cat that had been rubbed the wrong way.

As he crossed the room to the fireplace and deposited

the glasses on a small mahogany table, she rose and donned her silk negligee, then belted it tightly. "I understood this was my room," she said.

He filled the glasses with wine. "It is your room."

"I don't remember inviting you into it."

He raised a glass to his lips and took a sip of wine. "A husband has every right to enter his wife's room, Jess," he said gently. "Will you join me?" He held out a glass of wine.

Her hand went out to accept the glass before she remembered how cross she was. She snatched her hand back. "We have an agreement, Lucas, and I'm holding you to it."

A wicked gleam lit up Lucas's eyes. "Now what made you think that I wouldn't abide by our agreement?" He held up his glass of wine. "Did you think I would ply you with wine to have my wicked way with you? Jess, Jess," he admonished softly, and chuckled. "The wine isn't really for you. It's for the servants. In the morning, when they find two glasses here, they'll think that ours is a normal marriage. Otherwise, they're bound to talk, and that could be unpleasant."

That took the wind out of her sails. "Oh."

He studied her face. "I'm sorry about Ellie," he said. "I'm sorry that she ruined your gown."

And that deflated them even more. "You're sorry?"

He nodded.

"She did it on purpose, Lucas."

He shifted restlessly. "I know. But you have to understand how it is with her. She looks upon me . . . well . . . as a father figure. Jess, put yourself in her shoes. She's just a child. She lost both her parents, then her brother and his wife. It was a terrible shock to her when they all died. I've tried to make it up to her, but she still grieves for them. She resents you, of course, because she's afraid you will displace her, and she'll lose me, too. She'll get over it in time. Give her a chance, Jess."

Put like this, she began to feel guilty for resenting Ellie, but it didn't really change things.

She shook her head. "I feel sorry for her, Lucas, really I do. But I don't think you're helping by letting her get away with things."

He took her hand and patted it. "It's not such a tragedy, Jess. It's only a gown. You have plenty of others."

She snatched her hand away. "That's not the point. And it was my *wedding* gown." He was beginning to look worried, and that pleased her immensely. "My *wedding gown,* Lucas."

"I'll replace it."

"For your information," she said, "a wedding gown cannot be replaced."

"What's your point, Jess?"

In sheer frustration, she swung away from him, then swung back as something else occurred to her. "And what do you mean by telling Ellie that I would make you a pauper?"

"What?"

"Don't deny it. You told her I had ordered so many gowns, I would make you a pauper."

"It was a joke. And I was talking to my mother, you know, after she handed me all the bills for the garments she'd ordered. Ellie must have misunderstood."

Had Ellie misunderstood? It was possible, she supposed. "I don't know anything about adolescent girls," she said, "but—"

"But?"

"I was thinking about our convent boys. They need love, yes, but they also need discipline."

"Jess," he chided, "this isn't an orphanage. Ellie is a member of the family. I promised her brother that if anything happened to him, I would take care of her."

She said, "Yes, you had some kind of pact with your friends, didn't you? That you'd all take care of her . . . Perry told me."

His eyes went blank. "We were comrades. It was a promise we made to each other, not just to Philip. Are you suggesting that I palm Ellie off on Adrian or Rupert?"

"No!" she exclaimed. "That never entered my mind. That would be cruel."

"I'm glad you see it that way." He hesitated. "If you would only try to make a friend of her, I'm sure things would sort themselves out."

She tried to imagine herself making a friend of Ellie and she just couldn't see it. Until she got over her infatuation for Lucas, Ellie would always regard her as her enemy.

Lucas didn't really understand the problem. He thought Ellie saw him as a father figure. And he saw Ellie as a child. It was almost like history repeating itself, with Ellie taking her place, and herself taking Bella's.

The thought startled her, then made her shudder. She didn't want Ellie to dislike her as much as she had disliked Bella. There must be something she could do to win the girl over. But what? Sister Elvira, she thought. That's what she would do. She would write to Sister Elvira and ask her advice.

She let out a sigh. "I'll try," she said, "but don't get your hopes up."

"That's all I ask, Jess, that you'll try."

His smile could have melted a heart of stone, and where Lucas was concerned, her heart was already fragile. Suddenly, the trials of the last few hours became too much for her—Perry's words of wisdom, Ellie's spite, doubts about her Voice and Rodney Stone, and now her role as Lucas's wife. She just wanted to be alone.

She said crisply, "And now, if you don't mind, Lucas, I'd like to go to bed."

He grinned, and his eyes glinted wickedly. "Is this another hint, Jess? Are you offering to share my bed?"

She gasped. "I only meant—" She saw the twinkle in

his eyes and she ground her teeth together. "My mind doesn't work like yours, Lucas."

She turned her back on him, marched to the bed and flung herself down. "When I think of a bed, I think of sleep."

He set his glass on the table and wandered over to the bed. She strained away when he bent over her. Laughter lurked in his eyes. "Jess, it wouldn't matter what I said. I think you've got you-know-what on the brain right now."

She gave a disbelieving snort.

He laughed in sheer masculine enjoyment. "I'll prove it to you," he said. "What comes to mind when you think of a kitchen table?"

He was playing with her. Is this how married couples behaved? "A kitchen table?" she said. "That's easy. I think of—"

The image that flashed into her mind sent a wave of heat surging through her. She was breathing rapidly, remembering how she'd felt when he'd practically taken her on the kitchen table at Hawkshill. His powerful body had covered hers, the press of his weight pinning her to the table. And she had wanted it. He'd made her want it, just as he was making her want it now.

She looked up at him, and she knew he was reading her correctly. His expression was wiped clean of all amusement. There was a stillness about him; his features had hardened, his eyes had darkened. The strong pulse at his throat started an answering beat in her own body.

When his hand brushed her thigh, she let out a startled shriek, dodged away and came up on her feet. She had to say something, anything to break the charged atmosphere between them. "Chopping vegetables," she cried out.

He blinked slowly. "What?"

"When I think of a kitchen table, I think of chopping vegetables."

His lips twitched. "I didn't know nuns told lies. Shame on you, Jess."

She backed up a step, not because he'd moved, but because she felt overwhelmed by him. She was acutely aware of the strength and maleness of him, and the heat that seemed to radiate from his body to hers. He wanted her to be aware. She could see it in his eyes.

She had to put a stop to this. "What is it you want, Lucas?"

He lowered his head to hers. "Just a good-night kiss, Jess," he said, his voice husky. "Is that too much for a man to ask his wife on his wedding night?"

The light from the candle cast an intimate glow, warming her skin, opening her senses. She heard the soft rasp of his breathing, and her own breath caught. But it was his eyes that held her, eyes as dark as midnight, and just as dangerous. When his head dipped again, she moaned.

His firm, sensual lips curved in a faint smile. "It's only a kiss, Jess," he whispered.

His mouth touched hers, not threatening her, but in a tentative caress. Her stomach tightened and her knees went weak. She put her hands against his chest to push him away, and the rapid beat of his heart sent the blood pounding through her veins.

He took the kiss deeper, opening her mouth to the intimate possession of his tongue. She felt him tug the ribbon tying her braid back, then his hands combed through her hair, loosening it till it fell freely about her shoulders. She was aware, but only vaguely, that the logical part of her brain was telling her that she didn't want this. Her instincts were surer, stronger, and they were telling her the opposite.

Without breaking the kiss, he curved his fingers around her hand, slipped it inside the edges of his robe and pressed it to his bare chest. Warm masculine flesh and muscle quivered beneath the pads of her fingers. He shifted slightly, and his weight bore her back against the wall. She felt the hard thrust of his hips pressing against her and the last vestiges of her fears and reservations were submerged in a flood of pleasure.

Lucas pulled back and gazed down at her. Eyes as gray and misty as the North Sea gazed back at him. She wanted him as much as he wanted her.

He shook his head as he strove to gain control of himself. He had a reason for being here, but this wasn't it. He couldn't remember, not when his body was as hard as iron and urging him to take her. He had to slow down; he had to think. When he inhaled a long, calming breath, sanity gradually returned.

After his conversation with Adrian, he'd made up his mind that he wasn't going to be a stranger in his wife's bedroom. He didn't really want Jessica to lay down all the rules between them. But how had it come to this? He had flattened her against the wall, and even now he couldn't stop rubbing his bulging groin against her soft woman's flesh.

It had gone too far; he didn't know if he could let her go now. But if he didn't, there would be hell to pay in the morning.

With a resigned sigh, he straightened, but before he could step back, Jessica hooked one arm around his neck and arched her body into his.

"Jess?" he said on a strangled murmur.

When she made a soft sound of arousal, he kissed her. He kissed her brows, her cheeks, her ears, and her husky voice saying his name made him wild to have her. His hand spread out on the small of her back, arching her hips, and he rhythmically ground himself into her. He undid her negligee and filled his hands with the weight of her breasts. He crushed her to him and she molded herself to his hard length. At each small surrender, his passion soared.

When he lowered her to the bed, he wasn't thinking of the wisdom of what he was doing. This was the woman he'd wanted for more years than he cared to remember. It had always been Jess with him. He'd been too blind to see it. So many years to make up for. He would never let her go again.

He was positioning himself to take her when the doorknob rattled and someone knocked on the door. Lucas groaned, and raised his head. His breathing was labored, as was Jessica's. She blinked slowly as she came to herself.

"Jessica!" Ellie's voice, as clear as a bell, came to them from the other side of the door. "I know you're still up. I can see the light under your door."

Lucas swore under his breath.

Dazed, Jessica looked around her, then she gave a gasp of horror. She was on the bed, flat on her back, her feet touching the floor, and Lucas was planted between her thighs. She could feel his hard shaft pressing against her. Her only protection was the thin folds of her nightgown. Beneath his robe, he was naked.

He stifled a laugh. "Don't wriggle! For God's sake, don't wriggle, or I won't answer for the consequences."

"Jessica!" Ellie again. "Open the door. I want to talk to you."

Lucas chuckled. Jessica's face flamed scarlet. She moaned and shut her eyes.

Another voice joined Ellie's, Lucas's mother's. Her words were too low to be clear, but her tone was unmistakably sharp.

"But Aunt Rosemary, I only wanted to apologize to Jessica."

The voices receded, then there was silence.

Lucas was watching Jessica's face. "You can wriggle as much as you like now," he said.

She slammed her hands into his chest. It was like trying to move a brick wall. When he saw that she was serious, he frowned and rolled from her.

"Now what's wrong?" he asked moodily. Unsated desire was riding him hard. He'd been only a moment away from burying himself in her warm, willing body, and he didn't understand why they couldn't go back to where they'd left off.

Her voice was shaking. "I'm holding you to your promise, Lucas."

"My promise?" he demanded incredulously. "My promise? After what we just did?"

Wavering between tears of mortification and a strong desire to run and hide herself, she swallowed hard and nodded. She was awed; she was horrified. She had practically begged him to take her. She had practically forced herself on him. If Ellie hadn't knocked on the door, it would have been too late. Then she would be no more than a convenience to him. She wasn't asking for his love, but by all the saints, she would have his respect.

He made a vicious swipe with one hand. "To hell with my promise! I want you. And you were willing, more than willing. It's as simple as that."

No mention of love, she noticed. Not that she expected it. Not that she wanted it. She stuck her chin out. "Obviously, it's not as simple as that for me."

He glared at her. "It could be, if you'd only let yourself forget that you're a—"

"What?" she goaded dangerously when he hesitated.

He didn't want to quarrel with her, he wanted to go to bed with her. "A nun," he said mildly. "That's what I was going to say."

Her voice shook. "A dried-up stick of a nun is what you meant."

"Oh, for God's sake!"

"Mind your language!"

His frustration boiled over. "If you'd only come to bed with me, we wouldn't be having this stupid quarrel."

She ground her teeth together. "Bed! Is that all you can think about?"

"Yes," he yelled, making her jump. "And if you had a grain of honesty in you, you'd admit it's all you can think about, too."

Her lips were still burning from his kisses; her pulse was still hammering. He was telling the truth and she knew it, but nothing on God's earth was going to drag it out of her. "You don't know what I want," she said, trying to sound confident, wincing at the pathetic wobble in her voice.

"I do know," he said. "Oh, not from your words, Jess. Words can say anything. But your body doesn't lie to me."

His gaze dropped to her breasts. She felt a peculiar tightening where his eyes lingered and she looked down. The soft material of her negligee was stretched taut, and the tips of her breasts, like two plump strawberries, were straining at the seams.

"Yes," he said, and his voice was dark with raw sensuality. "Your breasts are begging for my mouth, and I want to take them."

She made a soft whimpering sound and folded her arms across her chest.

Lucas studied her for a long while and all his frustrations gradually seeped away. Her huge, expressive eyes were fear-bright and fixed on his face; her mouth trembled, her throat worked. He could see that he had made quite an impression on her, but not enough to overcome her virginal scruples, or whatever the hell it was that made her reluctant to surrender herself to him.

"It's going to come down to it sooner or later," he said.

She bit down on her lip.

He smiled grimly. "I'm not going to break my promise to you, but I'm not going to keep my hands off you, either. Not after this. That is asking too much."

No response from her.

He sighed. "Drink the wine," he said, "it will help you get to sleep. Good night, Jessica." And pushing past her, he made a leisurely exit.

Once he was in his own chamber, he poured himself a small measure of brandy and drank it back in two gulps. His heart was still pounding; his body was still primed to take her. He didn't know why women had to make everything so complicated.

When he started to pour another drink, he realized what he was doing and set his empty glass down with a thunk. Jess was the only woman who had ever driven him to drink.

He thought about the mother superior then thought about Adrian and he shook his head. Moments later, grinning ruefully, he poured himself another measure of brandy and began to sip it slowly.

It was her own panicked cry that awakened her. She lay there trembling, her heart racing, the blood pounding at all her pulse points. Realizing she'd been dreaming, she sobbed in relief and hauled herself up.

She'd been dreaming about a children's game, a game that had turned into a nightmare. In a few minutes, the dream would recede and she would go back to sleep.

But the dream didn't recede. It was still vividly etched in her mind, and she could not shake herself free of it. Resigned, she threw back the covers and swung her legs over the edge of the bed.

The room was almost in total darkness except for a sliver of pale light at one edge of the curtains. She didn't bother trying to use the tinderbox to light a candle. It was just too difficult and time-consuming. Rising, she went to the curtains and opened them.

Her windows looked out on Green Park, and though the darkness was edged with a predawn haze, everything was blurred. Only the lights of Buckingham House on the far side of the park stood out clearly.

She rubbed her neck to ease the knot of tension that had gathered there. She'd followed Lucas's advice; she'd drunk some of the wine before going to bed, and she wondered if that could be responsible for her nightmare. Even as the thought occurred to her, she discarded it.

Wine made people happy or it made them sick. It didn't leave them with a lingering sense of unease.

It wasn't unease. It was more dire than that. *Dread* was the word that came to her.

She found her negligee, slipped it on, and took a chair by the window. There was no point in going back to bed. She knew she wouldn't get a wink of sleep until she'd tried to sort through what she was feeling.

Her dream had started out well enough. They were all on the front lawn of Hawkshill, she and the sisters and the children, and they were playing a game, oranges and lemons. Everyone was laughing and talking at once, then the scene shifted suddenly. Hawkshill became a church and the children and nuns faded away. There was a big stone cross, *her* cross, in front of the church, and they played their game around it. But the players had all changed, and so had the words of the nursery rhyme.

One down and two to go, they chanted.

Lucas and Bella had joined hands to form the bridge, and everyone skipped under their joined hands. When she passed under the bridge, their arms descended, trying to catch her. She jumped away and when she looked back, she saw that they had caught Rodney Stone instead. Rodney Stone was led away, and the game started over.

She was panic-stricken. She knew this wasn't a game. The people who were caught out really would have their heads chopped off. She cried out for them to stop, then went tearing after Rodney Stone, through the church door and into the dark interior. There was no sign of him, but she saw a set of stone steps going down into the bowels of the earth. And she realized she was in her own tomb.

Then they came for her, all the guests who had been at her wedding. "Who is next, Sister Martha?" they chanted. "Who is next? Who is next?"

She jumped to her feet. "Oh God, no!" She wasn't aware she had spoken aloud. "Oh God, no!"

This wasn't her dream. It was her Voice's dream. And

she knew what it meant. Either her Voice had already murdered Rodney Stone, or he was planning to do it.

She stared blindly out the window as she summoned all her powers of reason to deny what her intuition told her. Lucas and Bella—that was Ellie's doing. She'd made them sound like a couple, and that's how they had appeared in her dream. As for Rodney Stone, she'd been thinking about him incessantly. And there was nothing sinister about the others. She'd seen them all earlier at her own wedding.

It was logical, but it did not convince her.

She took the chair again and stared into space. She hadn't heard her Voice in some time, and never quite like this. Maybe it wasn't her Voice. Maybe it was her own dream.

"Voice?" she whispered, opening her mind to him. "Voice?"

There was nothing there but a void.

CHAPTER
18

JESSICA PARTED THE MUSLIN DRAPES AND LOOKED down on the front courtyard. The carriage was waiting to drive Lucas's mother and Ellie to a musicale at Lady Bowes's house in Manchester Square. At the last minute, she had pleaded a headache. She had a different kind of engagement in mind tonight, a secret engagement.

She'd chosen her moment with care. Lucas wasn't here. He and some of his friends had gone out to Twickenham to take in a prizefight, and he wasn't expected home till the wee hours of the morning. She was glad he was gone. Lucas's eyes were too sharp. He wouldn't have been fooled by her headache, and might have suggested staying home to keep her company. Then she could never have kept her appointment with Perry.

There was flurry of activity below. As Mrs. Wilde and Ellie descended the front steps, a footman hurried to the carriage and held the door for them. Mrs. Wilde was first to enter. Ellie was right behind her, and with Ellie was a page, dressed in the Dundas livery. This was Pip, the ringleader of the boys at Hawkshill, and Sister Elvira's answer to the letter Jessica had sent her. The girl needed something outside herself to focus on, said Sister Elvira, and the experience would be good for Pip, too. The odd thing was, Pip and Ellie had taken to each other right away. And now, Ellie had taken Pip under her wing and had made his welfare her personal concern.

Ellie was no longer the sullen, willful child she had been, but she still hadn't warmed to Jessica. In fact, sometimes Ellie could be downright nasty.

Jessica was thinking about this when Ellie suddenly turned and looked up at the house. Jessica let the drape fall and took a quick step back, but not before she had seen the smile spread over Ellie's face. It was almost as though Ellie knew what she was up to.

She couldn't know. She and Perry had been very careful to make their plans during a walk in Green Park, when there was no one there to hear them. It was just her guilty conscience.

When the carriage drove through the front gates onto St. James's Place, Jessica let out an audible breath, turned on her heel and made for her own chamber on the other side of the house. She had another two hours to while away before darkness fell and she could keep her appointment with Perry. She cursed the long summer evenings that seemed to go on forever.

She was pacing when the knock came at her door. Her first guilty thought was that Lucas had returned early. She dived into the bed and hauled the covers up to her chin before calling out a wavering "Enter." It was only one of the maids with a supper tray for the "invalid." Jessica thanked her and after she had gone sat on the edge of the bed and looked at the clock.

Would the time never pass?

She looked at the supper tray on the table beside the bed. The aroma of something savory filled her nostrils. She was sure she couldn't eat a thing for nerves, but she lifted the silver lid that covered the plate just the same. Cook had outdone herself. Thinly sliced beefsteak in a spicy wine sauce, tiny roast potatoes and buttered Brussels sprouts sprinkled with almonds were all artfully laid out to tempt her appetite. And for dessert, her favorite, fruit trifle and cream.

Her stomach churned, reminding her that she had hardly had a bite all day. She'd been too keyed up. She drew a chair to the table, seated herself, picked up a fork and began to eat.

At Lady Bowes's musicale in Manchester Square, the guests were idling their way in to supper. There were fewer young men at this function than at balls, a fact that Ellie was loudly lamenting to her chaperon, Mrs. Wilde. They were filling their plates from side tables in the spacious formal dining room.

"Young men have odd notions about music," said Mrs. Wilde. "They think it's unmanly—especially with a prize-fight so nearby. Poor Hetty chose the wrong date for her party."

Her brows rose when she saw what Ellie was putting on her plate. "Strawberry ice?" she said. "I thought you hated ices."

Ellie dimpled. "It's for Pip," she said. "I promised him that if he could go for a whole week without saying any swear words, I would reward him. This is his reward."

Mrs. Wilde smiled as she watched Ellie go off to find her page. Since Pip had joined their household, her ward had become a far happier girl. The smile faded. But not, she had to admit, when Ellie was with Jessica. Ellie was jealous and there was more to it than her schoolgirl infatuation for Lucas. She'd always been the center of attention. Now her nose was out of joint, and she took it out on Jessica.

She blamed herself. She'd been so pleased when Ellie had come to live with them. Lucas no longer needed her;

Ellie had given her a new direction. She'd been the daughter she'd always wanted. She'd spoiled her and it was almost impossible to change the rules on her now.

Out of the corner of her eye, she saw Sir Matthew Paige enter the room. Noting that his head was turned away, she allowed herself one quick, comprehensive glance before looking down at her plate.

She didn't think there was a man alive who could match him for presence. There never had been and there never would be. He had an air about him, something vital and purposeful that he'd possessed even when he was a young man.

She chose a vacant spot at one end of the long dining table. Without haste, he made his way over to her and took the chair next to hers.

"Smile," he said, "or people will begin to wonder about us."

She smiled. "People are already wondering about us, Matt."

And her most of all. She'd thought they'd settled everything between them, but every time she turned around or looked up, he was there. And their eyes would meet and hold, and her spirits would lift.

Not again. Dear Lord, not again.

He looked up, arrested. "Who, for instance?"

"My daughter-in-law, Jessica. She's been asking questions about you. So has Ellie. Wherever we go, you are there also. Matt, you must stop singling me out like this. You know nothing can come of it."

"I know nothing of the sort," he retorted.

Her heart thundered against her breast, and she gripped her cutlery to stop her fingers trembling. It wasn't only his words that affected her, but the look he'd given her when he'd said them. Only Matt could seduce a woman with a look.

"Has your son said anything?" he asked briskly.

"No," she said. "Lucas has said nothing. Why do you ask?"

"I thought he might have warned you off, ordered you to stay away from me."

"Why would he? He knows there's no need. We are nothing to each other, Matt. Not now."

For a while, they ate in silence, then he said in a conversational tone, "Do you ever think about the future, Rodie, and what you have to look forward to?"

She didn't know how she managed to laugh, but she did. "I live in the present, Matt. I have my family and friends. I don't have time to think about the future."

"Your son is married now," he said. "He doesn't need you."

"There's my ward."

"I thought Ellie was your son's ward?"

"She needs a mother." Another laugh that cost her dearly. "And, God willing, there may be grandchildren soon."

"And you're going to devote the rest of your life to your family?"

"Isn't it enough?"

He shrugged carelessly. "You'll be living your life on the periphery of theirs. Don't you want something for yourself?"

"I'm happy as I am. Truly. In fact, many people would say my life is enviable. I have everything I want."

If she told any more lies, she was sure she would choke on them. Desperate now, she looked for some way of escape. There was none. Ellie was with a party of friends and they were carrying their plates into the next room. No one looked her way, or caught her eye. She had to search to find her poise.

Looking up, she said, "Matt, why don't you stop fencing with me and tell me what you really want."

He looked at her for a long moment, then nodded. "I want you," he said simply. "I still love you, you see, and I think you love me. We're free to marry now, and that's what I think we should do."

His words shocked her, but they also thrilled her. It was a long time before she said anything. "Matt, it's been fifteen years. Love dies."

He was looking at his glass of wine. "Mine didn't. Did yours?"

She couldn't force the words out. A yearning coiled deep inside her and spread to every cell in her body. He made her wish for things she knew she could never have.

He gave her a searching look and smiled. "I'm not suggesting that you give anything up, Rodie. How can our being together change what you have with your family? I want to give you things, not take them from you. We could tour the Continent, go to Florence, Rome, Paris— all the places we planned to visit when we were younger. Don't you remember?"

She remembered. Oh God, how she remembered. Sated with passion, they would lie entwined in each other's arms and make plans for the future. How could they have been so naïve?

Her own despair was forgotten when she looked into his eyes, beautiful, sad eyes, crystal blue and very, very fragile. She recognized the same vulnerabilities in him that were in her. She didn't want to hurt him, but she had to put an end to this.

"It's not me you love, Matt. It's the girl I used to be. That girl no longer exists. Look at me. Really look at me."

She knew what she was talking about. Ever since their conversation at Bella's ill-fated ball, she'd taken to studying her reflection, naked, before going to bed, and the sight hardly bolstered her confidence. He'd had a string of young, nubile mistresses over the years. And she was old.

His eyes crinkled at the corners. "Your beauty hasn't dimmed," he said. "It has matured and I find it much more interesting than when you were a girl."

"Matt, I'm not young anymore."

"Neither am I."

"I'm a . . ."—she hated to say the word—"a dowager, for pity's sake. I've heard the gossip about you and your mistresses, your lightskirts, your *affaires*. You could never be satisfied with me. If you want a companion on your tour, take Madaleina Cartier. I'm not saying this to hurt you. It's the truth and you know it."

"And what," he said, "shall my mistress and I talk about?"

"What?"

"If I take Madaleina to Florence, what shall we talk about?"

She didn't understand his question and shook her head.

"Rodie, I'm bored out of my mind with the younger generation. We've nothing in common, nothing to talk about. And mistresses have no conversation worth mentioning. You and I always had plenty to say to each other."

A flash of the old Rodie surfaced. She laughed. "That's not how I remember it."

He grinned. "That, too."

Somehow, all the awkwardness between them had slipped away, and she said easily, "We must have been mad not to know that what we did would hurt others."

"My wife never knew," he said, "and if she had, she wouldn't have cared. She didn't love me, Rodie. Even before she became an invalid, we were estranged. You know all this."

She looked beyond him for a moment, remembering. That's what had drawn them together in the first place. They'd been lonely, and feeling sorry for themselves. But he had less to feel guilty about than she, for her husband had always been kind to her, more like a father really.

"You never told me how it was for you," he said. "I received your note telling me you never wanted to see me again. And that was all. What happened afterward?"

"Does it matter now?"

"It does to me."

It did to her, too, but it was shattering to go back over old ground. These were the most painful memories of her life.

"What happened," she said, "was that I came to my senses. I realized that I was wrong in thinking I wasn't hurting anyone by . . ." She shook her head, not sure how to complete the sentence.

"Your son," he said, not without bitterness, "made you choose between him and me."

"Matt," she chided gently, "it wasn't that simple. You were still married. And I had a young son to consider. His welfare meant more to me than anything in the world."

"And those circumstances no longer apply." He gave her a moment to think about his words, then he smiled into her troubled eyes. "I'm not going to hurt you, Rodie. I'm going to court you. There's plenty of time to make up our minds about the future. Let's not try to overcome obstacles before we come to them."

When he left her, she felt the lack of his presence as though a light had gone out. It didn't matter, she told herself. She'd get used to it, as she'd got used to it once before. And she still had a son who meant more to her than anything in the world.

But in her heart, a spark of hope had been ignited.

Jessica saw the signal from her bedroom window. Perry had taken the lantern off the back porch and was waving it back and forth. She held her candle to the window, indicating that she had received his message. She had to wait another five minutes before setting off, to give him time to hail a hackney and have it ready. They had planned this business down to the last detail. Even their clothes were plain and serviceable so as not to attract attention to themselves.

The hackney was waiting for her in St. James's Place. Around the corner was St. James's Street where many of the exclusive gentlemen's clubs were and, as a precaution, Jessica was wearing a veiled bonnet. Perry opened the coach door, stretched out his hand and hauled her in. Then, sticking his head out the window, he gave the cab driver the directions to Rodney Stone's rooms in Drury Lane, just off the Strand.

"Did anyone see you leave the house?" he asked.

"No one," she assured him. "By eleven o'clock, most of the servants are in bed, and I slipped out a side door."

They lapsed into silence as the hackney turned the corner into Pall Mall, then Perry said, "I hate deceiving Lucas like this. What if he finds out we've sneaked off together? Can you imagine what he'll think?"

With more confidence than she was feeling, she said, "He won't find out, and if he does, he won't think anything. I'll tell him the truth."

Perry laughed, not very pleasantly. "Oh yes, the truth," he said. "And I'm sure he'll believe you. How did I ever let you talk me into this? We're housebreakers, that's what we are. Do you know what the authorities do to housebreakers? They transport them to the colonies."

"So we'll be careful not to get caught."

"But what if we *are* caught?"

"Then we'll tell them that we're acquainted with Rodney Stone and were worried when none of his friends could tell us where to find him."

"And so we broke into his house to look for his aunt's direction?"

She nodded. It was the truth—more or less. Rodney Stone had disappeared without a trace. Perry had done an excellent job of sleuthing and had discovered that Mr. Stone's London friends thought he was in Brighton and his Brighton friends thought he was in London. If he had disappeared, they said, it was probably because he had got into debt again and was lying low until his aunt bailed him out. But no one had ever met this aunt or could tell Perry where to find her.

She wanted to believe that everything was that simple.

When the hackney turned into Drury Lane, Perry pulled on the string and the coach rolled to a stop. He paid off the cab driver and with a hand on Jessica's elbow steered her in the direction of Water Street.

"Was it wise to pay off the cab?" she asked.

"This is the theater district," he answered. "There'll be plenty of cabs when we're done." He halted, and shook his head. "I must be mad. This is just like when we were children. You were always leading me astray."

Her eyes glinted with merriment. "Was I?" she said.

"Go on and laugh." His smile took the sting out of his words. "But as I remember, I was the one who got all the beatings." His tone altered. "Did you bring a tinderbox to light a candle?"

She patted her reticule. "Yes, but I'm not very good with it."

"Neither am I."

"Did you bring the jemmy?"

"The what?"

"The crowbar."

Perry patted his coat. "Right here."

"Then we're all set."

Rodney Stone's lodgings were on the ground floor. Perry knew his way around, since he'd been there that morning to look the place over. There was a landlady, a Tartar of a woman, he'd told Jessica, who wouldn't let him in the front door. Her rooms were right above Mr. Stone's, so they would have to keep very quiet.

Jessica kept watch while Perry used the crowbar to force one of the windows. That was the easy part. The difficult part was once they were inside, getting a flame started in Jessica's tinderbox so they could light a candle. After several minutes of fruitless striking flint to iron, in sheer desperation, Jessica tried the door to the hallway. There was a light shining under it, so she knew a lantern or candles were still lit. The door was locked but Perry finally managed to open it with one of Jessica's hairpins. After making sure no one was there, she took a lighted candle from a wall sconce and returned to Mr. Stone's rooms. It took only a moment to light the candles on the table, and another moment to replace the candle she had borrowed.

"My respect for housebreakers," said Perry, "has just gone up by several notches. I don't know how they do it."

"Hush," said Jessica. She was at the window, making sure the curtains were securely drawn.

She pointed to a chair, then to the door, and Perry obediently braced the back of the chair under the door handle. "That ought to stop them for all of two seconds," he muttered.

"Shh!" said Jessica.

She had her back to the window and was looking around the room. Her first impression was that though it was shabby, it was as neat as a new pin. There was very little furniture—a stuffed armchair by the grate, a small dining table with two chairs, a sideboard, and a bureau desk. There was no means of cooking which meant that Stone dined out a great deal or sent out to the various cook shops in the area and had his dinner sent over. Her second impression was that the place had not been lived in for many weeks. There was a dank, musty odor that cast a pall over everything. She brushed her finger along the table and left a trail like the wake of a ship.

As Perry began to open the bureau drawers, she took one of the candles and entered the bedchamber. Shadows flickered and danced on the wall. After closing the curtains, she turned and surveyed the tiny room. The bed was built into an alcove, giving a little more floor space. The only other furniture was an elaborate washstand with glass jars and bottles scattered over it, just like a lady's dressing table; a chair, and a great mahogany wardrobe-dresser.

She crossed to the wardrobe and opened the doors. Every shelf was stacked with garments—coats of every color, white lawn shirts, waistcoats, pantaloons, and white satin breeches. Her heart was beginning to race and she didn't know why. She shut the doors and opened one of the drawers underneath. Spanking fresh neckcloths smelling faintly of starch took up most of the space. There was also a pile of white lawn handkerchiefs embroidered with Mr. Stone's initials.

She stretched out a hand to touch them and quickly drew back. The fine hairs on the back of her neck were standing on end; her throat began to close up; there was a roaring in her ears. She forced herself to go on with it and, before she could change her mind, quickly pressed her hand to one monogrammed handkerchief. And she was instantly swept into her dream.

She saw a church and her wedding guests playing a game in the shadow of a cross. They caught Rodney Stone and led him off.

"No!" she said. "No!" And with a cry of panic, she turned and ran.

There was no one in the other room, but the door stood open. "Perry?" she quavered. "Perry?"

Silence.

She blew out her candle, threw it down on the table and ran through the door. Perry was sitting on the floor, slumped over. She took a step toward him, then another. Strong arms suddenly wrapped around her and her scream was cut off by someone's hand. A surge of pure terror galvanized Jessica and she fought with the ferocity of a captured wildcat. Her attacker was stronger, and he got hold of her in an armlock, subduing her struggles with pressure across her chest.

The man holding her yelled out, "I got the other blighter, Jack. In 'ere."

Perry was groaning as he slowly came to himself. He

rubbed the back of his head. A red-faced beefy man came through the front door. He had a cosh in his hand.

"Bow Street runners," said Perry, blinking up at Jessica. "I told you this would happen."

The constables took them to the Bow Street office for questioning, where they were locked up in separate cells to await the pleasure of the magistrate on duty. Nobody believed their story, nobody believed they were people of quality. The runners had been lying in wait for them all along, having been alerted by the landlady who had suspected something like this might happen when Perry had come to look the place over that morning. They weren't even dressed like people of quality, the constable said, but in plain, shabby garments. No. They were housebreakers, caught in the act, and all their protests fell on deaf ears.

Their luck changed when the magistrate finally condescended to see them. He recognized Perry as an old school chum of one of his sons. Perry played up the connection for all it was worth. He also played up his "friendship" with Rodney Stone, making him out to be another old school chum about whom they'd been worried. Not only did the magistrate let them go, but he also promised to investigate Rodney Stone's disappearance.

One of the runners had hailed a hackney for them. When they were sitting inside it, Perry finally spoke. "Don't look so upset, Jessica. I know we've been gone for three hours, but Lucas will never find out. You won't see him till breakfast, if then. That sporting crowd always spends the night carousing. I'd wager they're all as drunk as lords right this minute, and snoring their heads off. I just wish I were with them."

She hadn't been thinking about Lucas but about Mr. Stone, and the awful feeling that had come over her when she'd touched his handkerchief. The one good thing that had come out of all this was that the magistrate was going to look into Stone's disappearance.

"Did you find anything in Stone's desk?" she asked.

"Nothing, and that's what's so interesting," he said. "He's cleared everything out of it. Looks like he left in a hurry."

She thought about the rooms that were as neat as a new pin and the garments that were stacked in order in Stone's wardrobe. "If he'd left in a hurry," she said, "things would have been in a mess, and they weren't. Everything was in its place."

"Hmm. So what does that mean?"

"I don't know," she said. "I don't know."

When they arrived home, Perry walked her to the side entrance which led to the servants' quarters in the basement, and took his leave.

Though she knew the servants would be asleep now, her heart began to race as she climbed the servants' staircase. When she opened the door into the corridor, she paused to make sure the coast was clear. A few steps took her to her own chamber.

As soon as she closed the door, she went as limp as a rag. She was back in her own room and Lucas didn't ever have to know what had happened. Almost at once, she stiffened. The candles were still lit, and she was perfectly sure that she had doused them before going to meet Perry. She'd wanted everyone to think that she was asleep and must not be disturbed.

Her glance darted around the room, then flew to the dressing-room door. Under her horrified gaze, the handle turned and the door slowly opened. Lucas stood on the threshold. He had removed his coat, but apart from that he was fully dressed.

And his expression was dangerously calm.

A T FIRST, SHE JUST GAPED, THEN, COMING TO HER-
self, she made a lightning decision. The best form of
defense was attack. Squaring her shoulders, she made a
great show of removing her outer things and throwing
them over the back of a chair. "You told me," she said,
"not to expect you back till the wee hours of the morning."

"And I was told," he answered in a voice that was all
the more menacing for being polite, "that you were not at
the musicale because you were at home nursing a headache."

"You were at the musicale?"

He smiled unpleasantly. "I left a message with Ellie to
pass on to you. Didn't she tell you? I decided that as soon
as the fight was over, I'd look in at Lady Bowes's. After
all, I'm a newly married man. My friends would think it
odd if I did not make a few concessions to my bride."

She missed the sarcastic reference to his bride because
her mind had fastened on Ellie. She was remembering

Ellie's smile as she'd looked up at the house before entering the carriage. Ellie must have guessed she was up to something and had hoped Lucas would find her out. As he had.

"No, she didn't tell me," she said.

"No doubt she did not want to disturb you when you were indisposed."

"How like Ellie," she said sweetly, "to be concerned for my welfare."

"Yes, isn't it," he agreed amicably. "Do you know that Perry was indisposed, too?"

"Perry?" she quavered.

He nodded. "He wasn't at the fight because he had a . . . now what was it? . . . a cold, I believe he told Adrian. Quite a coincidence, wouldn't you agree, both you and Perry indisposed on the same evening?"

All this pleasantness was making her more nervous than she already was. She moistened her lips. "Coincidences do happen, you know."

He suddenly roared at her, making her jump. "Don't lie to me! You were with Perry tonight. So no more lies and no more evasions. I've seen the way he looks at you and follows you with his eyes. I want the truth, Jessica, and I want it now. What have you and Perry been up to?"

"The way his eyes . . . ?" Her teeth snapped together. "I hope you're not suggesting what I think you're suggesting!"

"You tell me."

He threw the words down like a gauntlet and she lost no time in picking it up. Her fears and guilt for having deceived him were swallowed up by a stronger emotion. Outrage. Her teeth were still clenched; her eyes snapped. She ground out, "Only a filthy mind like yours could believe that Perry and I are capable of such a thing."

He stared at her long and hard. His eyes were the first to break away. Swinging away from her, he raked his fingers through his hair. "Bloody hell, what am I supposed to think? Every time I turn around, yes, even in my own house, I'm falling over the young cub."

"He's my friend," she cried out, "*and* your cousin. Adrian is here, too, but I don't hear you complain about him."

"I'm not complaining." Frustration roughened his voice. "It's just that—"

"What?" she demanded when he hesitated.

He swung back to face her. "You shouldn't encourage him. Perry is young and susceptible."

She gasped. "I don't encourage him. I don't encourage any man!"

"And that's another thing. This situation between us is unnatural. If we had a normal marriage, Perry wouldn't be a problem."

"How can Perry be a problem?"

"You know what I mean. I don't know where I am with you. You won't let me come near you."

"You come to my room every night."

"Yes, and read a book while you mend and sew for your cursed convent boys."

"And we talk. I thought that was the point, that we should get to know each other better."

He said angrily, "I know what I said, but what I meant was . . ." He shook his head. "That's not what's important right now. What I want to know is where you and Perry were tonight, and what you were doing."

He was still angry but she no longer felt threatened by him. Apparently he'd decided there was nothing between her and Perry after all. She wanted to stay angry with him but she couldn't. After everything she'd been through, she wanted someone to talk to. And he looked so capable and solid, like a rock that nothing could erode. Just looking at him made her feel better.

She gave a teary sniff. "This has been one of the worst nights of my life," she said, "at least the life I remember.

Oh Lucas, for the last three hours, Perry and I have been locked up in Bow Street." She sat on the edge of the bed and looked tearfully up at him. "We were terrified that we would be transported to the colonies and our friends would never know what had happened to us."

"In Bow Street! For three hours! You and Perry?"

She nodded and sniffed again.

There was a long, baffled silence, then he began to laugh. He stopped when he saw the look of reproach in her eyes. Going down on his haunches, he took her hands in his. "My poor darling! How awful for you both. I'll have my attorneys sue those damn magistrates for wrongful arrest. If anyone has hurt you or insulted you, they'll pay for it."

His words acted on her like balm on a festering sore. "It wasn't that bad," she allowed. "The magistrate on duty recognized Perry and finally let us go."

He was frowning. "They must have arrested you for something."

She gulped. "They said we were housebreakers."

"Housebreakers? What made them think that?"

"They caught us breaking into Rodney Stone's house."

He dropped her hands and stood up. "What were you doing there?"

"We were trying to find Mr. Stone. We were looking for some clue to his whereabouts."

"Why?"

She spoke quickly, eagerly. "Do you know that no one knows where he is? The last his friends saw of him was before he set off for Chalford—you know, to attend Bella's ball. He hasn't been back to his lodgings in town. Don't you think that's odd?"

"No. Stone told me that he was going straight from Chalford to Brighton."

"But that's just it. His Brighton friends haven't seen him, either. Lucas, I'm afraid something bad has happened to him."

"Nonsense! I spoke to his aunt. She told me that he was deep in debt and she was letting him stew this time before helping him out. Obviously he's gone into hiding to escape his creditors."

"You met this aunt?" she asked incredulously. "When?"

"When you were recovering from your fall. What difference does it make?"

"What? Oh, Perry and I were beginning to doubt she existed. How did you find her?"

"Stone's landlady gave me her direction. Why?"

"She told Perry—"

"What?"

"It doesn't matter. Obviously, she didn't trust Perry. It was she who called in the runners."

"Would you mind telling me what the hell this is all about?"

She came off the bed because he was towering over her and that made her feel at a disadvantage. "What this means," she said, and she spoke quickly before she could change her mind, "is that I'm still not convinced that Rodney Stone is as innocent as you seem to think. No! You listen to me, Lucas Wilde! It all fits together, don't you see? He was in debt. Someone paid or offered to pay him a great deal of money to abduct me. And now Rodney Stone has disappeared."

"For the love of God!" He swung away from her and walked to the fireplace.

She went after him. "His rooms haven't been lived in for weeks," she said. "But his clothes are all there. Only his desk has been cleared out." Everything was beginning to fall into place in her mind. "Do you know what I think, Lucas? I think someone else cleared out his desk, someone who didn't want us to find an incriminating letter or message."

He said roughly, "I might believe you if you could give

me one good reason why anyone would wish to abduct you."

"Isn't it obvious? Because I was asking questions about my father's murder. The murderer must have wanted to frighten me off. Maybe I was getting too close."

"Don't tell me you're back to that again!"

"It's the only explanation that fits."

He lowered his head till they were practically nose to nose. "You're still trying to find out who murdered your father. That's what this is all about, isn't it?"

"Yes," she hissed.

There was a heartbeat of silence, then he said in a frighteningly soft tone, "Am I still a suspect, Jess? *Am* I?"

"If I thought you were the murderer, I wouldn't be here, now would I?"

"Then whom do you suspect?"

Their voices had dropped to a whisper, and a feeling of eeriness crept over her. He was as still as a sculpture. Only his eyes were alive, and they were watching her with an intensity that she could not hold. She stepped away from him.

"I suspect no one and I suspect everyone," she said. "But whoever did it must have had motive and opportunity."

He laughed harshly. "That's what you said about me once."

"You weren't the only one at the Black Swan that night."

"There must have been at least twenty other people who witnessed my fight with your father. Do you suspect all of them?"

"I wasn't thinking of them."

"Then who were you thinking of?"

"Adrian, Rupert, I don't know. You had dinner with them that night. And they left just before my father arrived. One of them could have done it."

She could see it in her mind's eye. They would have

seen her father enter the Black Swan and one of them could easily have taken up a position on the bridle path, lying in wait for him."

"That's preposterous. Do you know who you're talking about? These men are my friends—Adrian and Rupert. We went to school together and through the war together. I know them. And I'm telling you that neither of them could have murdered your father."

Put like that it did seem preposterous. She liked Rupert and Adrian, and she couldn't see them doing something so heinous.

People were such fools. They looked at him and saw exactly what he wanted them to see. No one had ever suspected him of murder.

"Jessica," he said, "these are honorable men. They would never have shot your father in the back, even if they had a motive for killing him."

She gave him a sharp look. "Maybe not, but I think you know more than you're telling me. What are you keeping from me?"

"God, this is insane! What could I be keeping from you?"

She was as intense as he. "I don't know, but I'm going to find out. Who are you protecting, Lucas?"

"Do you never listen?" His teeth were clenched and his hands had balled into fists. "The only person I'm protecting is you! You had the motive and opportunity. Isn't that what you're looking for? Then look no further than yourself."

"What motive?" she scoffed. "Everyone knows I thought the world of my father. He may not have been easy to get along with, but he was devoted to me and I to him. Everyone says so. I would never have done anything to hurt him. Tell me about this motive that was so compelling that I murdered my father. There isn't one, Lucas, and you know it!"

"Your admirable father," he said savagely, "wanted to

sell you into sexual bondage. He was going to auction you off as though you were a slave. Jess, your father would have sold you to the highest bidder to line his pockets."

She shook her head. "No," she whispered. "I don't believe you."

"You didn't know your father, Jess. You thought he was going to take you to London to help him run a gaming house. You begged me to help you and I promised you I would. But it was worse than that. What you didn't know was that he planned to sell you. There was going to be an auction . . ."

Memories too painful to contemplate swam at the border of her mind, but she didn't want to know them. "Liar!" she screamed and flung herself away from him.

He halted her flight by grabbing her shoulders, and she lashed out with her open palm. She would have hit him again if he had not captured her in his arms and held her flush against his body. But nothing could subdue the ferocity of emotions his words had stirred up.

"Liar!" she sobbed. "Liar!"

"Jess, Jess," he murmured soothingly. "Hush now. Stop this. Darling, you'll hurt yourself."

His soothing words only enraged her more, and her struggles to free herself became wilder. When she sank her teeth into his shoulder, he jerked himself free, then half carried, half dragged her to the bed. Forcing her down, he came down on top of her. The press of his weight succeeded at last in controlling her struggles, but it didn't make her soften toward him.

Between sobs and moans, she got out, "You wanted to hurt me. That's why you're saying all this. It isn't true. I know it isn't true. My father loved me. He loved me. That's why he kept me with him. He must have loved me. He must have."

His face was parchment white and his eyes were almost black. "I should never have told you. I never meant to. I may have been mistaken. I can't remember now. It was so long ago. Jess, Jess, don't take on so. Love, please! It doesn't matter now. After all this time, it can't possibly matter."

Though she knew he meant to comfort her, ~~each word~~ pierced her heart like a barbed hook. It must be true, or he would not be trying to take back his words. And it was all there in his face for her to read—guilt, remorse, anxiety, helplessness. He was sorry, now, that he had said so much.

It was true, then. Her father would have sold her to the highest bidder. She shouldn't be so shocked. The same thing had happened to some of their orphanage children, until they'd been rescued by the good Sisters of Charity.

His lips touched her forehead and she jerked herself away. "Don't touch me!" she cried, then a keening cry of despair tore from her throat, and she turned her face into the pillow, away from him, and wept.

She didn't know how long she had lain there, facedown on her bed like a broken doll. She heard him moving around the room and she heaved herself up. There was a large white handkerchief crumpled in her hand. She couldn't remember how it had got there, but she used it to mop her cheeks and blow her nose.

He was standing on the hearth, sipping what looked like brandy from a crystal glass, watching her over the rim, as though he were the mouse and she was the cat. It made a change.

"You can relax, Lucas," she said. "I've done all the crying I'm going to do. Now I want answers."

"Jess, it's late—"

"You started this."

He heaved his shoulders in a gesture of resignation and sat at the foot of the bed. "I'm sorry I shocked you like that," he said. "And you must know that I don't believe for one moment you murdered your father. That was said in anger."

She'd lost interest in finding out who had murdered her father, at least for the moment. It was her father she wanted to know about. And herself. "Tell me about the auction."

"I only know what your father told me. It was going to take place in London. I knew it had to be soon, because it was no secret that your father was drowning in debt."

"Who else knew about it?"

"No one else knew. If it had become known in Chalford, your father would have been strung up on the nearest post. No one liked him, Jess."

"Except me," she said bitterly. "How much money was involved?"

"I don't know. But I do know that your father thought that marriage to me was a catastrophe. I was only a poor soldier then. There would have been no marriage settlement to pay off his debts or money to set him up in style. He was angry when he entered the Black Swan, and crazy with anger when I . . ." He trailed to a halt.

She said coldly, "When you refused to marry me?"

"Jess, I had already asked Bella to marry me just a few hours before. I couldn't back out of it, not then. And I was angry with you for setting your father on me. You had lied, of course. You'd told him that you were no longer a virgin." He hesitated, then went on. "*Damaged goods* were the words I believe he used. It wasn't true, Jess."

"Don't worry, Lucas. You're not hurting my feelings. I want to understand my father, that's all. You came to see me that day. Tell me what happened."

"I came to see your father that morning, but I found you instead. I was angry with your father, violently angry, because of what Adrian had told me. You had become a recluse. You never went anywhere, never did anything. You had no friends. And your father didn't care. He had become an inveterate gambler and a drunkard and Hawkshill was going to ruin."

"No wonder you didn't want me to go to Bella's ball!" she said bitterly. "You were afraid everyone would cut me dead."

"That's not true. The people of Chalford have accepted you, Jess. They like you."

"Because of you! What I can't understand is why you cared, then or now."

"Why do you think?" he retorted. "Because there was always more between us than I was willing to admit."

She wasn't interested in what had once been between them. He had hurt her, and she thought she would never forgive him for doing it deliberately. "Just tell me what happened when you found me."

He looked at her for a moment then looked down at the glass in his hands. "You told me you were going to London with your father, that he would open a gaming house and you would be its drawing card. I wasn't really listening, not then. I didn't realize you were asking for my help. All I could think was that you would be a gaming-house wench and no better than the barmaids at the Black Swan." He shook his head and smiled in self-derision. "You have no idea what that did to me, Jess. I can only explain it by saying I went a little mad. I forgot about honor. I forgot about Bella. I . . ."

He took a long swallow of brandy before continuing. "I'm not proud of what happened next. But I frightened you, and that brought me to my senses. Then I listened to you. Unlike you, I could easily believe the worst of your father, and I was determined to get you away from Hawkshill. My mother was in London and I was going to send you there until I could think what to do about you."

"And I agreed?"

"I wasn't going to give you a choice."

"I begged you to marry me, didn't I?"

A muscle tensed in his jaw. "Yes."

It didn't matter, she told herself. It didn't matter. "Then what happened?"

"I went to see Bella late that afternoon."

She drew her knees up to her chin and hugged them to her. "And you proposed to her?"

Another derisory smile. "Yes. You told me how it would be, that I would come to regret it, but I wouldn't listen. It didn't take me long to discover that you were right. I'll never forget sitting in her drawing room like an ice sculpture, after she had accepted me, wondering why I felt so cold."

"Then you had dinner with your friends at the Black Swan. Where was my father that day?"

"He was in Oxford, I believe, selling the last of his stock. Jess, your father was always in debt."

"Tell me what happened when my father found you."

He sighed. "He found me alone and sat down beside me. He'd been drinking. At first, I couldn't make sense of what he was saying. I'd ruined all his grand plans, he said. Then he blurted it out. There were men in London who could buy and sell me ten times over, and they would pay handsomely to get you, as long as you were a virgin. Now that you were damaged goods . . . Jess, I think I've said enough."

There was a dull pain where her heart should have been. "The question is," she said, "did I hate my father enough to murder him?"

"I don't care if you did murder him," he said fiercely.

"So you think I did it?"

The anger went out of his eyes. "No, Jess. You could never kill anyone. You'd finally had your eyes opened. But in spite of what I said earlier, I don't think you hated your father even then. I think you would have forgiven him anything. You were always making excuses for him."

Something else occurred to her. "I could never have found work as a governess or a companion, could I, Lucas? I wasn't respectable enough. That's why I stayed with my father. What else could I do?" She bit down on her lip, and he reached for her.

"Jess—"

She jerked away from him and got to her feet. After wandering aimlessly around the room, she stopped at the window and drew back the curtains. Her eye was caught by her sapphire betrothal ring. "I once had a sapphire ring that I wore around my neck, didn't I, Lucas?" When he was silent, she turned to face him.

"You remember about the ring?" he said.

"No, Perry told me. Tell me about it."

"It was your mother's," he said, "and the only thing that you had of hers. It was your most precious possession."

"Did I lose it?"

"Why do you say that?"

"I remember, or I think I remember, coming to the Black Swan to find you to tell you about it."

He nodded. "You were distraught. And I promised to buy you another sapphire ring when I made my fortune. It didn't help. You didn't want another ring. Nothing could replace your mother's ring."

She said with sudden insight, "I didn't lose it. My father took it away from me and sold it. Didn't he?"

"I . . . I can't say for sure. It's possible."

"Tell me the truth. I have a right to know."

"Yes. He sold it, and gambled the money away. I found out he'd sold it to Lady Radford. You won't remember her. When she died last year, I bought the ring from the estate."

She looked down at her ring. "Are you telling me that this is my mother's ring?" she asked incredulously.

"Yes," he said simply.

Sudden tears stung her eyes and she turned her back on him. Any normal woman, she told herself, would be touched by his gesture. And she was touched, but she also felt horribly ashamed, and she couldn't explain it.

When she was sure she had control of her voice, she

said, "I tried to make everyone believe that my father spoiled me, but you never thought so, did you, Lucas?"

"No, I never thought so. It's what you wanted to believe, Jess, and you tried to make others believe it, too. He was a selfish man. Brutal in many ways. I never understood how he could have fathered a daughter like you. But you would never hear a word against him."

She gave a brittle laugh. "I'm much wiser now, you'll be happy to hear. I should have known how it was from my work with our children. You've no idea how much children will endure and still remain passionately loyal to parents whom you and I would consider loathsome."

"I understand," he said quietly.

She turned to face him. "You understand? *You understand?*" Her eyes were raw with pain. "You understand nothing! What do you know of a child's hunger for love? You were born to parents who loved you. You grew up anticipating everyone would like and admire you. And they do. You're the most popular man in Chalford. Ask the constable. Ask your attorney." Her breathing was becoming irregular and it punctuated each word as she tried to articulate her thoughts. "Just to see you at a ball is a real pleasure. Everyone should have so many friends. Don't tell me you understand, Lucas Wilde, because you could never understand what loneliness is."

He set aside his glass and came off the bed.

She went on. "Yes, I wanted to have someone in my life who once loved me and thought I was special. You have legions. Is one person too many to ask for myself?"

When her voice cracked, he started toward her.

"Don't think I'm wallowing in self-pity! It's not me I'm thinking about but the child I used to be. I've cried often enough for our orphanage children, so why shouldn't I cry for her?"

He had taken her in his arms, but she strained away from him. "What was wrong with me that no one could love me, not even my own father? Was I too wicked? What?"

She was ashamed of the tears that were streaming down her face and when he drew her close, she tried to push him away, but he wouldn't allow it. "Don't pity me," she cried out. "Don't you dare pity me!"

He cradled her in his arms, ignoring her feeble resistance, pressing chaste kisses to whatever part of her face she turned away from him. "You foolish girl," he murmured, "not to know what is staring you in the face. No, don't fight me, listen to me. You were never alone. *I* thought you were special. You don't know because you can't remember. Why do you think I was so enraged when I heard that you would become mistress of a gaming house?"

"You loved Bella," she cried. "It was always Bella with you."

He gave her a gentle shake. "Was it? I wanted it to be Bella. But when I was soldiering in Spain, it was your image that haunted me. No other woman's. I need hardly tell you that I was appalled. You were little more than a child, so I told myself. I had an understanding with Bella. I couldn't get out of marrying her. That would have been dishonorable. And I thought that what I felt for you would pass."

Startled, she stared up at him. "Dishonorable? That's an odd word to use."

"Not to me. It's how my father raised me. The only way I could get out of marrying Bella was if she released me from my promise. If things hadn't turned out the way they did, I would have asked her to break our engagement. Oh, I admit, I went a little crazy when you sent your father after me, but I would have come around to it soon enough. I needed time to come to terms with the fact that you were all grown-up, that it was no longer a sin to think of you the way I'd been thinking of you."

He paused, searching her face. "If you wanted to punish me, you succeeded. These last three years have been sheer hell without you. I've had bouts of despair, 'black spells' my friends call them, because I could not bear wondering what had become of you. I knew what would happen when I saw you again at Hawkshill. You're special to me, Jess. I'll never let you go. Don't you know that yet?"

She shook her head. "You married me because you were forced to."

"That merely hastened my plans. I would have asked you to marry me sooner or later. You're mine, Jess. Mine."

A lump formed in her throat and she swallowed.

He nodded. "And now that I've found you again, I'll never let you go." His voice turned husky. "You were never afraid to take chances, Jess. Take a chance now. Take a chance on me."

His fingers fanned across her cheeks and he cupped her face. His mouth brushed hers lightly, then with more pressure, parting her lips. Her lids grew heavy. She closed her eyes and leaned into him.

CHAPTER
20

H E'D MADE UP HIS MIND THAT WHEN THIS WAS OVER, she was going to know just how special she was. He ached for her, but there was more to it than pity. He was beset by a confusion of emotions. She was right about him. His life had always been easy. Though he'd been a soldier and had had his share of hardship and sorrow, he'd never known real loneliness. He couldn't begin to understand what Jess must have endured both then and now.

His lips grazed hers. When she opened her mouth to him, her taste and flavor spread over his tongue then raced like wildfire straight to his loins. Every muscle in his body contracted then expanded. He felt as though he were carved from iron. Breathing became difficult.

"Oh Jesus," he groaned, breaking the kiss, "this isn't what I want for you. I know, I know . . . I shouldn't blaspheme," and he took her lips again.

He didn't know why she was smiling. He was shaking. This was important. He didn't want to frighten her, or do anything to spoil it for her. And he would spoil it if he didn't get a hold of himself. He held on to that thought and gradually found his balance.

When she drew away, there was a question in her eyes. "You're different," she said.

His voice, though hoarse, held the hint of a smile. "Yes, I know."

"Why?"

"Because this is different. You're different." He shrugged helplessly, groping for words. "I thought I knew everything there was to know about making love with a woman, but with you, I feel like an untried youth. You're important to me, Jess, and I want this to be perfect for you. I've made mistakes with you, serious mistakes. I won't make them again."

When her brows lifted slowly, it occurred to him that he'd just made an unforgivable gaffe. A man didn't go to bed with one woman and raise the shades of his past loves.

Her eyes dropped away and she fingered his shirt. "You didn't act like an untried youth at Hawkshill when you practically took me on the kitchen table," she said.

He shifted uneasily. "I wish you would forget about that. As I told you, I've made mistakes with you, but I won't repeat them."

"Or when you flattened me against my kitchen wall, yes, with the sisters and children upstairs, and gave me a lesson in masculine anatomy. Lucas, that was very wicked."

Color crept into his cheeks. "I wish you would forget about that, too."

"Or," she went on persistently, "on our wedding night, when I was saved from a fate worse than death only because Ellie came to my door and interrupted you."

"Jess," he protested, then stopped. Her eyes were sparkling with mischief and her lips were twitching. It was a look that reminded him of the old Jess. "What?" he demanded.

"Lucas," she said, "you can't know how many times I have cursed Ellie for coming to my door precisely at that moment, or how often I've thought about that kitchen table and the anatomy lesson, and burned to know your touch again."

She was so much like the Jess he remembered—saucy, teasing him—that he did no more than stand there and stare.

She looped her arms around his neck and smiled into his eyes. "Lucas Wilde," she said, "don't be different or I won't know you. Just be yourself."

"Jess," he said softly. She was coming back to him. The old Jess was still there, just below the surface, and she was coming back to him. With a great whoop of laughter, he swung her into his arms and carried her to the bed. When he sprawled beside her with a foolish grin on his face, just drinking in the sight of her, he thought she might turn shy on him, but she didn't. Eyes locked on his, she began to undo the tiny buttons on her bodice.

"This seems familiar to me," she said. "I can't believe that this is my first time. I—" Her eyes dropped to the buttons she was undoing and her fingers stilled.

"What is it, Jess?"

She looked up at him with a frown in her eyes. "Lucas, tell me the truth. Were you and I ever lovers?"

"Not guilty! No, I swear it, Jess."

She looked down at her buttons and undid one, then another. When she stopped, her fingers were trembling. He saw the quick rise and fall of her breasts.

"Now what have I said?"

Her hand fluttered to her throat and she said in a shaken whisper, "I've done this before. I know I have."

He frowned. "Done what?"

She gulped. "I've been with a man."

"How could you have been with a man? It's impossible."

"You thought so once, didn't you? You came to Hawkshill and thought me no better than the maids at the Black Swan. That's what you told me."

"That's not what I said! I said that you would *become* no better than the barmaids at the Black Swan. In the future!"

"That doesn't prove anything!"

He threw up a hand in sheer frustration. "I can't believe the change in you. A minute ago, you were ready to fall into my arms. Now you're as cold as ice."

"A minute ago, I didn't have this horrid suspicion that I'd done this before."

He shook his head. "If that were the case, your father wouldn't have been so angry the night we quarreled."

"You mean the night you refused to marry me."

"He said I'd ruined you for other men. That's why he was so angry. If I'd already had you, you'd lost your value."

When she winced, he reached for her, but she twisted away from him and came off the bed. He went after her. He put a hand on her shoulder but she shook it off.

"What if," she said, turning to face him, "my father knew I wasn't a virgin and tried to palm me off on you? That's the kind of man he was, wasn't he?"

"Jess, don't torture yourself like this."

She said in an anguished whisper, "Where was I, Lucas, the night I ran away? Who was I with? How did I get to London?"

"I don't know, Jess. And I don't care."

"What if I was with some man? What if I couldn't help it?"

He writhed inside to even contemplate such a thing. In as calm a tone as he could manage, he said, "I'd kill any man who hurt you. But it wouldn't change anything. It would only matter to me if it mattered to you."

"What if I'd been willing? Would you mind then?"

"Jess," he said, "I'm not exactly without experience myself. Do you mind?"

"Yes," she said vehemently.

He smiled at this, a genuine smile. "Look," he said, "this is a new beginning for both of us. Whatever was in the past is over and done with. Let it go, Jess. Don't let it hurt you." He held out his arms. "Now, come here and let me love my wife."

Her eyes went wide. "Of course," she said. "You'll know whether I'm a virgin, won't you, Lucas? And I'll know, too."

"So?"

She said quickly, "I don't want to know."

"What!"

"I don't want to know."

"Jess, this is ridiculous. I've told you, I don't care one way or another, and neither should you."

She stared at him blindly for a long interval, then turned away with a little shake of her head. A terrible dread gripped her. Maybe there was more to her lurid past than Lucas guessed. Now that her illusions about her father had been shattered, anything seemed possible. She'd had a few illusions about herself, too. She didn't know if she was ready to face the truth about herself, not yet.

He could tell that she was hardly aware of his presence. She was sitting on the edge of the bed, lost in thought, and not happy thoughts either if her hands were anything to go by. She was wringing the bedspread as if she were a washerwoman.

He had to put a stop to this.

"You'll never be at peace," he said, "until you know the truth."

Startled by the sound of his voice, she looked up. He was unbuttoning his shirt. "Lucas, no," she said.

He ignored her interruption. "Or maybe it's me. Maybe I'm not the man you want."

Her lips flattened. "You know better than that. What are you doing?"

"I'm going to show you how foolish your fears are."

She watched in a kind of awed alarm as he stripped off his shirt and tossed it on the floor. Muscles bunched in his powerful arms and chest; skintight black trousers were molded to his long, muscular legs. He didn't look like the Lucas she knew. This man was too intimidating. She sucked in a breath when he came down on the bed beside her.

He exerted a slight pressure, bearing her backward. Her eyes jerked up to meet his. His look was searching, grave and, at the same time, reassuring. Her heart slowed a little as the tension seeped out of her. He was the same Lucas she knew after all.

"Don't look so stricken, Jess." He fingered her hair, pushing back stray tendrils from her face. "I'm your first and only lover, and I'm going to prove it to you."

Anxiety began to beat in her. She wasn't the girl he thought she was and soon he would know it. And in spite of what he said, she didn't believe it wouldn't matter to him. Look how it mattered to her.

While she lay there staring up at him, he began to undo the buttons on her bodice. When the backs of his fingers brushed against her breasts, he could feel her heart race in response, see the pulse that leapt in her throat. But panic moved in her eyes, the panic of a cornered wild thing, and he cupped her neck with one hand to prevent her from taking flight.

He smiled when she began to babble some nonsense about wanting to see a doctor to verify whether she'd ever been with a man. That they should delay this. That he hadn't thought it through. That she wasn't the girl he thought she was. That this was all wrong. That he would change toward her.

He stopped the rush of words by sealing her lips with a kiss. He held her still by pinning her with one leg thrown over hers. Ignoring her struggles, he began to court her with easy, casual touches, brushing his hand in slow, lingering caresses from breast to waist to thigh. He tasted desire on her lips, but he also tasted the underlying fear. Shifting slightly, he came down on top of her.

The heat of his body overwhelmed her, and still she felt numbingly cold. Pictures were forming in her mind. She wanted her hands on him. She wanted his hands on her. She wanted no clothes between them. She wanted him to pin her to the bed and take her. It was all so familiar, all so terribly, horribly familiar. And it was so wrong, it was so . . .

He knew the exact moment she lost control. She made a small whimpering sound at the back of her throat, then her breathing changed, became shallower, quicker, and the hands that were pushing him away suddenly clung to him, drawing him closer.

He kissed her eyes closed, he kissed her ears, the pulse at her throat, her lips. He was fascinated by her lips, how they trembled, softened, how sensitive they were, how responsive. Tears kept seeping from under her lashes, and he kissed these away, too. Nothing in his experience had prepared him for the sudden, fierce swell of possessiveness that surged through him or the bitter remorse that came in its wake. If he'd been a better man, more sensitive, if he'd followed his heart instead of his head, things would have turned out differently. She wouldn't have been alone and unprotected all these years. She wouldn't be plagued now with the specter of a past she couldn't remember. He didn't believe she had lost her innocence, but even if it were true, it didn't matter to him. As God was his witness, he refused to let it matter to him. Whether she'd had one lover or a score of lovers, she was still the same Jess.

When he kissed the tips of her breasts through the fabric of her gown, he could feel the surge of desire lash through her. He held his own passion rigidly in check. He wanted her to know how beautiful she was, how desirable. He had to convince her that no matter what was in her past, she would always be beautiful and desirable to him. Slowly, very slowly, he began to undress her.

Love-dazed, she stared up at him, but when he freed her from her gown and swept it to the floor, sanity returned in a blaze. She seized his wrists before he could begin on her petticoats. "Don't lie to me, Lucas. Tell me the truth. Have we ever been lovers?"

He shook his head. "Only in my dreams. I've waited years for you, Jess. Don't turn me away now."

He kissed her before she could begin to think coherently. Without severing the kiss, he removed the rest of her garments, then dragged the covers over them. His kisses became more intimate. He couldn't resist the tips of her breasts. At the first touch of his tongue, she shivered. When he sucked strongly, her back came off the bed. He pushed aside the bedclothes, and his mouth wandered to her ribs, the flat of her stomach, a small mole on the inside of her thigh. He smiled when he felt her shudder.

She wanted to think, think, think, but those clever hands and lips of his gave her no respite. She couldn't believe the things he was whispering in her ear. She wasn't that beautiful. She couldn't make him feel all the things he said he was feeling. He couldn't want her that much. Lies, truth, everything disintegrated in a surge of pleasure when he touched her there, between her thighs. Yesterday and tomorrow ceased to exist. Mind, soul and senses were aware of nothing but him.

He stood for a moment to pull off the rest of his clothes. When he came back to her, he kissed her with slow, deliberate kisses, and his hands moved over her, exploiting with a lover's caress all his newfound knowledge of her secret vulnerabilities. He wasn't going to give her time to think; he wasn't going to let her change her mind.

Blood began to pound through her veins in a slow, thick pulse. She grew restless. The room was too hot. Her lungs couldn't find enough air to breathe in. Her skin was damp. There were odd animal sounds coming from the back of her throat. Anticipation shivered through her. And she knew, she knew that whatever was in her past, she had never wanted like this. Never.

"Lucas?" she said urgently. "Lucas?"

He rose above her. Her fingers curled around his arms, clenching and unclenching, conveying her need. His blood was singing. Nudging her legs apart, he positioned himself to take her.

When she felt him go still, she focused her eyes on his face. Light and shadow from the flickering candles made his bones stand out starkly. His hair looked ink black. But it was his eyes that held her. There was a curiously intense look in them, angry and determined at the same time.

"Listen to me, Jess," he said fiercely. "This is the first time for both of us, do you understand? It's never been like this for me. Never. I won't let you spoil it for us. I don't care if you'd had other lovers. From this day on, I'll be your only lover, and you'll be mine. That's what counts. Believe it."

Sweet, he was so sweet, so good, that she no longer doubted she'd loved him as a girl. She loved him now. Twice in her life, she'd fallen in love with him, and if they were torn apart and met as strangers, she knew that she would fall in love with him again. She would always love him. But that would be her secret. She wasn't going to burden him with something he'd never asked for nor desired.

She framed his face with both hands and kissed him on the lips. He gave one short, explosive breath and slowly entered her. That first thrust sent shards of pain shooting through her entire body. She gasped. She couldn't speak, couldn't draw air into her lungs. He didn't understand. He wouldn't let her go, wouldn't stop. She dug her nails into his shoulders, trying to convey her distress. Something was wrong. This wasn't possible. She recognized that he was trying to be gentle, but it wasn't working. His words were soothing, but they hardly helped. She shoved, she bucked, trying to dislodge him, but he was immovable. She stopped struggling when she realized that with every movement to free herself, she only drove him deeper into her body. Then suddenly the burning pain receded to an uncomfortable fullness, and her whole body went slack.

He raised his head and looked down at her. Tears shimmered in her eyes, and her look was one of patent accusation. He couldn't find the breath to express what he was feeling, not yet. But she must have seen something in his eyes because her look changed and, as enlightenment dawned, her cheeks bloomed and a slow smile spread from ear to ear. Its brilliancy dazzled him.

"You're my first lover," she breathed out.

He sucked air into his lungs. "No," he corrected, "I'm your first and last lover. And that's how it's going to stay."

She touched a hand to his face, and a worried little frown came and went on her brow. "Are you all right?"

"I am now." He rested his brow on hers. "But I don't mind telling you, I *never* want to go through that again."

She giggled. "Lucas, do you know what I think?"

He could see that she was in a talking mood and had no conception of the sensual torments he was still suffering. She was hot and wet and incredibly tight, and he was ready to explode. He was appalled at how hard he had to fight to gather what was left of his control.

"I think—" she began.

He stopped her words with a kiss. When he slowly pressed into her, he heard the catch in her breath. Encouraged by that small sound of arousal, he began to move more forcefully, in deep, hard strokes. When she followed where he led, the smoldering fire in him flamed out of control. Her mouth was hungry. Her body was supple.

She was lifting herself to him, accepting him with utter abandon. He had dreamed of her like this. In so many hellholes in Spain, he had dreamed of her like this, wild and wanton with a hunger to match his own. Then he stopped thinking when he felt her begin to shudder in his arms. "Yes, love," he said hoarsely, fiercely. "Give in to me."

He felt her start of surprise as she went soaring over the crest, and as she convulsed beneath him, he gave himself up to the beat of his own body. There was nothing in the world but this; there was no one in the world but her.

She came awake slowly, and with eyes still closed, allowed impressions of place and time to sink into her. The sheets at her back were freshly laundered; her hair was spread out over the pillows; she could detect the flicker of candlelight on her eyelids; her body was warm and damp. There were scents that were unfamiliar to her. Love. Passion.

Memory returned in a rush and her eyes flew open. Lucas had pulled back the bedclothes, uncovering her to his gaze. He had donned his dressing robe and was sitting on the edge of the bed. His hand was resting on her breast, kneading it gently. As she watched, he lowered his head and blew a warm stream of air over one tensed nipple. She stifled the moan in her throat but he either sensed it or heard it. He looked up and smiled.

This was another Lucas she did not know. There was a sleepy look in his eyes, and a lazy slant to his smile. Lazy and sinfully, sinfully sensuous.

She wanted to reach out and pull him down beside her and show him that she could be sinfully, sinfully sensuous as well. And she would have, if she hadn't felt so shy. Just thinking about last night made her go hot all over.

He bent his head and kissed her, but before he could do more than press his lips to hers, she hauled herself up. There was something she must do before she lost her nerve. Last night, as she'd drifted into sleep, she'd felt so close to him, she'd wanted to share all her dark and ugly secrets. In fact, she'd made up her mind that that's what she'd do. She didn't want lies or half-truths to come between them. She wanted to be one with him. All she had to do now was say the words.

He sighed. "You've got that worried look in your eyes again. What is it this time? I thought you'd be happy, deliriously happy, to discover you had no lovers before me."

"Well, I am," she said.

"But?"

Her eyes slid away from his.

He tilted her chin up with one finger, forcing her to look at him. "But?" he repeated softly.

He was so straightforward, so transparently honest, while she was all shadows and dark mirrors, a mystery even to herself. He always thought the best of everyone. He could never conceive of anyone trying to deceive him. Her mind was beset by suspicion and distrust. Why couldn't she be more like him?

When he released her wrist, she unobtrusively edged under the covers. "Lucas," she said earnestly, and stopped. She couldn't just blurt the words out. She had to come at this slowly and carefully. She started over. "Lucas, you know I was run down by a carriage?" When he nodded, she went on. "Well, I think the accident did more than blot out my memory. I think it may have . . . affected my mind."

"I'm listening."

He was taking her seriously, and that encouraged her to go on. "Last night, everything seemed so familiar to me, as though I'd done it before. I knew what was going to happen, oh, seconds before it happened. I didn't know everything. I mean, I didn't know how I would feel. But I knew how you would touch me. I knew where everything was leading. Don't you think that's strange?"

"Not if your memory is coming back to you. Is it?"

"I . . . I don't know. There have been little things, but nothing of any significance. Nothing to explain this."

"Perhaps it's just a flash of recall."

"What does that mean?"

He grinned wickedly. "Well, you were very precocious for your years, and I was mad to have you, though I wouldn't admit it. It's fair to say we went too far a time or two back then. That's probably what's coming back to you."

She said indignantly, "I was precocious? You're years older than I! It isn't fair to blame me. And just how far did we go, Lucas Wilde? Mmm?"

His eyes were sparkling. Holding her gaze in his, he raised her hand and pressed a kiss to her open palm. "I swear, no further than we've gone since you came back to me, except for last night."

"And you've never undressed me?"

"Only in my dreams. Jess, you were a virgin. We proved it right here in this bed. I don't see what the problem is."

"The problem," she said, beginning to get edgy, "is that I don't know what's real and what's unreal anymore."

He kissed her on the lips. "Don't let yourself become obsessed with it. Your mind isn't deranged. I'd stake my life on it. You lost your memory. You've been cloistered in a convent for the last three years. You have no reference for sorting out what's real and unreal. Give it time and everything will fall into place. Jess, you're not abnormal. You've been through a harrowing experience, that's all."

Deranged. Abnormal. The words set off alarm bells inside her head. He wouldn't believe her. He would think she was insane. And he was wrong. As time passed, things weren't falling into place. They were becoming more confusing, more frightening. She wasn't thinking only of last night and how everything had seemed familiar to her. She'd wanted to tell him about Rodney Stone. Most of all, she'd wanted to tell him about her Voice. But there was no Voice, not now. And that seemed strange to her, too.

He was watching her, waiting for her to speak. The coward in her won the battle for control. She didn't want him to change toward her, or look at her with revulsion. And maybe, just maybe, he was right.

Lucas watched the play of emotions on her face and thought that he'd seen the same resigned look in the eyes of a wounded deer just before the hunters closed in for the kill. Then the look was gone and she was smiling brilliantly. Once that smile would have fooled him, but not now. She'd let him get too close to her.

"Jess, what is it?" His voice was soft, reassuring.

"Nothing. Nothing at all." Hers was brittle.

"Talk to me."

His eyes were intense on hers. She had to divert him or he would pry the truth out of her—just when she'd decided she didn't want him to know how abnormal she really was. Raising her arms, she flung back her head and ran her fingers through her hair. The covers slipped to her waist as she knew they would, exposing her breasts. The cursed man didn't even drop his eyes. He was still staring at her with that questioning look.

The tremulous smile she gave him wasn't all playacting. She brought his hand to her breast. "This is what's real," she said. "When you touch me, when you make love to me, I forget everything else. Make love to me, Lucas. Now."

There was a moment when he resisted. But the fingers on her breast flexed involuntarily and she shivered in arousal. He touched her again, deliberately, his thumb grazing her nipple, and her back arched off the pillows.

He quickly removed his hand. "Later. After we talk."

But he was wavering. She could see it in his dilating pupils, hear it in the sudden huskiness in his voice. His formidable control was slipping away.

"I don't want to talk." She hoped her smile was alluring. "Lucas, I ache for you. I want you. I need you."

She didn't wait for his response but slipped her hands inside his robe and pushed it from his shoulders. At the first brush of her fingers, every muscle in his body tensed. He didn't say anything or take her in his arms, and both his silence and stillness unnerved her. She didn't know the first thing about seducing a man. Maybe she was doing it all wrong.

With only blind instinct to guide her, she put her lips on his bare skin. His strangled groan of pleasure was the sweetest sound she had ever heard. Her confidence soared and she shoved him down on the bed and loomed over him.

He was a magnificent specimen of the male animal. But she already knew this. What was different was how she saw him. So much brute strength, so much blatant masculinity, and it was all held rigidly in check for her sake. In the act of love, he surrendered his power to her, and it was all hers to command.

She touched the male part of him and drew back violently when he suddenly reared up and tumbled her on the bed. His eyes were hot with passion, but laughter lurked in their depths.

"My love," he said, "there is only so much a man can take before he disgraces himself. The anticipation is killing me."

Then the smile left his eyes and there was only passion.

His mouth came down on hers, demanding, possessing, and she realized what a fool she had been to think she could have everything her own way. Surrender was a two-edged sword. Yield, his kiss told her. And she did, not because she was afraid of him, but because she reveled in everything that was masculine in his nature. She'd never felt more of a woman in her life.

"I've wanted you for years," he muttered. "I've

dreamed of you like this. I want to know all of you, every intimate inch."

He wasn't gentle, but she didn't want gentleness. They were both greedy, desperate, wild. Once, when he was too rough, she cried out. He went perfectly still and looked down at her with a stricken expression on his face.

"Now," she panted, "now," and she dug her nails into his shoulders, urging him to take her.

He laughed softly and covered her body with his. She cried out when he drove into her. Then he braced himself on his arms, making his penetration as deep as he could make it. Their eyes locked, then lost focus. Rational thought slipped away. She reached for him, and it was the signal he had been waiting for. Unchecked, he let the passion take them both, and the sudden blaze that engulfed them brought them to a shuddering, explosive climax. Then there was nothing but the sound of their own harsh breathing.

In the aftermath of spent passion, he wanted to talk. She wanted to sleep. He lay awake for a long while after, going over in his mind the conversation they'd had before they'd made love. She'd been on the point of telling him something, something that troubled her, but at the last moment, she'd had second thoughts. The more he thought about it, the more it seemed to him that she'd deliberately distracted him from pursuing the subject.

Her breathing was slow and even. He smoothed back her hair and adjusted her to the fit of his body. Her head rested in the hollow of his shoulder. His arms cradled her.

The familiar fierce possessiveness flooded through him. He was her lover now. She might not know it yet, but that changed everything between them.

"PERRY, IF IT WERE ANYONE BUT YOU, WE'D BE FACING each other at twenty paces with dueling pistols in our hands. You do realize that, don't you?"

Perry pulled at his neckcloth as though it had suddenly decided to choke him. Lucas was standing with his back to the window and the sunlight, though not blinding, made it difficult to read his expression. Lucas's voice didn't betray anything, either, and that made Perry highly nervous. He badly needed something to drink.

His eyes flitted around the room, one of the two rooms he rented above a draper's shop in Bond Street, and came to rest on the tray of decanters on a side table. They were all empty.

He cleared his throat. "I'm sorry I don't have anything to offer you to drink," he said lamely.

"I wouldn't accept it even if you had. Perry, this place is a pigsty. I don't know how you can live like this. Haven't you ever heard the word *hygiene*?"

Perry shut his eyes to the stack of dirty dishes on the

table and the muddle of books and dirty clothes that were heaped on every available surface. "Yes, well, we're not all earls with an army of servants to clear up after us," he said defensively.

"Good try, but it won't work. I'm your trustee, remember? I know what you can and can't afford. So where's your manservant?"

"He handed in his notice and I forgot to look for another. And I don't know why you're finding fault with me. I remember the rooms you and Adrian kept at Oxford. You couldn't lift anything without finding a maggot under it."

When Lucas laughed, Perry heaved a great sigh of relief. For the last half hour, he'd had to give Lucas an account of his escapade with Jessica the night before, and just listening to his own voice relate the story had made him seriously wonder whether he was a candidate for an insane asylum. He'd gone off in the dead of night with another man's wife. Not any man's wife, but Lucas's. And Lucas was a crack shot. He knew perfectly well that Lucas would not kill him if he challenged him to a duel. But he might decide to teach him a lesson by clipping off the tip of a finger. Or by parting his hair. Permanently.

Lucas said, "So what it comes down to is that *my wife*"—he emphasized the words and smiled when Perry winced—"is convinced that Mr. Stone has met with a bad end."

"And I agree with her," said Perry.

"At Bow Street they seem to think that he's hiding from his creditors." When Perry's head jerked up, Lucas nodded. "Oh yes, I've already been to Bow Street. I went there first thing this morning before coming here. I think that's the most likely explanation for Mr. Stone's disappearance, or he may have met with an accident. At any rate, it's the not knowing that is worrying Jessica." Lucas used the windowsill as a seat, and folded his arms across his chest. "And I don't like it when my wife is worried, Perry."

"No, of course not," said Perry, and something in Lucas's tone made him sit up straighter.

"I don't like it when she goes off on escapades all over town late at night when I'm not there to protect her."

Perry gulped. "I get your point."

"And I particularly don't like it when she's locked up in Bow Street like a common criminal."

Perry was silent.

Lucas let out a long, theatrical sigh. "I don't think Jess will have any peace of mind until she knows exactly what has happened to Stone. And that's where you come in, Perry. Let's find out who remembers him in Chalford. Who saw him last? Who saw him leave? I'd begin at the Rose and Crown, if I were you. That's where he was staying."

"Chalford! But I have things to do here and this could take days, weeks."

Lucas bared his teeth in a facsimile of a smile. "I think it might be beneficial all round if you and Jessica had a little holiday from each other."

He began to pull on his gloves. "And while you're in Chalford, there's something else you can do for me."

There was the sound of voices raised in anger from the street below, and Lucas turned to look out the window. A horse and cart had come out of a side street and were blocking the progress of a stream of carriages. He was about to turn away when his eyes fell on a lady and gentleman who were walking on the other side of the road. His mother was looking as pretty and animated as he had ever seen her. The object of her attentions was Sir Matthew Paige, and he had eyes only for her. Neither of them took any notice of the altercation between the carter and the coachman who were bellowing insults at each other.

"Well?" said Perry in a resigned tone. "What else do you want me to do?"

Lucas erased his frown and turned to face Perry. "When you're in Chalford, I want you to look up Bella. Get a list from her of all the gentlemen she gave those blank invitations to, the ones for her ball. Send it to me, and I'll go on from there. Oh, and talk to her butler. Maybe he remembers something."

"I don't see how that will help us find Mr. Stone."

"Perhaps it won't. But I'd like to know how he came to have an invitation to Bella's ball when no one seems to know him."

"I see what it is!" exclaimed Perry. "You're beginning to think there may be more to Mr. Stone than meets the eye."

"No," said Lucas. "I'm trying to pin everything down so that I can lay Jessica's fears to rest. That's all."

As he left Perry's lodgings, it occurred to him that he didn't want to believe there was anything sinister in Rodney Stone's disappearance because once he suspected foul play, it would open his mind to all sorts of possibilities he didn't want to think about. Or act upon.

When he came out on Bond Street, there was no sign of his mother or Sir Matthew. Sir Matthew was probably walking her home. His own errand would take him first to Rodney Stone's lodgings, then out to Hampstead, to talk to Mr. Stone's aunt again. Just as well. Lately, he'd been bumping into Sir Matthew Paige a tad too often for his liking and it was becoming difficult to keep his thoughts to himself.

Rosemary halted when she and Sir Matthew came to the iron gates of Dundas House. "Why don't you come in for a glass of sherry?" she said. "I'd like you to meet my daughter-in-law. She's not your typical young bride, Matt. She's likely to ask your help in placing her orphanage boys, or to solicit a donation for her convent." She laughed.

His smile was touched with irony. "I'd like to, Rodie, but I don't think your son would approve."

Her smile died. "Things have changed, Matt. You and Lucas are always polite to each other now when you meet."

"Don't let that deceive you. Your son still sees me as his mortal enemy."

She said quickly, "I'm sure you're wrong."

"Are you? Then why hasn't Lucas ever introduced me to his wife? There have been plenty of chances."

"Lucas is not here now. There's nothing to stop me introducing you to Jessica."

A look of impatience crossed his face. "Rodie, that's not the point, and you are being deliberately obtuse. There will never be a reconciliation between your son and me. You need to accept that."

She placed her hand on his sleeve and looked up at him with a plea in her eyes. "He needs time to get used to the idea that we'll be together. Be patient, Matt. Lucas isn't a boy now. He'll come round." When his features hardened, she cried, "We hurt him, Matt! All those years ago, we hurt him. It's not something he can easily forgive."

"I'm not interested in his forgiveness. I'm not ashamed that we were lovers. Our situation was intolerable. We found joy in each other, and I've lived without that joy for fifteen years. If my happiness depends on your son, tell me now. Then I'll know there is no hope for me."

A silence fell, and the slow thud of her heart seemed to toll like a death knell. A moment before, she'd felt the heat of the sun warming her skin. They'd been happy and flirtatious, content just to be together. Now the cold in his eyes frightened her. His face had a tense, hard look as though he expected a blow.

There would be no blow. She wasn't going to give up Matt a second time, not only for her sake, but more especially for his. In all the years they'd been apart, she hadn't really grasped what he had suffered. She'd been too caught up in her own guilt and grief. She'd known he'd had other women since her, many women, and she'd assumed he'd got over her far more quickly than she'd got over him. But it wasn't true. For all his affairs and mistresses, he had been more alone than she could ever have imagined. She'd had her son. All Matt had ever had was a wife who despised him.

She'd known all this, but those were only facts her brain had absorbed. Recently, her heart had taken his impression. He wasn't the invincible knight in shining armor she'd imagined him to be when she was young. He was a real man, with all the flaws and insecurities of a real man.

And she never wanted him to be alone again.

At last she whispered, "When I'm with you, everything seems simple."

"It *is* simple." His eyes blazed. "Rodie, let's not wait on anyone's convenience. Let's marry at once. What's to stop us eloping? I mean, right this minute? We could buy what we need on the way to Scotland, or wherever you want to go. Just once, let's think of ourselves. Or better yet, let's stop thinking and act on instinct."

She said lightly, "You don't mean that, Matt."

"I was never more serious in my life."

"Matt, I can't just leave everything on a whim. I have obligations, to my family, to my ward. You must see that."

"Those were the words, or words very like them, you wrote to me all those years ago. Nothing has really changed, has it, Rodie?"

"We were both married then—"

He interrupted before she could complete the sentence. "Yes, and have been paying for our sins ever since. And if your son has his way, we'll go on paying for the rest of our lives."

She said quietly, "All I'm asking is for a little time, not

for myself, but for my son. I don't want to hurt him, Matt, and I don't want to lose him."

There was a chill, resigned look in his eyes, and she knew what he was going to say before he spoke. "We've come full circle," he said. "I think I always knew what your answer would be. You'll always choose your son over me."

She cried, "Why do I have to choose between you?"

"Because he will make you."

He removed her hand from his arm and took a step back. "I thought my patience was limitless," he said, "but I see that I was wrong. In fact, I've come to the end of what I can tolerate. I was a fool to think I could resurrect the past, a fool to think you would change. It would have been better if I had stayed away. With us, there is always a penalty that must be paid."

The bitterness in his voice sent a shard of cold fear straight to her heart. "No . . . Matt . . . no. I'll talk to Lucas. I'll tell him about us. He may not like it, but he'll accept it. You'll see."

His smile was not reflected in his eyes. "It has been in my mind for some time," he said, "to see something of the world. I had hoped you would come with me."

"And I shall!" she cried passionately.

"Will you?" He was looking past her, toward the house. Some moments passed, and when he looked back at her, his eyes were blank. "There are some loose ends I must tie up before I leave. I don't know why I've kept on the house in Chalford." He nodded as though coming to a decision. "I should put it up for sale. I may never return to England."

The lump in her throat made it hard to find her voice. "Matt, what are you saying?"

He gave her a strange, unnatural smile. "Tomorrow morning," he said, "I shall go to Chalford. My business there may take a few days or it may take a little longer. I won't be returning to London. If you want me, Rodie, you know where to find me."

"You're giving me an ultimatum?"

"No. I think you've already made your decision."

As he struck out toward St. James's Street, she put her hand on the cold iron gate to steady herself. A passing carriage blocked her view, and when it went by, he was gone.

She entered the house filled with resolve. Lucas must be made to understand that Matt was not the villain he made him out to be. It was time to forgive and forget. And no one was perfect. With a little goodwill all round, everything would work out for the best.

As she crossed to the stairs, she heard a noise in the library. Thinking it was Lucas, she changed direction, knocked on the door and entered. It wasn't Lucas who was sitting at the desk, but Jessica.

"Jessica, what are you doing?"

Jessica looked up with a start, but when she saw who it was, she smiled. "I gave Lucas a letter to frank, a letter for Anne Rankin, but now I want to add something to it. It must be here somewhere." She indicated the pile of letters that were strewn across the desk.

Rosemary came further into the room. "I think you're too late. I believe he took all the letters with him this morning when he went out. Do you know when he'll be back?"

Jessica sat back in Lucas's great leather chair and studied her mother-in-law. There was a strained look about her she hadn't noticed when she'd first entered the library. "He said he had some errands to run but he'll be here for dinner. Rosemary, are you all right?"

Rosemary brushed a hand over her eyes. "A slight headache. Nothing that wearing my spectacles won't cure. Vanity will be my undoing." When she smiled, Jessica smiled with her. "Is Ellie home?"

Jessica shook her head. "Bella came up to town unexpectedly to do some shopping, and she and Ellie went out together."

"No doubt Ellie will give us all the details of her outing over dinner. Bella is all she ever talks about. I wish Lucas . . ." She broke off and sighed. "Well, Lucas won't, so there's no point in raising the subject."

When Rosemary left, Jessica let out a slow breath. She knew that her mother-in-law was disappointed that she and Ellie had not become friends. Maybe she should do more. But it didn't seem to matter what she did, Ellie continued to rebuff every overture. Today's shopping expedition was an example. Jessica had invited herself along by saying that it would give her the chance to return her books to the circulating library. It turned out that Bella and Ellie were walking in the opposite direction, to pay a call on Bella's dressmaker. She hadn't pressed the point when she saw that she wasn't wanted. That never helped. All it did was get Ellie's back up.

Sighing, she looked down at the letters she'd been going through and began to put them in order. Yesterday, she wouldn't have had the confidence to enter her husband's book room and go through his personal things. But now that they were lovers, everything had changed.

She sat for a long time, a little smile tucking up the corners of her mouth, just thinking about Lucas. He made her feel warm and cherished. Right this minute, he was making inquiries about Rodney Stone, not because he thought anything had happened to him, but because he wanted to set her mind at rest. If she would have peace of mind only by producing Mr. Stone, he'd told her, then that's what he would do.

When she stood up to leave, her hand brushed against something and a sheet of vellum fluttered to the floor. She wasn't deliberately prying, she told herself; she didn't think it right to read her husband's personal correspondence. But when she saw her own name, her eyes read on with a will of their own.

It was a letter from Lucas's attorney informing him that, as instructed, he'd paid out various sums of money from the trust fund he'd set up for Jessica Hayward. The names of the recipients were Rupert Haig and Adrian Wilde.

She folded the letter and placed it on top of Lucas's correspondence. He'd told her that he'd borrowed money from his friends to buy Hawkshill. It seemed odd that he would wait so long before paying off the debt.

Deep in thought, she left the room.

Jessica sank onto her bed and began to braid her hair. She was remembering how she had awakened that morning, in this very bed, in her husband's arms, savoring the intimacy she shared with him. She'd felt happy and hopeful and unafraid. All that had disappeared during a dinner filled with tension. Her mother-in-law was distracted, Ellie subdued, and Lucas's mind obviously elsewhere. Then Rosemary had made an innocuous remark and the atmosphere between mother and son became charged.

"Sir Matthew," Rosemary said, "is putting his place in Chalford up for sale. I thought it would be nice if we gave a party for him, you know, for all our Chalford friends."

Without looking up, Lucas replied, "I didn't know Sir Matthew had any friends."

"Lucas," said Rosemary, "you know that's not true. Sir Matthew is very well liked."

"Not by me."

The coolness in his voice surprised Jessica, and she groped in her mind for a remark that would ease the tension. "He was very kind to me," she said, "that night at the Haigs' place when I fell, and he found me."

"Sir Matthew Paige," said Lucas evenly, "is one person who will never cross the threshold of any house of mine."

He was looking at his mother as he spoke, and Jessica felt as though she were seeing the face of a stranger. "Lucas—"

He held up a hand. "Why don't you and Ellie take your coffee in the drawing room, Jessica? I think my mother has something she wishes to say to me. We'll join you later."

"But Lucas—"

"Now."

The word was softly spoken, but it was a command for all that. She and Ellie left at once, but neither Lucas nor his mother joined them. It was left to a servant to tell them that Mrs. Wilde had retired to her room, and his lordship had gone out.

All the vague promise of things to come that had buoyed her up during the day evaporated into thin air, leaving a void in its place. She'd thought she knew Lucas, understood him, was close to him, but clearly what she knew was only the tip of the iceberg.

Perhaps it wasn't possible to truly know anyone. No one was transparent. Everyone wore a mask. But Lucas hadn't been wearing a mask when he'd spoken to his mother. She did not think she would ever forget the cruel, hard set of his features, or the coldness in his voice.

She lay awake for a long time, waiting for him to come to her, but he never appeared. And in the morning, it was as if the contretemps over dinner had never taken place. Life went on as before. If smiles faded, they were quickly restored. No one apologized. No explanations were offered.

And no one mentioned Sir Matthew's name.

CHAPTER
22

THE CONVENT OF THE SISTERS OF CHARITY WAS LO-
cated a short distance from Fleet Street, near the
Temple Bar. The houses here were squalid and crowded
to the rafters. Taverns proliferated. Vice flourished. Respectable citizens passed through the streets in the safety
of their carriages, unless they were officers of the law or
the nuns from the convent. The former were given a wide
berth, and the latter were treated with a kind of affection-
ate tolerance. The nuns were known to be softhearted,
and anyone who tried to harm them knew that he would
have an angry mob howling for his blood.

Jessica had not severed her ties to the convent. As the
wife of an earl, she was in a position to enlist the resources
of people who could make a real difference to the sisters'
work, both financially and in a practical way, by offering
jobs for their older children. But what she liked best was
to come to the convent, as her social engagements allowed,
and spend time with the younger children in the nursery.

This was one of these days. Lucas had left the house

early on some business and was not expected back till evening. Rosemary was spending a few days with friends in Canterbury. And Ellie was with Bella. That meant the day belonged to her to do what she pleased.

She was on her knees, bathing one of the babies, when Sister Brigid brought a visitor to see her.

"Miss Bragge," said Sister Brigid, and gave a telling sniff.

Jessica was in the act of lifting little Sarah from the tub and could not turn around to see who had entered. She thought she must have misheard the name in the confusion. It was feeding time and several babies were exercising their lungs at full pitch.

Having swaddled Sarah in a towel, she turned to look at her visitor. When she saw that it really was Ellie, she was surprised. She'd invited Ellie to tour the convent several times, and the invitation had been steadfastly refused. This, of course, was Bella's influence. Bella's heart was too tender to witness the sufferings of these unfortunate children, so she claimed, and Ellie had decided she felt the same.

Jessica tucked Sarah firmly into the crook of one arm and rose to her feet. "Where is Bella?"

"She left this morning for Chalford."

"For Chalford? Then who brought you here?"

"I brought myself in a hackney. Jessica, it's Pip. I don't know where he is."

Jessica knew how close Ellie was to her page, but Ellie's distress surprised her. "One of the servants has probably sent him on an errand. If I know Pip, he'll be back before his next meal is due."

"Oh, if that were only it!" cried Ellie. Her face crumpled and she burst into tears.

Jessica brought Ellie to her former cell and she waited until the fit of weeping had run its course before beginning to question her. She'd already gathered that Ellie believed Pip had run away, and that he might have taken refuge at the convent.

"I don't believe he's run away," Jessica said bracingly, "but even if he has, it wouldn't be the first time. Girls are much easier to manage. That's why we send them to our school in Chelsea. Girls want to learn, you see. Sometimes I think boys are born just to cause trouble."

There was no answering smile from Ellie, but she did try to compose herself. She blew her nose with the handkerchief Jessica had given her, and dabbed her eyes. She was sitting on the cot, and Jessica was sitting on the only chair.

"He's only eight," said Ellie wretchedly.

"But much wiser than his years."

Ellie looked up, and for the first time since entering the cell, allowed her eyes to meet Jessica's. "Jessica," she said, "did you really live in this place for three years?"

"Yes. Why?"

Ellie shrugged. "It's so . . . grim."

"That's because you are comparing it with how *you* live. If you could see the wretched hovels these children come from, you would look at our convent with different eyes. This is a place of hope for them. Without the love and devotion of the nuns, their fate would truly be grim. Now tell me about Pip."

Ellie looked down at the handkerchief she was tying into knots. "I failed him, Jessica," she said in a small, contrite voice.

Jessica seriously doubted it. There was much about Ellie that she could fault, but not how the girl had interested herself in her page's welfare. Ellie had kept up Pip's lessons and seen to it that the other servants made allowances for his background.

"How did you fail him?" she asked.

"I knew he was worried about his brother." Ellie looked up, her eyes filled with misery. "I wanted to tell you three nights ago, but I didn't know how to begin."

"Pip has several brothers. Which one do you mean?"

"His younger brother, Martin. He went to work for Rupert as a stable boy."

Jessica nodded. "Martin has always wanted to work with horses. Not that he knows the first thing about them. Go on."

"The thing is, Bella thought, after I wrote to her about Pip, that she would like a page, too. So, she made Martin her page." The trickle of words became a spate. "But Martin broke things and Bella was angry. She punished him and he ran away. But Bella didn't care. She went back to Chalford without even trying to find him. And this morning,"—she swallowed hard—"Pip didn't bring me my chocolate, and no one knows where he is."

"Martin is missing, too?"

"Yes."

"How long have you known?"

Ellie's eyes dropped away. "The day I went shopping with Bella."

For a moment, Jessica was speechless, then she jumped to her feet. "So that's why you were so silent at dinner that night! A little boy has been missing for three days, and you didn't think to tell me?"

"Bella said that he was only playing truant. She said he would come back, and it would teach him a lesson when he found that she'd gone back to Chalford without him. Bella said that he'd come back when he was hungry."

" 'Bella said'," snapped Jessica. "What does Bella know about these children? What does she know about living on the streets of London? What does Bella know about what children who find themselves in desperate straits will do just to stay alive?"

Ellie's voice was tortured. "Jessica, I didn't know."

"Oh, yes you did! That night at dinner, you were having an attack of conscience, but I was too blind to see it. Because of your dislike of me, no, your *hatred* of me, you let two innocent children suffer. You were right in saying you failed Pip. When you didn't try to find his brother, what choice did he have but to look for him himself."

Tears were streaming down Ellie's cheeks. "I'm sorry, Jessica. I'm so sorry."

"Spare me," Jessica snapped.

She began to undo the buttons on her gown. Ellie was too chastened to say anything. She sat there in misery as Jessica threw off her gown and began to dress in the nun's habit that hung on a hook on the back of the door. When Jessica reached for the wimple, Ellie cleared her throat.

"Jessica," she whispered at last, "what are we going to do about Pip and Martin?"

"I'll find them," said Jessica. She was at the scrap of a mirror on the wall, adjusting her wimple so that no hair showed.

Ellie said, "I'd like to come with you."

"Oh no." Jessica turned to face her. "I shall be going into places you could never imagine existed. And I don't want you to see them or what goes on there. Besides, Lucas would be enraged if he thought I'd permitted you to see such dens of vice, never mind enter them."

"But I want to make amends."

Now that she was primed for action, Jessica's anger had abated somewhat. "Perhaps you do, but I have more important things to think about than your peace of mind."

"But—"

"No! You're going to go home and wait for me there. What you can do is pray—pray for those boys, Ellie. Now come along."

They parted in the vestibule. Ellie was left in Sister Brigid's care while Jessica, accompanied by two other nuns and a burly porter, walked toward Fleet Street.

Ellie broke the silence. "I didn't know that you were in London, Sister Brigid."

"I won't be here for much longer," said Sister Brigid.

"We novices take turns, a month here, a month at Hawkshill."

"I see."

"There's a hackney stand at the corner of Fleet Street," said Sister Brigid. "When they come to it, they'll send a hackney for you." Seeing the tortured look on Ellie's face, the nun unbent a little. "Sister Martha knows what she's doing, and she's well loved in these parts. She'll find your boys."

"Sister Martha?" said Ellie.

"Jessica. Lady Dundas."

"She really is a nun?"

"Did you ever doubt it?"

"Well, no, but Bella said—" Ellie stopped in mid-sentence.

"Yes?"

"It doesn't matter what Bella said." Ellie turned to face Sister Brigid. "I wasn't very kind to you in Chalford when you were nursing Jessica. I behaved like a child. I hope you will forgive me. I'm so sorry. I wish there was something I could do to make it up to you."

There was a moment of complete silence, then Sister Brigid smiled and said softly, "I absolve you on one condition."

"What condition?"

"Save those words for Sister Martha."

Tired and weary, and still in her nun's habit, Jessica arrived home just as dusk was falling. Ellie was watching from an upstairs window, and when she saw Pip jump down from the hackney, she picked up her skirts and went tearing out of the room. When she got to the front door, a footman was carrying Pip's brother into the house.

"Martin is suffering from exhaustion," said Jessica quietly. "I know, the stench is awful, but that's because he's been cooped up in a sewer for the last three days. It could have been worse. Believe me, it could have been much worse."

She broke off to issue orders as a wide-eyed, staring maid came forward. There was bathwater to be drawn, and nightclothes to be laid out for the boys and a tray of whatever Cook had in the kitchen to tempt their appetites.

"Has Lucas come home?" she asked Ellie.

"Not yet."

"Good. That will give me time to tidy myself before he sees me."

Ellie grabbed Pip's hand as they ascended the stairs, but he wrested it from her grasp to demonstrate just how Sister Martha had made her hand into a fist and planted it on old Scurvy's nose.

"She drew 'is cork, that's wot she dun. Ooh, it wuz lovely. There wuz blood everywhere!"

"Who is Scurvy?" asked Ellie.

"Scurvy," said Jessica, "is a tosher, you know, a sewer scavenger. They can make a good living from what they find in the sewers. The trouble is, the sewers are sometimes impassable for grown men. That's when they use small boys. But they won't be using Martin again."

"Did you really hit him, Jessica?" asked Ellie, torn between horror and admiration.

"It was an accident. He bent his head at the wrong moment."

At this, Pip chortled and Martin roused himself enough to smile.

The story gradually unfolded in Jessica's bedroom as the boys were made ready for bed. Jessica and the nuns had tracked the boys' foster mother to a gin house. At first she'd denied having seen the boys, but when Jessica threatened to make a citizen's arrest and take the woman straight to the magistrates, she'd confessed that Martin had turned up three days before and she'd promptly apprenticed him to old Scurvy, the sewer scavenger. As for

Pip, he'd gone off to try and rescue his brother, and she couldn't remember when she'd last seen him.

"Finding the mother was the easy part," said Jessica. "The hard part was finding Scurvy. There are so many sewers that empty along that stretch of the Thames. If Pip hadn't seen me and called out, it might have taken us days to find them."

She was kneeling by the copper tub to bathe the boys, and held out a washcloth to Ellie. "I'll do Martin," she said. "You can do Pip."

Ellie looked at the washcloth for a moment before gingerly accepting it. Misunderstanding the girl's hesitation, Jessica said, "They're used to being bathed by the nuns, so there's no false modesty here."

Ellie looked at the boys. Their knees were tucked up to their chins and their eyelids were drooping. Pip was relatively clean, but Martin, who was much smaller than Pip, looked like a little doll that had been dipped in a tub of grease then rolled in soot. Tears stung her eyes.

Quickly kneeling, she said, "You'll have to show me what to do."

Jessica laughed. "Just think of them as potatoes with their skins on, and scrub away."

Opening his eyes at that moment, Martin exclaimed, "Did you see 'er, Pip? A facer. Right on the nose! That's good ole Sister Martha for you." And he demonstrated by plunging his fist into the bathwater and sending a plume of water flying.

After the boys were carried upstairs and put to bed and her own room was cleared, Jessica changed into a gown and rang for a footman. Not long after, he returned with a decanter of brandy and two glasses.

"You look," she said, eyeing Ellie as she poured out the brandy, "as though you could do with a glass of Sister Dolores's famous elixir."

In fact, Ellie looked to Jessica to be on the point of

exhaustion. There was very little color in her cheeks, and the dark circles under her eyes looked like bruises. Her mouth trembled, and quick tears came and went at the slightest provocation. The girl obviously had spent several sleepless nights worrying, and now that the worrying was over, she was ready to collapse.

"This is a poor substitute for the elixir," said Jessica, handing Ellie a glass of brandy, "but it will have to do. Drink it! It will do you good, then it's off to bed with you."

While Ellie obediently sipped the brandy, Jessica plunked herself down on the opposite armchair flanking the grate. "No," she said, when Ellie made a face and tried to set her glass aside. "I know the taste is awful, but it really will do you good. Just think of it as medicine."

Ellie picked up her glass again, took a minuscule sip, then gave a teary sniff. After another sip, she said, "Jessica, how can people do this to children?"

"For money," Jessica said. "A pittance for a slave. That's what it amounts to. And it's all perfectly legal. Pip and Martin are fortunate that they are charges of the diocese, else I would have had a real fight on my hands."

Another silence as Ellie digested this, then, in a low, vibrant tone, "I think the nuns must be saints to do what you did today. I had no idea that you ran such risks. I thought you spent all your time in the convent."

"Now don't go making me out to be something I am not. I'm not a saint. I'd only disillusion you in the end."

Ellie flushed and looked down at her glass. "You're thinking of Bella. I can't believe how I set such store by her. She didn't care at all what happened to Martin." Her laugh cracked. "Just listen to me! I knew and I did nothing! So I'm no better than Bella."

Jessica said quietly, "I didn't mean what I said earlier. I was so worried about the boys, I spoke without thinking."

"I deserved it."

294 / ELIZABETH THORNTON

"Ellie, if we're going to blame ourselves, I have to shoulder my share."

Startled, Ellie looked up. "What do you have to blame yourself for?"

Jessica shrugged. "I knew you were upset about something these last few days. I should have come right out and asked you what was wrong, but my pride got in the way. I was afraid of another rebuff. So you see, I'm guilty, too."

These words had the opposite effect to what Jessica intended. Tears flooded Ellie's eyes, and she felt for her handkerchief, then mopped her cheeks. When she lifted her head, there was a look of entreaty in her expression. "Every day I expected Bella to tell me that Martin had come home. After all, he lived in a fine house; he was warm and dry, and had plenty to eat."

"That's true. But life in Bella's stately mansion had suddenly become intolerable for poor Martin."

"She must have done something *dreadful* to make him run away to that horrible creature who calls herself his foster mother."

"Oh, she did."

"What?"

"Bella called him a bad word."

Ellie looked puzzled. "What bad word?"

"The most abhorrent word a small boy can be called. Yes, though it pains me to say it, Bella said the forbidden word."

"What word?" breathed Ellie.

"Baby," said Jessica.

Ellie straightened. "Baby?"

"Yes. But that's not the worst of it. She went further. She stopped using his name altogether and called him 'Baby' instead because, as she said, only a baby would let things slip through his fingers. All the servants began calling him 'Baby,' too. What self-respecting boy could live with that?"

Ellie began to laugh. "I thought she must have had him whipped or worse."

"Oh, Martin would have cheerfully suffered a whipping. He might have boasted about it. But this touched his pride, and he was ashamed."

The smile on Ellie's face suddenly died, and she hung her head. After a moment, her shoulders began to heave as she tried to choke back the sobs. Jessica quickly crossed to her, knelt down and wrapped her in her arms.

"There, there," she said. "Everything worked out for the best. And now that we've found Martin, we'll keep him with us. That ought to make Pip happy."

Ellie's words were almost incoherent. "Oh, Jessica! I've been so cruel to you. I don't d-deserve your friendship."

"Yes, well, if we had to deserve our friends, nobody would have any, would they?"

"You don't understand! I did something awful."

"What did you do?"

"I burned down your wagon . . . to frighten you away . . . and later I . . . I came into your room when I thought you were sleeping. I swear, Jessica, I wasn't going to hurt you with the scissors. I was going to cut the bed-drapes, just to frighten you, you know, to show you that you weren't wanted."

Jessica took a moment to absorb Ellie's words, then she said incredulously, "*You* set our wagon on fire? And that was *you* in my room at Haig House?"

Ellie gulped and nodded.

"But . . . I don't understand. At Haig House, I smelled roses, Bella's perfume."

"I may have been wearing it. I don't know. I can't remember. You . . . you didn't think I was Bella, did you?"

"I'm afraid I did. And when our wagon burned, we thought it was the work of some local boys."

"Oh, God! Now do you see how wicked I am?"

"It's all right, it's all right," Jessica crooned as the sobs became deeper, harsher. "I forgive you. From what I've heard, I was no better at your age. Young love makes fools of us all."

Ellie screwed up her face as the words tumbled out. "That's not it! It was because of Jane. I felt as though I were betraying her. I couldn't allow myself to like you. But Jane was good like you. She would never have blamed you for what your father did." The spate of words turned into a torrent. "And I felt so guilty. Maybe I could have s-stopped her. There must have been something I could have done. But I never suspected that she would drown herself. I s-swear it!"

"Jane? Who is Jane?"

"My brother's wife."

Jessica sat back on her heels. She remembered Jane Bragge's grave in Saint Luke's churchyard, and later Lucas's mother telling her that the young woman had accidentally drowned. She remembered something else. Philip Bragge, Jane's husband, had died at Waterloo, leaving Ellie alone in the world, until Lucas had become her guardian.

She stared at Ellie's bent head. "No, Ellie," she said, "I'm sure you're wrong. It was an accident."

"That's what everyone thinks," Ellie cried. "But I know what I know."

Jessica felt a numbness creeping over her. Jane Bragge and her father? She didn't want to think about it; she was afraid to think about it. She said faintly, "You resented me because you were infatuated with Lucas."

"No," Ellie sobbed. "I hated you because your name was Hayward! I hated you because of what your father did to Jane!"

Long minutes passed. Gradually, Ellie's sobs diminished to teary sniffs. Finally, she raised her head. Her throat worked and she swallowed. "I've said too much," she whispered. "I should never have told you."

Jessica said, "What did my father do to Jane?" Ellie

shook her head, but Jessica read the answer in her anguished expression. "Did he rape her?"

Ellie drew in a breath and fresh tears welled in her eyes. "Yes," she whispered.

Jessica felt her heart contract, but there was no real sense of shock. Some hidden part of her mind had already made the connection. "Did Jane tell you?"

"No."

"Oh, Ellie, were you there when it happened?"

"No. But I overheard Lucas and the others talking about it."

"Lucas?"

Ellie nodded.

Jessica took her chair again, picked up her glass and took a long, fortifying swallow. She was surprised at how calm and collected she sounded. "Drink the brandy, Ellie, then take your time and tell me everything from the very beginning."

Ellie obediently sipped from her glass. Her head was bowed, and she kept her eyes down. At length, she began to speak. "Lucas had just come home from the war," she said. "And Judge Hicks and his wife had taken me in until it was decided where I should go. They came out to talk to the judge. I wasn't wanted, so I went out to the barn to play with the new kittens. They were in the loft. Afterward, Lucas and the others came into the barn. They didn't know I was there. And that's when I heard about Jane."

Jessica said softly, "Who came into the barn, Ellie?"

"Lucas and Adrian and Rupert."

"Go on."

Ellie drew in a breath. "They were talking about Jane. They said that she had drowned herself."

"But how could they have known when no one else knew?"

"She'd left a letter for my brother. Rupert had it. I didn't understand what it all meant, not then."

"I see. And what did they decide to do about it?"

Ellie didn't answer for a moment. She darted Jessica a glance, then looked down again. "They . . . they talked about punishing your father. They talked about calling him out, or horsewhipping him or . . . or something. It was a matter of honor, they said."

"What? All of them were going to punish my father?"

Ellie shook her head. "No, they drew straws to see which one would do it."

"They drew straws," said Jessica.

Ellie was too innocent to understand the significance of what she'd just revealed. *They talked about calling him out or horsewhipping him or something.* It was the "or something" they had finally settled on. And they'd drawn straws to see who should do it.

In her mind's eye, she could see the scene in the barn as if she'd been Ellie. She would have been looking through the open trapdoor. How handsome and debonair those young men newly returned from the war would have appeared in a young girl's eyes. How noble and honorable. They would have talked in a civilized way. Ellie would never have understood the innuendos. And if something had struck an odd note, she wouldn't have believed it.

They considered themselves honorable men, Jessica supposed. They'd held fast to their pact. They'd provided for Ellie. They'd also provided for her. But they wouldn't have provided for her unless they'd thought she had a claim on them. It didn't take much imagination to figure out what that claim was. Why hadn't she seen it before?

Now she understood the letter from Lucas's attorney. When Lucas had married her, he'd become her sole protector and provider. That's why he'd paid off his friends.

She didn't feel any strong emotion—no anger or revulsion or fear. She supposed that most people would think that justice had been served. A wicked man had met with his just deserts. If she felt revulsion, it was for her father.

Her regret and compassion were for the poor girl who had suffered at his hands.

Looking up, she said, "Who got the short straw, Ellie?"

Ellie shook her head. "I don't know."

"It was Lucas, wasn't it?" said Jessica gently.

Misery swam in Ellie's eyes. "Yes," she whispered.

Another revelation that had no power to shock her. She'd already made that connection, too. The words came easily. "Don't look so worried, Ellie. Nothing came of it. There was no duel. Lucas did not horsewhip my father. My father had many enemies. Obviously, someone else got to him first."

Ellie's face cleared, and she let out a long, shivery sigh.

"Does anyone else know what you've told me?" asked Jessica.

"No. I couldn't tell anyone in case . . ." Ellie swallowed. "If Jane drowned herself—if she did it deliberately—well, she couldn't be buried in the church graveyard."

"I don't know who makes up these stupid rules, but I'm sure God will punish them in His own good time. I'm glad you told me about Jane. All the same, I think we should keep it to ourselves, not only for Jane's sake, but also for Lucas's."

Ellie cried passionately. "I would never do anything to hurt Lucas, Jessica."

"I know, dear, I know. And neither would I."

"You won't tell him that I told you, will you, Jessica? I mean, it sounds as though I meant to betray him, and I never would."

"No, I won't tell him. As I said, it will be our little secret. Now, let's get you into bed."

After she'd put Ellie to bed, she prowled through the house like a restless cat, reviewing in her mind everything she'd learned from Ellie. At first, she could think of noth-

300 / ELIZABETH THORNTON

ing but Jane Bragge and the torments she must have suffered before she'd taken her own life. And the more she thought of Jane, the more she despised her own father.

Yet, she could not condone what Lucas had done, though she could understand it. He'd been a soldier. After the carnage at Waterloo, where so many of England's brightest and best had perished, what could the life of one wicked, wicked man mean to him?

Her one comfort was that this was an isolated case that could never be repeated. It was over and done with. It was in the past. There was no reason to fear for the future.

But it wasn't one isolated case. Rodney Stone was missing, and no one knew what had happened to him.

"No," she whispered despairingly. "Lucas isn't my Voice."

But she didn't believe her own words.

CHAPTER
23

I T WAS A LITTLE AFTER MIDNIGHT WHEN LUCAS AR-
rived home. He walked into his library and suddenly
halted. Jessica was curled up on the sofa fast asleep. There
was a fire burning low in the grate and several candles
were still lit.

He stood for a moment or two, silently contemplating
her. Ever since he'd received an express letter from Perry
early that morning, he'd checked and rechecked every
inconsequential piece of information he had on Rodney
Stone, and now his mood was dangerously brittle. On
almost every point, Jess had been right. She'd known
more about Stone than his own aunt and his friends.
There had to be a reason for her knowing so much, and
the only reason that came to him was that she had known
Stone from before. Then why hadn't she told him?

He crossed to a tray of decanters on a side table and
poured himself a measure of brandy. Then he turned to
stare at Jessica again. Candlelight softly gilded her skin.
Her hair was in disarray and long wanton threads of gold

clung to her cheeks and throat. The lace kerchief that she'd decorously tucked into the edges of her low-cut bodice had parted, revealing the creamy swell of her breasts.

So much loveliness and innocence had always had the power to stir his protective instincts, even in the act of love. Especially in the act of love.

He took a second long swallow from the glass in his hand, and his lips flattened. He didn't want to protect her, not now. He wanted to take her, possess her, master her, so that she would learn once and for all that he had some rights where she was concerned. He was her husband. He wasn't her pet dog to be coddled or distracted as the mood struck her.

It rankled that she hadn't been completely honest with him.

His third swallow emptied his glass and he set it down on the table with a jarring snap. Jessica's lashes quivered, and she slowly opened her eyes.

Levering herself on one elbow, she looked around the room in a daze, and her eyes came to rest on Lucas.

"What time is it?" she asked drowsily and drew herself up.

There was no answer.

Something about his silence struck an odd note, and she shook off her languor. He was staring at her with such intensity that her breath caught. This was Lucas, the man she loved, yet she hardly recognized him. Though it was warm in front of the fire, her blood chilled. He couldn't possibly know what she'd learned from Ellie. Then why was he looking at her with that hard, set look on his face?

She couldn't breathe, couldn't move. His inflexible dark stare seemed to pin her in place. She had to say something to break the unnerving silence that bound them together, but the words that formed on her tongue died unsaid. A shiver that had nothing to do with fear passed over her. And knowledge as old as Eve began to seep into her.

He must have seen something in her eyes for there was a subtle change in him. His eyelids drooped, and a faint smile softened the harsh line of his mouth. Then he began to remove his neckcloth. After tossing it on the nearest chair, he threw off his coat and started on the buttons of his waistcoat.

"Lucas—"

"No. No words, Jess. I've gone beyond that."

Her heart lurched when he crossed to the sofa. His breathing was audible and his nostrils were flared. And still those burning eyes held her as securely as any bonds. It flashed through her mind that if she tried to escape him he would stop her. He was out of control, an irresistible force bent on overwhelming her.

The naked hunger in his eyes ignited an answering hunger in her. Excitement speared through her, and she slowly sank back on her elbows. Only then did he release her from his stare.

His gaze dropped to her parted lips, then moved over her slowly, lingering on the pulse at her throat, her breasts and the long sweep of her legs entangled in her skirts. When he went down on his haunches beside her, she stifled a moan at the back of her throat.

In a low, driven tone, he told her that he was done with allowing her to have everything her own way. She was made for him, made for this. As he disrobed her, he told her in husky, broken whispers that this was how he wanted her, open and vulnerable to him, helpless to deny him anything. And she *was* helpless, as he proved over and over again. Her body had become an instrument for their mutual pleasure, and he knew just how to play it. It was a long, long time before he bore her down to the carpeted floor, then, quickly rising, he stripped out of his clothes.

Breathless and dazed by so much passion, she gazed up

at him. There was a moment of profound silence as their eyes locked. He held himself perfectly still, and it came to her that while she shamelessly reveled in his lovemaking, he was having second thoughts.

"Lucas," she whispered, holding her arms out to him.

As if it were the signal he'd been waiting for, he came down on top of her. There was a moment when she savored the press of his weight, then he drove into her with such ferocity that they both cried out. His kisses were desperate; his hands urgent, and she gave herself up to him without reservation.

"Lucas," she whispered as she felt the power of him fill her whole world, just as he filled her body. Thoughts raced through her mind, but she refused to be swayed by them. She didn't care who or what he was. She didn't care what he had done. She would protect him. She loved him. She loved him. *Lucas,* she thought, *Lucas,* and her throat tightened.

At the end, when her body shattered under the driving pressure of his, it seemed that her heart shattered also. Her shoulders began to heave in great, shuddering sobs, and she dissolved in a flood of tears.

He pulled from her and scooped her into his arms. "Jess, sweetheart, don't take on so. I didn't mean to frighten you." With his back against the sofa, he held her curled into him, her head angled against his shoulder. His hands ran over her ceaselessly, and he pressed chaste kisses to her brow, her eyes, her cheeks. "I thought you understood. I thought it was what you wanted, too."

He didn't know where the soothing words were coming from, but he knew he wasn't telling her the whole truth. He hadn't wanted to frighten her so much as get her attention. He'd wanted to let her know that he was a force to be reckoned with. The trouble was, he'd let things go too far.

"It doesn't have to be that way," he said softly. "I can be as gentle and restrained a lover as you want me to be."

Her tears dried and she tilted her head to look up at him. "I did understand," she said. "It was what I wanted because it's what *you* wanted. And you didn't frighten me, Lucas," then as an afterthought, "well, only a little, at first."

He expelled a pent-up breath. "Then why the tears?" And dipping his head, he kissed one errant tear at the corner of her mouth.

"Because . . ." She turned her head slightly and their lips met.

"Because?" He cupped the back of her neck with one hand to hold her in place. His lips brushed hers, no more than a gentle pressure. "Because?" he repeated softly.

Because she loved him. Because she feared the past and was terrified of the future. But she couldn't tell him anything. "Because . . . I didn't know it could be like this." She paused. "It was awesome." And that was the truth. "You were awesome. Because . . ." She sucked in a breath when she felt his hand on her breast, then she moaned as his fingers plucked one nipple erect, then the other.

"Because?" he prompted.

"Lucas," she said weakly, "what are you doing?"

His hands on her flanks had eased her into position astride his lap. "I'm making love to my wife," he said, "the way it's supposed to be."

He lavished her with slow, easy caresses and words that made her heart sing. "I love you," he said. "I love you, Jess."

She gave him back the words he wanted, the words she ached to say. "I love you, too, Lucas. I love you."

It was almost perfect.

"So what do you wish to say to me?" she asked.

They were sitting at the little table in her parlor, now dressed in their night robes, drinking tea. Lucas had let her know he had something particular he wished to say to

306 / ELIZABETH THORNTON

her, and that if they went to bed, he feared he would never get around to talking. He said this with a roguish grin, but she wasn't fooled. Lucas detested tea, so this must be serious.

"No," said Lucas, grimacing as the concoction he always referred to in his mind as "mare's water" passed over his tongue. "You first. You waited up for me. Why?"

She took a reviving sip of tea before answering. "I had this idea," she said, "and I couldn't wait to share it with you." She paused, going over the little speech she had rehearsed in her mind while she'd waited for him to come home.

"And?"

She tried to sound both animated and eager. "You suggested once that we should go to Paris for our honeymoon."

"And you said you didn't want to go anywhere."

"Well, I've changed my mind, only . . . I want to do more than see Paris. What's to stop us spending, oh, six months on the Continent or longer, you know, making the grand tour?"

"You want to leave England."

"Well, I want to see the world. I'm such a provincial, Lucas. I feel out of place with your sophisticated friends. A grand tour would broaden my experience, be a real education."

He took another sip of tea. "How odd," he said. "Everyone seems to be talking about visiting the Continent. You. My mother. Bella. I wonder whether Ellie would like to go, too?"

"It wouldn't surprise me. Lucas, you may find this hard to believe, but Ellie and I are friends now." And she gave him a judiciously edited account of the day's events.

She spoke mostly to his back. He was at the tea trolley and had found the decanter of sherry that was kept on the bottom shelf. When he held it up to her she shook her head. He rejoined her at the table. To cover a sudden attack of nerves, Jessica reached for the teapot and refilled her cup.

He said abruptly, "How soon do you wish to leave England, Jess?"

A wrong note if ever she'd heard one.

"As soon as possible."

His tone was dry. "Would tomorrow be too soon for you?"

She laughed. "Tomorrow would be lovely if it could be arranged. We could go ahead of the others, and Ellie and your mother could join us in a week or two."

"No, that's not convenient. I have business in Chalford. But you need not wait for me."

Her heart skipped a beat. "I wouldn't dream of going without you. I mean, what kind of honeymoon is that? And . . . and what business do you have in Chalford?"

"That's what I wanted to talk to you about. An express arrived from Perry early this morning while you were sleeping."

"An express?" she said as though she'd never heard of such a thing.

"A letter that was delivered by special messenger."

His eyes were speculative and she felt a peculiar sensation stealing over her. He was as wary of her as she was of him. "It must have been important," she said carefully.

"It was. It's about Rodney Stone. Jess, you were right. He never left Chalford."

"He's dead," she said tonelessly.

"No one knows that for sure, but the authorities are beginning to suspect foul play. It seems that Mr. Stone was last seen by a lock keeper, on the towpath, making for the old priory. No one saw him after that, not at the Rose and Crown and not at the hostelry."

"A lock keeper?" she said.

"The man who regulates the old weir. Mr. Frome is lock keeper at Saint Martha's Cross. He remembers Stone because he saw him in the taproom of the Rose and

Crown earlier that evening. He thought Stone was just going for a walk along the towpath."

Saint Martha's Cross. Where had she heard that before? She had an instant and vivid impression of a stone cross in front of a church and a children's game that wasn't a game at all. Those who were caught really were being led off to have their heads chopped off.

Saint Martha's Cross. Until that moment, she'd never heard of it. But Rodney Stone had been seen by the lock keeper at Saint Martha's Cross. And in her dream, they'd played their terrifying game around a stone cross that had cast a ghastly distorted shadow.

One down and two to go. One down and two to go.

Who is next, Sister Martha? Sister Martha?

They looked at him and saw exactly what he wanted them to see. No one had ever suspected him of murder. He could do it again.

Who drew the short straw, Ellie? Who? Who?

It was Lucas. It was Lucas. Lucas.

"No!"

She came to herself to find that Lucas was pouring sherry down her throat. She shoved his hand away and reached for her teacup. Uncaring of the scalding hot liquid, she greedily gulped down the tea. Quick tears of pain stung her eyes.

Lucas was frowning. "I'm sorry I shocked you," he said.

"When did he disappear?"

"Right after he came to see you at Bella's."

"When I was convalescing from my fall?"

"Yes."

"And Saint Martha's Cross? Where is it? I mean, is there a cross?"

"Not now. But the locals still remember where it used to be. It was in the old priory grounds. Constable Clay and his men combed the ruins but there's no sign of Stone."

She fought down her nausea. Priory. Church. A sacred building—that's all she'd known in her dream. Lucas was speaking again, and she tried to still her thoughts to listen to him.

"After I received Perry's letter, I decided to delve a little deeper into Mr. Stone's affairs. I visited his bank. It turns out that Stone came into some money before he went to Chalford. Contrary to what all his friends believe, he has no debts. He paid off his creditors before leaving town. I went to see his aunt again, and she has no more idea than I of where the money came from, unless he won it at cards."

He shook his head. "Jess, you suspected that Stone was going to abduct you."

"It seemed to me at the time that he meant to abduct me. But you said that I panicked."

"You mentioned that someone may have paid him to do it."

"Did I? I can't remember."

"And you also suspected that foul play might be involved in his disappearance when everyone else was convinced he was hiding from his creditors. How could you have known all this?"

"I didn't know. It was only when Perry discovered that none of Stone's friends knew what had happened to him that I . . . that we both began to suspect the worst."

"But why should you care? Why did you go to his rooms, Jess? What were you looking for?"

"I wasn't looking for anything. Perry and I were worried about him, that's all."

"And you found nothing?"

"No. If you don't believe me, ask Perry."

"I believe you, Jess. I always believe you when you give me a straight answer."

He rose and went to stand in front of the fire. With his back to her, he said, "In his letter to me, Perry says that there's a rumor going around that there was a woman with Stone the night before Bella's ball."

"Woman? What woman?"

"I don't know. No one seems to know her name. Maybe she doesn't exist."

He turned suddenly and she came under his hard, searching stare. Panic edged into her mind and the room began to swim.

"Jess," he said gently, "you're not keeping anything from me, are you? You have told me all you know? Anything less could be dangerous. You do realize that, don't you? If Stone was murdered, God only knows what may happen next. That's why I don't want you anywhere near Chalford."

"I don't know anything," she said, and to her horror, her voice caught on a sob.

He came to stand beside her and his face was the picture of concern. It was the face of a good man. How could she think what she was thinking?

Yet, everything rang so true, everything was falling into place. And things she'd never thought about were taking on a new significance. He'd married her, surprising everyone. He'd literally forced her into marriage. What better way to keep an eye on a woman who was asking too many dangerous questions?

And a wife could not testify against her own husband.

When he reached for her, she drew back violently. "Jess," he said, "sweetheart," and he swept her up in his arms. "I shouldn't have told you about Stone. It's all been too much for you."

She could feel the steady beat of his heart against her breast and the bunching of powerful masculine muscles as he adjusted her in his arms. "Don't go to Chalford," she said, and she could hear the naked fear in her voice. "Stay here with me."

"I have to go. Don't worry, love, I know how to take care of myself."

"Then let me come with you."

"No."

"But why do you have to go?"

"Perry is there. And I'd like to clear up this business about Mr. Stone."

"But—"

He kissed her swiftly, silencing her. "It's all arranged. Adrian and I set off early tomorrow. I won't be gone for long."

He carried her into her chamber and put her to bed. After extinguishing the candles, he joined her there. "You're cold," he said. "Here, let me warm you."

He made love to her, not as they'd made love before, but a gentle blending of their bodies that had more to do with comforting than pleasure. She felt safe in his arms, and that seemed wrong to her. But she couldn't help what she was feeling. Right or wrong, she loved him with her whole heart.

When she felt the rhythmic rise and fall of his chest, she untangled herself from his arms and slipped from the bed. After donning her robe, she entered the dressing room. Guided only by her sense of touch, she found what she was looking for in the bottom drawer of Lucas's dresser. It was a pistol, primed and ready for use, in the event of thieves breaking into the house.

Swiftly rising, she returned to her own chamber and hid the gun in her writing table. Then she went to one of the long windows and looked out. Buckingham House, with its cheery lights, winked at her, signaling that all was right with the world.

She put a hand to her mouth to stifle a panicked sob. She had to be strong. She couldn't allow herself to be overcome by emotion. Oh, if only she had a particle of the resolution she'd possessed when she'd set off from the convent to return to Hawkshill! Everything had seemed simpler then. Her one thought had been to stop a murderer from murdering again.

She'd come full circle, but it was all so different. She hadn't know then that she would fall in love with her Voice.

"Voice," she whispered into the silence, "I won't let you do this. Turn back before it's too late."

She felt a flicker of awareness, but no more than that, no suspicion, no recognition.

Voice? she repeated silently, more insistently, testing him, testing herself. But there was no need to test herself, not now. Her Voice existed just as surely as she did.

She opened her mind to him. *Voice? Voice?*

Lucas stirred and she crossed to him. "Jess? Jess? I love you."

At his softly murmured words, something inside her quietly shattered. Clever, clever Lucas. There was no weapon he would not use to quell her suspicions. But he was too late. They weren't suspicions now. They were convictions. She could forgive him her father, but not Rodney Stone, and not his next victim.

I will stop you, Lucas. I will. I will.

Her own words mocked her.

"Jess, come back to bed."

She crawled in beside him, and his arms immediately wrapped around her. As he caressed her body, she lay perfectly still, willing herself not to respond to him, not this time.

He raised his head. "Jess, what is it? What's wrong?"

"Nothing," she murmured, and she put her arms around his shoulders.

"Then love me. Love me, Jess."

Her resistance died away. It was impossible to deny her own heart. "Lucas," she whispered helplessly, hopelessly, when he entered her. "Lucas." Her body did not share the reservations of her mind. It welcomed him, answered him when he demanded more from her. At the crisis, she gave a cry of despair and the tears welled over.

He was infinitely gentle as their passion ebbed. There was a smile in his voice. "I know, I know. It was awesome."

She lay there quietly, waiting for him to fall asleep, thinking, thinking, thinking.

In the morning, when she awakened, Lucas was gone. She didn't wait to don her robe, but ran out of her chamber in only her nightgown. She met a footman on the stairs. To her repeated and insistent inquiries, he faltered out that the master had left for Chalford early that morning with his cousin, Mr. Adrian Wilde.

An hour later, Jessica and her maid were in the carriage and on their way to Chalford.

CHAPTER
24

SHE STOPPED FOR THE NIGHT AT THE BLACK BOAR, JUST a few miles before Chalford. Though no one knew her in these parts, just to be on the safe side, she wore a veil and kept it in place until she and her maid were shown to their room. If it had been possible she wouldn't have brought a maid with her. She wanted to be alone. She didn't have the energy to make small talk. She was doing things in secret and stealth. A maid only complicated matters. But a maid was also an indispensable accessory for a lady who was traveling on the road. Not to have brought Sadie would have invited speculation at every inn they stopped at on the way.

Her bed was comfortable, but she could not get to sleep. She tried to pray, but no words came. She listened, but there was nothing there but an incomprehensible void. Wide-eyed, she lay staring at the ceiling, her mind frozen, impenetrable to thought or emotion.

In the morning, she roused herself enough to put on a performance for her maid. She told Sadie she had some business in the area that would take her an hour or two to complete. When she returned, they would go on to the Lodge together.

She debated whether to take Lucas's pistol with her and decided that where she was going, it wasn't necessary. Besides, it was so unwieldy, she didn't know how she could conceal it. And when she went to the Lodge to confront Lucas, she would not go alone.

A hired coach took her into Chalford and set her down only a mile from her destination. Perhaps she was being too cautious, but she didn't want anyone to see where she was going or what she was doing. This was something she had to do by herself. After paying off the driver, she walked toward St. Luke's church, but as soon as the coach drove off and she knew that no one was watching her, she turned off the main road and made for the towpath that followed the river.

As small things registered in her mind, she felt herself begin to thaw, but she put a guard on her thoughts. She could tolerate only so much, and she was close to the breaking point. Whatever she could see and touch were the only things she allowed herself to think about.

There was a light mist rising, a heat vapor that drifted off the river and veiled either shore. It wasn't a dense mist, and she could still see ripples cutting the surface of the water. There were no barges on the river, plying their trade to Henley and London. No punts or boats. The sun was obscured by clouds, and a light drizzle had begun to fall. She passed a neat little cottage beside a weir. This must be where the lock keeper had seen Rodney Stone on his last walk along the towpath.

Not long after, she came to a fork in the path, and she left the river and began to climb, but it was a gentle incline, a slow, steady sweep that shouldn't have made her breath catch. At the summit, she paused to take in the vista. On her left, looking out over the valley, was Haig House. From her vantage point, she could also see the pavilion that she'd been making for the night Rodney Stone had pursued her. She tried to let that thought slip by unexamined, but the barb was too deep and she felt it twist. If Rodney Stone had been following Lucas's orders that night, then Lucas . . .

She shied away from the thought before she could complete it. None of that mattered now. She had to stop Lucas. That took precedence over everything. All else— her lost love, lost hopes, broken dreams—could be wept over later.

A light froth of mist floated in front of her eyes, then rapidly dissipated. Suddenly, a bird burst into song and she glanced around fearfully. A thrush on an ancient rowan soared upward, and she raised her eyes to follow its flight. She felt the rain on her face, heard the wind soughing in the topmost branches of the trees, and her own breath shuddered through her in a broken little sob.

She stood there for a long time, her face turned up to the rain. A shaft of sun drifted across her face, warming her, then vanished behind a bank of clouds. She closed her eyes and prayed.

When she opened her eyes, she felt calmer. No one else could stop Lucas, only she. No one loved him as she loved him. And this day was inevitable. She'd known it for a long, long time. This was why she'd been sent back to Hawkshill.

Turning from Haig House, she now looked at the object of all her dread, the ruined priory. It was situated far below Haig House, concealed by thick stands of trees. That's why she had never seen it before. And there wasn't much to see. All that remained of this once-flourishing monastery were crumbling stone walls and the tower.

But there was more here than could be seen by the naked eye.

The mist was rapidly rising, not only from the river, but also from the earth itself. It was a veil she welcomed, heaven-sent. She could explore the ruins without fear of detection.

When she started down the other side of the incline, Haig House was shrouded in a swirl of vapor.

The path made a sharp turn to the left, well before the priory, then climbed steeply toward the trees that concealed the road. Jessica picked up her skirts, veered off the path and waded through a patch of newly scythed grass to the low stone wall that enclosed the ruins. It took her only a moment to navigate it.

She had known that what she would see would be the "church" of her dream, but all the same, it gave her an eerie feeling. Here, on this bare slab of stone, the cross had stood. To her right was the rectory, though all that remained of it was its stone pulpit and foundation. The cloisters and dormitories had vanished long since and were now replaced by a close-cropped stretch of grass. And it was right here, on the stretch of turf, that her wedding guests had played their game.

A shiver ran over her when she approached the main building. This was where Rodney Stone was taken to have his head chopped off. It was a ruin now, but it hadn't been a ruin in her dream. Or maybe it had been. All she'd had were impressions.

One down and two to go. The unholy litany drummed inside her brain.

Who was the next victim? Who?

She glanced involuntarily over her shoulder toward Haig House. Mist swirled in front of her like a sheet of transparent gauze. The silence was stretched taut, as if the whole of creation was holding its breath to see what she would do next.

Quickly turning, she passed through the stone archway and into the nave. The archway and its tower were almost intact but she could just as easily have entered the nave by climbing over a pile of rubble. She'd entered by the tower door without thinking and she realized now that she was retracing everything that had happened in her dream.

Above her, where once the vaulted roof had hung like a canopy, was the open sky; beneath her feet were flagstones; ahead was the chancel where the high altar had stood. She passed white marble statues in niches and effigies of knights carved into the walls. The mist cast a ghostly pall, sometimes obscuring her vision, sometimes lifting to reveal the sad splendor of a long-ago era. But she didn't need eyes to see what she'd come for. She was seeing things with an inner eye.

She approached the chancel with dread churning inside her. Each step heightened her senses to a razor-sharp edge. The hem of her garments was damp and clinging; she could smell wood smoke and the sweet scent of newly mown hay; the rain had stopped; a dog barked off in the distance; someone was watching her.

Her heart leapt and she jerked her head round. From his perch on top of one of the walls, a squirrel sat contemplating her as he calmly chewed on an ear of wheat. It took a long while for her heartbeat to return to normal.

She found what she was looking for in a small bay off the chancel. Like the tower entrance, this part of the building was well preserved, and here too the floor was flagstones.

In the very center of the floor, in solitary splendor, was a stone tomb, with the effigy of a woman, hands clasped in prayer, reclining in her final repose.

"Saint Martha," Jessica said, barely mouthing the words. "Saint Martha's crypt." The tomb in her dream.

And the final resting place of Rodney Stone.

A great sob tore at her throat, but she choked it back. She couldn't stop to worry about how it would all end. She couldn't think of Lucas. Too much was at stake.

Ruthlessly suppressing all emotion, she examined Saint Martha's tomb. It wasn't a coffin, but rather a marker to indicate the crypt that would lie beneath it. In her dream, there had been a set of stone steps leading down into the bowels of the earth.

She examined the tomb from all angles. She touched first one sculptured detail then another. She tugged, she pulled. Nothing happened. Finally, she sat back on her heels. There must be something she was missing.

She looked around the small bay and her eyes came to rest on a life-sized relief of the saint set in one wall. Rising, she walked to the wall and examined the sculpture. Saint Martha stood beneath a foliated cross with a fish in one hand and a lamp in the other, but it was the cross with its intricate halo that held Jessica's eyes. This was the cross of her dream.

She saw now that this slab of stone was not part of the wall but was attached to it, much like a painting. She ran her fingers around the bottom edge. A draft of cool air fanned over them. With mounting excitement, she began to twist, press and pull every projection she could get her fingers around. She was just about to give up when she touched the Latin inscription at Saint Martha's feet. It moved, or so she thought. When she pulled on it hard, it twisted to the side and she heard a grating sound, as if a key had turned in a lock.

Pulse racing, heart hammering, she splayed her hands on the stone sculpture and pushed hard. It wheezed, resisted, then slowly swung inward.

She'd found her steps. They led down into an icy, inky darkness.

Adrian was yawning when he entered the breakfast room of Walton Lodge. Lucas was already there, seated at the table. After helping himself from the servers on the sideboard, Adrian joined him.

"Where is Perry?" asked Lucas.

"Having a bath." Adrian glanced at the clock. "So what is the agenda for this morning?"

"I suggest that the first thing you do is get dressed."

Adrian looked down at his dressing robe and grinned. "Why? There are no ladies here to take offense, just we men, like in the good old days."

"Were they good old days? I'm beginning to wonder about that."

Adrian's smile faded and he looked at Lucas more closely. "You sound," he said, "as though you got up on the wrong side of the bed. What's wrong, Lucas?"

"What's wrong," said Lucas, throwing down his napkin, "is exactly what I told you on the way down here." He began to tick things off on his fingers. "First, Rodney Stone is missing, and foul play is suspected. Secondly, according to Perry, the butler at Haig House kept all the cards for Bella's ball. He remembers Rodney Stone particularly because he was a dandy, but there is no card now with Stone's name on it. So what happened to it? Third, there is a rumor going around about Stone and a woman he came down to see, but no one knows the identity of this mysterious woman, nor do they know where the rumor originated. Fourthly, my wife believes that Stone was paid to frighten her so that she would stop asking questions about her father's death. I could go on and on." Lucas looked off into space and said in a different tone of voice, "I tell you, Adrian, there's something very strange at work here, something that goes back to the night William Hayward died."

Adrian reached for the coffeepot and poured himself a cup of coffee before responding. "I can't see it myself. What I think is that Stone has gone off to the wilds of Scotland or something, and that when he turns up, as I'm sure he will, he'll explain everything."

Lucas said, "That may well be, but I'm not taking any chances until I question him in person."

"Chances on what?"

"Chances on something happening to Jessica."

Adrian was shocked into swallowing a mouthful of

scalding hot coffee. "Are you serious?" he demanded incredulously. "Who would wish to harm Jessica?"

"Whoever murdered her father."

There was a long silence as Adrian digested this. Finally, he shook his head. "You're not suggesting that one of us would do anything to hurt Jessica?"

"I don't know, Adrian. I don't know what I think anymore."

"But it was you . . . that is . . . if you didn't . . . I don't understand."

Lucas's eyes blazed with sudden anger, but he kept his voice low. "I did not execute William Hayward. Yes, I know, I drew the short straw, but I did not go through with it. I told you at the time that I wouldn't go through with it, that I couldn't. What I want to know is—who did?"

"If you didn't do it, then it wasn't Rupert or me."

Lucas was silent.

Adrian lifted his head and his eyes were as hard as Lucas's. "And what if," he said softly, "one of us did take matters into his own hands? Would you betray him to the authorities? Would you go back on your word to your comrades? Where do your loyalties lie, Lucas?"

Lucas moved like lightning. His hand closed around Adrian's arm, and coffee cup and coffee went flying. Neither man paid any attention to the porcelain cup that smashed to fragments or the spreading coffee stain on the pristine white tablecloth.

In a low, driven voice, Lucas said, "Nothing comes before my wife, do you understand? Not the past, not our friendship, not an oath I swore on my immortal soul. Nothing! And if I discover that someone has tried to hurt Jessica, or frighten her, no matter who it is, that person has become my mortal enemy, and I shall deal with him accordingly. Do I make myself clear?"

He released Adrian's arm and, suddenly rising, went to look out of the window, inwardly cursing himself for taking his frustrations out on Adrian. He felt helpless, that was the problem, helpless and deeply uneasy by what had come to light, not only with his own investigation of Stone, but with what Perry had told him the night before. An invitation card was missing. He knew that Bella's butler, Verney, was a stickler for detail. If he said the card was missing, then someone must have taken it. But the thing that disturbed him most of all was Perry's disclosure about the rumor that was going the rounds. It was Jessica's name that was being bandied about. She was the "mystery woman" that Stone had come to see. And if Stone turned up murdered, the next rumor that would go around was that Jessica was implicated.

He was glad, now, that he'd left her safely in London.

He turned to face Adrian and managed a smile. "I'm sorry," he said, "I shouldn't take my frustrations out on you. You asked about the agenda for today. We're to meet Rupert at his place later this morning. But before that, I want to speak with the driver of the carriage Stone hired that night. Jessica insisted that he saw her. Maybe he's lying. Maybe he has something to hide."

Adrian was still rubbing the arm Lucas had grabbed. "Why Rupert's place? Why not invite him here?"

"Because I want to question his butler as well. And I want to look over the priory."

Both men spoke at the same time.

"Lucas—"

"Adrian—"

The door opened and the butler entered, "Milord," he said, "her ladyship's maid is here."

The butler held the door wide, and Sadie entered. Lucas recognized her as Jessica's abigail. "What the devil are you doing in Chalford?" he demanded.

The little maid flushed at her master's hostile tone and began to tremble. "I came with her ladyship," she said, and promptly burst into tears.

The butler took over. "There's a hackney driver here

as well, milord. He says he drove her ladyship to Saint Luke's, and watched to make sure that she entered the church. But her ladyship did not enter the church. She took the path that goes by the old priory."

"I'll get dressed," said Adrian.

Lucas was already striding for the door.

She made the sign of the cross before she climbed over the ledge to the first step. Once there, she hesitated, overcome by a chilling, nauseating terror. It wasn't only dread of what she would find in the crypt that gripped her. She hadn't given a thought to providing herself with a candle or a lantern. She'd been too overwrought.

She heard a faint sound—a horse on the bridle path? Some small creature passing through?—and her head jerked. Mist swirled around, blanketing the walls of the priory in a ghostly shroud. Whoever she'd heard was now silent. Drawing in a deep breath, her back pressed hard against the stone wall, she began to descend the stairs.

When she reached the bottom, her foot touched hard-packed earth. She hesitated, absorbing as much as she could through her senses. The air was cold and clammy, but what she had feared most did not transpire. She'd steeled herself for the stench of putrefying flesh, but there was no stench. Nevertheless she was convinced Rodney Stone's body was here because she was sure that her dream had come to her straight from the mind of the murderer. What she did not know was what state of decay it would be in.

She peered into the gloom. The darkness swallowed up the light a few feet in front of her face. Though there was nothing to be seen, her imagination was seeing things that made her flesh creep. A crypt was a place of burial. God only knew what she would find, and she wasn't as brave as she had hoped she would be.

A few deep breaths calmed her a little, and it was then,

as she was inhaling, that she became aware of something she had not noticed before. The faint essence of something sweet and cloying hung on the air, the scent of a flower. Roses.

Thoughts raced through her mind in rapid confusion, then there was only one thought. "Bella," she sobbed softly.

The word echoed back to her in a mocking refrain.

She held her breath and listened. There wasn't a sound to be heard. With one hand on the stone wall, she began to inch forward. It might have been her imagination, but the scent of roses seemed to intensify. She was edging close to panic when her foot stepped on some small, soft object. With a cry of fright, she stepped to the side. The smell of roses filled her nostrils. It took every particle of her control to force herself down on her haunches. Slowly putting out her hands, she felt for the object she had trampled. It was the head of a rose. Her fingers closed around it convulsively.

"Oh, Bella," she breathed out.

She crouched there, shaken and horrified, staring into the black depths of the crypt, and the same eerie feeling that had overtaken her in Rodney Stone's rooms engulfed her now and her whole body began to shake. She tried to scream, but all that came out of her mouth was a terrified whimper. Like a wild thing in a panic, she started to her feet and fled.

She tore up those stairs as though the demons of hell were after her, out through the bay—and straight into the arms of a figure who came out of the mist.

"Jessica!" said Lucas, and his arms closed around her like a trap.

A scream tore from her throat. Twisting and turning, she tried to fight him off, but his arms only tightened till she could scarcely breathe. When she stopped struggling, the brutal pressure of his arms eased.

"Jess, what is it?" He looked over her shoulder toward the crypt. "What are you running from?"

Murderer! she wanted to scream, but pure animal instinct rushed in to protect her. But her instincts could not mend her broken heart. He had known that she was in Chalford, had known exactly where to find her. There was only one way he could have known. He must be her Voice, and he could read *her* as easily as she could read him.

She'd thought that she'd resigned herself to the fact that Lucas and her Voice were one and the same person, but now she saw how wrong she had been. She'd been clinging to the faint hope that by some miracle she would be proved wrong. With the death of all hope, something inside her quietly slipped into despair.

"Jess, tell me," he said, and he gave her a shake to loosen her tongue.

"In there," she choked out, pointing to the crypt. "In there."

"You found Rodney Stone's body? Where? Show me, Jess."

He would kill her, too, and no one would ever know where to find her. "Why, Lucas? Why?"

"Who can say how a murderer's mind works? All I know is he's got to be stopped. Now show me where you found the body."

Yes, he had to be stopped, and she was the only one who could do it.

They would play out the charade to its bitter end. Clinging to him like a woman in the grip of hysteria, she began to babble. It was all an act to allay his suspicions, but it seemed to work. His arm tightened protectively around her and his words were soothing. And that was all an act, too.

At the entrance to Saint Martha's crypt, they halted.

Lucas was staring at the hole in the wall as though he'd never seen it before. He was a consummate actor.

She put a finger to her lips and whispered shakily, "There's someone down there. I hit him with a rock. I think I may have stunned him."

Lucas frowned at her. "Stay here," he ordered, and reaching into his coat pocket, he produced a pistol.

He had taken her bait. She must be a consummate actress, too. She waited until he had disappeared from sight, then, reaching inward, she grabbed for the edge of the door and began to pull. She heard his exclamation of surprise, then the tread of his boots as he tried to intercept her. The stone door was heavy, but sheer terror gave her strength.

It was only as the door slammed shut that she realized how foolish she had been. Unlike her, Lucas would know how to get out of the crypt. Obviously, he came and went as he pleased. All she had done was gain a little time for herself.

On that thought, she whirled around and took off. She instinctively avoided the straight route out of the ruins and leapt for one of the low walls. She reached the top, but the slab under her feet tilted, and she pitched forward onto the ground. Her head cracked against one of the boulders that littered the area. Winded, stunned and shaken, she lay there like a lifeless doll.

She didn't know how long she lay there before she became aware of her surroundings. She blinked rapidly and, rolling to her side, curled into a ball and moaned as though a knife had pierced straight through her heart. It had all come back to her. Memories—bitter, galling memories—were flooding her brain and she was drowning in them. Lucas was her Voice! Lucas was her Voice! And he had tried to murder her once before. That's why she'd run away from Hawkshill.

And history was repeating itself.

She didn't care. Nothing mattered anymore. No one mattered, not even herself. She'd credited him with a few scruples. She'd thought he cared for her, but that was a lie. He'd wanted to silence her because she knew too much.

There were no tears, only dry, choking sobs. She couldn't stop the shivering. Her teeth were chattering. If Lucas had come upon her then, she could not have done a thing to save herself.

Time passed and she slowly came back to the present. She gave a bitter, shaken laugh. How many times had she prayed to have her memory restored? She'd been better off as she was. God was more compassionate than she'd known.

He had to be stopped. First her father, then Rodney Stone, and now Bella. She hadn't found Bella's body, but in that moment of terror in the crypt, when she'd sensed the malevolence of the murderer, Bella's image had been seared into her mind.

Her mission had come to nothing. She had failed, failed, *failed*. If only she hadn't trusted him, Bella would still be alive.

She dragged herself to her knees, then to her feet. She mustn't allow herself to give in to despair. Her own private hell would still be there waiting for her when this was all over.

There was a whisper of sound from the other side of the wall, then, "Jessica?"

Lucas!

Ignoring her aching head and chattering teeth, she took off.

Haig House was the only place of refuge close by. Lucas would know that, too. He would try to cut her off. No matter. She had no choice. She had to go on. If she could only slip by him unseen, she could find Rupert. He would know what to do.

She paused for a moment, looking toward the path,

hoping to see Lucas's horse tethered there so that she could use it to make her escape. There was nothing to be seen but a froth of vapor shrouding the hedgerows, and the walls of the priory's boundaries. And even if she were to see the horse, she couldn't be sure that Lucas was not there, waiting to pounce on her.

Her eyes scanned the way ahead. The mist obscured her view, but that was a blessing. It would conceal her from the eyes of predators. She looked over her shoulder. What was he *doing?* What was he waiting for?

"Jessica . . ."

A bubble of panic rose in her throat, and she was off and running.

When she reached the trees, she paused for breath. She looked behind her, but there was no sign or sound of pursuit, no thundering of hoofbeats crossing the turf. She would have to go where a horse could not follow.

She cupped her hands to her eyes and sagged against the trunk of a tree. A droplet of moisture splashed on her face. She looked up. Raindrops had gathered on the boughs and were dripping onto her. Her coat wasn't soaked but it was uncomfortably damp. Her soft leather half boots were caked with mud and stained beyond repair. Until that moment, she'd been dry-eyed, but the sight of the water marks on her new boots broke the tenuous thread of her control.

She choked back the sobs and angrily dashed away the tears. She had to get a grip on herself, she had to concentrate. Moving quietly and quickly, she passed through the belt of trees and came to the road. Up above was Haig House, but it too was lost in the mist. Nothing and no one were stirring. On that thought, she dashed across the road to the shelter of the trees on the other side.

From that point on, the going became harder, and the climb exacted a toll. By the time she reached the summit, she had a stitch in her side, her calves ached, and her breathing was labored. But all her aches and pains went out of her mind when the house suddenly loomed up in front of her.

It looked so safe and solid, something normal in a world gone mad. Checking to see that the coast was clear, she dashed across the turf.

C H A P T E R
25

SHE RAN THROUGH THE SHRUBBERY THAT GREW ALONG
the foundations of the house, then embraced the stone
wall as if it were her lover. One moment of relief was all
she allowed herself. It wasn't over yet, and Lucas could
still intercept her. On that sobering thought, she sank
down and tried to get her bearings.

The mist here was less dense, held at bay by a breeze
that wafted over the downs. But whenever the breeze
died down, the mist rolled in again. She was at the side of
the house, not far from where the marquee for Bella's ball
had been set up. All that stood between her and the terrace with its glass entrance doors was the conservatory.

She stayed there for a long time, listening. There were
small sounds—the drip of water from the roof into a
puddle; a forlorn songbird—but there was nothing to
alarm her. She got to her feet, then moving quickly and
silently, began to make her way to the terrace. She had
just drawn level with the conservatory when the door
opened and Rupert came out. He was more surprised

than she. She had frozen like a sculpture. He dropped the clay pot he was holding. It fell with a thud on the grass, and though it didn't break, the rose in it snapped in two.

"Jessica!" he exclaimed. "I didn't know you were in Chalford. My God! What's happened to you?"

She looked down at herself. She looked a fright, but that didn't matter. Raising her eyes, she gazed up at him. No man loved a woman more than Rupert loved Bella, and she was just about to bring his world down upon his ears.

She said feebly, "I'm sorry about the rose."

"The rose?"

She pointed to the ground, at the rose that had snapped in two.

He picked it up. "Don't be. It won't be wasted," and he shortened the stem and tucked it into the pin on the lapel of his coat. "Now come into the house, and tell me what's happened."

In answer, she grasped him by the arm and dragged him into the conservatory. Roses of every hue were set out in tiers everywhere the eye could see. The scent made her shiver. There were two stone benches just inside the door. He led her to one and made her sit. His look of puzzlement had changed to one of consternation.

"What is it, Jessica?"

"Does the door lock?"

He nodded.

"Please, Rupert, lock it. L . . . Lucas is after me."

His brows rose, but he did as she asked. When he came back to her, he said, "Now what's all this about you and Lucas? Have you had a falling-out?"

"Rupert," she said, groping for a way of softening the blow, "when did you last see Bella?"

"What does this have to do with Bella?"

"Please! Answer me!"

He frowned at her harsh tone. "Four days ago when

she went off on a shopping spree to town. Didn't you see her there?"

"Yes, but she left yesterday to return to Chalford. She should have been here by now."

"If I know Bella, she's probably stopped off somewhere to visit friends. No need to look so worried, my dear. Now, tell me about you and Lucas."

His words did not reassure her. She'd sensed her Voice's presence in the crypt. He'd been there recently. And Bella's perfume had permeated the air.

She swallowed past the constriction in her throat. "Rupert, I know that what I'm about to say will shock you, but please hear me out. Lucas is a murderer. No! Listen to me! He killed my father. I was there. I saw him. He tried to kill me, too. And Rupert, oh Rupert, I'm almost sure he's killed Bella. I've just come from the old priory. I found a way into Saint Martha's crypt. I was looking for Rodney Stone's body. There was no light, but I could smell Bella's perfume. And I found a rose. She must be there, don't you see?"

His face and lips had gone deathly white.

"I feared something like this would happen," she went on, "but I never thought his next victim would be Bella. We've got to stop him. I locked him in the crypt, but that was some time ago. He won't be there now. And I heard him calling my name."

"You went into the crypt?" he said and paused. "Jessica, what are you talking about?"

She jumped to her feet, walked to the glass door and peered out. "He'll know that there's nowhere I can go but here. He could be here at any moment. He may be here now. He's armed and dangerous." The last was wrung from her. "Oh, Rupert, what are we going to do?"

Her words died when she turned to look at Rupert. He was bent over, holding his head between his hands.

She sat down beside him and put a comforting hand on his arm. "Rupert, you've got to stop him. But be careful.

Lucas is dangerous. I'm sorry, I'm so sorry. It's all my fault."

"Jessica!" He raised his head. "Bella can't be dead. And what's this about Rodney Stone? You're confused. I know you are. Now calm yourself, and tell me exactly what happened. What were you doing in the priory? And don't tell me Lucas has murdered anyone because I won't believe it."

She *was* on the verge of panic, and his reluctance to believe her wasn't helping. Realizing she would only make matters worse if she did not calm down, she quickly related the events of that morning. But all the while, she kept darting a look out the windows.

When she stopped speaking, he said, "Jessica, you're in a panic for nothing. Bella has her maid with her, as well as four stalwart coachmen and my carriage. Has something happened to them too?"

"I don't know," she cried. "Perhaps she came here in secret to meet Lucas."

He shook his head. "I can't believe that."

"Then why was there a rose in the crypt?"

"What rose?"

She felt in her pockets, but all she produced were her gloves. She set them aside and dug deeper. There was no rose. "I think I must have dropped it when I fell."

"When your memory came back to you?"

"Yes."

"And you locked Lucas in the crypt."

"Yes!" she cried out. "Rupert, I'm not deranged! I'm telling you the truth. I swear it. Rodney Stone's body is there, and Bella . . . oh God, I think something must have happened to her too."

Suddenly rising, he walked to the glass door and looked out. With his back to her, he said, "The wind is rising and the mist is clearing. There's no sign of Lucas. I don't think he found a way out of the crypt, Jessica. I think he must still be in there."

He swung round so suddenly that she jumped. He smiled. "You know," he said, "you're going to look very foolish if I send for the constable and Bella arrives home an hour later. And how will Lucas feel, knowing that his wife has accused him of murder? I think we should go down there now and let him out of the crypt before this goes any further."

Constable? She hadn't thought of sending for the constable. That's not what she wanted. She didn't know what she wanted. She only knew that Lucas had to be stopped.

He unlocked the glass door and opened it. "There's something else you're not taking into account. Lucas arrived at the priory after you. If I send for the constable and he finds Stone's body buried in the crypt, he may accuse you of the murder."

His eyes narrowed on her face, then he looked down at his feet to see what she was staring at. The rose had fallen out of his lapel.

Jessica jerked her eyes up to meet his.

Sighing, he shut the door and bent to retrieve the rose. Petals broke away and floated to the floor.

She tried to say something, but her tongue had stuck to the roof of her mouth.

"That was careless of me," he said, and he crushed the rose in his hand then threw it away. "But that's not all, is it? What else did I say, Jessica?"

She looked into his eyes and knew that lying would not save her. She had given herself away and now he knew that she had found him out. Making the movement as unthreatening as she could, she slowly rose to her feet. "When I entered the crypt," she said, "I wondered why there was no smell of putrefying flesh. You've just told me why. You buried Rodney Stone's body in the earth floor, didn't you, Rupert?"

"So, that's it." He smiled ruefully. "I'm sorry. I didn't want to frighten you. I wanted to get this over and done with before you realized what was happening."

He was going to kill her. She saw at once that it wasn't a sudden decision. He'd had every intention of doing away with her from the moment she'd accosted him outside the conservatory. And the moment she knew that, everything became clear to her.

"You're my Voice," she said.

"Voice?" He cocked his head to one side. "That's not how I would describe it. You came into my mind uninvited. I wondered about it a time or two, oh, years ago, but not seriously. I thought my imagination was playing tricks on me. All that changed the night your father died."

"Yes," she said, as memories flooded her mind. "At first, you couldn't believe that I was reading you. You didn't want to believe it. But you could not shut your mind to me."

"And," he said softly, "I was terrified."

"So you came after me and tried to murder me. I didn't see you, you know, not clearly. So you were quite safe."

He spoke without passion, and his words were all the more lethal because of it. "Safe? I think not. Try to see it from my point of view. I would always be afraid of your power to read me. My whole life through, I would be afraid. There's no way I can guard myself against you. Not completely. How can I live with that?"

She said wonderingly, "But why you? Why not someone else's mind? I thought it was Lucas's mind I could read. When I was a girl growing up, I was sure of it."

"Then you were mistaken. It had to be my mind. You and I are related, you see. Oh, not closely, cousins three or four times removed. Our common ancestor is Great-great-uncle Albert. I suspected it must be something like that, so I looked into it after you ran away from Hawkshill. It's all written down in the family annals. Uncle Albert was the black sheep of the family. He was cast out without a penny many years ago, and from what I can

336 / ELIZABETH THORNTON

gather, deservedly so. He hadn't the least notion of what he owed to the name he bore."

"We're related?" she said, trying to absorb the thought.

"There's even a physical resemblance between us. Haven't you noticed? We have the same hair and eyes."

Though she heard every word, another part of her mind was on Lucas. What had she done? Oh, God, what had she done?

"Lucas won't help you, Jessica. It will take him hours to find his way out of the crypt, as I should know."

Her eyes flared.

"No," he said, "I'm not reading your mind. I simply guessed you'd be thinking about him. You see, it's only the females in our family who have the . . . 'gift,' shall we call it for want of a better word? Oh, we males are sensitive, but we haven't the same power, and not everyone has it. As you may imagine, my grandfather was appalled. He thought it was an abomination, and I agree with him. It was a secret we kept closely guarded within the family."

He didn't look like a murderer. He didn't sound like a murderer. Even in this macabre nightmare of a conversation, he was as gracious and charming as she'd ever seen him.

People were such fools. They looked at him and saw exactly what he wanted them to see. No one had ever suspected him of murder. He was too clever for them.

She had a flash of recall, Rupert at Bella's side, the picture of the devoted husband. Everyone knew how Rupert spoiled Bella. No man loved a woman more.

"It's time, Jessica."

Having murdered once, he could do it again. In fact, he would do it again. A shudder ran over her. "Bella was to be your next victim. You were going to kill your wife. And you would have killed her if I hadn't come back to Hawkshill."

"True. You have no idea how terrified I was when you

reappeared. For three years, I'd assumed you were either dead or were so far away that you were no longer a threat to me. Then I started having these little twitches, and that worried me. I remember the day I made up my mind to murder Bella. I had the strangest feeling that I'd spoken aloud."

"I was at vespers," she said. "I knew my Voice was going to murder again, but that's all I knew."

"When I heard you'd lost your memory, I hoped you had lost your powers as well, or that they were so weakened that I was safe from you. But I soon discovered that wasn't the case." He laughed. "You were careless, Jessica. You left me with one of your own thoughts once."

"I remember," she said. "I was on the bridle path, thinking about how you had murdered my father. I knew I had given myself away. What did I do?"

"It was the house," he said. "I saw Haig House in the distance. But it was different. I couldn't see it clearly. And I didn't think of it as my house, but as some rich man's house. Then I knew, I *knew* you had slipped into my mind. After that, I became even more vigilant, and kept my guard up at all times. You have no idea how wearing that can be."

"You didn't succeed. I sensed your anger the night I ran from Mr. Stone."

"Yes. When I'm in the grip of strong emotions, it's almost impossible to keep you out of my mind. That's why I decided to postpone my plans for Bella until I had dealt with you."

The words were torn from her. "Why, Rupert? Why did you do all this?"

He answered her gently. "We haven't got time to go into it. And I don't think I could ever make you understand." He paused then went on. "You must see that I can't let you live. But I promise, I'm going to make this as easy and as painless as possible. You see, I like you. I really like you. There's no malice in what I must do. I have no choice. It's as simple as that."

Her whole body tensed to defend herself. "You won't get away with it. Lucas knows that I'll come here. He'll tear this place apart until he finds me."

"I'm aware of that. But give me credit for some intelligence. It will be a tragic accident, a fall from the cliff, when your mind was deranged. I shall tell the constable you were here, of course, and when Lucas comes out of the crypt, he'll substantiate my story. You weren't yourself; you were raving like a lunatic."

He opened the door. "Your only chance is to get to the crypt and let Lucas out before I can stop you. Call it a sporting chance. But if I catch you, I'll break your neck."

Her terror wouldn't have been so complete if he hadn't looked and sounded so normal. But he wasn't deranged. He was simply a charming, cold-blooded killer.

Panic was beating at the edges of her mind. He wasn't giving her a sporting chance. She could never hope to outrun him.

She licked her lips. "And if I refuse to run?"

"Then we'll finish it right here. Of course, that would be an inconvenience to me. I'd have to carry your body to the bluff. But the mist would give me cover. Nobody would be the wiser. And I wouldn't count on help from the servants, even if you run into any. I shall simply tell them that you're deranged and take you away." He waited a moment, and when she remained immobile, sighed and said, "Look, I'll make this easy for you."

Leaving the door open, he walked to the far end of one of the aisles. He was a good twenty feet away, his back still turned to her, when she sprang forward and leapt through the door.

She instinctively turned toward the terrace. If she could get inside the house, she could find servants and demand their help. But into her mind flashed the sure and certain knowledge that the terrace doors were locked. She was reading him! She was reading him just as if he were shouting his thoughts aloud. He couldn't shield his thoughts from her when he was in the grip of strong emotions. Turning aside, she headed into the shelter of the trees.

She could hear the pounding of his steps gaining on her, and sheer animal terror lent her speed. She was on a path, one of the famous walks of Haig House. What she didn't know was where the path was in relation to everything else. It was one thing to skirt a bluff in the mist but quite another to find a safe way down when a murderer was hard on her heels. If she left the path, she might go hurtling over the cliff.

Where was she? Dear God, where was she?

Bubbles of panic rose in her throat. She was going to die. He was going to kill her and nobody would ever know. Then he would kill Bella.

She was panic-stricken, but another emotion began to rise in her. It mustn't end like this. She'd been given a mission. The sisters said it was ordained. *Oh, Lucas. Oh, Lucas. What have I done?*

Read him! The thought suddenly seized her. *Read him!* And as easily as slipping into a bath of water, she slipped into Rupert's mind.

He was reliving the night she'd run from Rodney Stone. He'd remembered how he'd helped carry her in the improvised stretcher, along this very path, pretending to be concerned when what he'd really wanted to do was finish her off. If only he'd got to her first! But this time he had cornered her. Soon, it would be over. She couldn't escape him now.

A map, he was giving her a map, just as he'd given her a map of her father's murder. They were on the path that led to the pavilion. There was no way down for the next mile, only a sheer drop to the rocks below. And when they came out on the pavilion, one hard shove would send her toppling over.

She was trapped, and she had no one to blame but herself. If she'd wanted to be an accessory to her own murder, she couldn't have done more to help him. He'd asked her all those questions to make sure that he was in the clear and that there was no one there to save her. And like an idiot, she'd told him everything. If that were not enough, she'd played right into his hands the moment she'd leapt out of the conservatory and made for the terrace doors. This was the way he'd hoped she would take. There was no way down at this point, unless she went over the bluff.

Or, she could go up.

She discarded that thought almost as soon as it occurred to her. He would only stop her. Even now, he was holding himself in check, allowing her to outstrip him because she was going exactly where he wanted her to go. The moment she veered off course, he would pounce on her and drag her to the edge of the bluff.

The mist was thicker at this point, sheltered from the breeze by the trees that grew close to the path. *Good cover,* he'd called it, and it would be good cover if she could put some space between them. If she could only put some distance between them she could hide and wait for help to arrive.

She was tiring. Her lungs were bursting. The muscles in her legs were cramping brutally. She had to disable him, she had to find a way to even the odds. She ran the race of her life, her eyes desperately searching for deliverance.

A terrified whimper caught in her throat. Ahead of her, a sudden gust of air had dissipated the mist, carrying it off in a wild dervish.

And she could see the roof of the pavilion!

It was sheer animal instinct that made her balk at going to her death like a lamb to the slaughter. Her strength was almost spent, but she found an inner reserve that galvanized her into motion. With the agility of a gazelle, she leapt off the path and into the undergrowth. She heard Rupert's grunt of surprise, felt him check, then he turned to come after her. He called her name and the sound of it acted on her like a spark to dry powder. Oblivious of briers and the thorns from brambles, she shot through the undergrowth.

The fear of death sharpened all her senses. She knew where she was! She was traveling in reverse the route she'd come when she'd run from Rodney Stone. There was a map inside her head. She could see it as clearly as if she were reading a chart in her hand. She was making for the depression she'd fallen into when she'd run from Stone.

She had a chance, a slim chance if she could stay the course.

He was reaching for her. She saw it in her mind's eye. Those powerful hands were reaching for her. She was almost there. She was almost there . . .

Now!

She dropped to her knees so suddenly that he could not save himself. The hands that were reaching for her flailed the air, but his momentum carried him forward. He stumbled over her and went flying into the depression. She hoped he had broken a leg or brained himself on a boulder. She didn't wait to find out. Like a wounded, hunted animal, she crawled away on her hands and knees.

She didn't think she had the strength to rise, but when she heard him laughing softly, with a will of their own, her limbs began to move.

"Jessica," he said, his voice coming to her from the depression. "Why are you doing this? You're only prolonging the agony. You know it can end in only one way."

Terrified as she was, she still spared a moment to read him. He was winded and his ankle hurt, but it wasn't serious. It wouldn't stop him coming after her. She stifled a whimper of terror and looked around for a place to hide. He would expect her to get as far from the bluff as possible. So she would do the unexpected. Crouched over, she carefully inched her way toward the bluff.

Peering over the edge, she scanned the rock face for a ledge, anything that could give her shelter. The mist thinned, and she saw a ledge no bigger than a toehold, about ten feet down.

He was beginning to stir. She could sense it all through her body. On that desperate thought, she slipped over the edge of the bluff and held on for dear life. Then, quietly, cautiously, she felt for a toehold. When she found it, she searched with her dangling foot for another. When both feet were secure, she groped for something to hang on to, then inch by slow inch, she began to lower herself to the ledge.

"Jessica?"

She flattened herself against the rock face, scraping her knees, but she hardly noticed. Her breath was suspended in her lungs as she waited for him to appear above her.

"I know you're hiding close by. You can't escape me."

She heard him move away from her, then she heard nothing. Heart hammering, groping for crevices, she slowly continued her descent.

Under her foot, a rock suddenly gave way and went slithering down the slope, taking other rocks with it. She strangled her scream, but the sound of the rocks falling reverberated in the silence like a thousand echoes. Arms straining, every muscle tensed, she desperately sought for another hold. She found it just as Rupert's head appeared above her.

He was kneeling on one leg on the turf, close to the edge. Tendrils of mist clung to his shoulders. The breeze ruffled his blond hair and curled it into wisps. When he saw her, he flattened himself on the ground and reached out with both arms. He was going to dislodge her hands and send her hurtling into space.

As those hands came closer, nausea overcame her and her head swam. It wasn't courage that made her give up her handholds, but panic. Clinging to the rock face with only her nails, inexorably, she began to slip. She cried out when her feet came to rest on the strip of ledge she'd spied earlier. Not knowing if it could bear her weight, she frantically groped for crevices, projections—anything she could dig her fingers into to bear some of her weight.

"Jessica."

She looked up.

"Why are you doing this?" He shook his head sorrowfully then he was gone.

She knew he'd be back. It was only a matter of time before he'd be back. She had to put more distance between them. She released one of her handholds to search for another, and the ledge beneath her feet began to give way under the burden of her weight. It was no use. She couldn't go down, and she couldn't go up. She was trapped.

She heard him approach the edge of the bluff and she looked up. He loomed above her, poised to catapult a great boulder that he held above his head. She cowered against the cliff, but she couldn't tear her eyes away.

"I admire your pluck," he said. "I really do. And strange as it may sound, I bear you no ill will."

"You're mad," she cried.

"No. I'm desperate."

"Then you're evil through and through."

Her words seemed to shake him, but only momentarily. His whole body tensed as he braced himself to make the throw. It never came. She heard a thundering as if a regiment of cavalry was on the move. Then she heard the rush of feet, and men shouting. Rupert was wrenched back from the edge of the precipice. It seemed like forever before another man appeared above her.

Lucas, grim and white-faced, stared down at her.

He flattened himself on the turf and wriggled forward, both hands extended. "Easy now," he said. "Let's do this one step at a time. Give me your right hand, Jess."

Now that he was here, her nerve completely deserted her. Tears welled up. "I don't think I can."

"Now!" he commanded, and she gave him her hand.

It was over in a matter of minutes. She was hauled up and set down on the turf. Adrian and Perry were there with drawn pistols. Rupert was grinning sheepishly.

Jessica hardly spared Rupert a glance. She was watching Lucas. She wanted to throw herself into his arms, and beg his forgiveness for locking him in the crypt. The look in his eyes held her back.

"Put up your pistols," he told Adrian and Perry.

He came to stand an arm's length from Rupert.

Rupert said, "I suggest that we repair to the house and settle this in a civilized manner."

Lucas sent him to his knees with a blow to the stomach, then he hauled him up by the collar. "By all means," he snarled, "let us repair to the house. But don't expect me to be civilized." Then he sent Rupert sprawling. "Move!" he roared. "Adrian, watch him."

Then he came to Jessica and swept her up in his arms. She buried her face against his chest and let the tears come.

CHAPTER
26

THE FIRST THING LUCAS DID ON ENTERING HAIG House was to send one servant to fetch the constable, and another to have Rupert's carriage brought round to take Jessica home. She would have none of it, and after a short argument, he entered the library and set her on a sofa, then removed his coat and wrapped it around her shoulders. But his eyes did not meet hers.

Once Rupert was in his own sanctum, a change came over him. Though he had not been cowed on the way up, he'd been silent and thoughtful. Now, he took charge of things, assuming the role of host, asking Perry to hand round the brandy decanter. With the exception of Rupert, everyone declined.

He sat at his desk, cradling his glass in both hands. Lucas stood by the empty grate, one arm supported by the solid oak mantel. Adrian stood with his back to one of the small windows. Jessica and Perry sat on the sofa on one side of the fireplace. No one said anything. All eyes were on Rupert.

He said, "I could deny everything, and there is nothing any of you could say in a court of law that would convict me of murder. But I don't want this to go to a court of law, so I'm going to tell you everything."

Lucas said harshly, "You tried to murder Jessica and we here are all witnesses. So don't think you're going to get away with this."

"All I'm saying," replied Rupert, "is that I don't think this will go to a court of law, leastways, I hope not."

Jessica's eyes flew to Lucas, then to Adrian. Their faces were grim, but neither of them contradicted Rupert. This wasn't going to go to a court of law. She couldn't believe that they would let Rupert get off scot-free. Once they knew what he'd done, they would change their minds.

She shivered, and smiled at Perry when he patted her hand, but it was a teary smile. He was the only one there who seemed to understand what she was feeling. But there was more to her despondency than that. She could have borne her aches and pains and her blinding headache if Lucas would only look at her. Not once since he'd pulled her from the cliff face had he given her more than a passing glance.

Rupert was speaking again. "You might say," he said, looking at Lucas, "that we wouldn't be here now if you had done your duty three years ago. We had a pact, Lucas. You drew the short straw, then you reneged on your promise. When you asked us to meet you at the Black Swan that night, it never occurred to me that you would go back on your word. I was furious, and when I passed Hayward on the way out, I decided to take matters into my own hands. One of us had to remember what we owed our fallen comrade."

Lucas said, "Our pact had nothing to do with murder, nor would Philip have asked it of us. He wasn't like that. Our vow was to look after the ones who were left if anything should happen to us in battle. It was a mistake to draw straws, a mistake I soon came to regret. Murder is the act of an outlaw."

"It wasn't murder," said Rupert curtly. "It was an execution. We all know what manner of man Hayward was. We all know what he did to Philip's wife. He deserved to die."

"That isn't the point. We were all in this together, and we all agreed to call it off. You broke faith with us, Rupert."

Adrian said, "You shot Hayward in the back."

Rupert turned his head to look at Adrian and said indifferently, "To throw the authorities off the scent, in case they became suspicious. No one would believe that I would stoop to such a thing. But I repeat, it was an execution, and I'm not sorry I did it. Someone had to."

Jessica felt herself recoil in horror. She knew now more than ever that her father was anything but a good man. Perhaps he had deserved to die for what he had done to Jane Bragge. But by his admission, Rupert had stooped to the same level as her father, if not lower. What was so chilling was that he could not see it. And it did something to her, to hear them talking so coldly about her father. He was her father, and she had loved him in spite of everything.

Lucas said quietly, "And Rodney Stone? I suppose that was his grave we found in the crypt?"

"We?" asked Rupert.

"Adrian and I. It was Adrian who heard me shouting and opened the crypt door."

Rupert gave a low laugh. "My, how the fates have conspired against me! If you had been alone in that crypt with the door shut, it would have taken you hours to find a way out. The door is not an exit. There's another way out that leads to the river. My grandfather modified the crypt when he dabbled in smuggling, oh, in a very small way, you understand. Only for himself and a few friends." He clicked his tongue. "Jessica, you did not tell me that Adrian was here, too."

"I saw you," said Adrian, looking at Jessica, "and called your name, but you didn't respond."

She shrank into Lucas's coat. "I . . . I was in a panic."

Lucas went on as though this aside had not taken place. "The earth in one corner of the crypt had been freshly turned over. Is that where you buried Rodney Stone?"

Rupert inclined his head. "I buried him there when Jessica was convalescing from her fall."

The implication that he had murdered him there too was not lost on anyone, and there was a complete and abrupt silence before Lucas went on. "Explain how Rodney Stone fits into this, Rupert."

Rupert took a healthy swallow from his glass and said, "You have to understand first of all that Jessica was a great trial to me. You see, she can read my mind, and I mean that quite literally. I don't have time to go into all the details. Jessica can explain it to you later, after . . . well, she'll explain everything later."

Perry broke in at this point. "Dash it all, Jess, do you mean to say that it was all true, when we were children and everything, that you really are a bit of a witch?"

"I wouldn't go that far," she said miserably, not daring to look at anyone. "My intuition is sharper than most people's. And there was only one mind I could ever see into, and then, only rarely. But I never knew whose mind it was." She darted a lightning glance at Lucas. Nothing showed in his face, neither aversion nor understanding.

A memory came to her vividly—Lucas telling her, quite savagely, when she was a young girl that if she continued to play her games, all her friends would spurn her. Normal people did not wish to associate with witches. After that, she'd been too ashamed to let anyone know that she was different.

Adrian said, "I seem to remember hearing something to that effect, oh, years ago. Lucas, didn't you—"

"Yes," said Lucas, "I did, but I thought Jessica was playacting."

"I wasn't playacting."

"So it would seem. Does this mean that you remember everything before you ran away from Hawkshill?"

"I fell in the priory when I was running away from . . . that is, I banged my head on a rock, and when I came to myself, I began to remember things. I'm not sure yet if my memory has completely returned."

"I see. Rupert, you were telling us about Rodney Stone."

So much for the miracle of recovering her memory. She felt like a naughty child who had been reproved with a slap on the wrist. Once again, Perry reached out and patted her hand and she felt a little better.

"If," said Rupert, "Jessica had not possessed this cursed talent, she would have been quite safe. I admire her. I like her. I always have. I mean that quite sincerely."

Lucas repeated evenly, "Tell us about Rodney Stone."

"I met him in London, and later, when I saw I would never be free of Jessica, I hired him to abduct her. I was afraid to act for myself, in case she would read me. But it all went wrong. Jessica . . . I don't know. She sensed something."

"Stone was to abduct her," said Lucas. "Then what?"

Rupert said nothing, but looked down at the glass he was aimlessly shifting from hand to hand.

Lucas said suddenly, "My God, I don't believe this!"

It was a long time before anyone spoke, then Adrian said, "But why was it necessary to abduct her? Why not simply kill her in the house or in the grounds?"

"Because," said Rupert, "it was too risky! Because there were too many people wandering around and I could not leave my guests for long. What difference does it make now?"

He looked at Jessica and she knew why. She was reading his mind, seeing clearly how the whole thing was
plotted. "There were two carriages," she said. "You questioned the wrong driver, Lucas. Stone would have
stunned me when I entered the first carriage, then he
would have driven me to the crypt and locked me in for
Rupert to deal with later. That carriage would have
driven away and Stone would have walked back to Haig
House. He would have mingled with the guests and left
in the carriage that had brought him to the ball. The
driver you questioned was above suspicion and would
have given Stone an alibi, as, in fact, he did." She looked
down at her hands. "I will say this. Rodney Stone did not
know that he was to be an accomplice to murder. He
thought Rupert wanted me for . . . for . . ."

Lucas spoke as though the words were strangling him.
"You would have murdered her and buried her body in
the crypt. She would have disappeared again, and I would
never have known what had happened to her."

Another long silence ensued, then Lucas said, "Tell us
about the carriage that was to be used in Jessica's abduction."

Rupert drained his glass. "Stone arranged that part,"
he said. "The driver was some petty criminal who was
paid to keep his mouth shut. He didn't know about me,
and I didn't know him."

"So if he were apprehended," said Lucas, "he could
only lead us back to Stone?"

Rupert nodded.

"If Jessica had not sensed something . . ." Lucas
broke off and turned his face away. "And I didn't believe
her."

Adrian said quietly, "Tell us what you sensed, Jessica,
when Stone tried to get you into the carriage."

She blinked rapidly. "Something malevolent, I don't
know, but it was the same feeling that came over me in

Rodney Stone's rooms when Perry and I were there, and again this morning, in the crypt."

"Try to be precise," said Lucas quietly.

He wasn't looking at her, but she sensed the rigid control he was imposing on himself. She looked down at her bruised and bloodied fingers and ragged nails. "I hardly know how to explain it," she said. "I sense that something is very wrong. And I get impressions, fragments of dreams." She looked at Rupert. "You went to Stone's rooms, and you were in the crypt quite recently."

He nodded. "I was covering my tracks, making sure I'd left no clue that would incriminate me. I knew I'd been careless, but that was because I never expected anyone to question Stone's disappearance."

She shuddered and hugged herself with her arms.

Lucas said, "I suppose you meant to murder Stone from the first?"

Rupert shrugged. "If I'd allowed him to live, he would have been too great a threat to me. Lucas, he was a nothing. He was despicable, and no loss to the world."

Lucas showed no emotion. "His aunt would not agree with you. But if, as you say, Jessica can read your mind, what was to stop her knowing you had murdered Stone?"

"For one thing, she was sedated, and for another, I was more vigilant. She can't read my thoughts at will."

"Sedated?" said Lucas.

"I doctored her medicine with laudanum. It was the only way I could have her in my house and feel safe. And I wasn't taking any chances when I got rid of Stone."

Lucas's hand clenched into a fist. Jessica was remembering Sister Dolores's elixir and how groggy she'd been. And all the time it was Rupert's doing. That's why she'd been so weary. It was only after she'd left Haig House that she'd started to get well again.

Another long silence, then Lucas said, "It was you who gave Stone an invitation to Bella's ball?"

"I filled in his name in my own hand. That was a

stupid mistake. But as I said, I never expected anyone to question Stone's disappearance."

"And you found the card and destroyed it?"

Rupert inclined his head.

"You started the rumor that Stone was coming to Chalford to be with some woman?"

"Yes."

"To divert suspicion from yourself?"

"Yes."

"On to Jessica, in fact."

"Yes. If she accused me, I thought people would take my word over hers. And it almost worked. Had you not caught me red-handed, had you not come upon us on the bluff precisely when you did, you would never have suspected me, no matter what Jessica said."

Lucas looked at Jessica. Without inflection he said, "You're wrong, Rupert. I would have taken Jessica's word over anyone's."

At any other time, these words would have thrilled her. Now, they scourged her.

He watched her for a moment, then he turned back to Rupert. "I should have listened to her. She always suspected Stone."

"I'll say," said Perry in a voice that burned with indignation. "It was Jess who kept asking questions about him. If she had left it alone, so would we."

Lucas said, "How did you know about the crypt, Jessica?"

There it was again, "Jessica," when he always called her "Jess." That was how low she had sunk in his opinion. "It came to me in fragments of a dream," she said. "I thought it was my dream, but later, I came to think it had come from . . . from my Voice."

"That's what I was to her," said Rupert, "A Voice, not a person. But you must see my dilemma. It was only a matter of time before she unmasked me."

Adrian made a sudden movement with his hand, and everyone turned to look at him.

"What?" asked Lucas.

"All this just to cover William Hayward's murder? I hardly think so. There's got to be more to it than that. We had a pact. If one was accused, the others would have protected him. We would have given each other an alibi. Jessica would have been laughed out of court if she'd sworn that Rupert was guilty because she could read his mind. There's got to be more to it than that."

"You say that," said Rupert, "because it's not your mind she can read. Can you imagine how tiresome it is keeping a guard on your thoughts? For the most part, I kept her at bay, but one can't always be vigilant. And that first time, when I panicked . . ." His voice trailed away.

"What first time?" asked Lucas.

Rupert looked at him blankly and shook his head. "It doesn't matter."

In a tight little voice, Jessica said, "The night he murdered my father. I saw him, though not clearly. But his mind was open to me, and I could feel his hatred and rage. He knew I was inside his mind and he came after me. He would have murdered me too if he'd caught me."

"I panicked," said Rupert. "She was there. She had seen me kill her father. She was reading my mind like an open book. Naturally, I went for her. But she eluded me."

She eluded me. This did not describe the horror of the next few hours. He'd hunted her down as if she were a wounded animal that he'd wanted to put out of its misery. That's what had been so horrible. She'd felt his compassion and his regret, and it had made her sick to her stomach. At the same time, her heart had shattered because she thought he was Lucas.

She'd escaped by hiding on one of the river barges that was being loaded with farm produce for sale in London. She'd concealed herself in a bin of potatoes. It was near dawn before the barge cast off, and late afternoon the next day when they docked in London. She remembered wandering the streets in a daze. Her father was dead because of her, and Lucas would kill her, too. And blind to everything but her own misery, she'd stepped in front of a moving carriage.

"And," said Adrian, "that's why you've done all this—just to cover your tracks?"

"No," said Jessica. "He's planning another murder."

With a dry little laugh, Rupert rose and went to the table with the crystal decanters. After refilling his glass, he took his seat again. "I see," he said, "that I'm to be spared nothing."

"Whose murder?" asked Lucas.

"Bella's, of course," replied Rupert. "But I see from your expression you've already guessed it. Did you see through all my little ploys and stratagems, Lucas?" A sneer crept into his voice. "Or do you imagine that I love my wife? I despise her and that is no exaggeration." He put his glass to his lips and almost drained it. "To think," he said, "I chose her to be mistress of my ancestral home. My mother would turn in her grave if she could see the woman who has replaced her. Bella is vulgar from the tips of her fingers to her painted toes. She has no heart, and no taste. She has the mind of a child. Try and carry on a conversation with her and see what I mean. She has only one topic of conversation and that is Bella. Not that any of us thought the less of her for that when we were rivals for her affections. But we were young and foolish then."

He set down his glass with a snap. "She has no appreciation for this house and its history. Nor does she want to learn. She despises my tenants and their wives because they have honest dirt under their nails. I assure you, the feeling is mutual."

He stopped suddenly and shook his head. "Don't you think I know, Lucas, that both you and Adrian thank your lucky stars that I was the one she married? I tell you, I had not been married a month before I knew what a fool I'd been, but I endured for three years before I decided to do something about it. I had murdered once, I thought, and I could do it again. No. I *would* do it again."

He looked at Jessica and said softly, "But you were there, even then, weren't you, Jessica, listening to my thoughts, learning my secrets?"

"That's not how it works," she said. "Your thoughts come to me in blurred pictures and sensations." She looked at Lucas. "I'd heard my Voice before, describing what I know now was my father's murder. But this time it was different. It told me there would be another murder. From the moment I returned to Hawkshill, I had only one thought in my mind—how to prevent it."

"And to think you've saved Bella!" exclaimed Rupert with a laugh. "What an irony! You always hated her when you were a girl. And she has never had anything good to say about you. That's the trouble with Bella. She never recognizes quality."

Lucas's mouth twisted. "So you made up your mind to murder Jessica."

"I had no choice."

"And how were you going to do it, after the debacle with Stone?"

"I hadn't the foggiest idea. I knew I couldn't make any plans in case she got wind of them. It would have to be something I devised on the spur of the moment. When she walked out of the mist today, alone, with no one to protect her, I thought luck was on my side." He drained his glass. "I wanted it to be quick and painless. I didn't want her to suffer. But she was too clever for me."

"And Bella?" said Lucas. "What plans had you made for her?"

Rupert clasped his hands and looked down at them. "I had promised her a trip to the Continent. It's something she has always wanted. I would have arranged an accident, something, I don't know." He looked up. "Lucas, I am not a cruel man. She wouldn't have suffered."

There was an odd little silence, then he said, "Time is passing, Lucas, and I've told you everything. I think you, Adrian and I have matters to discuss among ourselves."

Lucas seemed to stir himself, as though his mind had been miles away. He ignored Rupert and turned to Perry. "See that Jessica gets home safely. No. On second thought, take her to Hawkshill. The nuns are there. They'll look after her. And Perry, stay with her. I don't want anyone badgering her with questions. Understood?"

"Understood," replied Perry quietly.

Jessica felt her heart constrict. "I don't want to go to Hawkshill," she said. "I want to go to the Lodge."

Lucas shook his head. "There's no one there to look after you. I'll look in on you later. Perry?"

She made a halfhearted protest, but Perry's arm went around her shoulders. "Come on, Jess," he said, and helped her to her feet. "If you're up to it, you can take my horse and I'll take Adrian's."

There was a strained look in Perry's eyes that made her uneasy, but when he saw her studying him, his expression cleared. At the door, she turned back to look at the men who had been such close friends, and she had the uncanny feeling that she was looking at statues. No one moved. If they were breathing, she wouldn't have known it. No one looked at her.

She slipped out of Lucas's coat and laid it on a chair. Then Perry ushered her out of the room.

CHAPTER
27

WHEN THE DOOR CLOSED, ADRIAN WALKED TO IT and turned the key in the lock. He then went to the window and looked out. "We don't have much time," he said.

Lucas remained where he was, staring at Rupert. And under that stare, Rupert flushed. "I don't think," said Lucas slowly, "that I ever knew you."

"You knew me," said Rupert. "And I'm the same person I always was. God, Lucas, how can you look at me like that? You know what Hayward was. Do you think Jessica is going to waste any tears on him now that her memory has returned? I don't think so. He was a careless, unfeeling father. And don't waste your sympathies on Stone, either. Do you imagine I would have cut off the life of some promising young man? He was a wastrel. He would have done anything for money. As for Bella, you despise her as much as I do. I've seen it in your face when you've thought yourself unobserved. Do you think I wanted to be tied to such a woman for the rest of my life?"

"Will you listen to yourself? These are *people* you're talking about, for God's sake, not vermin!"

Rupert sneered. "And weren't the French people, too? Yet we killed them as though they were vermin and they did the same to us. Having wept bitter tears for some of the finest comrades who ever fell in battle while the scum of the earth got off scot-free, you'll pardon me if I don't shed tears for people who have no claim on my sympathies."

"And Jessica?" said Lucas in a queer, tight voice.

Rupert looked down at his desk and began to riffle through some papers. "Jessica is my one regret. However, I will say this. If I'd known that you loved her, I would never have embarked on this course. But you see, Lucas, you hid it so well. I always thought you felt sorry for her. I wish I had known how it was before it was too late to turn back."

Adrian spoke over his shoulder. "He's here! Constable Clay is here."

"I fear," said Rupert, "I must beg a favor of you, Lucas. I don't have a pistol in my library. Will you lend me yours?"

Lucas spoke through his teeth. "I'd like to see you hang from the highest gibbet for what you tried to do to Jessica."

"No doubt. Then if you won't do it for me, do it for her sake."

They heard footsteps in the hallway. There was a knock at the door. The handle turned. "Sir?" A pause, then in an aside, "I know they are in there, Constable."

This time someone pounded on the door, and the doorknob rattled. "Open the door at once." Constable Clay's voice. "Do you hear? Lucas? What the devil is going on in there?"

"Lucas," said Rupert, "leave me some honor. For friendship's sake?" He held out his hand palm up.

Lucas felt himself suddenly transported. Inseparable—he, Adrian, Rupert and Philip—that's what they'd been. They were boys again, carefree, pounding up and down the stairs of this very house. On his fourteenth birthday, a surprise party on the lawns of Haig House, and later, a loan to buy his commission and so many kindnesses in between. *For friendship's sake,* Rupert would say. It was a loose translation of the Haig motto. Loyalty, that's what it was all about.

His eyes suddenly teared. How could it have come to this? Wild thoughts darted through his mind as he tried to find an answer to his own question. There was no answer. There was only bitter, bitter regret.

There was no time to debate the rights and wrongs of what he should do. And still he hesitated. Whoever raised a hand against Jessica was his mortal enemy. He wanted to kill Rupert with his bare hands. He wanted—

"For friendship's sake," Rupert repeated, and there were tears in his eyes, too.

Lucas came to his decision. Quickly crossing to the desk, he put his pistol into Rupert's hand. "I'll make everything right," he said, "but I must know how Stone died."

"I broke his neck."

Something slammed into the door and a panel shattered.

A look passed between the two men. Rupert mouthed the words, "Forgive me, my friend."

The door burst inward as the gun went off.

A mile away, Jessica felt as though a sun had exploded behind her eyes.

She sensed something and turned to her side. Moonlight gilded the familiar objects of her room. On the table beside her bed was a prayer book and a glass carafe filled with water.

"Lucas," she whispered, and hauled herself up.

He was sitting in the only chair in the room, in semi-darkness, his legs stretched out in front of him. He stirred when she said his name, and slowly rising, came to the bed. His face was to the window and she could just make out the harsh set of his features, the unsmiling mouth, eyes that were like gouges against the pallor of his skin.

"He's dead," she said softly, "isn't he?"

He sat on the edge of the bed. "He killed himself with my pistol."

A breath shivered out of her. She was too much on edge to ask how it had happened. She didn't want to know, and maybe she would never want to know. "What did you tell the constable?"

He said something short and violent under his breath. "How well you know us! You're right, of course. We closed ranks yet again, to protect one of our own."

This was said with so much bitterness that she put out a hand to comfort him, but she let it fall away. There was something about him that told her the gesture would not be welcomed.

"I told him," he said, "that Rupert believed Stone had insulted you when you were a guest of his house. They quarreled. Stone fell against the fire fender and broke his neck. Rupert panicked and buried his body in the crypt. I discovered the grave and taxed him with it. Rather than face the disgrace, he killed himself."

She swallowed hard. "I see. And did Constable Clay believe you?"

"No, he didn't believe me. There were too many gaps in my story. The crypt for one. No one knew there was a way into it, and I could not give a satisfactory account of how I'd stumbled upon it. But whatever Constable Clay suspects, he can prove nothing, not unless you tell him what you know."

"I see," she said again, not knowing what he wanted her to say.

He rose abruptly and paced to the window. "If you think about it," he said, "this is the best solution. This protects everyone, not just Rupert. If I'd handed him over to the constable, everything would have had to come out—what your father did to Jane Bragge, Rodney Stone's part in this—you see what I mean. Innocent people would have been hurt."

"I understand."

"Do you?" He swung to face her. "You're very forgiving. My God, Jess, he almost had you! Up there on the cliff? If we hadn't found you when we did, it would be *your* body that the undertakers would be laying out right now."

She flinched and looked down at her hands. They felt oily from the salve Sister Dolores had rubbed on all the cuts and abrasions she'd sustained while trying to climb down the cliff face. Without being aware of what she was doing, she began to massage them. "You never told me," she said, "how you found me."

"Luck! Sheer luck!" His voice was so savage that her head snapped back. She watched him warily as he walked to the end of the bed. "I knew you would make for Haig House. Where else could you go? But when we arrived, the servants had not seen you. All they could tell us was that Rupert was in the conservatory. But he wasn't in the conservatory. What we found were your gloves. And I knew then, I knew—"

There was a long silence. He looked exactly as she'd seen him when she'd left Rupert's library—unmoving as a statue.

He expelled a long breath. "We fanned out," he said. "I took the path to the pavilion. I don't know why. When we heard rocks falling, we all converged on the sound. Do you know how lucky you were that we were on horseback? Do you realize how close you came to losing your life? Can you imagine how I felt? Why, Jessica? Why did you do it?" He made a small sound of derision. "What a stupid question! You thought I was the murderer. There's no other explanation. You thought I had murdered your father. You thought I had arranged things with Rodney Stone to abduct you and God knows what else. You thought I was going to murder again. You thought I was your Voice."

She felt as though the darkest, ugliest part of her soul had been prized out of her and brought into the glaring light. Her throat tightened alarmingly. "Please, Lucas, try to understand. Ellie told me about the straws. She saw and heard everything. And I always knew that if I could discover who had murdered my father I would know who my Voice was. Don't you see, I knew he was going to murder again, and I had to stop him."

"When did Ellie tell you about the straws?"

She couldn't think. Night and day had not had much meaning for her since she'd found out. "Our last night in London."

"And before that, did you suspect me of murder then?"

"No," she cried out. "No, I swear it. I suppose I always sensed you were hiding something, something to do with your pact. I understood about Ellie, but I could not understand how I came into it. I read the letter from your attorney. I know that Adrian and Rupert gave you the money to buy Hawkshill. But I don't know why."

"Why do you think?" he said wearily. "You were part of the pact. If I had died in battle, the others would have taken care of you. I made them swear to it. And later, if anything happened to me and you came back, I didn't want you with nothing to live on. Yes, Rupert and Adrian helped me scrape the money together for Hawkshill. I had supposed that they felt guilty for having considered executing your father. And Rupert . . ." He paused. "Rupert insisted on it. And now I see why."

"Lucas . . ." Her voice died away. She couldn't find the words to tell him how his constancy shamed her.

"Why didn't you confide in me? Why, Jess?"

"What could I say? That I heard voices? That I had visions? I was afraid you would think I was mad. I don't know. I tried to tell you. I just couldn't find the right words."

"You found the right words in Rupert's library."

Biting her lip, she looked away. "I had no choice. I had to tell you. But would you have believed me if Rupert hadn't confirmed what I said?"

"Yes," he said simply.

"Lucas," she said, groping for the words that would soften him. "Try to understand. When you appeared at the priory, I was shaken. I was sure Rodney Stone's body was there and that my Voice had put the thought in my mind. What else could I think but that you were my Voice, and you'd come to stop me?"

"I see what you mean. It never occurred to you, I suppose, that I was worried out of my mind and had come to find you? Do I seem unreasonable? Well, maybe I have a right to be. It's not every day that a man is betrayed by the two people he trusts most in the world."

His manner chilled her more than his words. He sounded so formal, and not like the Lucas she knew. If only he would curse, blaspheme, go on a rampage, she would weep with joy.

"I'm sorry," he said, "I'm not myself. You've been through a terrible ordeal. This discussion can wait for another day."

"No." She shook her head vigorously. "I want it to be over and done with. I can't bear this . . . . misunderstanding between us. What is it you wish to know?"

He propped one shoulder against the bedpost. "Tell me about your Voice. Tell me why you thought it was I. When did it first come to you? I don't know. Just tell me about it."

She took a moment to gather her thoughts. In little more than a whisper, she began to speak. "I called it my Voice because I didn't know what else to call it. It came to me in impressions and pictures, not words. I suppose I was first aware of it when you began to take an interest in me. You must understand, Rupert's thoughts were not violent then. He thought I was pretty, that I was clever, and that I was quality. I thought it must be you I was reading. I mean, I was hardly aware of Rupert. You were the only one who meant anything to me. I couldn't talk to you about it because you had made it quite clear that you regarded this . . . talent . . . with extreme distaste."

"But why Rupert?"

"We were related, or so he told me." And she went on to tell him all that Rupert had told her.

Many minutes went by before he spoke again. "Tell me about the night you ran away from Hawkshill. Did you tell your father we were lovers? Did you send him to find me?"

"Yes," she said softly. "I thought, believed, you loved me, whatever you said. And I thought Bella would not marry you if the story that we were lovers got out. She was too proud."

Swallowing the tears in her throat, she went on. "I didn't do it only for myself. I did it for you, oh, not so that you would marry me, but so that you wouldn't marry Bella. You didn't know her as I knew her. She was cruel. She was a liar and a cheat, and, oh—all the things Rupert said. I knew you could never be happy with her."

She let out a pent-up breath before continuing. "Then, I don't know, I sensed something, and I was terribly afraid. I was on my way to your house, thinking that's where my father had gone, when something came over me. I knew it was my Voice. Lucas, I thought it was you. You were angry, maddened, but that's what I expected after what I'd done. Then it changed. Murder, it told me. Oh God, it was awful. I ran down the bridle path to stop you, but I was too late. I don't know exactly what happened next, except that the murderer came after me, and all the time, I thought it was you. You weren't going to give up. Nothing but my death would satisfy you."

She had to swallow several times before going on to tell him how she had managed to escape, and how it had ended with a carriage running her down in front of the convent.

Another endless silence ensued. He shifted slightly and there was an odd note in his voice. "You sensed that Rupert was sorry he had to kill you?"

She nodded. "He was telling the truth. Back there at Haig House? He was telling the truth. He feared and hated this horrible talent I have, but he didn't hate me."

From another part of the house, the sound of a child's cry came to them. The wind rattled the windowpanes. Along the corridor a door opened and shut.

Lucas let out a long sigh. "Try to get some sleep, Jess. I'll look in again tomorrow."

She tried one last time to break through the barrier he had erected against her. "Let me come with you. I don't want you to be alone. I know how much Rupert's friendship meant to you. I'm sorry, Lucas. I'm truly sorry."

"I believe you mean that."

"I do."

For the first time, his voice betrayed all the strain he had been under. "It's best if you stay with the nuns for now. Adrian and I have much to do. We have to get our story straight. There'll be an inquest, of course, and we have to arrange Stone's funeral as well as Rupert's."

"Where will Rupert be buried?"

"At the priory. There have been Haigs buried there for over two hundred years. The church may object because he took his own life, and that's something else Adrian and I will have to deal with, so you see, I won't have much time to give to you."

She couldn't argue with him. She understood only too

well. Their grief for Rupert would be exclusive, and she would only be in the way. She understood, but it still hurt.

"Till tomorrow, then," she said.

"Good night, Jess."

When the door closed and she was alone, she kept the tears at bay by retracing in her mind everything that had happened since that evening at vespers when she'd learned that her Voice would murder again. She'd made mistakes, but if she had to do it over, she didn't see how she could do anything differently. She was sorry about Rodney Stone, bitterly sorry. But she hadn't failed altogether. She'd stopped a murderer from murdering again.

Bella. Rupert's words came back to her. *What an irony.* And it was an irony. All the trials and tribulations she had endured had been for the sake of a woman she thoroughly detested. Bella! Of all people!

That's when she began to cry.

CHAPTER
28

ROSEMARY LEFT JESSICA AND ELLIE TAKING TEA IN the Lodge's morning room, and went in search of Lucas. She found him in his study, stuffing papers and documents into the leather grip she had given him on his last birthday. She knew this wasn't the best time to have a conversation with her son. They'd just returned home from the priory after Rupert's funeral service. Lucas had taken his friend's death very hard, in fact, they all had. And now that he was executor of Rupert's estate, he was leaving within the hour with Bella to consult with Rupert's attorneys in London.

In normal circumstances, she would have kept her peace until he returned, but he was expected to be away for at least a week, and what she had to say could not keep for a week. No, nor for another day.

"Mother," he said, when he caught sight of her, "come in." He shut the grip and fastened it. "I'm relying on you to keep an eye on Jessica while I'm away. This has all been a terrible ordeal for her. See that she gets plenty of rest, and try to make her eat. These last few days, all she has done is pick at her food."

"I'm afraid I can't oblige you this time, Lucas," she said. "You see, I won't be here."

He looked up with a frown. "What do you mean, you won't be here?"

"I'll be with Sir Matthew Paige, that is, if he'll still have me after the shabby way I've treated him."

She came farther into the room, but she did not take a chair. Lucas was standing, and she felt that she would be at a disadvantage if she allowed him to tower over her. And to take a chair would put her, at least in her own mind, in the unflattering role of a supplicant. This time, she was asking for no favors. This time, she was telling her son how it would be.

"I see," he said.

"I hope you do. I did when I saw Matt there, at Rupert's funeral." Despite her best efforts, tears sprang to her eyes. "He didn't look well. He looked old. I wouldn't have known him. It broke my heart to see him like that."

"He's a drunkard, Mother. That's all it is."

She said sadly, "I wonder if you can hear the sneer in your voice? Well, I suppose I shouldn't be surprised. You've called Matt a lot worse than that—villain, adulterer, lecher. To you, he's always been lower than vermin."

Lucas flinched as if she had struck him. His mother didn't notice. She'd found a handkerchief and was dabbing at her eyes.

"I don't want to quarrel with you, Lucas. I've come to say goodbye. You told me that Matt was one person who would never cross the threshold of your house, and you never say anything you don't mean. According to you, Matt is beneath contempt. Well, so must I be. We both wronged your father. But I will say one thing: I think your father would have been far more forgiving than you."

She moved closer. "I've always been very proud of you, Lucas. And I want you to know that I do love you, even when you're wrong. And you are wrong in this. To you, everything is simple. How could it be otherwise? You've led a charmed life."

He made a movement with one hand, and she stopped speaking. "Jess said something very similar to me once," he said.

"And she was right. Some of us are not as fortunate as you. Life isn't kind to everyone, and yes, sometimes we make wrong choices and have to pay the consequences. But that doesn't mean we're beneath contempt. You look at Matt and you see a drunkard and a libertine, but there's more to people than meets the eye, if only you would . . ."

All the color had drained out of his face, and she broke off to say, "Oh, my dear, I'm sorry. You were thinking of Rupert, of course. But no one could have possibly known he would take his own life. You can't blame yourself. His own wife was as shocked as anyone, and if Rupert didn't confide in Bella, who would he confide in?"

He said nothing to this, and eventually she went on. "Well, I think I've said enough. I shall send for my things later if that's all right with you. And you need not worry about me. In spite of what you think, I know Matt will make me happy. But that's not the important thing. What matters to me is that he should be happy, and I'm going to do everything in my power to see that he is. Goodbye, my dear. I shall miss you all very much." And with a teary sob, she turned away.

She was at the door before Lucas had the presence of mind to go after her. "Mother," he said, "you will always be welcome in any house of mine."

She shook her head. "How could I be comfortable, knowing that I had to leave Matt at the door because my son thinks he is a rodent or something equally horrid? You must see that I couldn't do that to him."

She opened the door.

"Mother!" He crossed to her.

"What is it, Lucas?"

"I don't think anything of the sort!"

"Don't you?" She peered up at him. "I'm only repeating what I've heard you say."

"Perhaps I thought that once, but—"

"But what?"

He hesitated. "I don't know anything anymore," he said. "You're right, Mother, and I was wrong."

"What do you mean?"

He swallowed. "I'm not saying that Sir Matthew and I can ever be friends, not close friends, that is, but—" He floundered then found his stride. "If you were there to smooth things over, we might get along tolerably well."

There was a moment of mystified silence, then Rosemary's face crumpled, and she burst into tears.

Rosemary was not to be put off by the frowns and evasions of a mere manservant. "You must be Breame," she said warmly. "Sir Matthew has told me so much about you."

The frown softened. "Thank you, ma'am."

"And he's not at home, you say?"

"No, ma'am."

"Fine. I'll wait for him in his library."

Having established her credentials, she sailed past the startled servant and made straight for the only door off that great square entrance hall that was closed. She'd made the right choice as she discovered the moment she opened the door and a cloud of tobacco smoke floated out.

Sir Matthew was sprawled in one of the armchairs that flanked the grate. There was an empty bottle at his feet and a glass of amber liquid in one hand. In the other hand, he held a slim cigar. His neckcloth was askew, his jacket was wrinkled. The lines in his face seemed deeper, harsher, and his eyes were dull and flat. But it was his pallor that made her heart tighten.

When he saw her, he rose unsteadily to his feet. "Rodie?" He spoke as though he'd seen a ghost.

Breame opened his mouth to say something, then checked himself. He looked at the two unmoving figures who were intent only on each other and, with a little smile, he bowed himself out of the room and quietly shut the door.

The sound of the door latch brought Rosemary to life. She walked to the long window and opened it wide. "I thought," she said, "you came down to Chalford to sell this place? I understood that you were soon to embark on a grand tour?"

When she turned to him, she saw that he had dispensed with the glass and cigar and was making an effort to tidy himself.

"Here, let me do that." She crossed to him and began to arrange his neckcloth. "Matt," she said softly, faintly reproving, "you really must take better care of yourself."

He pushed her hands away and put some distance between them. He was scowling at her. "What the devil are you doing here?"

She wavered a little under the ferocity of his scowl. "I saw you at Rupert's funeral. I thought you looked unwell."

"And never said one word to me, or looked at me, or gave any indication that you knew I was there. I might as well have been invisible."

"Matt—"

"But I suppose that was to be expected. I should be used to it by now. Your son was there and when that paragon of every virtue known to man raises an eyebrow, you run to his heel like a tame dog." He pressed a hand to his eyes and shook his head. "Forgive me. You've caught me at a bad moment. Breame will show you out."

She ignored the dismissal. "Matt, Anne Rankin told

me that you've become a recluse, that you never go anywhere or see anyone. Everyone was surprised to see you at Rupert's funeral."

His sneer was pronounced. "And I daresay your son thought it was gall on my part to show my face among decent people. Well, you may run home and tell him how right he is about me. I'm a profligate and a drunkard. That should make him happy."

"I can't tell him anything. He's on his way to London, but—"

"I might have known it. You wouldn't be here if there was the slightest chance that he would get wind of it. Am I supposed to be flattered?"

Her temper flared. "You're supposed to be silent and listen to me!"

Her outburst had the desired effect. He folded his arms across his chest and supported himself by leaning against the edge of a library table.

Encouraged by his silence, she began on the little speech she had rehearsed on the way over. "Lucas has changed, Matt. I think, no, I know Rupert's death has affected him profoundly. It's shaken his complacency. Well, it's shaken everyone's complacency, hasn't it? Rupert didn't seem the type to take his own life, and all over a tragic accident. I think it's made Lucas wonder if he should have been more sensitive, more aware of his friend's state of mind. It's softened him, that's what I wanted to say."

She smiled as the recollection of her last conversation with Lucas came back to her, and the smile was still in place when she approached Sir Matthew. "The thing is, he has given us his blessing, Matt. We can be married as soon as you like."

The look he blazed at her was so savage that she recoiled from it.

"He's given us his blessing! Who asked for it? Not I! Well, it's not enough. I never wanted you on those terms, so you can tell Dundas his generous offer has been refused." Suddenly straightening, he yelled, "Breame!"

The manservant entered the room almost before the echo of his name had died away, and there could be no doubt that he'd been eavesdropping on the other side of the door.

"Breame," said Sir Matthew, "show Mrs. Wilde out."

"Yes, sir." Breame looked at Rosemary mournfully, and his look spoke volumes. "This way, Mrs. Wilde."

"I'm not going anywhere," she declared. "Breame, kindly fetch a pot of coffee for Sir Matthew, oh yes, and while you're at it, have Cook make up a tray of sandwiches. That will be all."

"Yes, ma'am."

"Breame!" roared Sir Matthew.

"Yes, sir, at once, sir," said Breame and he whisked himself out of the room.

Sir Matthew glared at the closed door and set his jaw. He turned his head and now glared at Rosemary. "I don't know what you hope to gain by this."

Rosemary was at the other window, struggling to open it. "And I don't know how you can breathe in this fog." She kept her tone light and chatty. "Are you very fond of those cigars, Matt?"

"Very!" he replied truculently.

The window opened and she inhaled a long breath. "Then I suppose I shall just have to get used to them."

Her confidence was more show than substance, but when she turned suddenly and caught the look in his eyes, a look he instantly veiled, her nerves steadied.

"Matt, sit down," she said. "I have something I wish to say to you."

"I won't have you on anyone's sufferance, Rodie," he said savagely, then less savagely, "I won't have you on anyone's sufferance."

She was silent and unsmiling. Sighing, he took an upright chair beside the library table. She took the chair next to his.

"Matt, you didn't give me a chance to answer your question. It wasn't a question, though, was it? It was a reproof. I didn't speak to you at Rupert's funeral because my heart was breaking, and I knew that if I said anything I would burst into tears. You looked so wretched, so . . . neglected, and I could not bear it."

His eyes were fixed on the floor. She sat looking at her clasped hands.

She went on. "Duty has always been, well, my guiding principle, I suppose you could say."

His tone was gruff. "As I discovered to my cost."

"Sometimes I failed in my duty, but I always knew it was something to aim for."

"Rodie, where is all this leading?"

She smiled. "Patience, Matt. When I saw you today, I realized, for the first time, that there was no one in the whole world with a greater claim on me than you. And I had failed you."

He looked up with a question in his eyes.

"I had not understood it till that moment. I'd always felt guilty, I suppose, for the past, and that guilt made me blind to what I owed you. All my life, I've tried to be dutiful, and it was hard. With you, it wouldn't be hard. With you, it would be easy, and I think that's why I distrusted my feelings. But I've learned my lesson. I won't fail you again. Am I making sense?"

"No," he said.

"Well, perhaps this is something you can understand. I told my son today that I would never enter his house if you were not welcome there. I told him that my place was with you, and that if he could not accept that, then we should say goodbye. And he said that he thought you and he might manage to get along tolerably well. And that's where it stands, Matt."

He said hoarsely, "You chose me over him?"

"Yes, my darling. I chose you. And if you still want me, I'll marry you as soon as you like. Where you go, I shall go. And I promise to be a loving, dutiful wife."

"Rodie." His voice cracked. "Oh Rodie." And he reached for her.

Breame entered at that moment bearing a tray with cups and saucers. He stood immobile for a moment or two, staring at the couple who were locked in a passionate embrace. Then he did a little pirouette and slipped away unseen with a big smile on his face.

Ten days later, Jessica was in the morning room, curled up on a window seat, when Ellie walked in. She folded the letter she'd received that morning from Lucas and looked curiously at the parcel Ellie carried under one arm.

Ellie set the parcel on the table. "I passed the lovebirds on my way up from Hawkshill," she said. "Jessica, don't you think it's strange that people that old can be in love? They were holding hands as they walked along the bridle path."

"Sir Matthew and Rosemary aren't *that* old," said Jessica. "And people can fall in love at any age. As for holding hands, I think it's charming."

"I've never seen you and Lucas holding hands. Is that a letter from him?"

"Yes. It came this morning."

"What does he say?"

"He says that he doesn't think Bella will ever come back to Chalford."

"Well, that's no loss, if you want my opinion."

"Ellie," said Jessica, not wishing to pursue this topic of conversation, "what's in the parcel?"

Ellie flashed her an impish grin, but her eyes were shy. "It's for you, Jessica. I . . . hope you like it. Lucas said you would."

"Lucas?"

"Before he went away." Ellie went to the sideboard,

opened a drawer and returned with a pair of scissors. "Cut the string," she said.

Jessica took the scissors from Ellie and obediently cut the string. Then she carefully unwrapped the paper. Inside was her wedding dress.

"I don't understand," she said.

Ellie shook the dress out and held it up to the light. "Well, what do you think?"

Jessica's hands traced the front of the gown. There wasn't a mark or stain on it, nothing to show that a glass of strawberry cordial had been spilled over it. "It's perfect. How did you get the stain out?"

"The stain wouldn't come out. We had to replace the front panel. It was Lucas's idea. He got a matching piece of material from your dressmaker and Aunt Rosemary showed me how to make a pattern and cut it out. I've been at it for ages, but when we heard that Father Howie was back in London, I worked twice as hard. I don't want you to think I did it all by myself. The nuns helped me. You can wear it next week, you know, when Father Howie comes out to perform the service."

Jessica couldn't tear her eyes away from her wedding dress. "It looks like new," she said.

Ellie frowned. "What's wrong, Jessica?"

Jessica fished in her pocket, found her handkerchief and blew her nose. "Nothing is wrong," she said. "I couldn't be more delighted. Thank you, Ellie. It was very thoughtful of you."

Ellie's gaze faltered and her smile slipped. "No it wasn't. It was the least I could do, and you know it. I was beastly to you."

There was an oddly appealing look in Ellie's eyes, and Jessica couldn't help responding to it. "I won't say you weren't beastly, because we both know it would be a lie. But if you wanted to do something to please me, you hit on the right thing."

Ellie beamed.

"Now tell me about Father Howie. I didn't know he was coming to Chalford."

"Didn't you? Lucas told me in one of his letters. You never did get round to having your marriage blessed or whatever it is. Lucas said I should make a push to get your gown finished for the ceremony."

"Lucas arranged all this, without a word to me?"

"Oh dear," said Ellie, "I hope it wasn't supposed to be a surprise and I've spoiled it."

"Knowing Lucas," said Jessica, "I think he has merely forgotten to mention it."

There was a step in the hall and the sound of Perry's voice calling for Ellie. A moment later, he entered the morning room. "Morning, Jessica," he said. "Well, brat"—looking at Ellie—"are you ready for your driving lesson?"

Ellie blushed, stammered something incoherent, and tucked her hand in the crook of Perry's arm. He gave her a bashful grin and they went off together, leaving Jessica staring.

Ellie and Perry? When had that happened?

She picked up the letter she had received from Lucas. There was nothing in it that could not be broadcast by the town crier. Romance was in the air, and the only personal message she had from her husband was a recipe for a restorative to bring the color back to her cheeks.

She made her way upstairs with her wedding gown carefully draped over her arms. After laying it on the back of a chair, she smoothed her hands over the delicate material, then took a step back to admire it. So much had happened since she had last worn it.

She knelt in front of the chair and let the memories take her.

A long time later, when she descended the stairs, she was dressed in her riding habit.

CHAPTER
29

THEY LEFT THE CLOSE-CROPPED TURF BEHIND THEM the steadier they climbed. It was good to be outside, good to feel the wind in her face and the sun on her back, and the sure, swift motions of the horse beneath her. There was the scent of meadowsweet and willow herb in her nostrils and the muted sound of hooves as they struck the earth. There was nothing like this, *nothing,* and she didn't know how she could have forgotten it.

This was one of the few rewards that had come to her since she'd regained her memory, not that she could ride, but that she could ride fearlessly, as though she'd been born to it. And she had been born to it. When she'd had no memory to guide her, the picture she'd formed of life with her father at Hawkshill had been slightly off center. No one had told her that her father was Irish. No one had told her of the good years, when he was sober and industrious, and had trained horses for his livelihood. Everyone remembered the bad years, when the drink and gaming had taken hold of him and he'd let everything slide.

She'd ridden more prize horses by the time she was an adolescent than most men had ridden in their entire lives. There wasn't a thing she didn't know about the care of horses. She knew about poultices and mashes and foaling and farriers. But she hadn't known how to read. She hadn't known how to mix with people. She'd been wild and unruly. That's what people remembered. And that's what had brought Lucas Wilde into her life.

How could she have resisted him? There was no one else who cared what happened to her, not during those lean years when her father became a drunkard. Lucas was right about that, too. It was mere bravado on her part that made her spin tales of how her father spoiled her. There were no presents, no silk underthings, only a box on the ear when she got in his way. She became very adept at keeping out of her father's reach. Until she was fully grown and his avaricious mind calculated how he could turn a profit on her. And Lucas would never have allowed that to happen.

Lucas. She'd loved him from that moment, on the church steps, when he'd intervened to save her from two spiteful girls who'd tried to shame her because she couldn't read. It seemed that she had made a laughing-stock of herself in church by "reading" her Bible upside down. Lucas said that only clever people could do that, and had proved it by reading his own Bible upside down. A look had passed between them, and though he hadn't known it, that was when she had given him her heart.

Poor Lucas. He couldn't have known what fancies she'd woven around him just because he was nice to her. He couldn't turn around but she was there, "by accident," so that she could bask in his company. He'd had no idea that she watched his comings and goings from Hawks-hill's hayloft. Looking back, she could see that he'd been amused by her antics, then not so amused when he'd started to court Bella. But she could never have seen him go to someone like Bella.

That wasn't how she'd felt about Bella at first. She'd known, deep down, that she, herself, could never have Lucas. He was too far above her. And when Bella had appeared on the scene, she'd resigned herself to the inevitable. Lucas was Prince Charming; Bella was a princess. They were right for each other.

It was only natural that she would turn her attention to Bella, and what her strange powers told her made her shudder in revulsion. Bella was a liar and a cheat. She was a thief. If she took it into her head that someone had slighted her, she paid that person back tenfold. Governesses, servants, friends—all paid a penalty for some imagined slight. And no one paid a bigger penalty than the poor footman who had been sent to the colonies for Bella's crime.

Jessica had tried to save him. She'd told Sir Henry about the jeweler's shop where Bella sold her trinkets and all he'd done was threaten to have her transported, too, if she breathed a word of it to anyone. And her father had been bribed to make sure she kept her mouth shut.

She hadn't saved the footman, but she'd made up her mind to save Lucas, whatever the cost to herself. That's why she had sent her father after Lucas that night. She'd known Bella would never marry a man who had betrayed her.

She knew now why she hadn't been a blushing bride on her wedding night. After Lucas had come home from the war, when he'd come out to Hawkshill looking for her father, he'd found her in the hayloft. Their memories of that encounter were entirely different. He'd been furious and had called her a gaming-house wench. Then he'd kissed her, and she'd melted with love for him. Only Lucas could have mistaken her trembling for fear. Then he'd pushed her away and called himself some ugly names.

She'd spent the next few hours reliving every moment of that kiss, yes, and had taken it one step further in her mind and wished it could happen again. That's the memory that had come back to her on her wedding night. That's why she had known so much and only so much.

Oh, if only she'd been older and had had more experience. If only Lucas hadn't been so determined to stand by Bella. If only . . . if only . . .

She laughed when she realized where her thoughts had taken her. These were not the thoughts of a nun.

On a hilly rise, she drew rein and turned her mount to look out over the lush valley. The Thames was a broad ribbon of silver with dark specks of barges on their way up or downstream. Checkered fields were interspersed with dense woodlands. To the east lay the clustered roofs and spires of Chalford. Haig House and the priory were beyond the town and concealed from view by a bend in the river.

No shiver of apprehension shuddered through her now. It was finished. There were no shadows in her mind, no shades or ghosts. She was free at last. She lifted her face to the wind and gave her horse its head.

They hurtled down slopes and leapt over hedges. Then up, up they went, leaving trees and hedgerows behind, cresting a series of gentle rises toward the highest point on the downs. A stone wall barred their way, but Jessica did not slacken their pace. She'd been out on Juniper every morning and knew he could easily take the obstacle. As his long limbs stretched out, she bent low in the saddle.

"Yes, you beauty," she whispered. "Yes."

His ears flickered in response and powerful muscles bunched and strained as the wall loomed up in front of them. He was gathering himself to make the jump when a hare suddenly darted out from the wall and leapt away. Juniper faltered, reared up and came to a plunging, quivering halt. Jessica went flying over the wall.

She lay there, spread-eagle, gazing up at the sky. Winded wasn't the word for it. She felt as though her lungs had collapsed. She struggled to suck in air, and just when she thought she would suffocate, her lungs inflated like a broken-down wheezing bellows.

She was hauling herself up when a horse and rider came sailing over the wall. The rider was out of the saddle and running toward her before his mount had come to a stop.

As he came closer, she was surprised to see that it was Lucas. He'd told her in his letter that he wouldn't be home before the end of the week.

"Jess!" He went down on his knees and began to feel for broken bones. "Are you all right? Have you hurt yourself? For God's sake, say something!"

"I'm fine," she said. "The fall winded me, that's all."

"You're fine?"

She nodded.

"Hell and the devil!" he suddenly roared. "Who gave you permission to ride Juniper? It takes a grown man to keep him under control. And what are you doing so far from home with no groom to attend you? What if you'd broken a limb? What if someone had come upon you and robbed you, or worse? Do you never learn?"

Her dignity was wounded, and she opened her mouth to defend herself when she saw that his hands were shaking and that his eyes were leaping with fear as much as anger. A memory came to her—one of their boys had fallen out of an apple tree and, after she'd made sure he was unharmed, she'd wanted to give him a good shaking. Instead, she'd burst into tears.

She came up on her knees and cupped his face with both hands. "Lucas, I'm sorry. You're right. I should have asked someone to come with me. In future, I'll be more careful, I promise."

Her words made no impression on him. "And where the hell was your famous intuition?" he thundered. "This wall is a death trap! It's already killed one man and maimed several. Couldn't you sense it? Couldn't you feel it?"

She should have. She would have in the old days. "No," she said. "I didn't sense anything," and as the knowledge speared through her, she smiled brilliantly. "It's not there. I think I've lost it."

The smile was a mistake. His hands seized her shoulders and she steeled herself for the shaking she was sure he would administer, when suddenly a change came over him. He said her name on a broken whisper and crushed her in his arms.

When they drew apart, they stared at each other for a long moment, then they began to tear off their clothes. And on the open hillside, with the sun beating down on them, they came together in a storm of emotion. Words were superfluous. Words couldn't describe what they were feeling or make everything right between them. Words took too long. They would come to that later. This was a better way, this primitive bonding that surpassed everything. They celebrated life and the joy of being together. There was nothing in the world but themselves.

"Jess!" said Lucas a long while later. "I can't believe we did that." He was lying on his back, one arm thrown over his eyes.

Jessica was curled into him, and her breath tickled his armpit. "Neither can I."

Their eyes met and they both smiled.

"You're home early," she said.

"So would you be if you'd been with Bella for the last ten days." His smile faded. "That's not the reason. I missed you."

"And I missed you."

His fingers played with her hair. "I take it," he said seriously, "from what passed between us just now, that you've forgiven me?"

"Forgiven you?" She pulled herself up. "Forgiven you for what?"

"For that stupid pact; for blind loyalty to my friends; for letting things go so far." His mouth twisted. "If only

I'd listened to you from the very beginning. But I never dreamed that you were in any danger, I swear it."

She could see that he'd been brooding about things and that he wasn't looking for an easy absolution. Whatever he was about to tell her was important to him, something he had to get off his chest.

"Why didn't you listen to me?" she said.

He pulled to a sitting position and loosely clasped his knees. "Because I didn't want you stirring things up. I wasn't protecting my friends. I was trying to protect you and Ellie. I didn't want everything to come out, what your father had done to Jane, and that she had taken her own life. And God forgive me, I didn't care that your father had been murdered. I thought it was no less than he deserved."

She said softly, "Was Jane with child?"

He nodded. "She feared the disgrace. Everyone would have known it could not have been Philip's child."

He turned his head to look at her. "But I swear to you, Jess, it never crossed my mind that one of my close friends was behind everything, not at first. I trusted Rupert. We were all men of honor; we held to a certain code, Rupert most of all. I never suspected him until that last day, and even then, I was reluctant to believe it. Only a coward would shoot a man in the back, and Rupert was no coward." He shrugged helplessly. "He was an exemplary soldier, fearless in battle. His men worshiped him. Just listen to me!" he burst out. "Even now, knowing what he was and what he would have done to you, I'm still making excuses for him."

"He was your friend," she said quietly. "It's natural."

"A friend I never truly knew! I don't think I shall ever forget those moments in his library when he tried to justify what he had done. The way he separated people into the deserving and the undeserving! The way he manipulated us all! It sickened me, yet . . ."

"Yet?"

He made a grimace of distaste. "Later, I came to see that there was only a fine line dividing me from Rupert. No, I haven't murdered anyone, not with my hands, but I've manipulated people, and made them pay in other ways. My mother for one. And Sir Matthew. I thought I knew what honor and loyalty were all about, now I don't know anything. After Rupert, I'll never be the same again."

She didn't ask about his mother and Sir Matthew, because she didn't want to distract him. But she'd already worked everything out a long time ago.

Eventually, he said, "There's something else you should know. I wasn't honest with you, Jess. When I gave Rupert my pistol, I wasn't thinking of protecting the innocent. I was thinking only of Rupert. He was my friend, and I couldn't let him down. In spite of everything, I couldn't hand him over to the authorities. Can you understand that?"

"Only too well."

"You do?"

She nodded. "You see, my darling, I'm no better than you."

His head came up.

She nodded. "When Ellie told me about the straws, I was convinced that you had murdered my father, and of course, that you would murder again. I never seriously considered handing you over to the authorities to be dealt with by the law. Don't you remember, I suggested that we go on a grand tour? I wanted you away, out of England, to a safe place. When that didn't work, I crept into the dressing room and got your pistol."

"You got my pistol," he said blankly.

"I thought, hoped, if worse came to worst, that I would have the courage to kill you myself."

"Kill me!" He straightened. "You would have killed me?"

"Of course I wouldn't have killed you. You're still

alive, aren't you? All I'm saying is that I understand why you acted as you did. I don't know why you want my forgiveness, but you have it. Unconditionally. And Rupert wasn't all bad. You loved him. Love can't suddenly turn to hate, as I should know. Lucas, don't be so hard on yourself."

He plucked a blade of grass and began to chew on it. The silence was comfortable, and she closed her eyes just savoring this moment of closeness. He turned on his side and drew the blade of grass along the line of her throat.

"It still rubs me, you know," he said moodily. "No, that's too strong. It bothers me a little."

They'd come to the hard part, and she said carefully, "That . . . that I thought you were the murderer? That I locked you in the crypt and ran from you? That I didn't confide in you?"

"No," he said. "I've thought that over and I can see that you thought you had good reason."

She couldn't believe that she was getting off this easily. "Then what bothers you?"

He looked up at her. "That you and Rupert had this special bond. I mean, why not with me? That's what I can't understand. I've loved you for years. He was indifferent to you. I'm not finding fault or anything like that. I know you didn't *choose* to have this bond with Rupert. I suppose I'm, well, jealous. I'll get over it."

"Bond?" she said stupidly, incredulously, then her voice rose to a shriek. "*Bond*?" She jumped to her feet. "It was a shackle, a horrible, horrible shackle. It was like being in prison! No. It was worse than prison. It was my own private hell. And now I'm free. Can you understand that? I'm my own person. I'm free, free, free."

Joy welled up in her and could not be contained. She raised her arms and face to the sun. "I'm free," she said, over and over, in a litany of praise, "I'm free."

And there among the long sweet grasses that grew in profusion along the ridge, Jessica danced in naked splendor with only the song of a lone heron to accompany her. Awed and alarmed by the spectacle, Lucas bounded up and tried to capture her in his arms, but she would not be captured. Lucas gave up and watched his wife cavort and dip and prance till her breath was spent.

When she came back to him, she poked him in the chest with her index finger. "I'm warning you," she said, "I'm warning you, Lucas Wilde, if you ever try to get inside my head—" She stopped to suck in air.

"What?" he demanded.

"I really will shoot you and I won't have to think twice about it. We're two normal people, do you hear? And when we want to converse, we do what normal people do. We talk. *Talk*, Lucas Wilde. So you'd better learn how to do it."

"I promise I'll learn."

"And when we're apart, we'll write to each other. And don't tell me about the weather, or what you had for breakfast or dinner. Tell me what you're thinking and feeling. You've been gone for ten days, torturing yourself about Rupert and . . . and everything, and wrote not one word of what you were feeling to me."

"So I'm not a letter writer." He threw up his hands. "All right, all right, I'll do better in future."

"And . . . and it wouldn't hurt if we held hands once in a while."

"Give me your hand."

She gave him her hand. "And you're going to learn the steps of all the dances and dance every dance at a ball."

"Now, Jess, that is going . . . all right, I promise."

"And tell me you love me."

"I love you."

"Often."

"I love you, I love you."

When she paused for breath, he said, "May I be permitted to make a small suggestion?"

She inclined her head.

"I know a better way." And with a great whoop of laughter, he pounced on her and wrestled her to the ground.

The mother superior adjusted her wimple as the words of Father Howie's homily washed over her. It was hot on the lawns of Hawkshill, but there was no single room in the house big enough to accommodate all the children, and Sister Martha particularly wanted them present for the ceremony. She and her handsome young husband were kneeling on cushions as Father Howie blessed their union. At long last, thought the Reverend Mother, Sister Martha had found her true vocation. The girl was altogether different. One only had to look at her to know it. She glowed with happiness and something that went deeper than happiness. The girl had found her life. It was as simple as that.

The Reverend Mother's eyes shifted to Lucas. He seemed like a very nice, very pleasant young man, but of course, there must be a lot more to him than that. He must be remarkable to have won the heart of Sister Martha. The main thing was, he was deeply in love. He would make Martha happy. She had known *that* when he'd come to see her at the convent to enlist her aid in persuading Martha to marry him. It was evident to her that he loved both Martha and the girl she had once been, and that her little protégée would be safe with him. And how right she had been. No, she wasn't sorry she had written that letter giving Martha a push in the right direction.

A long time ago, she'd had the oddest feeling that Sister Martha's coming to their little convent had been ordained. Now, as she looked around the sea of faces that were turned up to watch the ceremony, she was convinced of it. Hawkshill prospered. Their children were as robust as the tall wheat that ripened in the fields. The sisters were happy and industrious. Without Martha, none of this would have been possible.

Her eyes wandered to the small group of guests who were clustered in the shade of an oak tree. There were only five of them, Lord Dundas's mother and her new husband, Sir Matthew something-or-other; two cousins, and his ward, Ellie. Perhaps it was mere fancy on her part, but she sensed that Martha's coming to Hawkshill had touched their lives as well.

She turned her head and frowned at Sisters Dolores and Elvira. They were standing beside Joseph, but where he was serious and silent, they were twittering like two budgies and she knew what that meant. On catching her look, they instantly closed their little beaks. When the service was over, she wandered over to them.

"What is it this time, Sister Elvira?" she said.

The nuns were silent.

"Well, out with it. Are we betting on how soon their first child will be born or what?"

The sisters exchanged a look of consternation.

"Well?"

Sister Elvira, who saw at once that the Reverend Mother would not be put off, said, "We weren't laying bets, Reverend Mother. You see, we both have this uncanny feeling that Jessica's first child will be born nine months from this very day."

The mother superior clasped her hands, closed her eyes and turned her face up to the sun. She'd always considered herself a bit of a holy witch, and she sensed that all the signs were propitious. She opened her eyes. "You may well be right," she said, then turning to Joseph, "I'll lay you odds, four to one, that their first child will be a boy."

"You knows I never bets on a sure thing," he said, and grinned.

With a little smile and a bow, the Reverend Mother made her way past the gaping nuns toward the group of well-wishers who surrounded the radiant couple.

Return to Dianne Nolten
951-242-8136
1-25-14 / 1-27-14

ABOUT THE AUTHOR

ELIZABETH THORNTON holds a diploma in education and a degree in Classics. Before writing women's fiction she was a school teacher and a lay minister in the Presbyterian Church. *You Only Love Twice* is her tenth historical novel. Ms. Thornton has been nominated for and received numerous awards, among them the Romantic Times Trophy Award for Best New Historical Regency Author, and Best Historical Regency. She has been a finalist in the Romance Writers of America Rita Contest for Best Historical Romance of the year. Though she was born and educated in Scotland, she now lives in Canada with her husband. They have three sons and five grandchildren.

Ms. Thornton enjoys hearing from her readers. Her e-mail address is <thornton@pangea.ca> or visit her at her home page:

> http://www.pangea.ca/~thornton

or write to her:

> P.O. Box 69001 RPO Tuxedo Park
> Winnipeg MB R3P 2G9
> Canada

If you cherished

YOU ONLY LOVE TWICE

Get swept away with nationally bestselling author

ELIZABETH THORNTON

in her next sensational romance,
a tour de force of passion and suspense . . .

*"Elizabeth Thornton writes complex, compelling stories; her
characters are always full-dimensional, her plots intelligent,
and the chemistry between the hero and the heroine really
zings. I buy her books on the basis of her name alone,
because she always delivers."*
—New York Times *bestselling author Linda Howard*

COMING SOON FROM BANTAM BOOKS

(Read on for an exciting sneak preview . . .)

Abbie tried to bring her thoughts round to the question her partner had asked, something about her brother, George, but her mind wasn't functioning properly. She was still reeling from the look Hugh had blazed at her. He was angry, and she thought she knew why. Her well-meaning family had, in all likelihood, tried to pressure him into asking for her hand in marriage. This is what she'd feared had happened, and Hugh's smoldering look confirmed it. Perhaps he thought that she had put them up to it! Somehow, she had to persuade him that marriage was the last thing on her mind.

"No," she answered mechanically, as the steps of the dance brought her level with her partner. "George is not in Bath. He may have decided to stop off in London on his way home from Paris, or he might have met some friends and gone off with them."

Mr. Horton? Morton? shook his head, but the steps of the dance separated them and she didn't catch his reply nor did she care. She had far more important things to worry about than George's whereabouts. George came and went as he pleased. He would turn up eventually, he always did. Her most pressing problem was how to salvage her friendship with Hugh.

When the dance ended, she looked around for Hugh. He was in conversation with Olivia and Major Danvers, a very serious conversation by all appearances. Pinning a smile on her face, Abbie hurried over. As she drew near them, her steps slowed to a halt. Hugh's face was in profile, and she had the oddest sensation, much like the one she had experienced when they were first introduced all those months ago. A lock of dark hair fell across his broad brow; his features looked as though they were carved out of marble; his coat hugged a pair of powerful masculine shoulders; muscles bunched in his arms as he leaned over to take a paper from Major Danvers's hand.

Roman centurion, she thought, and swallowed.

The awesome impression faded when Hugh slipped on his wire-rimmed spectacles and began to read. Roman centurions were not equipped with spectacles but with great metal shields and swords. Hugh was no warrior. He was a scholarly gentleman who had ruined his eyes by spending too much time with his books. The spectacles were vastly reassuring. He was still the same Hugh, still the best friend a girl ever had.

"Hugh," she said with unnatural brightness, "you're back."

He turned his head slowly and his tawny eyes gazed at her over the rim of his spectacles. "As you see," he said.

It seemed to Abbie that there was a moment of awkwardness, and she tried to cover it by looking around for somewhere to sit. Every chair and settee was occupied. Hugh solved her dilemma. He rose and held up the paper he'd been reading.

"I shall put this with the rest of the accounts," he said, looking at Major Danvers, then turning to Abbie. "Come along, Abbie. After I've taken care of this, I'll take you to the tea room for refreshments."

A look passed between Abbie and Miss Fairbairn. *I told you so,* Olivia was saying. It was her belief that Hugh was too sensible to be swayed by Abbie's meddlesome family, and too naive to understand their hints.

"What were you and Olivia talking about?" asked Abbie as they left the ballroom.

"The Trojan War."

There was something dry about his tone, and she looked at him quickly. His expression gave nothing away. Deciding she must have been mistaken, she tried again. "What did Major Danvers give you?"

"A bill for candles," he replied. "If we continue to use up candles at this rate, we may have to raise subscriptions."

Hugh was treasurer of the committee that had oversight of the Assembly Rooms, and he took his responsibilities very seriously. Abbie was in the habit of teasing him about it, but on this occasion she felt shy and said nothing.

The office was just off the main entrance. Hugh took a candelabra from one of the hall tables, unlocked the door, and ushered Abbie inside. While he went to the desk and riffled through some papers, she wandered around the room, looking at the pictures on the wall, but she wasn't as casual as she pretended to be. She still sensed an awkwardness between them and wasn't sure whether it originated with herself or with Hugh.

"Hugh," she said, turning suddenly, "I—"

"Who was the young man you were dancing with?"

"What?"

He looked up from the folder of papers he'd been reading. "The young man you were dancing with? I don't think I know him."

"Oh, he's George's friend. Harry Morton or Horton. I can't remember which."

"George?"

"My brother."

"Your brother's friend." The set of Hugh's mouth softened a little. "And you don't know his name?"

"George has many friends, and you know how hopeless I am with names."

"But you never forget a face."

It was a private joke. Hugh was referring to the time Abbie had made a social blunder when she'd been introduced to one of Bath's leading citizens and claimed she remembered him and his daughter from somewhere. The "somewhere" turned out to be a hotel on the outskirts of Reading at a time when the gentleman had told his wife he was with his mother in Falmouth. There was no daughter.

"Hugh," she said, "why aren't you wearing your spectacles?"

"I only wear them when the light is bad." He indicated the candelabra. "When I have a direct light, I can see perfectly well. Why do you ask?"

"No reason. It's just that you look different without them."

Now she knew where the awkwardness between them originated. It was with her. Her damnable family had put ideas in her head. She wasn't seeing Hugh as her best friend but as the romantic figure Harriet had described. She had to rein in her imagination before she spoiled everything.

"What is it, Abbie? Why do you stare at me like that?"

"You haven't told me what you think of my new gown," she said, then stifled a groan. This wasn't how she'd planned to put their friendship back on the right footing. The question was too personal. She should have asked him about his books or the state of the Assembly's finances. Dear Lord, what must he be thinking?

Hugh was thinking that he'd deliberately engineered this private tête-à-tête to question Abbie about Paris, to determine what she'd done to arouse the suspicions of a member of His Majesty's Intelligence Service. But when he saw the swift rise and fall of her breasts and heard the slight hiatus in her breathing, his thoughts changed direction. At long last, Abbie was seeing him as a man.

Easy, he told himself, *slowly.* This was Abbie. Her boldness was all show. She wasn't nearly as worldly as she liked to think she was. In fact, she wasn't worldly at all. She didn't know the first thing about men. *Easy,* he told himself again, as he felt his body quicken in anticipation. He wanted to tempt her, not terrify her.

As casually as he could manage, he dropped the paper he was holding and slowly crossed to her. "Your new gown?" he said. "I think your gown is"—his eyes moved over her slowly—"charming. Quite rustic, in fact. Is this the rage in Paris, this shepherdess's getup? It suits you, Abbie."

"Shepherdess!" Her confusion was swamped by a tide of indignation. She glanced down at her gown. "It's no such thing! I don't know why I asked for your opinion. You've never shown the slightest interest in ladies' fashions."

"Oh, I don't know." He smiled into her eyes. "I occasionally think of other things besides Roman ruins and the price of candles. I'm not as dull as you think, Abbie."

There flashed into her mind a picture of Barbara Munro, the beautiful actress whom Harriet insisted was once Hugh's mistress. She'd laughed herself silly when she'd had time to think about it. She doubted that Hugh had entertained a carnal thought in his life. He was too wrapped up in his intellectual pursuits. But she didn't feel like laughing now.

His eyes had narrowed on her face, not the clear, guileless eyes she knew so well, but cat's eyes, sharp and watchful, seeing everything.

When he tried to take her hands, she took a quick step back and rushed into speech. "I don't think you're dull. Someone has to think of Roman ruins and the price of candles." She came to an abrupt halt. This was going from bad to worse.

"Praise indeed," he said dryly. "Shame the devil, Abbie, and tell the truth. Don't you find me too tame for you?"

Guilty color flooded her cheeks. Those were her very words! But she'd never uttered them to another soul.

"I see," he said and, with a whimsical smile, returned to the desk.

"Oh, Hugh!" Abbie went after him, cut to the quick to think that she'd hurt his feelings. "You don't understand."

"What don't I understand?" He propped himself against the desk, folded his arms across his chest, and regarded her steadily.

"Your friendship means a great deal to me. Hugh, you know how much I admire you and enjoy your company. I wouldn't want anything to spoil what we have."

"What could spoil it?"

She answered with feeling, "My family, for a start." When he made no response to this, she foundered a little before going on. "They came to see me last week, and . . . and . . . they've got the wrong idea about us. Oh, I should have foreseen how their minds would work. I should have known better than to ask you to carry letters for me." She touched a hand to his sleeve and quickly withdrew it. "Was it very bad, Hugh? Did they . . . well . . . did they ask you a lot of personal questions?"

"Well, they did, but I found your family quite charming." He paused, "Oh, I see what it is. They feared I was going to ask you to marry me, and they posted down to Bath to warn you off. Is that it?"

A look of consternation crossed her face. "Feared? It was no such thing! They *hoped* you were going to ask me to marry you, and they came to try and persuade me to bring you up to scratch. Hugh, they think that at seven-and-twenty, I'm an old maid. They don't care who I marry, just as long as—" She covered her mouth with her hand and peeked up at him. "That didn't come out the way . . . that is . . . that's not what I meant."

"Oh, don't apologize. You've always been frank with me, Abbie. That's one of the things I like about you. But this is interesting. Tell me what you said to your family."

"I told them the truth."

"That I have ice in my veins, and that no warm-blooded female would ever be interested in a dull stick like me?"

When she began to protest, he waved her to silence. "Not all women are like you, Abbie. As a rule, they're not interested in the breadth of my knowledge, the scope of my interests, or my prodigious . . . ah . . . intelligence. They want a man who knows how to charm a woman."

She shot him a quick look, but there was no hint of humor in his eyes. That shouldn't have surprised her. Hugh didn't have much of a sense of humor. She said, "All you lack is practice, Hugh, and that is easily come by."

"Is it? Now there's a thought. Would you mind, Abbie, if I practiced with you? I mean, we are friends, and I know you won't get the wrong idea if I make a fool of myself."

She'd never seen him look so uncertain. Not only did that look stir her softer feelings, but it also made her realize what a fool she'd been. This was Hugh. He hadn't changed. She'd allowed her family to put ideas in her head, and her lurid imagination had done the rest. Poor Hugh. He really was a sweet man.

"Of course I don't mind," she said. "What else are friends for?"

"You won't take offense?"

"How could I take offense when you would only be following my advice?"

"That settles it, then."

With that, he tipped up her chin and kissed her.

She froze. This wasn't what she had had in mind, but it was no more than a slight pressure of his lips on hers, then it was over.

"How did I do?" he asked.

She dimpled up at him. "Hugh," she said, "I'm not your grandmother. If you're going to steal a kiss from a lady, do try to put a little feeling into it. Here, let me show you how it's done."

She placed both his hands on her waist, then slipped one hand around his neck and exerted a little pressure to bring his head down. When he resisted, she looked up at him with a question in her eyes.

"You feel good in my arms, Abbie," he said. "Do I feel good to you?"

She had been concentrating on the mechanics of the kiss, but now that he'd made her think about it, she couldn't deny that she liked being in his arms. In fact, she liked everything about Hugh—the broad shoulders, the manly features, the thick black hair that looked as though a woman's fingers had just played with it. But she especially liked his mouth. It was full-lipped, firmly molded, and made for kissing.

A shiver of feminine awareness rippled through her. Dear Lord, where had that thought come from? This was Hugh, her best friend. She was doing it again, letting her imagination run away with her.

His lips settled on hers, and whatever she'd been about to say was swept away in a flood of sensation. He angled her head back, and the pressure of his mouth increased, opening her lips to his. She felt his hands kneading her waist, the flare of her hips, her back, then his arms wrapped around her, bringing her hard against the full length of his body. He left her mouth to kiss her brows, her cheeks, her throat. She sucked in a breath when he nipped her ear with his sharp teeth, then she moaned when he bent her back and kissed the swell of her breasts.

He kissed her again and again, each kiss more desperate than the last. Abbie had never known such passion. Her skin was hot, her blood was on fire, her whole body shivered in anticipation. She wanted more, more, more.

The kiss ended as suddenly as it had begun. One moment she was in his arms and the next he had set her away from him. Dazed, she stared up at him.

"How was I this time, Abbie?" he asked.

"What?" She steadied herself with one hand on the desk.

"Did I put enough feeling into it? You did say to put a little more feeling into it, didn't you?"

She looked around that small, candlelit room as though she'd never seen it before. It was like awakening from a dream. As she gradually came to herself, she touched her fingers to her burning lips, then looked up at Hugh with mounting horror. How could she have let things go so far? What must he think of her? How could they ever be natural with each other after this? And it was all her fault.

She cleared the huskiness from her voice but she

could do nothing about her burning cheeks. "Hugh, what can I say?"

His eyes anxiously searched hers. "Was I so bad?"

She blinked slowly. "No. You were . . . very good."

"Oh, I can't take all the credit," he said modestly. "You're quite the accomplished actress, Abbie. But I think I managed my part quite well too."

As comprehension gradually dawned, the worry frown on her brow vanished and she gave him a brilliant smile. "You did very well, Hugh. Very well indeed. In fact, you were quite convincing."

"And so were you," he said, and smiled. "So were you, Abbie."

He kept up a flow of small talk as he ushered her out of the room, but he didn't know what he was blethering about, and he doubted that Abbie knew either. He'd given her something to think about, and could tell from her surreptitious glances that his strategy was paying off. It was beginning to register with Miss Abigail Vayle that there was more to old stick-in-the-mud Hugh than his prodigious brain.

In bed, Abbie pulled the covers up to her chin and composed herself for sleep. Thoughts of Hugh tried to intrude but she ruthlessly suppressed them. She wasn't up to examining all the ins and outs of what had passed between them at the ball. She tried counting sheep but there was no relief there. Little Bo Peep kept making a nuisance of herself. Gritting her teeth, Abbie turned on her side and kept Hugh at bay by thinking of her brother. He'd met friends in Paris, George had told her. He would stay on for another week or two, then he would make for—now what exactly had he said?

She was searching for the words that escaped her when she suddenly plunged into sleep, and straight into

Hugh's arms. He was kissing her passionately, making her experience all those thrilling sensations she'd experienced in his office. Her skin was hot, her bones had turned to water She wanted more, more, more. But Hugh was shocked. *I've never had a carnal thought in my life,* he said. *I was only playing a part. After the spectacle you have made of yourself, we can never go back to being friends. You're an old maid, Abbie. An old maid. An old maid.*

All at once, his hands were around her throat and she could hardly breathe. He was going to kill her! She was suffocating! She tried to scream, but no sound came. And as suddenly as she'd plunged into sleep, she awakened to a nightmare.

The pressure on her aching mouth eased a little. "That's better," whispered the man who was kneeling over her. "I'm going to let you go, but one cheep out of you, and I'll slit your throat. Do you understand?"

She nodded her head vigorously. A moment later, the hand was removed from her mouth, but she could feel the sharp point of the knife pricking her throat. There was no candle lit, but impressions were bombarding all her senses. Her assailant was a big man and he smelled of cologne. Though he spoke in the cultured accents of an English gentleman, he had calluses on the tips of his fingers. She could tell he had entered her room by the window because the cold night air ruffled the muslin drapes and the pages of the book she kept on the table by her bed.

Her heart was pounding so hard that she could hear each terrified beat. "I keep my money in the clothes press," she choked out.

"Shut your mouth and listen," he snarled. "We want the book Colette passed to you in Paris. Where is it?"

"Colette?" Her thoughts spun off in every direction. "Who is Colette?"

He slapped her so hard that her lip split and her teeth jarred. Tears of pain and terror welled in her eyes.

"Don't make this hard on yourself, Miss Vayle," said that hateful voice. "We know you have the book. We know you want to sell it to the highest bidder. So here's our offer. Your brother's life for the book Colette gave you."

She was horribly afraid of what he would do to her if she denied knowing Colette again. There was a cold brutality about him that warned her he enjoyed inflicting pain. She swallowed the blood in her mouth as her mind groped frantically to make sense of what was happening.

She didn't know any Colette, but she'd been in Paris with George and Olivia. And she had bought books, a whole trunk of books for the little business she had set up. But those books were not in Bath. They were locked up at the customs house in Dover.

She felt rather than saw the movement as he raised his hand to strike her again, and she blurted out, "The book isn't here. If you kill me, you'll never find it." Then the full horror of his words cut through her panic. "What have you done to my brother?" she cried out.

His hand instantly covered her mouth, mashing her lips against her teeth. "Keep your voice down!" His lips were so close to her ear that she felt his warm breath fan across her cheek, and her stomach heaved. "I won't hesitate to kill your companion if she comes to investigate. Do you understand?"

She nodded and once again found herself released. She was still mortally afraid, but her mind was working like quicksilver, adding things up, making connections. One thing stood out clearly. The truth would not save her or George. They would be safe only as long as her assailant thought she had Colette's book to trade.

"A book for your brother's life," he whispered. "Most people would think that was a bargain. Where is the book, Miss Vayle?"

Though she was beginning to believe that George really had been abducted by this man and his accomplices, she said, playing for time, "How can I be sure that you have George? Last time I saw him, he was in Paris."

"When you give me the book, I'll take you to him."

"And murder us both the minute you have the book in your hands?" She was alarmed at her own temerity, and even more alarmed at the thought of what he would do if she didn't get a grip on herself. "Oh, no. That's not how we'll play this out."

There was a long silence, then he said, "Go on."

She couldn't go on because she didn't know how to extricate herself and George from this horrible nightmare. If only she had more time. "It will take me some time to get hold of the book," she said. "As I told you, it's not here. It's . . . it's in my bank vault in London."

"London?"

"And I'm the only one who can get it." That ought to buy her a reprieve of several days. Then she would have time to get help or come up with a plan to save George. "And when I have the book, we'll make the exchange on neutral ground. But first, you have to prove to me that you have my brother."

He laughed softly. "You're such a suspicious character, Miss Vayle. What do you want me to do, cut off his little finger and send it to you?"

Fear for George's safety made her reckless. "Two can play at threats."

Her words had a profound effect. She could sense it

in the way he tensed and sucked in a breath. His voice was dangerously quiet when he spoke. "If you go to our competitors, I promise you, Miss Vayle, we'll cut up your brother and send him to you in pieces."

Her words were bold but her voice shook. "If you harm a hair of George's head, your competitors will have the book Colette gave me before you can turn around. Do I make myself clear?"

"Very clear, Miss Vayle."

"Good. Then you'll bring me a letter in George's hand to prove that he's unharmed, and after that we'll work out the details of the exchange."

Genuine admiration colored his voice. "You are a very clever operator, Miss Vayle, very clever indeed, for a woman. Just a word of warning. Remember what we did to Jerome and Colette when they crossed us."

She had to ask. "What did you do to them?"

He answered pleasantly. "We skinned Jerome alive, but we were more merciful with Colette. We merely put a bullet in her brain."

Now she knew she was going to be sick.

"Don't take anyone into your confidence," he said. "We'll be watching you, Miss Vayle, and at the first hint of trouble, we'll cut our losses."

She believed him. A wave of despair washed through her. If she didn't have the book he wanted, how could she hope to save her brother? One false step on her part and it would be all over for George.

"I—" she said and got no further. Pain exploded through her head, and she sank back onto the pillows as blackness engulfed her.